Steel Girls
in the *Blitz*

Michelle Rawlins

ONE PLACE. MANY STORIES

This novel is entirely a work of fiction. The names, characters
and incidents portrayed in it are the work of the author's
imagination. Any resemblance to actual persons, living or
dead, events or localities is entirely coincidental.

HQ
An imprint of HarperCollins*Publishers* Ltd
1 London Bridge Street
London SE1 9GF

www.harpercollins.co.uk

HarperCollins*Publishers*
Macken House, 39/40 Mayor Street Upper,
Dublin 1, D01 C9W8, Ireland

This edition 2024

1
First published in Great Britain by
HQ, an imprint of HarperCollins*Publishers* Ltd 2024

Copyright © Michelle Rawlins 2024

Michelle Rawlins asserts the moral right to be
identified as the author of this work.
A catalogue record for this book is
available from the British Library.

ISBN: 978-0-00-859853-2

MIX
Paper | Supporting
responsible forestry
FSC™ C007454

This book contains FSC™ certified paper and other controlled
sources to ensure responsible forest management.

For more information visit: www.harpercollins.co.uk/green

Typeset in Sabon by HarperCollins*Publishers* India

Printed and Bound in the UK using 100%
Renewable Electricity at CPI Group (UK) Ltd

For the late Florence Temperton & Gwen Bryan,
who gave so much and asked for so little.

Prologue

Sunday, 15 December 1940

Staring at the burning building, a crescendo of flames against the darkness of the night, Archie was momentarily paralyzed. Bricks were tumbling heavily onto one another, and windows were cracking and smashing as they were blown out, scattering razor-sharp shards of glass across the debris-laden road.

The cacophony of ear-splitting noise around him abruptly alerted Archie to the fact his beloved city was under attack. The Luftwaffe were soaring the skies overhead and explosions were erupting around him. The street he had known like the back of his hand was unrecognizable. Houses were obliterated, reduced to ugly piles of rubble, and the hustle and bustle of life had all but gone.

'Archie. Are you okay?' came a familiar voice.

Archie glanced up. The look of fear on his friend's face told him all he needed to know. Hitler had done his worst. He'd finally attacked the everyday people of Sheffield; brought havoc and destruction to the people he loved most in the world.

'Can you stand up? Are you hurt?' the voice, etched with desperation and concern, asked.

Was he in pain? Archie didn't know. His body had frozen into some form of restricting paralysis. But part of him didn't want to move. If he stayed still, maybe he would wake up and the devastating scene around him would dissipate as quickly as a nightmare vanished as soon as you opened your eyes. But the terror-filled voice continued.

'Archie, do you need help? Do you want me to get someone?'

Who? Who would he get?

'No. It's okay.' Archie stumbled to his feet, his body weak and his head pounding, but he managed to force his fragile body up, gripping the arm which was offered.

'What shall I do?' the frightened voice asked.

Archie knew he had to take charge. This was his job after all, what he'd been trained to do, but as he tried to process the utter carnage around him, his thoughts scrambled.

He looked straight ahead, the unimaginable sight directly in front of Archie, arresting him.

'No!' he screamed. 'We've got to save them.'

'We can't,' came that voice again. 'It's too late.'

Chapter 1

'What about this one?' Patty trilled excitedly, as she picked up a pale pink dress and matching jacket from the rail in Banners. 'You would look lovely in this.'

'Mmmm,' Hattie mused. 'I'm not sure. I was thinking something a little more traditional, but it would really suit you.'

'Me?' Patty said in surprise, although she did silently agree the outfit was her colour, but determined to be the dutiful maid of honour, she insisted, 'We are looking for *you*. You need to find something. You're getting hitched in a week.'

'I know, but you need something to wear too, and you love pink.'

'I can't upstage the bride,' Patty protested, despite the fact the more she looked at the pretty ensemble, the more she liked it. 'I'm not getting an outfit until you decide on something.'

Ever since Hattie's fiancé, John, had written the previous month, to say he had been granted weekend leave from his role in mortar-bomb training at Salisbury Plain, and to instruct Hattie to go and get a marriage licence, it had been all actions go.

Patty had fussed around her best friend like an old mother hen, insisting they went shopping for outfits, practised different hair-dos and redid her make-up more times than Hattie had fingers. Betty and Ivy had insisted they would take charge of the wedding tea and Dolly had offered to make the cake. The ceremony had been booked for the following Saturday at Holy Trinity Church in Darnall, although the vicar had explained it would be a quick affair, as the number of special licences to exchange vows had soared since war had begun. Hattie didn't mind. All she cared about was becoming Mrs Harrison. It was the start of a new future and hopefully one that would eventually mean she wouldn't have to be trapped in the same house as her increasingly violent dad, whose volatile mood swings left both Hattie and her mum constantly walking on eggshells.

'Did you think any more about wearing your mum's dress? You are a similar size. I bet it wouldn't take much altering. My mom is a dab hand with a needle and thread. I bet she could nip it in for you.'

'I did want to, but she doesn't want me to. She says it's a bad omen and my marriage could end up as miserable as hers. I have insisted that I borrow her veil, though. It would feel so wrong not to wear something of my mum's on my wedding day.'

'Oh, Hatts,' Patty gasped, putting the outfit back on the rail, and squeezing her friend's slender arm. 'I wish you'd told me more about your dad.'

'I'm sorry.' Hattie smiled weakly. 'I hate talking about it. Coming to work and spending time with you all is the best tonic and I was happy to leave everything with my dad at home. I can't ever really forget about it, but I can put it away for a few hours every day.'

After Ivy's end-of-summer garden party, Patty had vowed to be a better friend to Hattie, and actually listen. Over the last few weeks, sharing several pots of tea and visits to Banners for wedding attire, Hattie had started to open up about her dad's drunken episodes.

'It's all right. I understand. And talking about escapism, let's not ruin today. If it kills me, we are not leaving this shop until you have the perfect dress. Now come on.' Patty linked her arm through Hattie's and ushered her to a nearby area of the women's clothing section which boasted a small but eye-catching array of beautiful wedding outfits.

Fingering the delicate dresses, a mixture of silk, lace, satin and heavy cotton, Patty finally pulled out a simple, but intricately bodied ivory gown.

'What do you think?'

Hattie eyed the exquisite dress, with its full-length sleeves and high neck, perfect for an autumnal wedding. The pearlescent buttons down the back, the tailored cut and the calf length were exactly what she'd envisaged. 'I love it,' Hattie whispered.

'Reyt then. You must try it on.'

Ten minutes later Hattie emerged from the changing room looking every bit the blushing bride. 'It was made for you!' Patty trilled. 'John will be in heaven when he sees you. You look stunning.'

'Do you think?' Hattie felt a twinge of excitement. A flutter of somersaulting butterflies in her tummy making her giddy as the realization kicked in: she was getting married in a week's time.

'Yes! You look an absolute picture. John will die with happiness.'

'Okay.' Hattie giggled. 'You've convinced me, but you must get the pink outfit too. Go and get it quickly and try it on.'

Delighted, Patty didn't have to be asked twice, especially after spending most of her week in mucky, dust-covered overalls. After a quick change, the two girls stood in front of the full-length department-store mirror, grinning at the reflections staring back at them.

'Hatts!' Patty exclaimed, their radiant images filling them both with joy. 'Can you believe it? You're getting married!'

'I must admit, I do have to keep pinching myself. It still doesn't feel real. I don't think it will until the day itself.'

'I bet. I'd be exactly the same but it's going to be the best day.'

'I hope so,' Hattie whispered, taking Patty's hand in her own and squeezing it tight. 'I just can't wait to see John. I know I got to see him in June, but it feels like an age ago.'

'It was four months ago. It is a chuffin' age. Will you get a honeymoon?'

'Not straightaway. John has only been granted a weekend pass but hopefully he will get some leave in the next few months, and we might be able to do something nice.'

'That will be something to look forward to,' Patty said, determined to keep the mood buoyant.

'It will! Right, we better go and pay for these outfits. I don't suppose we can stand here forever.'

'Hatts?'

'Before you even suggest it,' Hattie jumped in, instinctively reading her friend's mind. 'John's mum has been in touch. He has sent money to pay for most things.'

'Are you sure? I'm happy to pay for my own outfit. It's not like it will gather dust in m' wardrobe. I'll definitely be wearing it again.'

'Positive. I must admit I was a bit surprised too, but Rita said he'd been putting money aside for a while. I think he probably realized my dad spent every spare penny me and my mum put away and didn't want me to worry.'

'He really is a good 'un, isn't he?'

'He is. I do feel very lucky.'

'And I'm sure your John feels exactly the same.' With that, a grin as big as the moon appeared across Hattie's face. 'Oh, Patty. I know I keep saying it, but I do feel like the happiest girl alive.'

'And as I keep telling you,' Patty replied, plonking a kiss on Hattie's cheek, 'it's no less than you deserve.'

Another trill of excitement shot through Hattie. Her life had felt like a continual battle for so long, it really was wonderful knowing things were turning a corner, and a hopeful one at that.

Ten minutes later Hattie and Patty were at the till, the ecstatic looks on their faces perfectly simulating how gladdened they both felt. Then to the bemusement of Hattie, Patty erupted into a fit of giggles.

'I know I look like the cat that's got the cream but what's suddenly tickled you?' Hattie laughed.

'Well' – Patty chuckled – 'I thought I might be able to give you this next Saturday, but I don't suppose there's any harm in you having it now. Besides which, I'm not sure how I can buy it without you seeing.'

'Buy what?'

'This!' Patty pulled her left arm from behind her back, and in her hand was a lacy pale-blue garter.

'Patty!' Hattie blushed, her eyes widening in astonishment.

'I couldn't resist, and let's face it, you need something blue.'

'You are a case.'

'I'm sure John won't be complaining.' Patty winked, a hint of mischief in her voice, despite the fact that when it came down to it, apart from the animated and lively banter she'd heard in the canteen at Vickers, she was utterly clueless as to what happened on a couple's wedding night.

'Shall I take those?' the immaculately turned-out, older and rather prim-looking sales assistant asked, rather curtly.

'Er yes. Thank you,' Hattie muttered, the colour of her cheeks deepening from pink to crimson.

A few minutes later, Hattie and Patty were making their way out of Banners. 'Well, she was a bit prissy,' Patty hooted. 'She's clearly forgotten what it's like to be young! Did you see the way she held the garter, as if it was some sort of forbidden garment?'

'She was rather straight-laced.'

'It was worth it to see her face, though!'

'You are a one.' Hattie laughed, as they made their way down Attercliffe Road. 'Anyway, thank you for this afternoon. I really have had a lovely time and I finally feel as though I can actually get married next weekend.'

'Oh, Hatts! It's going to be the best,' Patty said, linking her arm through her friend's as they passed Charnley's, on the corner of Bodmin Street, where a queue of eager children were queuing up for ices, taking advantage of the early autumn sun. 'Next week is going to feel the longest ever at work.' A week working at Vickers, operating a great, heaving, mucky crane, was not how Patty would ideally like to spend the week leading up to her best friend's wedding.

'I'm just glad the bosses agreed to let us all have Saturday morning off work. We only got the eleven o'clock slot because someone else had cancelled.'

'It would have been pretty mean of them to say no, what with all the overtime we are putting in. I can't remember the last time I finished before six o'clock in the week.'

'That's true but I'm grateful all the same.'

'What time is your John due home on Friday night? Have you heard?'

'Not yet, but I'm hoping it won't be too late. It would be nice to see him before Saturday, even if it's only for an hour or so. I told him I should be back from work at six thirty at the latest.'

'Well, don't you be having a late night.' Patty winked with a cheeky glint, as she gave Hattie a playful nudge in the ribs. 'You need to be as fresh as a daisy on Saturday morning. I don't want you looking anything but the glowing bride.'

'I can assure you the only reason I won't get any sleep will be if nerves take over, which I'm sure they probably will.'

'I'll forgive you for that. I don't think I'd sleep a wink either.'

As the two women got to the point where they had

to fork off in different directions, Hattie unlinked herself from Patty, and gave her a tight hug. 'Thank you again. You really have made today very special.'

'Well, I wouldn't be a reyt good best friend or maid of honour if I let you walk down the aisle in any old dress, would I?'

'Even so. It really has been lovely.'

'Don't mention it. I've enjoyed every minute.' Patty smiled, as Hattie released her from the affectionate embrace. 'Right, I'll see you Monday and make sure you have a break tomorrow. Next week will be non-stop.'

'I will, and you,' Hattie replied, waving with her free hand, the other laden down with shopping bags.

With a spring in her step, Hattie happily tottered the rest of the way home in a contented daydream, as she tried to envisage what her wedding day would be like. Hattie imagined John, looking tall and dapper, in his Army uniform and tried to visualise the look of surprise on his face when he saw her in her dress for the first time. She prayed she wouldn't trip on her heels as she made her way down the aisle or stumble on her vows. The butterflies in her tummy, which had once again returned, fluttered as she quietly practised saying 'I do' and John slipping her wedding ring on her finger.

But as she opened the back door, letting herself into the West Street house she had grown up in, her joyful thoughts came to an abrupt end.

'Look what the cat's dragged in,' her dad snarled, eyeing

Hattie up and down, the contempt in his tone palpable. 'Lady Muck herself. Feeling all grand are we, now yer getting yerself wed.' The last sage remark, a statement more than a question. 'Marrying into the Harrisons. You'll be turning yer nose up at the likes of us once you've got that ring on yer chuffin' finger.'

All the elation Hattie had felt, just moments earlier, after finally choosing her wedding outfit, deflated quicker than a popped balloon. It wasn't even five o'clock but by how much her dad was slurring his words, he'd obviously gone straight to the pub after his early shift down the pit had finished.

'Vinny, let Hattie be,' his downtrodden wife pleaded. 'She's only just walked through the door.'

'Don't you bloody well start,' Vinny snapped, glaring contemptuously at Diane. 'And I don't know why yer even sticking up for her. She'll be gone once she's said I do. You'll never see her. She'll be off to live in that bloody grand house up Firth Park.'

'Dad!' Hattie protested. 'Stop it. I'm not going anywhere for the time being.'

It was true John's parents did have a nice semi-detached house in one of the better parts of Sheffield. His dad had worked his way up the ranks at Smith's Brewery into a senior position and John had been following in his footsteps before war had broken out, but Hattie had no intention of leaving her mum until her future husband was home for good.

'We'll see,' Vinny droned on. 'Anyhow, who says you'll be welcome here after next week. Yer won't be my responsibility anymore. I'll be glad to be shot of yer. You've always been a snooty little so and so.'

'Vinny!' Diane gasped. 'How can you say such a thing about your own daughter.'

'It's okay, Mum,' Hattie interrupted, knowing any retaliation would only fuel her dad's drunken rage. 'Why don't I take my bags upstairs and then I'll make us a cuppa and start tea.'

'That's right,' Vinny shouted, slamming his fist on the kitchen table. 'Just ignore me, like I'm not bloody well here. Well, let me tell you, I am here and while you live under my roof you can have the bloody decency to show me some respect.'

Hattie took a quiet intake of breath. She'd secretly hoped her dad would still be out when she got home, so she could show her mum her wedding dress, but there was no chance of a nice evening now. Once her dad started there was no rest until he took himself off to bed or passed out, drunk.

'Sorry,' Hattie said, forcing herself to sound genuine, in an exhausted bid to try and dilute her dad's raging anger, despite how much she despised him in that moment.

'I should chuffin' well think so,' he ranted.

Deflated, Hattie stepped through the kitchen into the hall, all the excitement she'd felt while shopping

13

with Patty now extinguished. *Please don't let him ruin my wedding*, she thought, making her way upstairs, the reserve of sympathy she normally felt for her dad now empty.

Chapter 2

Saturday, 12 October 1940

'Thank goodness you're here.' Hattie exhaled, letting her friend in the back door.

'Is everything all right?' Patty asked, praying nothing had gone wrong at the last minute.

'Yes. No. Sorry. Yes. I'm just a bag of nerves and my tummy is turning somersaults.'

'I've told her this is completely normal,' Hattie's mum, Diane, who was stood by the cooker, interjected. 'Would you like a cuppa, luv, while the pair of you are getting ready?'

'That would be grand, Mrs Johnson, thank you.'

'Diane! You have known me for long enough to know that.'

'Sorry.' Patty smiled. 'I hope you are going to join us while we get changed and do our hair and make-up.'

'I better make Vinny his bacon sandwich first. He'll not be best impressed if he doesn't get his breakfast.'

Patty shot Hattie a glance but knew better than to make a big fuss, today of all days. 'Well, make sure you come and join us when you can.'

'I will, luv. Thank you.'

Five minutes later the two girls were in Hattie's bedroom, where their outfits hung resplendently on the back of the door.

'Right. It's nine o'clock. We have two hours to get you ready and to that church on time. I would say you should be fashionably late but it's probably not a good idea to miss yer slot.'

'No!' Hattie laughed. 'I dread to think when John will next get leave.'

'Did you see him last night?'

'I did. Only for an hour. He popped in after he got off the train.'

'How was he?'

'He's put some weight back on after France, so looked really well. I think after Dunkirk, the Salisbury Plain feels like heaven.'

'I bet. Was he excited about today?'

'Yes. He was quite giddy. He'd found a jeweller near to where he's based and bought the rings, so at least I got to see them before today.'

'What are they like?' Patty asked, sweeping Hattie's thick brown hair into rollers.

'Very simple gold bands, exactly what I hoped for.'

'And dare I ask how yer dad's been the last day or so?'

Hattie had arrived at work on Monday fed up and anxious, but her friends had rallied and assured her they wouldn't let Hattie's dad ruin her big day.

'A bit snappy but nothing out of the ordinary. I just hope he doesn't start drinking early today and ruin everything. I wouldn't put anything past him.'

'He won't!' Patty said adamantly, determined nothing was going to ruin her best friend's special day. She hadn't told Hattie, but Patty had spoken to her dad and her foreman, Frank, at the factory, who had agreed to keep on eye on Vinny. She wasn't really sure what that meant in reality but did feel confident they would discreetly defuse a situation if Vinny showed any signs of causing a scene.

'Right, that's your hair in rollers. Why don't we do our make-up while it's setting?'

By quarter to eleven, the two girls, looking as pretty as a picture, were standing at Hattie's front door, as the pick-up car John had arranged, pulled up.

'Enjoy every minute,' Diane whispered as she gave Hattie's hand a squeeze, as she and Vinny made their way outside.

'Thanks, Mum.' Hattie reached out and put her other hand over hers, which was shaking ever so slightly.

'You look lovely,' Patty complimented Diane, sensing she needed a bit of a booster, knowing Vinny probably hadn't even looked sideways at her. Hattie had insisted on taking her mum shopping a couple of weeks earlier and had treated her to an emerald-green knitted dress that emphasized her petite figure.

'Thank you, luv' – Diane nodded – 'but it's you two girls who look beautiful.'

Before anyone could answer, the conversation was interrupted by a gentle honk of a horn as a bright blue Ford Deluxe pulled up, a silk-white ribbon stretching from the bonnet to the wing mirrors.

'Your chariot awaits,' came the familiar voice through the driver's side window. John had told Hattie his oldest friend and best man, Mark, would be collecting them to taxi them to the church.

'You go in the front, Dad,' Hattie suggested. 'The three of us can squeeze in the back.'

Once they were all comfortably encased, Mark set off. 'Is John okay?' Hattie asked, knowing the two men would have spent the morning together.

'I should imagine he's a bit like you. Touch of the old nerves but take it from me, Hattie, he can't wait to make you his wife. And can I just say, he's in for a treat. You three ladies look gorgeous.'

'Aren't you the charmer.' Patty giggled. Then touching her friend's arm, she asked, 'Are you feeling okay?'

'I think so. Still got butterflies but it's a nice feeling.'

'That's exactly how it should be, luv,' Diane, who was on the other side of her daughter, reassured her.

In what felt like the blink of an eye, Mark pulled up outside the Darnall Parish Church. Despite the autumn drizzle that had plagued Sheffield for most of the week, the sun had broken through the clouds, making a welcome appearance.

'Oh, look.' Hattie pointed to the front of the old stone

church, where a newly married bride and groom were making their way down the drive, surrounded by a crowd of smiling guests. 'It looks like the last wedding has just finished.'

'We better get a shift on in that case,' Mark encouraged, already opening his door. 'The vicar gave firm instructions we couldn't even be a minute late!'

'This is it,' Patty squealed, giving Hattie's hand a final squeeze. 'It's really happening.'

'I can hardly believe it,' came the whispered reply, as Hattie, Patty and Diane all clambered out of the car, taking care not to scuff or mark their immaculate outfits.

At the gates to the church, after the previous wedding party had spilled out onto the road, Vinny positioned himself next to his daughter. 'Shall we?' he gestured affectionately, opening his right arm into a triangle, inviting his daughter to join him.

'Yes.' Hattie nodded, a pang of emotion coursing through her, as she remembered how as a little girl, her dad would sit Hattie on his knee and sing her nursery rhymes. *Why can't he always be like this?* But she also knew this wasn't the time or place to try to make sense of her dad's volatile mood swings, simply grateful that today, at least, he was every bit the father she needed him to be.

The fatherly act of kindness hadn't been lost on Patty or Diane either; the two women exchanging a warm smile, both relieved that Vinny was doing the right thing on his daughter's big day.

'Right, I'll go and get a seat,' Diane said, pecking her daughter on the cheek. 'Enjoy every second, luv. You look beautiful. John is a very lucky man.'

'Thanks, Mum,' Hattie whispered, her voice faltering ever so slightly.

'Come on, Diane. I'll walk in with you,' Mark offered, leading her away, conscious if they didn't get going, the vicar would end up stumbling over his words as he raced through the whole ceremony. 'Besides which, we get the best seats in the house and a perfect view of the glowing bride from the front row.'

A minute or so later, Hattie, supported by Vinny, with Patty following closely behind, entered the doors of the church. The congregation fell silent, every pair of eyes on Hattie, and the organ player burst into life; the upbeat traditional Richard Wagner notes of 'Here Comes the Bride' now echoing around the draughty old building.

A bag of nerves, Hattie forced herself to look up from her ivory leather shoes, to gaze through the fine netting of her veil, borrowed from her mum. And there was John, standing by the altar looking tall and dashingly handsome in his razor-sharp ironed and starched military uniform. Even from the other end of the church she could see the familiar glint in his eye and huge smile. *He's really here and I'm actually getting married.*

Hattie remembered her mum's advice and savoured every moment as she slowly made her way down the aisle, catching glimpses of all her friends from Vickers, whose delighted faces bestowed how happy they were for her. When she reached John, Vinny gently released his daughter, taking a seat next to Diane, and Patty, just as she'd rehearsed, dutifully took the simple bouquet of pink and white roses from Hattie.

'We have gathered here today to join in matrimony John Edmund Harrison and Hattie Diane Johnson,' the vicar began.

Hattie barely heard the words which followed, or the hymns sang, so in a state of joyful elation was she, although at one point she could have sworn the vicar missed a few words out of the sermon, his words falling from his lips much quicker than usual. But she didn't care. As long as she was with her beloved John, nothing else mattered.

'Do you John Edmund Harrison take Hattie Diane Johnson to be your lawful wedded wife?'

'I do,' John replied firmly.

Then slightly averting his eyes, the vicar addressed the question to Hattie.

'I do!' She grinned.

As she and John carefully placed their wedding rings on each other's fingers, Hattie thought she would burst with happiness. The moment she had dreamt of, now a reality.

'You may kiss the bride.'

John lifted Hattie's veil, leant over and placed his lips upon hers, the sweet, loving kiss causing every part of her body to tingle. 'I love you, Mrs Harrison,' he said, when he reluctantly pulled away, squeezing his new wife's hands a little tight.

'And I love you.'

With that, a jubilant round of applause, interspersed with several gleeful 'oohs' and 'ahs', echoed around the church.

After signing the official register, Hattie and John made their way outside. 'Here they are,' Patty trilled, alerting the rest of the guests to raise their arms and shower the newlyweds with handfuls of confetti.

'My goodness.' Hattie giggled, turning to John, who was equally as amused.

'You did it. You really got married,' Patty exclaimed as the delighted couple made their way down the steps, just in time to let the guests for the next wedding make their way into the church.

'We did.' Hattie grinned. 'I'm still not sure I can quite believe it.'

'You better had,' John proclaimed in mock jest, affectionately placing his arm around his wife's shoulders.

'Right, is it time for some scran?' Mark asked the crowd as they made their way onto the pavement; aware another eager couple would be keen to take their slot to exchange vows.

'Have you forgotten already?' John said, rolling his eyes. 'We're just going to have our photo taken before we join everyone in the church hall.' The photoshoot had been a wedding present from John's mum and dad, who had insisted on providing the special keepsake of the day.

'Of course. I'll nip you two and Patty down to the photographer's studio and then come and collect both lots of parents.'

It was an hour later before the wedding party arrived back to enjoy their wedding reception, just as Betty, Daisy and the rest of the gang were putting the finishing touches to the hall.

Nipping in ahead of Hattie and John, Patty looked for Archie. 'Is everything ready?' she mouthed. A quick nod confirmed all she needed to know. Patty and her friends had been planning the post-ceremony party ever since Hattie had announced the date.

Quickly accepting a glass of port and lemon from Betty, Patty took her position as the guests all gathered in a horseshoe in the middle of the hall. As the bride and groom entered the room, which had been decorated with an array of homemade bunting, glasses were raised, and a triumphant cheer erupted.

'To Hattie and John!'

'My goodness,' Hattie gasped, taking in the welcoming scene. All her friends from Vickers, their families, her parents and John's relatives were smiling back at them. The day just kept getting better.

After what had been a tumultuous year, to see everyone smiling and looking so relaxed was utterly wonderful.

'Here you go,' Betty said, handing the happy couple

champagne glasses, the translucent, fizzy liquid bubbling over the rims.

'Oooh' Hattie exclaimed. 'Thank you. I don't think I've had champagne before.'

'Well, your wedding day is the perfect time to start.'

'Where did it come from?'

'My parents had a couple of bottles in the cellar and insisted we opened them today.' John smiled.

Hattie took a delicate sip. 'Oh!' She laughed, the bubbles hitting the back of her throat. 'It's rather nice, isn't it? I could get used to this.'

'Not on a turner's wage packet you won't!' Patty interrupted, bustling over to her friend.

'This is true,' Hattie agreed. 'Anyway, I just wanted to say thank you.'

'What on earth for?'

'For everything over the last few weeks and especially this morning when I was a bag of nerves. I don't think I'd have got to the church without you.'

'Well, I would be failing in my duties if I let you miss your big day!'

'I should be thanking you too,' John interjected. 'I think I'd have been more than a bit miffed if Hattie hadn't arrived at the church.'

Hattie looked up at John, her enormous smile confirming how utterly elated she felt.

'Right,' John said. 'I think we better go and chat to everyone and thank them for all of this.'

As well as their guests who had donned their finest attire – the women in their best dresses and the men looking dapper in pressed suits – along each side of the hall was a row of tables adorned with a vast selection of sumptuous-looking food. There was a spectacular array of vegetable quiches, beef sandwiches, bowls of boiled eggs, scones, jam tarts and, centre stage, a two-tier iced wedding cake, decorated with dried red rose petals. A feast fit for King George VI himself. And one section of the table was piled with neatly wrapped gifts, a mass of brown paper, ribbons and bows.

'Yes,' Hattie enthused, then looking to Betty asked, 'am I right in thinking, you, Dolly and Ivy are responsible for this?'

Betty nodded. 'You know how much they like an occasion to cook for. They were all in their element.'

'Did I hear my name?' asked Dolly, who in all her finery – a navy knitted dress and a delicate pearlescent clip in her brown hair – had approached the newlyweds.

'I just wanted to say thank you,' Hattie said. 'Did you make the cake? It looks beautiful.'

'Ah, it was m' pleasure, duck. My gift to you both.'

'That's incredibly kind,' Hattie said, touched that the good-hearted canteen manager could be so generous, despite only knowing her a matter of months. 'Where on earth did you get all the ingredients?'

'You know me. A bit of begging here, bartering there and a few visits to couple of folk who owed me a favour or two.' It was a well-known secret; Dolly had her finger in all sorts of pies and could get most things she needed off the black market.

'As Hattie said, we really are very grateful,' John reiterated.

'Don't mention it, duck. Anyway, enough of that. Congratulations! You both look a picture.' Then clinking her glass gently against Hattie's, she added: 'You deserve this, duck. I wish you both a lifetime of happiness.'

Hattie sensed Dolly had guessed, long before everyone else at Vickers, how difficult things had been at home, always offering a listening ear if she needed someone to natter to, but for today at least her dad was on his best behaviour, although she was aware the day was still young.

'You do that,' Ivy conferred, breaking Hattie's silent fears. Ivy, looking immaculate in her tailored burgundy velvet dress accompanied by a pearl necklace, had come to join the little group.

'You are all so kind.' Hattie blushed. The newly married couple repeated how grateful they were, thanking Ivy for all her hard work for the sumptuous and generous buffet.

Modest to a fault, Ivy politely waved off the compliments. 'I had a lot of helpers and the late summer meant Frank and I had had quite the harvest. I'm glad to put it to good use. There's a little something for your bottom drawer on the table too,' she added as she glanced towards the table holding the neatly positioned wedding presents.

'There was no need. You have done enough,' Hattie said.

'If I can't spoil a couple on their special day, there's something very wrong.'

Before Hattie could argue, more and more guests gathered around her and John to relay their best wishes.

'You really do make a lovely couple,' said Nancy, who look transformed in her deep-red dress, her blonde curls falling onto her shoulders, as she pecked Hattie on the cheek. 'Are you enjoying your special day?'

'I really am. It's a dream come true. I keep having to pinch myself.'

'That's exactly how it should be, luv.'

As the group of well-wishers around the couple increased, Dolly touched Hattie's arm. 'I'll leave you to it, luv, but where's your mum? I thought I'd go and introduce myself and have a natter.'

Hattie scanned the busy hall, which was now full of friends and relatives celebrating, and a dozen or so children, dashing among the legs, as they chased one another around, their infectious laughter reverberating off the walls.

'She's over there.' Hattie indicated to where her parents were stood with John's, near the drinks table. 'Please God, don't let him get a taste of it today.'

Almost reading her mind, Dolly replied, 'You just enjoy your day, duck. I'll go and have a natter.'

'Thank you,' Hattie whispered. She instinctively knew

this was Dolly's way of keeping an eye on her dad, as well as making sure her mum could enjoy the day too.

'It will be okay,' John said discreetly in Hattie's ear. 'Mark and my dad promised to make sure he didn't have too much to drink.'

'Thank you.'

'No need to thank me. I just want you to enjoy every second of today and not worry about a thing.'

And for the next few hours, that's exactly what Hattie did. In between sips of the delicious champagne, she and John circulated the room, chatting to their guests and even managing to enjoy a slice of quiche and a jam tart.

Then, as the couple stood next to the beautiful cake, John picked up a silver knife and gently tapped it against his glass.

'Time for a speech,' Mark reiterated, clapping his hand against his thigh.

A hush came over the room as all eyes turned to the bride and groom, even the children who were having a competitive game of marbles in a corner of the hall, brought their challenge to a temporary halt.

'First of all,' John began, looking from his wife to the expectant guests, 'I just wanted to thank you all for coming here today to help us celebrate our big day. It really does mean a lot. Now, I won't go on for too long . . .'

'Thank God!' Mark shrilled, encouraging a ripple of laughter.

'All right,' John replied, taking the quip in good

humour. 'Anyway, I just wanted to raise a toast to my beautiful wife.'

The laughter was now replaced by a chorus of 'aws'.

'Without Hattie, and my family, I don't know how I'd have survived this year, especially Dunkirk. It was only the thought of coming home to the people I loved that kept me going.'

The heartfelt words, which commanded a respectful and dignified silence, sent a shiver down Nancy's spine, as her own husband, who had been left psychologically scarred after France, tightly wrapped his arm around her waist.

'But I don't want to dwell on the war today.'

'Hear, hear!' Mark echoed, supported by several claps of encouragement.

'Instead,' John continued, 'I wanted to say thank you again and ask you all to charge your glasses.' Then turning to Hattie, he added, 'I really am the luckiest man in the world.'

'To John and Hattie,' came the enthusiastic response, followed by more clinking of glasses and cheers of delight.

For the next few hours, the hall was full of laughter as the guests enjoyed the day, momentarily forgetting about the rest of the world and the atrocities Hitler was responsible for. A gramophone was fired up, and John led Hattie into the centre of the hall. They swayed along to Bing Crosby's 'Only Forever', Hattie closing her eyes and resting her head on her husband's shoulder, but as a feeling of pure, unadulterated happiness consumed her, a niggling feeling crept in. Vinny had managed to stay sober today, but Hattie knew it was only a matter of time before her dad reached for a pint glass and his anger spilled out.

Chapter 3

'Here you are, duck,' Dolly enthused as she made her way over to the table in the Vickers canteen where her steelworker friends were sitting.

Dolly had grown very fond of the women since they all started working as crane drivers and in the turner's yard. Her respect for these feisty women held no bounds. Nancy was juggling a full-time job, as well as caring for her two young children, Patty had been forced to grow up as the atrocities of war had caused her to accept that life wasn't just a rollercoaster of dances, clothes-shopping and choosing the best lippy. And Hattie, well, she might have enjoyed the happiest day of her life, but Dolly knew she was quietly coping with a drunken and oppressive father.

And as for Betty, despite only being in her early twenties, she was always the first to help anyone in need. Between juggling her work at the Women's Voluntary Service and organizing winter care packages for the Allied troops, she rarely allowed her worries about her fiancé,

William, who was away training to be a pilot, to bring her down. Then there was Daisy, who had joined the steelworks as her mum, Josie, struggled with her health, but had managed to remain strong, with the support of all her new friends.

'I just wanted to come and say, again, what a grand day Saturday was. You must still be walking on cloud nine?' Dolly said to Hattie.

'I am a bit.' She grinned. 'It still feels like a dream.'

'Ah. I'm sure, duck! It really was a lovely occasion.'

'Does it feel any different, being married?' Patty chirped.

'It does, in some ways.'

'What like?'

'Well. It's just nice knowing me and John will always be together, even if we are apart, right now. It's like, I know we have got a long future together, when this war is finally over.'

'That's lovely, duck. And just how it should be,' Dolly replied, as she gave the stainless-steel tea urn a gentle shake, to check if it needed topping up. 'Did you enjoy the rest of the weekend?'

'We did. John's parents invited me, my mum and dad over for Sunday lunch, which was nice.'

'And yer dad. Was everything okay?'

Hattie nodded, taking the final bite of her beef sandwich, made from the leftovers of yesterday's meal. 'He was. Well, at least I think he was. He had a couple of beers with his lunch, then Mum took him home. I stayed at John's last night, so I could see him before he left for the train station this morning, so I haven't been home yet. I just hope he didn't carry on when he got back.'

'What was that like?' Patty interjected. 'Yer know, staying at John's.'

Hattie blushed. 'It was, er . . . well, it was fine. Lovely in fact.'

'Spare the girl her blushes,' Dolly protested, throwing Patty a mockingly stern look. Then turning to Hattie, she asked, 'It can't have been easy saying goodbye again, duck?'

'It wasn't, but I just keep reminding myself how lucky I am. At least John is only a couple of hundred miles away. I'm hoping he'll get home again soon.'

'That's the spirit. What are yer plans now? Will you stay with John's parents?'

'No. They said I could, but I don't want to leave Mum on her own with my dad. I'd rather keep an eye on her.'

'I understand, duck.' Dolly nodded, but not wanting to spoil the mood, she added, 'Did you get the chance to open all your gifts? I noticed there was quite the haul.'

'My goodness. Yes. Everyone was so generous. Thank you, again, for all your presents. You are all so kind. And, Dolly, you have just reminded me,' Hattie said, reaching down to pick up her haversack. 'The cake must have taken you so long. It was delicious. There was quite a lot left, so I've brought you all in another slice each.'

'Oooh,' Patty said, eagerly, her eyes widening, helping

herself to a piece of the delicious fruit cake. 'I'll not turn that down. My sarnie barely touched the sides.'

'You're as bad as your Tom Tom.' Archie laughed.

'I'll let you know I've been working hard all morning. A girl's got to eat. You wouldn't want me fainting on yer, would you?'

'Ah. You're very welcome, duck,' Dolly commented, finally getting a chance to answer. 'It was a pleasure. I'm just glad it went down well.'

'It did. And thank you, everyone else. You were all so kind. We've got plenty of bedding, towels and cutlery for when we finally get a house of our own.'

'You can never have enough,' Nancy, who had bought Hattie and John a patchwork eiderdown, replied. 'Bert and I still use the presents we were given on our wedding day.'

'How is your Bert?' Hattie asked. 'He seemed to be in good spirits on Saturday.'

It had been nearly ten weeks since Bert had returned to Sheffield from Dunkirk a broken man, after eleven months at war, the atrocities of what he'd witnessed and endured leaving him psychologically and physically broken. Nancy had naively believed her husband would arrive home happy at the thought of being reunited with his family, which in many ways he had, but what she had underestimated is the damage serving in France had done to him. For weeks he'd barely spoken, and during every air raid, had buried his head in his hands, unable to cope with the screeching of the German aircraft overhead or the terrifying ear-piercing bangs, indicating the Luftwaffe were bombing their beloved city. The debilitating gunshot wound Bert had suffered to his right leg not only meant that he hadn't initially slept upstairs with Nancy, but that he was deemed medically unfit to serve in the Army and had been discharged. His pride and self-esteem had taken a battering and it was only when Frank had suggested Bert could join the Home Guard a spark of his old self had returned.

'He's actually going up to Manor Field today to start with the Home Guard,' Nancy announced, proudly. Ever since Ivy's end-of-summer garden party, her *old* husband had gradually started to return to her. He might not have felt strong enough to tell her what exactly had happened while he had been missing in France, but the dark moods, which had left him distant and snappy, had gradually reduced, and the kind and caring Bert she knew and loved was resurfacing.

'That's wonderful,' Betty responded, delighted for her friend after watching how the devastating impact of war had left Nancy feeling helpless and scared. 'You must be over the moon.'

'I am.' Nancy beamed. 'I think it will give Bert the purpose he needs.' Then turning to Frank, who was sat at the opposite end of the table next to Archie, she added, 'Thank you. Whatever you said to Bert in the pub that day, it did the trick.'

'Not at all, duck. I'm just glad he's feeling a bit more chipper.'

'And what about William, Betty?' Nancy asked. 'Have you heard from him lately?'

Betty's fiancé had been stationed in Canada while he trained to be an RAF pilot.

'I have actually,' she replied, neatly folding the brown greaseproof paper Ivy had wrapped her egg sandwiches in that morning. 'He's on his way back to England!'

'What?' Patty gasped, wiping away the detritus of crumbs that had collected around her mouth. 'You kept that quiet.'

'I only got the letter on Saturday. Can you believe he's been to Hollywood?'

'Where the films are made?' Patty asked, in awe.

'Yes! They were all given a few days' leave before coming home. And wait until you hear this. When they got there, Deanna Durbin was recording her new picture and she put on a bit of a performance for them all! Can you believe it?'

'Jammy sod!' Archie said.

'Oi!' Patty shrilled, the tiniest surge of jealousy pricking her. Deanna Durbin was the epitome of the *girl next door*, with her innocent, sweet smile and enviable natural beauty.

'Don't tell me you haven't ogled over Clarke Gable!'

'Mmmm,' Patty mouthed, conceding she too had admired the good-looking heart-throbs that had burst onto the screen at the Pavilion in Attercliffe.

'When's he due back, duck?' Dolly asked, tactfully diverting the conversation to avoid one of Patty's infamous sulks.

'As far as I know he could be back already. He posted the letter from Moncton in Canada, telling me he was just about to get on a train to New York, where *The Queen Elizabeth* liner would be waiting to bring him and the rest of his troop back to Gourock in Scotland.'

'Oh, Betty. That's wonderful news!' Nancy exclaimed. She knew how much her friend had missed her fiancé. 'It sounds like you might get to see him soon.'

'Yes. I hope so.' But what Betty didn't say, determined to try and stay positive, is that in many ways she had felt happier when William was in Canada. He might have been soaring above the skies in those cumbersome machines, which seemed to somehow defy gravity, but he wasn't fighting Jerry and going into combat with the Luftwaffe.

Over the last two months, England had taken a battering. Hitler had instructed his air force to bombard Blighty at an increasingly terrifying frequency. London was being heavily targeted night after night, the sirens alerting the city at least once a day that Jerry was on his way. Hundreds of German fighter planes dropped thousands of bombs, destroying the East End, killing countless innocent civilians and leaving even more homeless. Sheffield hadn't escaped Hitler's mission. The casualties hadn't been anywhere near as prolific, but lives had been lost and many others were left relying on relatives and the authorities to put a roof over their heads. Betty was astute enough to realize once her William was fully trained, it would be his job to go into battle against them.

Despite her normally stoic attitude, the horrifying thought sent shivers down her spine and caused her to wake up in a cold sweat in the middle of the night. But Betty was also pragmatic enough to know, despite how much she wished she could, there wasn't a single thing she could do about it and she just needed to concentrate on the here and now. She'd followed William's advice to try and enjoy life more and taken Daisy up on her offer for trips to the pictures and The Skates and the odd shopping trip. Still, she never turned down any overtime at the factory, and she put in several hours a week at the WVS depot in Fulwood, where volunteers were making bandages and other medical supplies for hospitals.

'Try not to worry,' Daisy quietly said, discreetly touching Betty's arm. The two women had become firm friends and Betty had confided in her friend about her worries.

'Thank you.' Betty nodded, taking the last mouthful of her now tepid mug of tea, reminding herself she was still one of the lucky ones. She had a roof over her head and a sweetheart that, with any luck, she would soon be able to hold in her arms.

Chapter 4

'No arguments, but I'd like to get this round,' Hattie insisted, as she, Patty, Betty, Nancy, Daisy and Dolly made their way to their usual corner in The Welly.

'You don't need to do that, duck,' Dolly immediately protested, knowing Hattie had taken the role at Vickers so she could help her mum with the household budget, to compensate for the amount her dad squandered in the pub.

'It's okay. I'd like to,' Hattie replied. 'It's my way of saying thank you for everything you all did to make my wedding day so special.'

After finally relenting and accepting Hattie's offer, the group of friends were sitting in their usual corner, all nursing a welcome drink, after another long week. 'Cheers m'dears,' Dolly said, raising her glass of pale ale.

'Yes. Cheers,' Nancy answered, quickly followed by the rest of the group. 'Thank you for the drink, Hattie, but there really was no need.'

'It's just a little thank you. You were all so kind and

put in so much effort.' Turning to Betty, she added, 'The tablecloth and lovely matching napkins are very pretty, with the little daisies embroidered into them. I am going to send thank-you notes, but would you let Ivy and Frank know how grateful I am for the glasses. And, Daisy, the vase is beautiful.'

'Ahem,' Patty interrupted.

'I was just getting to you! I love the photo frame. As soon as we get our picture back from the photographers, I'm going to pop it in straightaway.'

'I thought it might be nice for your wedding photo.'

'It will.' Then addressing the rest of the table, Hattie said: 'I really am ever so touched, and John was quite overwhelmed too by everyone's generosity. He wanted me to thank you all.'

'You're very welcome,' Betty replied. 'If you can't get spoilt on your wedding day, there's something very wrong. Are you still walking in the clouds?'

'I suppose I am rather. I can't believe it will be a week, tomorrow, since I got married. Although, what with all the overtime, this week has brought me back down to earth with a bang.'

'I'm sure, but at least we only have half a day left and then we're done until Monday.'

'Thank the chuffin' Lord,' Patty sighed, stifling a yawn. 'I'm shattered.'

'This weekend certainly will feel a little different. It was so nice getting dressed up last Saturday and having something to celebrate. This weekend won't be quite the same,' Betty commented.

Nancy nodded, taking a delicate sip of her port and lemon. 'Has anyone got anything nice planned for this weekend?'

'I've promised our Sally and Emily I'll take them to the library tomorrow afternoon and then I think Archie is taking me to the pictures,' Patty said. 'How about everyone else?'

'Dolly and I are nipping to the WVS tomorrow afternoon, and then I said I'd help Ivy and Frank in the garden on Sunday before the weather turns cold,' Betty explained.

'Any more news from William yet?'

'No, but hopefully it won't be too much longer. I know it can take up to a couple of weeks to cross the Atlantic but I'm assuming he must be nearly back by now.'

'I'll keep everything crossed you hear from him soon,' Nancy said, before turning to Dolly. 'How about you? Anything nice lined up?'

'Nothing will top last weekend, but I can't complain. I've got m' lovely granddaughters on Sunday and I've promised we'll do some crafts. They are just the tonic after a full week at work and it gives my daughters-in-law a break for a few hours.'

'Aw, that will be nice. I'm sure they appreciate it. Have you heard from your sons recently?'

'I have, duck. They are still on a ship somewhere. They

couldn't say where, but at least I know they are safe and well. That's all that matters.'

'It really is,' Nancy agreed.

'How's your Bert got on this week with the Home Guard?' Dolly asked.

'Really well. I think it's given him a boost. It sounds like Bert's skills are just what they need. He says they will be using him to train up some of the younger lads.'

'Isn't that grand? Where's he stationed at?'

'Not far. Just off Beaumont Road at Manor Field. I am pleased. I think Bert would have struggled if they didn't have a role for him. If it wasn't for his leg injury, I know he would have been back on the front line. He needs to be able to do something, so this is the perfect solution.' Nancy didn't vocalize her thoughts, as she didn't want to come across as thoughtless in front of her friends, but there was a tiny element of her that was almost grateful Bert had been hurt, forcing him to be discharged from the Army. This way he could be at home with her, Billy and Linda, allowing for some semblance of normality.

'I'm sure he'll be an asset to them,' Dolly enthused. 'Men like your Bert are a credit to the country.'

'Thank you, luv. That's kind of you to say.'

'What about you, Hatts?' Patty asked. 'Anything planned for the weekend? I haven't owt on this Sunday if you fancy meeting up?'

'That would be nice. I'm going to take Mum out

tomorrow afternoon for a little treat, but apart from that I'm free.'

'Shall we meet up at The Skates?' Patty was determined to make more of an effort with Hattie, after she'd realized how hard it was at home for her. 'I should warn you, though, I might have m' sisters with me.'

'That would be lovely and the more the merrier. Does anyone else fancy it?'

'I could ask our Polly and Annie too,' Daisy chirped. 'They will never turn down roller-skating.'

'I'd have loved to,' Nancy interjected, 'but I'm cooking for Doris and her brood. It's the least I can do after what she's done for me over the last year.'

'I'll see how I get on,' Betty added. 'If the weeding doesn't take too long, I'll pop along.'

'That's a date then,' Patty said, draining her glass. 'Right, I'm sorry to be a party pooper, but I better get off. Dad said he is treating us all to a chippy tea, so I don't want to miss that.'

'And I better get back. I've not seen much of our Billy and Linda this week. I promised I would be back for bedtime stories.'

'Don't worry. I could do with an early night,' Dolly said, pulling on her coat, a chill now creeping in as autumn replaced summer. 'Thanks again for the drink, Hattie. Next one is on me.'

'As I say. It was just a little thank you.' What Hattie hadn't said was she'd been grateful for a reason to stay out of the house a bit longer. Despite her dad being on his best behaviour for her wedding, he'd been in a vile mood all week, fuelled by his nightly visits to the pub. She hated leaving her mum at home with him, but if she was honest with herself, part of her dreaded going home.

Knowing she had little choice, after waving her friends goodbye, Hattie put one foot in front of the other and made her way home, hoping her dad would either be in the pub, although that only delayed the inevitable fallout, or was already passed out on the couch, but as she opened the back door, Hattie knew before she'd even stepped over the doorstep, which it was to be.

'Where's m' dinner, woman,' Vinny growled. 'What's a man got to do to get a flamin' hot meal in this house?'

'It's in the oven,' Diane sighed, exasperated. 'I didn't know what time you'd be back.'

'Don't you start with yer smart-arse answers.' Vinny slammed his fist on the kitchen table as he dropped heavily into one of the chairs. 'I've already heard enough from that stupid bloody landlord. Jumped-up idiot.'

Hattie took a deep breath, any faint hope of a peaceful evening, after what had been a wonderful hour in the pub, obliterated.

'Oh, here she is. Making an appearance. Lady bloody muck.' Vinny scowled as Hattie hung her coat and gas mask on one of the hooks next to the back door.

'Leave the girl be, Vin,' Diane said, carefully lifting a casserole dish out of the oven.

'Don't you tell me what to do in my own house,' Vinny barked, already on his feet, his face red with rage. 'The little bitch thinks she's better than us now that she's married into that snooty bloody family.'

Hattie had been expecting the attack. She knew her dad would think she'd married above her station, just because John's dad wore a suit to the office and his mum had never had to work, or *get her hands dirty*, as her dad liked to remind her.

'Why don't you sit back down, Vin. I've got you a beef stew here. Have it while it's still hot.'

'Beef! Who are you trying to kid?' Vinny was centimetres from Diane's face, spit projecting from his mouth as he roared his obscenities. 'I can't remember the last time you put any 'alf decent meat in m' dinner. I don't know why I'm bloody married to yer. Yer as useless as her.' Vinny turned his head to sneer at Hattie, who closed her eyes in despair. If her dad didn't spend every spare penny, or more, staring into an empty pint glass, they might have a bit of spare money for better cuts of meat when rations allowed.

'Don't you shut yer eyes on me, yer jumped-up little madam.' Vinny rounded on his daughter, his whole body tensing in rage. Hattie froze. She'd lost count of the number of times her dad had taken his anger out on her mum, but he'd never aimed his drunken anger at her before.

'Vinny!' Diane gasped instinctively, her maternal instinct immediately kicking in.

In a flash, Vinny about-turned, his arms flaying indiscriminately, as fury at being reproached soared through him. 'What?' he yelled, swiping his clenched fist at Diane, narrowly missing his wife's face but causing the red-hot casserole to hurtle from her hands. It fell in slow motion, before exploding with colossal force onto the floor, the gloopy mixture of gravy and vegetables erupting across the kitchen. The volcanic splatter, which hit every wall and cupboard and covered the normally impeccably clean floor, momentarily stunned Vinny. But his vitriolic verbal assault was short-lived. 'Yer silly bloody cow. Now look what you've done. What am I supposed to eat now?' he screamed, without a single ounce of remorse. 'Give me some money. I'm going to the chippy.'

Diane, who was now silent, heavy tears cascading down her blotchy cheeks, slowly shook her head. 'I haven't got any. I spent the last of what I had in the butcher's today.'

On your dinner, Hattie thought, an amalgamation of disgust and fear leaving her frozen to the spot. She knew one wrong word and her dad could destroy anything in sight, and her mum would, yet again, bear the brunt of it.

'Don't lie to me. I know you hide it around the house. Where have you bloody well hidden it this time?'

'There's nothing left.' In fact, there was less than nothing. Every penny Diane had tried to squirrel away, in socks, under floorboards and behind bags of flour, Vinny had somehow found, leaving his wife terrified she wouldn't have enough to cover the following week's bills.

'Yer lying,' Vinny stormed, his cheeks reddening in rage.

'I promise. I'm not, Vin,' Diane sobbed, her whole body trembling. 'I'd give you it if I had it.'

'Give me it,' Vinny demanded, grabbing his wife by the shoulders, his thick, grubby fingers digging through her jumper, squeezing Diane's skin. 'I know you have some.'

'Dad!' Hattie gasped, finding her voice. 'Mum's not lying. Let go of her. You're hurting her.'

'I might have guessed you two would be in bloody cahoots,' Vinny spat, spinning around to face his daughter. 'The pair of yer lying to me after everything I've done for yer both. Putting a roof over yer heads and putting food on the table. You'd be nothin' without me.'

Hattie clenched her eyes shut. There would be no reasoning with her dad. He was too far gone to talk any sense into him. Instead, she reached into her bag and pulled out her purse and took out a few coins. 'Take this,' she muttered, pushing the money into her dad's hand.

Vinny stared at his daughter, a mixture of astonishment and shock. Hattie had never given him money before, nor had he sunk so low to ask. For a few seconds he didn't say a word, as his daughter's unexpected gesture attempted to infiltrate his fuddled mind. A knowing glance passed between them – Vinny knew he'd crossed an invisible line, but he was too drunk to recognise how low he'd stooped. He quickly snapped his dirty, sausage-like fingers around the coins, which despite how much he'd already downed that night he'd guessed would be enough for another pint if he only bought some scraps from the chip shop.

'About time you upped yer keep,' Vinny quipped, a weak and shallow attempt to defend his own despicable actions. His selfish mission accomplished, he shoved the cash in his pocket and staggered across the kitchen and out the back door. The loud slam caused Hattie to shudder in horror. What sort of monster had her dad become?

As soon as he'd left, Diane erupted into tears, dropping her head into her hands, the enormity of her husband's latest violent mood swing consuming her.

'It's all right,' Hattie said, rushing to her mum's side. 'Don't cry. He'll be gone for at least a couple of hours.'

'You shouldn't have to see this,' Diane sobbed. 'This isn't how it should be. I'm your mum. I should be protecting you. You shouldn't have to look after me.'

'You don't have to worry about that,' Hattie said gently, guiding her mum to a chair. 'I'm an adult. We need to look after each other.'

'Oh, Hattie. I feel like I've let you down.'

Hattie wrapped her arms tightly around her mum. 'You mustn't think like that. You could never let me down. You're the best mum, and only mum, I could ever want. It's Dad that has let us both down.'

'I wish I'd had the strength to leave him years ago when his drinking really took hold. I just didn't know how to. I just kept thinking, praying even, he would get better. I've been so naive.'

'You haven't, Mum. How were you to know he would get worse? You did what any of us would.'

'Well, that's not got me very far. I've made a reyt mess of my life.'

'Come on,' Hattie said firmly. As much as she felt utterly drained by her dad's latest episode, her inner strength kicked in. She couldn't let her mum fall apart. 'There's absolutely no point thinking about the ifs and maybes. It won't change anything.'

Diane lifted her head from her daughter's chest. 'Oh, luv,' she cried. 'What would I do without you?'

'We make a good team,' Hattie said, with as much fortitude as she could muster. 'Right, I know we shouldn't have to, but let's get this mess cleaned up and then I'll make us a cuppa and fix us something else for dinner.'

'I'm not sure there's anything else in, luv.'

'Let me worry about that,' Hattie reassured her mum. 'I'm sure I can find us something.'

Forty minutes later, the kitchen restored to its former, pre-apocalyptic state, Hattie brought a freshly made pot of tea to the now immaculate table. 'You really are an absolute blessing.' Diane smiled gratefully.

'I've managed to slice the bread thinly enough to make us a couple of Spam sandwiches too,' Hattie added. 'It's not much but it will keep us both going. I can nip to the shops in the morning.'

'Thank you,' Diane repeated. 'And I know I've already said it, but I really am sorry.'

'You have nothing to apologise for. We'll find a way of getting through this together.'

Hattie knew there was no point in hoping her dad would change. That ship had well and truly sailed. Instead, she needed to focus on trying to keep her mum safe. As much as Hattie would have wanted to move in with John as soon as they'd got married, she was glad, for the time being at least, she was here to support her mum, who she realized, with increasing alarm, may not survive without her.

Chapter 5

Sunday, 20 October 1940

'You're here,' Patty trilled, welcoming Hattie in through the back door. 'I didn't see you after work yesterday, so I wasn't sure you would still make it.'

'If I'm honest, I wasn't sure myself.'

Patty threw her friend a quizzical glance, but as she took in her pale pallor, and exhausted expression, she realized, instantly, something was up. 'It's not John, is it?' she asked, urgently. 'Have you heard from him? Has summat happened?'

'No. No. It's nothing like that,' Hattie sighed, taking off her anorak and hanging it off the back of the kitchen chair, which she promptly slumped into.

'Well, what is it then? You look shattered.'

'I am pretty tired,' Hattie admitted, the mere mention of the word causing her to yawn.

'Do you want to talk about it?'

'Oh, there's not much to say really. It's just Dad. He's been on another one of his drinking sprees this weekend.

My mum is at her wit's end. She's terrified of upsetting him in case he flies into a rage.'

'Was this last night?' Patty asked, tentatively.

'He started Friday but then took himself out yesterday afternoon.'

Patty listened quietly as Hattie repeated the awful events of the weekend. Although her dad hadn't exploded to the same velocity after he'd got home last night, he'd still accused her mum of being a 'good f' nothin' useless bitch' when his dinner wasn't waiting, piping hot, on the table for him. Terrified he would erupt again, Diane had rushed around making him a sausage sandwich, while he'd verbally assaulted her with one insult after another. Hattie had desperately wanted to interfere, to tell her dad to stop, but she knew, from experience, it would only fuel his volatile temper.

'I'm so sorry,' Patty said, when Hattie finished reliving the upsetting events of the last forty-eight hours. She genuinely couldn't begin to imagine how Hattie must feel. Patty had been blessed with two loving parents and been brought up in a calm and happy household. Her mum and dad might have the odd light-hearted quibble, but she had never heard either of them raise their voices, let alone lose their temper.

'It's okay. It's not your fault,' Hattie replied, her shoulders slumping. 'I just didn't get much sleep. I'm hoping Dad will turn in early tonight, and I can catch up before work tomorrow, but I know that's probably wishful thinking.'

'Is there anything I can do?' Patty asked, racking her brains for a way to make life a little easier for her friend. She'd vowed to herself, after realizing how hard life was at home for Hattie, she would be more supportive and less self-absorbed.

'I really don't think there is,' Hattie replied, shaking her head. 'I'm not sure there is anything anyone can do. My dad isn't going to listen to anyone, and Mum feels trapped. I just need to try and keep her spirits up when I can, but it's easier said than done.'

'Did you manage to take her out for a treat yesterday?'

'Sort of. We managed a quick cuppa and shared a cake at Browns but I ended up going shopping for extra food, after Dad's temper caused Friday night's stew, which should have lasted a couple of days, to end up in the bin.'

Momentarily stumped for words, Patty quickly digested what her friend was telling her. Hattie's home life really was a world apart from her own, and she was at a loss to know how to make things any easier for her friend. 'You know, you and your mum are welcome here any time, even if it's just for a bit of a breather for a few hours,' Patty finally offered. 'I know it's not much, but the kettle is always on. And, you know what my mom is like, she is always happy to see you.'

'Thanks, Patty. That's ever so kind of you. I might take you up on the offer if it all gets too much.' But Hattie knew, despite Patty's thoughtful gesture, it was going to take a lot more than a few hours' respite to try and help her mum achieve the life she deserved.

'Did I hear my name being mentioned?' Angie said, interrupting Hattie's thoughts. 'Oh hello, luv. I thought I could hear our Patty nattering away. She said you were coming over, before going to The Skates.'

'Hello, Angie. I'm not too bad, thank you,' Hattie replied, too tired to repeat the whole story again. 'How are you?'

'I can't complain. Our Tom Tom, by some miracle, has just had a nap, so I managed to put my feet up in the front room for half an hour.'

'I'm sure that was well deserved.'

'I don't know about that, luv, but I reyt enjoyed it. I could get used to it, but there's no way this little terror would let me get away with it.' Angie glanced towards her son, who was perched on her hip, his sleepy face nuzzled into his mum's soft shoulder.

'I can guarantee he won't.' Patty laughed, gently squeezing her little brother's chubby cheeks. 'He's got more energy than the lot of us put together.'

'Yer not wrong there, luv,' Angie agreed. 'Now, Hattie, has our Patty made you a cuppa?'

'Sorry. I was just about to,' Patty interjected. 'It'll have to be a quick one, mind, we are meeting everyone else in a bit.'

'Plenty of time.' Angie grinned, handing Tom Tom to Patty, and heading towards the kettle.

Forty-five minutes later, the two friends, flanked by

Patty's sisters, greeted Daisy and her siblings, as well as Dolly and her two granddaughters.

'No sign of Betty?' Dolly asked, more than stated.

'I'm here,' came Betty's familiar voice, as she strode up Church Lane. 'Sorry, Ivy insisted I sit down and have a Sunday dinner after hours in the garden.'

'You have been busy!' Dolly grinned, not that any of the women would expect anything less.

'It keeps me out of mischief,' Betty replied.

'Heaven forbid you just relax,' Patty joked.

'You know what I'm like,' Betty answered, taking the comment in the good-natured spirit it was meant.

'Right. Shall we get inside? It's getting a bit nippy out here,' Patty suggested, pulling her coat tighter around her body.

'Yes, let's get in,' Dolly agreed. 'These two are desperate to have a go, aren't you?' she added, smiling at her granddaughters, their enthusiastic nods acting as an answer.

After the rest of the group had all changed into their roller-skates, Dolly offered to look after bags and coats. 'I think I'm probably twenty years too old for this malarkey,' she said, laughing, as the other women promised to take good care of her granddaughters.

'I'll keep them downstairs in Mugs Alley to begin with,' Hattie promised. 'It can get a bit fast upstairs.'

'I'll stay with you.' Daisy nodded. 'My sisters are still a bit wobbly.'

'Well, enjoy yourselves.' Dolly grinned, giving her granddaughters each a peck on the top of their heads, before perching on one of the ringside benches. 'I'll be right here watching.'

For the next hour and a half, the group of friends, siblings and little girls laughed and giggled as they skated, even building up enough confidence to let go of Hattie's hands for a few seconds at a time. As for Hattie, she managed to put her dad out of her mind for those precious ninety minutes, and simply enjoy revelling in some much-needed fun.

Then, when the girls had finally tired, the three of them came to a standstill next to Dolly.

'Well, weren't you two marvellous?' Dolly said. 'Did you enjoy it?'

'Yes,' came her granddaughters' identical reply in perfect unison.

'Can we come again?' Lucy asked.

'I think we can manage that,' their nannan affirmed. 'As long as Hattie, here, doesn't mind coming too. I reckon I'd be lucky to last ten seconds before landing flat on m' face!'

'It would be a pleasure,' Hattie confirmed. 'They have been as good as gold, and it was just what I needed.'

Helping her granddaughters out of their roller-skates, Dolly turned to Hattie. 'Is everything all right, luv? I didn't like to say earlier, but you do look a bit worn out.'

'I won't lie. It's been a difficult weekend with my dad.'

'Would you like to talk about it?'

Hattie glanced at the two little girls, who were now

buckling up the brass-coloured clasps of their identical, well-polished brown leather shoes. The last thing she would want to do is taint their innocent outlook on life. 'Maybe not right now but I'm sure I'll see you in the week in the canteen.'

Dolly nodded, instinctively understanding whatever it was that had caused Hattie to look as though she hadn't slept a wink wasn't suitable listening material for Lucy and Milly. 'Make sure you do, duck. It's amazing what a tonic a cuppa and a chat can be.'

'I promise,' Hattie replied gratefully. For years, she had tried to keep her dad's drunken misdemeanours a secret, only sharing them with John, but she realized, now, more than ever, if she was ever going to find a way to help her poor, downtrodden mum, she needed the help and support of her friends.

Deep in thought after hugging Dolly and the rest of her friends goodbye, Hattie made her way home, but as she turned onto her street, the high-pitched screeching of the air-raid sirens suddenly alerted her to the fact her mum was at home alone with her dad, and no doubt battling to persuade him to get to the community shelter. Quickening her step, Hattie burst into a run.

Chapter 6

'Mum,' Hattie said, her tone indicating the urgency of her plea, as she rushed into the house. 'We have to go.'

Diane looked at her husband, her eyes bestowing what she daren't actually say.

'I'm not going anywhere,' Vinny said, adamantly.

The air-raid sirens had been screeching for several minutes, a constant reminder Hitler had no intention of easing off his stampede through Europe.

'I can't leave him, luv,' Diane whispered as Hattie tried to give her mum her gas mask, coat and hat.

Hattie knew no matter what she said, she wouldn't persuade her mum. Despite how appallingly her dad treated her mum, she had unwavering loyalty.

'What if something happens?'

Hattie nodded, resigned, knowing her mum would not change her mind.

'Let's at least get under the stairs.'

'Okay, luv.' Then turning to her husband, Diane added. 'Vinny?'

'I'm not moving an inch,' he barked, burying his head deeper into that week's copy of the *Sheffield Telegraph and Independent*.

'Come on, Mum,' Hattie insisted, touching her mum's arm, appalled by her dad's selfish actions.

Diane reluctantly followed her daughter to the tiny cubby hole they had used as a shelter since war had broken out, but not before she glanced over her shoulder one final time, in the hope she could somehow persuade Vinny. In his usual obstinate way, he didn't even look up.

'I'm sorry,' Diane whispered as she sat down on the cushions she had placed in there months earlier. Her eyes adapted to the darkness, with only a torch emanating the dimmest of light.

'It's not you who should be apologizing,' Hattie replied, placing her hand over her mum's, which, as it always did during a raid, was shaking uncontrollably, her nerves shot to pieces.

With every explosion, Diane shuddered. All Hattie could do was pray the raid would be over sooner rather than later, and hope, with all her might, by some miracle, they would survive the night in one piece.

Just over a mile away, Nancy pulled Linda onto her knee and wrapped herself around Billy, as they squeezed into the communal shelter. Although Bert wasn't as visibly shaken by the bombs they could hear dropping over

Sheffield, he still found the raids hard, each bang bringing back haunting memories of what he'd witnessed in the race against time at Dunkirk.

'We'll be okay,' Nancy mouthed to her husband, who was sat opposite her, next to Patty's dad, Bill, who always made sure he looked out for Bert as the sirens echoed around the city.

Bert nodded, but didn't trust himself to say anything, desperate to keep a hold on the fear coursing through his body. The nightmares and flashbacks still hadn't eased, visions of his friends being killed, victims of German bullets, as they made their way through the French countryside.

The end of the summer and early autumn had seen Sheffield, like most major cities up and down the country, targeted on a nearly nightly basis. Countless houses had been left uninhabitable, schools had been damaged and churches now had holes in their roofs, a constant reminder that the Luftwaffe weren't ignoring the city. But parishioners had worked hard to repair the church the best they could so weddings and services could still go ahead.

Farther along the bench Nancy had propped herself on, Angie and Patty, who, along with her friends, had rushed from The Skates to the communal shelter, were comforting Tom Tom, his elder brother and sisters, as they shared a tub of biscuits.

'Do you think Archie will be okay?' Patty asked her mom, her mind wandering to the ifs and maybes.

'He's a sensible lad,' Angie reassured her daughter. 'He's not daft. He'll do what it takes to keep himself and everyone else safe.'

'Chuffin' Hitler,' Patty whispered, vociferating the thoughts of everyone else in the shelter.

As usual card games started up, dominoes were taken out and the children played with dolls, toy cars and marbles as a distraction. Still, the hours passed by slowly. It was after midnight when the all-clear finally sounded, and the warden on duty opened the door, letting everyone out, the events of the night unclear.

'How are you all?' Dolly asked, as she plonked herself down on a free chair at the table where her friends had gathered in the factory canteen for lunch on Monday.

'Not s' bad, duck, despite yesterday's sirens. I thought they would never end,' Frank replied.

'Tell me about it,' Dolly yawned, 'I didn't 'alf struggle to get to sleep afterwards.'

'I know what yer mean,' the weary-faced foreman agreed. 'I could have certainly done with an extra couple of hours. Some of the fellas were telling me incendiary bombs were dropped in Shiregreen.'

'Was anybody hurt?' Dolly asked, instinctively.

'I don't think so, thankfully. By some miracle it sounds like houses were missed and they landed on the waste ground on Standon Road, not far from the Barrage Balloon Headquarters. The lads were saying it's left a great twenty-foot-long crater that's about six feet deep.'

'I heard someone else say a bomb landed on the golf course at Concord Park,' Archie added.

'Dear me,' Dolly sighed, 'but rather they land there than on some poor soul's house.'

'I won't argue with you there, duck.' Frank nodded.

'It did seem to go on forever last night, though.' Patty yawned. 'It was the early hours when we got to bed. I'll be holding m' eyes open with matchsticks. Between dashing to the shelter and then our Tom Tom waking me up before six, I feel like I could fall asleep standing up.'

'Get another brew down yer, duck,' Dolly encouraged. 'It should be well and truly brewed by now. It will help get you through the afternoon if nothing else.'

'Thanks, Dolly. I think I might just do that,' Patty added, standing up with her empty mug. 'Anyone else fancy a top-up?'

'Well, if you're offering.' Archie grinned.

'Go on then, duck. I'll have another,' Frank added. 'It's a long time until six o'clock and even longer until I get home.'

'More overtime,' Patty groaned. 'Did you have to remind me.'

'Sorry, duck,' Frank sympathized. 'There doesn't seem to be any let-up. The orders aren't slowing down. In fact, if anything, we are under pressure to get everything out quicker.'

Nancy quietly counted her blessings. Working for the Home Guard came with risks, but at least Bert was back with her in Sheffield. Despite the air raids, having her husband home had made life feel a lot easier.

'Any word from your William?' Dolly asked, turning to Betty.

'I have actually. There was a letter waiting for me last night when I got home.'

'Really?' Daisy quizzed. 'You didn't say.'

'Sorry. It was such a rush clocking in this morning I didn't get chance.'

'Is he finally back in England?'

'Yes! He's actually in Harrogate. At least he was when he wrote the letter that arrived yesterday.'

'Harrogate!' Daisy repeated. 'That's only the other side of Yorkshire.'

'I know. I can't quite believe it myself. And to top it off, he has been billeted to the rather grand Majestic Hotel.'

'Really? I'm not an expert but that doesn't sound like typical RAF quarters.'

'I don't think it is! Apparently, the RAF have taken it over to house aircrew and staff.'

'Maybe I should have joined the RAF! I'm clearly in the wrong job,' Patty groaned. 'I don't know owt about the Majestic but I'm sure it's a damn sight cleaner than those mucky girders we're parked next to in the cranes. I swear there's a foot of dust and grime in them. I bet they don't have that at the Majestic!'

'Patty!' Archie retorted. 'William is training to be a pilot. I don't think we can begrudge him a tiny bit of luxury, and I should imagine it's not all feather pillows and luxury eiderdowns.'

'I was just saying,' Patty said, shaking her head at Archie's reproach.

'Anyway, I'm sure it must be lovely knowing he's back on home ground?' Daisy commented, hoping to divert the conversation and prevent Patty from getting herself into one of her little melodramas. 'Did William say anything else?'

'Only that he had a bit of a choppy voyage back from America across the Atlantic, but I think in a small way he rather enjoyed it.'

'How long did it take?' Patty asked, oblivious to how big the Atlantic even was, and keen to show she wasn't trying to dominate the conversation. 'Has he been at sea for weeks on end?'

'Actually, he said it only took about five days.'

'Really? But America is on the other side of the world!'

'I guess modern transportation is better than it's ever been. William did say it was rather a grand ship.'

'In what way?' The thought of any form of luxury yet again piquing Patty's attention.

'Apparently it is one of the largest ships in the world, and there were ballrooms and huge dining rooms that they were allowed to nosy about in.'

'Did they have any dances?' Patty asked, her eyes lighting up.

'No!' Betty chuckled. 'It wasn't a holiday. They just used some of the best ships out of necessity.'

'What a shame. Seems such a waste.'

Betty shook her head bemused. Sometimes she really did wonder what went on in Patty's mind but surmised it must be lovely to have such a rose-tinted outlook on the world, even if there was a war raging across Europe.

'I'm glad he's all right, duck,' Dolly commented. 'It must be a weight off your mind.'

'Yes. Yes, it is,' Betty agreed.

What she didn't add, to avoid worrying Dolly, whose sons were in the middle of an ocean somewhere, was that William and the rest of the airmen spent most of their time on the lookout for German U-boats. Instead, Betty nodded as she took a sip of her new steaming mug of tea that Patty had topped up, hoping her quick response hid her real feelings. The reality was she wasn't sure how she felt.

'He might get some leave soon?' Nancy suggested hopefully, knowing only too well how hard it is to be separated from someone you love so dearly.

'Yes. That would be nice. It seems odd that he is virtually in the same county but still feels such a long way away.'

'I can understand that,' Nancy empathized, the memories of Bert being in hospital in Portsmouth still fresh in her mind. After eleven months of being away at war, he had finally got back to England after being shot in his leg on his way to Dunkirk, causing him to be separated from the rest of his battalion. 'I'll keep everything crossed,' Nancy added. 'It would be wonderful for you to see each other.'

'Thank you. And how's your Bert getting on?'

'Actually. Really well. I've seen a massive change in him over the last couple of weeks. He still gets shook up when the sirens go off, but he's really enjoying his new role. I think it's given him a sense of worth again.'

'Are you allowed to say what he's doing with the Home Guard?' Betty asked.

'From what I can gather he's helping with combat training at the moment.'

'And he's okay with that? It's not causing him any horrible flashbacks? Sorry, I hope that doesn't sound tactless.'

'Not at all. I know exactly what you mean. I was a bit worried when Bert first told me what he was doing, but if anything, it seems to be helping. I know it sounds the wrong way round, and I can't say it's not affecting him at all, but I think the fact he's feeling useful is overriding some of the memories at least.'

'Well, that's a good thing,' Betty encouraged. 'As long as he's all right, that's all that matters.'

'Thanks, Betty,' Nancy said gratefully. 'It really has made the world of difference.'

'Is it Bert's lot that have been removing all the street signs across Sheffield?' Frank asked, putting his now-empty mug back on the table. 'I saw a few blokes in what I thought were Home Guard uniforms dismantling some signposts at the weekend when I nipped to get some new chicken wire for the hen coop.'

'Oh, yes.' Nancy chuckled. 'Bert did mention something about that.'

'What on earth are they doing that for?' Patty asked. 'It's hard enough of a night with only a dim torch to see where yer going, with no streetlights. Are they really trying to confuse us?'

'Oh, Patts!' Archie laughed, putting his hand on her shoulder. 'It's not meant to confuse *us*.'

'Well, they're doing a good job of trying. Who else would they be trying to send the wrong way?'

The friends all exchanged a knowing look, a shared sense of utter astonishment.

'It's in case the Germans invade,' Nancy explained tactfully. 'It's Hitler's lot they want to confuse, not you.'

An expression of realization passed over Patty's face. 'Could that really happen?'

'Well, it's hard to say, duck,' Frank said. 'Hitler is certainly trying his best to get us all to succumb with his constant nightly bombardments. London has taken some nasty blows, but I reckon our RAF are giving him a run for his money. And because we are an island, we are not as easy to get to as the other countries on the Continent. They would have to get to us via the sea and that's not as easy as it sounds.'

Although Frank sounded confident, it was only because he didn't want to worry the rest of the gang, who were all, in one way or another, coping with so much. If the truth be known, he really had no idea what the future held.

'Chuffin' 'eck,' Patty gasped. 'That's a bit depressing. I wish I hadn't asked.'

'Nobody knows what's around the corner,' Frank said wistfully as he stood up, indicating dinnertime was over, 'but one thing is for sure, we've already proved Hitler can't just send his Luftwaffe and think we'll stick our hands in the air and surrender. He's underestimated what a force us Brits are to be reckoned with.'

As the friends made their way back to work, each one of them was lost in their own thoughts. Betty and Hattie fretted about their William and John, Patty for Archie and his nightly patrols, and Nancy, who was eternally grateful Bert was back in Sheffield, started to wonder how safe their city really was.

Chapter 7

Saturday, 26 October 1940

'William!' Betty exclaimed, as she opened the front door and stared back at her fiancé, dressed in his perfectly starched blue uniform, a smile on his face as big as the Cheshire cat's. 'What on earth are you doing here?'

'I thought I'd surprise you. And by the look on your face, I think I've succeeded.'

'You certainly have.'

'Come here,' William said, his arms open wide.

Betty didn't have to be asked twice. She stepped over the doorstep and into William's embrace. As she wrapped her arms around her fiancé's athletic body, calmness, mixed with overwhelming happiness, settled over her. For so long her mind had been a flurry of conflicting emotions. She had hoped William would stay in Canada, where he would be safer away from Hitler's Luftwaffe, for as long as possible, but on the other hand she missed her fiancé with every fibre of her being. But now he was here, a moment Betty hadn't even dared dream about, she didn't want to let him go ever again.

'That's more like it.' William chuckled, as he held Betty tight. 'I can't tell you how much I've been looking forward to holding you again.'

'I haven't dared even think about it,' Betty whispered, her eyes brimming with tears.

'You dafty,' William said. He released his arms from around Betty's slender back, and gently tilted her face to his, before tenderly kissing her on the lips. 'I was always coming back to you,' he added, as their lips parted.

'I know,' Betty sighed. 'I just wanted you to stay safe.'

'I've told you,' William started. 'I am going to be the best pilot the RAF has ever seen. You just need to trust me.'

Betty knew this wasn't the time to tell William her worries, determined not to spoil the moment. Instead, she leant up, looked into her fiancé's sparkling brown eyes and kissed him again, savouring the taste of his sweet lips and how wonderful it felt.

'Going away clearly has some advantages if this is the welcome home I have to look forward to,' William teased when they drew apart for the second time. 'I could get used to this.'

'William Smith,' Betty admonished, gently tapping him on the arm.

'Right, are you going to invite me in? I couldn't half do with a sit down and a bite to eat if anything is going.'

'Of course. Sorry. Come on in.' Betty stepped backwards into the hall, indicating for William to join her.

'Ivy and Frank are in the kitchen. We were just about to sit down for some dinner. There's plenty. You know what Ivy is like.'

'Are you sure she won't mind? Only I dumped my bag at my mum and dad's, had a quick cuppa and told them I would be back later.'

'Not at all,' Betty enthused. 'You know Ivy. She loves nothing more than feeding someone up.'

'What's that?' came a voice from the end of the hall. 'Did I just hear my . . .' But before Ivy finished her sentence, she too took in the familiar figure. 'My goodness. William! You're back.' Then popping her head back into the kitchen, she added, 'Frank. Come and see who's here.'

The next few minutes passed in a furore of hugs, handshakes and back clapping, as William was greeted by Ivy and Frank, who were as delighted as Betty to see the young RAF trainee pilot back on home ground.

'You will stay for lunch, won't you?' Ivy asked, as the tantalizing smell of bacon and eggs emanated from the kitchen.

'I was hoping you'd offer.' William grinned, throwing Betty a quick wink. 'I'm absolutely starving. My stomach has been rumbling for the last two hours.'

'You've come to the right place then, son,' Frank enthuscd. 'There's always more than enough to go round.'

'Of course,' William acknowledged. 'Betty told me in her letters about the hens, especially Houdini, and the veggie patch. It sounds like you have all been busy.'

'They keep me on my toes!' Frank chuckled. 'Not that I'm complaining. I've got rather attached to the hens.'

'The number of eggs they produce, I'm not surprised,' Betty commented.

'Talking of eggs,' Ivy interrupted. 'I've poached a couple for me and you, Betty, and there's plenty of bacon for these two.'

Five minutes later, the group were sitting around the kitchen table tucking into the hot, and much appreciated, lunch. 'So, William,' Frank asked in between mouthfuls, 'how are you finding the RAF?'

William's eyes lit up, evidence that his lifelong dream to be a pilot hadn't faltered, despite months of being away from home. 'It's been quite the hoot up to now. I have to admit, though, during one of my last flights in Canada, I wasn't actually sure I'd get my pilot wings.'

'What do you mean?' Betty quizzed.

William took a mouthful of his tea and explained, 'I'd set off and it was pretty nippy but nothing I was overly concerned about. I was over Montana and still needed to fly for another two hours to complete my final stage. Anyway, I was drifting about just looking for anything interesting, when the weather really started to turn.'

'In what way?' Ivy asked tentatively.

'It was my own fault. I hadn't realized storm clouds were approaching and I was a long way off from the airfield. I ended up following the route of the Canadian Pacific Railway to keep me on track, but the storm clouds were getting closer. I was still about ten miles from base but estimated the storm was five miles away. I'm not too proud to say, I was getting a tad nervous.'

'That sounds a bit hairy, son.' Frank frowned, with a look of concern.

'I have to say, I was incredibly relieved when my camp came into sight.'

'I'm sure.' Frank nodded. 'I assume you landed that plane of yours okay?'

'I did, but by the time I reached the airfield there were quite a few planes queuing up to land, so we had to just circle around for a while. The storm had turned into a pretty fierce blizzard by then and visibility was down to less than twenty yards. Then as I landed and started to taxi my port engine decided to give up the ghost and I had to abandon the old bird.'

'Thank goodness you got back to the airfield,' Ivy gasped.

'I know. I wouldn't like to think what could have happened if I'd been stuck over unfriendly territory with only one engine working! Anyway, my last flight in Canada was memorable to say the least.'

'Yes,' Ivy replied, as she glanced at Betty, whose elated smile had now been replaced by a somewhat sombre expression.

Betty had listened quietly and didn't know whether to

feel relieved that William had the expertise to land the great hunk of a plane safely or terrified at what was still to come. The RAF had been doing their best to hold their own against the Luftwaffe, during what was being labelled The Battle of Britain, but they had suffered heavy losses too during the raids, which had dominated the skies for the last few months. Blinking away the intrusive thoughts, Betty cut into her perfectly cooked poached egg, allowing the vibrant orange yolk to ooze into her thick piece of wholemeal toast. She desperately tried to stave off her worries, determined to enjoy the little time she had with William.

Sensing Betty's apprehension, Ivy added, 'So, William. Will you be in Harrogate for long? From what Betty tells us you are being accommodated in one of the best hotels in town.'

'It is rather a step up from the dorms at the training centre in Canada,' William replied. 'There are still crystal chandeliers hanging from the ceilings and the bathrooms have marble sinks. The beds are a darn sight comfier too.'

'Make the most of it, son.' Frank grinned. 'You deserve it after all that training. It's not very often we get to see how the other 'alf live.'

'I don't think you do too bad, Frank Brown,' Ivy quipped, in mock jest.

'Oh 'eck! Look what you've started, William.' Frank chuckled, taking the comment in the spirit it was meant.

Then turning to Ivy, he added, 'You can say that again, pet. I'm one lucky fella.' It was true, ever since he and Ivy had got together, his life had been turned round. He hadn't felt love like it since his wife Mary had died and couldn't imagine life without Ivy. He spent far more time at her house than he did in his own tired and neglected two-up, two-down terrace in Attercliffe, but hadn't quite built up the courage to take their relationship to the next stage.

'You will say anything to get yourself out of a tight spot.' Ivy laughed, raising her eyebrows, as she reached across the table to lift the teapot, ready to top up everyone's cups.

'Anyway,' Frank said, picking up what was left of his bacon sandwich, 'before I dig myself into a deeper hole, will you be in Harrogate for a while, William?'

Betty glanced across at her fiancé, hopefully. The thought of him being so close, even if it was just for a little while longer, was something she hadn't dwelt on.

William wasn't daft, and knew his lovely, sweet Bet, who would never stop him pursuing his ambition to become a fully fledged RAF pilot, would also be waiting with bated breath for his reply. Tactfully, he chose his words carefully. 'To be honest, I'm not sure. We haven't been told what the next stage is. At the moment, though, we seem to have lots of lectures and be sent on lots of marches to keep us fit.'

'Will they allow you any more weekend leave?' Betty

asked, before she could stop the eager words leaving her lips.

'I hope so,' William replied optimistically, placing his hand on hers next to him. 'I think the bosses know we are all keen to spend a bit of time at home, before . . .' He stopped and silently reproached himself for his very near slip-up. There was no need to say the words, the reports of air raids across the country causing death and devastation were on everyone's mind. Although London's East End and Docklands had taken the biggest battering, Coventry, Manchester, Liverpool, Southampton and Birmingham, as well as Sheffield, had been frequently targeted.

'Well, that would be wonderful,' Ivy interjected encouragingly, determined to keep the mood buoyant for Betty's sake. After losing her own fiancé, Lewin, in the Great War, she knew Betty would be worrying herself sick about what lay in store for William. 'You will be welcome here whenever you get some time off.'

'Thank you, Mrs Wallis.'

'Ivy! Please. There's absolutely no need for such formalities.'

'Okay,' William agreed. 'And I will definitely take you up on that offer, especially after that delicious bacon sandwich. It was heavenly and just what I needed.'

'Right, Frank,' Ivy said, standing up. 'I think we have some jobs to do in the garden.'

Frank didn't have to be asked twice, taking the hint

that William and Betty would appreciate a bit of time to themselves.

'I'll make you a fresh pot of tea,' Ivy said, as she collected up the empty china plates.

'Actually,' William said. 'I thought Betty and I could go for a little walk, while the weather holds. It's nippy but at least the sun is shining.'

'Oh yes, I'd like that,' Betty replied, keen for some fresh air, hoping the distraction would stop her mind from wandering off into a darker place.

'Let me make you a quick flask of tea,' Ivy insisted, already popping the kettle on.

Ten minutes later, coats on and with a bag holding a flask and a little tin of homemade biscuits, Betty and William made their way down Collinson Street.

'Where are we going?' Betty asked.

'You'll see,' William teased, tightening his grip around his fiancée's shoulder.

Betty didn't have to wait long as William directed her into the local park. 'Oh,' she whispered, warm memories flooding her mind, her imposing worries momentarily vanishing. Ever since the pair had started courting, they had regularly spent weekend afternoons strolling around the tree-lined green space.

'Let's go and sit down and enjoy that tea Ivy made us,' William suggested. 'I want to talk to you.'

Here we go, Betty thought, assuming her beloved William was about to announce his next terrifying posting.

'Remember this?' William asked, as he indicated for Betty to sit down on a bench overlooking a leaf-strewn lawn, a sure sign autumn had well and truly arrived.

How could Betty forget? This was the exact spot where William had proposed a year earlier, just one month after war had broken out and, just like now, he'd surprised her by turning up without any prior warning. Recalling the special moment, Betty instinctively fiddled with her sapphire and diamond engagement ring.

'Remember what I promised you back then?' William prompted.

Betty turned to face her very earnest-looking fiancé, but she was too scared to speak, frightened her words would be overtaken with tears and a jumble of mixed-up and confusing emotions.

'Come here,' William said tenderly, pulling Betty close to him, so her head rested on his firm shoulder. He squeezed his arm between the dip of Betty's slender back and the hard cold metal of the bench, before adding, 'I made you a promise when I proposed.'

Betty turned to face William, fighting to stop the tears which were desperately trying to escape from the corner of her eyes. With his free hand, William took hold of Betty's gloved fingers and entwined them with his on her lap. 'I told you then, and I will say it again now. I love you with all my heart and I will make sure I survive this war so I can get back to you and we can get married and spend the rest of our lives together.'

'Oh,' Betty gasped, unable to hold back the stem of tears any longer.

'Please don't cry,' William whispered, his heart aching at the sight of Betty looking so upset. This was the last thing he wanted today after they hadn't seen each other for so long. It was supposed to be a day of happiness, not upset and angst.

'I'm sorry. I didn't mean to. I just . . .' but Betty couldn't finish her sentence, knowing if she did, she would be at risk of completely breaking down.

'It's all right,' William soothed, hoping to somehow alleviate Betty's fears, even though he realized she had every reason to fret. William wasn't daft. He was all too aware of why Betty was worried. The life of a pilot was a precarious one, but William had refused to allow himself to think about the risks he would have to take when he was finally given the go ahead to defend Britain against Hitler's Luftwaffe. If he allowed himself to go down that road, there's every chance his determination to fight Jerry might falter. No. He had to stay strong and finish what he'd set out to do. From being a little boy, he'd dreamt of becoming a pilot and he wasn't about to give up now, even if it meant his future was unpredictable – to say the least. His country needed him, and he wasn't about to abandon his duty. Summing up all his strength, William took a deep breath.

'I will come home,' he said, his voice steady and strong. 'I will get through this.'

Betty released her hands from William's and took a white handkerchief delicately embroidered with miniature pink flowers from her leather handbag. 'Of course, you will,' she affirmed, desperately trying to pull herself together, knowing, despite how anxious she felt, what William needed now was reassurance, not dramatics. This godforsaken war was hard enough without Betty instilling any doubt into her fiancé's mind. 'You will be the best pilot the RAF has ever seen,' she added, parroting the mantra William had sworn by since the day he'd signed up.

'That's my girl,' William enthused optimistically, even if he also knew, in his heart of hearts, they were both simply trying to bolster the other, as they simultaneously worked hard to bat away the fears, which were doing a damn good job of trying to invade the periphery of their minds.

Betty nodded, painting on a smile, as she wiped away the cascading rivulet of tears, which had left a streaky line down her perfectly made-up face. 'I didn't mean to get into a fluster,' she said. 'I'm just feeling a little overwhelmed and emotional with you showing up out of the blue. I've missed you so much and hadn't dared imagine when I might see you again. And now you are here. I suppose I got myself into a bit of a state.'

'I know and I'm sorry. If I could have got word to you, I would have,' William replied, keen to try and enjoy the rest of the time he and Betty had together.

'Please don't worry about that,' Betty answered, her voice returning to normal. 'I'm just so glad to see you.'

'As am I,' William replied, before taking his fiancée's flushed face in his hands and tenderly kissing her on the lips. As the couple embraced, Betty closed her eyes and vowed not to let her feelings get the better of her again, but instead to savour the deliciously sweet moment.

Chapter 8

Monday, 28 October 1940

'I can't believe your William came to see you!' Patty trilled, as the gang of workers listened in delight to Betty's news as they ate their dinner. 'You must have been over the moon.'

'It was a lovely surprise,' Betty agreed, but the inflection in her voice was at odds with her words.

'Did he tell you if he would be in Harrogate for long?' Hattie asked, knowing only too well how special it was to see the man you loved, but also aware of the longing that followed when you had to say goodbye. Although it had only been just over a fortnight since she and John had got married, it already felt so much longer.

'He wasn't completely sure but thinks he could be there for a little while at least.'

'So, you might get to see him again soon?' Patty quizzed, oblivious to the subtle hint that Betty wasn't her normal optimistic self.

'I hope so but I'm trying not to get my hopes up in case he can't get back again.'

She and William had managed to spend a few precious hours together after Ivy had cooked them all a Sunday roast. Betty had managed to stay upbeat, somehow transporting her fears to the back of her mind, determined not to dampen the little time they had together. After another walk around the local park, William had promised he would do his best to come and see her again soon.

'I'm sure he will get back as soon as he can,' Nancy added, in a bid to bolster her normally stoic friend.

'I'm sorry,' Betty apologized, aware that she might not be coming across as thrilled as her friends would expect her to be. 'It really was a lovely couple of days. I think I'm just missing William more than ever today after such an eventful weekend.'

'I completely understand.' Hattie empathized. 'I know exactly how you feel. It can feel a little disorientating after such a happy time.'

Daisy looked at her two friends in turn. Neither of them were the type to complain, but it was obvious they were both struggling. 'How about we do something nice this weekend?' she suggested. 'I'm not saying it will compensate for William and John not being here, but it might help a little.'

'I'd be up for that,' Patty jumped in, her eyes lighting up at the idea of a bit of fun. 'What are you thinking?'

Nancy, Betty and Hattie swapped a bemused glance, knowing Patty didn't intentionally overtake the conversation.

'I was wondering if we should have a night out at the City Hall on Saturday for a change. It might be nice to get our glad rags on and have a little dance.'

'Oooh yes!' Patty enthused, before her friends could get a word in. 'Any excuse to get dressed up. What do yer all reckon? Hatts and Betty, do you fancy it? Archie is on air-raid duty this weekend, so I'd definitely be up for swapping out of these mucky overalls and getting my glad rags on.'

'Guilty as charged,' Archie said, taking a mouthful of his tea. 'But you girls should go out. You'll have a great time.'

'I might leave you all to it,' Nancy said, apologetically. 'I'd feel a bit guilty leaving Bert at home. Our Billy and Linda will be keen for me to be at home too and if I'm honest, I'm not sure I've got the energy to go dancing after a week here.'

'Of course,' Daisy replied. 'That's completely understandable.' Then turning to Betty, she added, 'What do you think? Do you fancy a girls' night out?'

Betty pondered the idea. She wasn't really in the mood for gadding about, but she also knew, from experience, no good would come from staying at home feeling miserable. The last thing she needed to do was dwell for too long on the ifs and maybes of the consequences of this damnable war or when she might see her beloved fiancé again. And wasn't William always encouraging her to have some fun when she could, vociferating she needed to let her hair down to balance how hard she worked? Maybe a night dancing would be just the tonic.

'Okay,' she answered, in response to Patty's question. 'It does sound like fun and it's not often we get the chance to don a dress and put on a bit of lippy.'

'Speak for yerself,' Patty, who took every opportunity she could to persuade Archie they needed a night out, chided.

'You are a case' – Daisy grinned – 'but I'm glad you can both make it.'

'How about you, Hatts?' Patty asked, realizing her friend hadn't answered Daisy.

'I'm not sure. Can I let you know later in the week?'

Despite her excitement at the thought of a night on the tiles, Patty wasn't completely oblivious to her friend's situation. 'Is everything all right?'

'Yes. I'm just always a bit tired by Saturday afternoon,' Hattie lied. She didn't want to bring the mood down. Her dad was still drinking away most of the household income, leaving her mum a nervous wreck that they wouldn't be able to pay the bills. Hattie had willingly agreed to as much overtime as Frank offered, knowing the extra wages would help compensate for the money her dad squandered in the pub. Although a night out sounded fun, Hattie knew the money she would spend could be better used helping with the shopping or paying the coal man, anything to keep the talisman from the door. Besides which, she wasn't sure she wanted to leave her mum alone with her dad, whose drunken tempers showed no signs of diminishing.

'Okay,' Patty replied, understanding Hattie might need a friendly ear. 'Maybe we could just meet for a cuppa and a cake on Saturday after we finish work.'

'I'd like that.' Hattie nodded, grateful her friend hadn't pushed the issue.

As the group tucked into the rest of their snap, Dolly wandered over for her usual dinnertime catch-up. 'Did I hear chatter of a night out?' she probed.

'These young 'uns are all off dancing at the weekend.' Frank grinned. 'Sheffield won't know what's hit 'em.'

'Hey,' Patty protested, 'I think what you mean is Sheffield is in for a reyt treat!'

'Not too good of a treat, I hope,' Archie said in mock consternation.

'Don't worry, Archie. I'll keep a good eye on Patty for you,' Daisy said, laughing.

'Excuse me!' Patty retorted. 'I am sat here, yer know. And there will be absolutely no need to keep an eye on me!'

'We're only teasing.' Archie grinned, throwing Patty a wink, as he playfully nudged her in the ribs.

'Are you going along to this night out?' Dolly asked Nancy.

'No. I think I'm going to curl up in my pyjamas and enjoy a quiet night in with Bert and the kids. I don't think I've got the energy to keep up. I'd be asleep by nine o'clock.'

'I'm with you there, luv,' Dolly agreed, sweeping up a couple of empty mugs. 'Anyone for a top-up?'

'Go on then, duck,' Frank replied. 'I am a bit parched today. All that dust. It doesn't 'alf stick in the back of yer throat.'

'Try being up a crane,' Patty jumped in. 'I don't think those girders have ever been cleaned. The dust is about a foot thick.'

'Sorry about that,' Frank sighed. 'Par for the course, I'm afraid. I'm not sure I'd find a cleaner in the land who would be willing to shimmy along those railings to give them a clean.'

'Is Vickers in need of any cleaners?' Hattie wasn't sure if she'd meant to say the words out loud or in her head, but they had passed from her lips before she could stop herself.

'You're not thinking of a second job are you, duck?' Frank asked, slightly confused. 'I thought you'd be sick of the place, what with all the overtime at the moment.'

'Oh no! Sorry. It wasn't for me.' Hattie's cheeks blushed as her friends all turned to face her. 'It was, I just thought someone I know might be after a bit of extra work.'

Patty looked at her friend. She suspected she knew exactly who Hattie was thinking of but had the good sense not to push the subject, realizing her oldest friend was hesitating about saying anything else. She wasn't the only one who had picked up on it. As the conversation turned to more excited chatter about Saturday night, Dolly plopped herself down next to Hattie, and handed her a fresh cuppa.

'Are you okay, luv?'

'Yes. Yes. I'm fine. Just a bit tired but aren't we all.'

'Well yes, but what I meant is the cleaning job. Am I right in thinking you had your mum in mind?'

'That obvious?' Hattie replied.

'Maybe not to everyone, but I know you have said things have been tough at home, so I just surmised.'

'It is hard. There's no point in lying. My poor mum is living on a knife-edge while my dad drinks himself into an oblivion every night.'

'I'm sorry,' Dolly sympathized. 'But if it makes it any easier to talk about it, I really do know what you and your mum are going through.'

Hattie gave Dolly a quizzical look. 'You do?'

'Afraid so, duck. I was married to a drinker, and I've seen more than my fair share of what the demon booze can do to a person.'

'I'm sorry,' Hattie said. 'I had no idea.'

'There's no way you could have, luv. I don't talk about it much. It wasn't a happy time. I'm just glad that part of my life is well and truly over.'

'Gosh. I feel awful now, harping on about my own problems,' Hattie sighed, guilt coursing through her. 'I really wouldn't have said anything if I'd have realized.'

'Now, enough of that,' Dolly chastised. 'That's the

whole point. I never told a soul and a reyt old mess that left me in.'

Hattie had always sensed Dolly had wanted to help her. She'd just assumed she was being motherly, and it was part of her caring nature; never once thinking Dolly had also had to cope with an alcoholic family member. 'I'm glad that whatever happened it's all over now.'

'Aye, me too, duck. But that's not what I wanted to say. I'm more concerned about you and your mum. Is there anything I can do to help?'

'That's ever so kind of you, Dolly, but I really don't think there is. I'm not sure there is anything anyone can do. I hoped for a long time he would eventually stop drinking but I realize, now, that's never likely to happen. He can't go a day without a drink.'

'Sounds familiar. I lived in hope for a long time, but it nearly killed me in the end.'

'Really?'

'Afraid so, luv. I'll tell you about it one day, but the reason I've even mentioned this is because I hate thinking of you and your mum suffering. It's a horrible life. No one should have to live like that. You and your mum deserve better.'

'It's my mum I'm worried about,' Hattie agreed. 'Eventually John will come home, and I guess we'll move in together, but I can't leave Mum in that house by herself with Dad. I don't like even going out with the girls. I'm frightened he'll . . .' But Hattie couldn't finish the sentence, not daring to tempt fate.

'It's okay,' Dolly said, patting Hattie's hand gently. 'I understand. Please let me try and help if I can.'

'That's so nice of you, but honestly, I'm really not sure what you can do. Mum has got a couple of cleaning jobs already. I just thought if there was something full time here, it might get her out of the house more and earn a bit of extra cash. We've been trying to hide what spare money we have from my dad, but he always seems to find it.'

'Aw, I remember that all too well,' Dolly mused, painful memories of her own selfish husband flashing through her mind. 'An alcoholic will move heaven and earth to pay for their next drink. It's a flamin' wicked addiction and they will stop at nothing.'

'You're not wrong,' Hattie agreed. 'I just wish I could help mum. I feel like she is trapped in this horrible life forever.'

'I know it's hard to imagine but it doesn't always have to be like this for her.'

'What do you mean?' Hattie found it impossible to envisage how her mum wouldn't always be beholden to her dad.

'Well, to start off with, I think I might be able to do one better than the offer of a cleaning job.'

'Really?'

'Yes. Now Nancy is back on the cranes, I'm a bit short-staffed here. The factory is getting busier by the week, which means there's an even greater demand for hot meals, especially while they are subsidized, and it means folk can have something here and save their rations.'

Hattie contemplated Dolly's suggestion. It would mean her mum could give up her cleaning jobs, where she worked herself into the ground for next to nothing. Not only that, but it would also mean she would be surrounded by people who genuinely cared all day. Her mum had gradually lost all her friends after they stopped popping in, wary of Vinny's erratic mood swings. Not that Hattie could blame them, there were nights she dreaded going home too, but she knew she couldn't leave her mum to the mercy of her dad's drunken outbursts.

'That's so kind of you,' Hattie replied gratefully. 'I can speak to Mum. I'm just worried she'll be a bit embarrassed, and then, that my dad won't like her being out of the house all day.'

Hattie didn't need to explain. Dolly understood. She'd suffered the same battles. The thought of anyone knowing her husband drank himself into a stupor most days, then used his fists to take his delirious thoughts out on her, left her introverted and fearful of the humiliation that would follow.

'Listen, duck. Believe me when I tell you I've been there and still wear the scars. The last thing I would ever want to do is cause your poor mum any more upset. From what I can gather she's been through enough already.'

'She really has.' Hattie sighed in agreement. 'I just want her to be happy. She deserves so much better.'

'I don't doubt it, luv. And so do you for that matter.'

'Thank you, but as I say, I can see my way out.'

'Well, how about you drop the hint there's a job here and if she agrees, I promise you, I won't breathe a word of what you have told me about your dad. It goes without saying Josie's lips would be sealed too. Neither of us would want to add to your mum's worries, but I would like to help, if I can, by giving her a job and somewhere safe where she can be surrounded by people.'

Hattie bit back the tears that were building in the back of her eyes. Patty had always told her what a lovely group of people she worked with, but Hattie had never imagined when she'd joined Vickers, that they would take her into their fold as quickly and fondly as they had. 'Thank you,' Hattie repeated, her shaky voice barely more than a whisper. 'You really are so kind and thoughtful.'

'Don't mention it, luv.' Dolly nodded, reassuringly patting Hattie's slightly trembling hand. 'I don't like to hear of anyone suffering.'

'I'll speak to Mum and let you know what she says, if that's okay. It might take her a little while to get her head around the idea, so I understand if you need to get in a replacement for Nancy in the meantime.'

'Don't you be worrying about that. We can manage until your mum makes a decision.'

'Reyt, I'm afraid we need to get back to it.' Frank's announcement pierced Hattie's thoughts and put an end to their conversation.

'I'll definitely talk to her,' Hattie reiterated to Dolly, standing up and packing into her bag the small biscuit tin that had held her dinner.

'What was that about?' Patty asked, pushing her chair under the table, catching the back end of Dolly's comment.

'I'll tell you over that cuppa and cake,' Hattie promised, as the pair zig-zagged their way back through the canteen.

'Sounds cryptic,' Patty commented.

'Just complicated,' Hattie replied, 'but I promise I'll explain.'

'Okay.' Patty smiled, sensing Hattie just needed time to digest what she and Dolly had been talking about.

As the two women separated off to their own sections of the factory, Hattie sighed deeply. She knew in her heart of hearts a job at Vickers would be the best thing that could happen to her mum, but whether her dad would agree was another matter. And if he did, would the extra wages just be fuelling his drinking? Why couldn't anything ever be easy?

Chapter 9

'What do you fancy, Hatts?' Patty asked her friend as they sat down at a table in a corner of Browns tea room.

'A nice hot pot of tea would be lovely. I know the factory is roasting but the walk has left me feeling all shivery.'

'I know what you mean,' Patty agreed. 'The weather has really turned. I hunted out my hat and gloves this morning.'

'I don't blame you. It's really chilly.'

'Shall we have something to eat too?' Patty asked. 'I don't know about you but I'm starvin'. My mum made me eat a bowl of porridge when I got up, but my stomach has been rumbling most of the morning.'

'We could share a cake?' Hattie suggested.

'Never mind sharing. We should have one each!'

'I could do with saving some money and if I'm honest, I don't think I could manage a full one.'

'Really?' The word left Patty's mouth quicker than she had time to process Hattie's comment.

'I'm just trying to be careful. My dad is spending money quicker than Mum and I can earn it.'

'I'm sorry.' Patty sympathized, concerned by how much pressure her friend was under.

'It's not your fault.' Hattie smiled weakly. 'My dad is a law to himself.'

'I take it things aren't getting any better?'

'No.' Hattie shook her head. 'Quite the opposite in fact.'

'In what way? Is he drinking even more?'

'I think so. He gets home later, and most nights can barely walk, but he still manages to have a go at my mum.'

Patty hated thinking of what a torrid time Hattie and her mum were having. 'Is there anything I can do? You know you only have to say.'

'Thanks, Patty, but I don't think there is. I never thought I'd ever say this, but I can barely look at my dad these days. I get so angry when I see him falling about all over the place. I really don't recognize him anymore.'

'I don't know what to say,' Patty said, feeling utterly useless. 'Is he still managing to get up for work?'

'Only just. My mum has to virtually drag him out of bed most mornings and, of course, then he snaps at her. He's so selfish and isn't in the least bit grateful, despite how much my mum does to help him, let alone the fact he spends every penny and more of what she earns.'

Before Patty could answer, a waitress in a perfectly starched white apron, approached the table. 'What can I get you both?' she asked, holding a notepad in one hand and a pen in the other.

'We'll definitely have a big pot of tea to share,' Patty started. Then turning to Hattie, she added, 'What do you fancy to eat?'

Hattie peered down at the menu again, mentally calculating how much she could afford, knowing she needed to give her mum as much of her wages as possible.

Sensing Hattie's trepidation, Patty took the lead. 'Could we have two bowls of your vegetable soup please?'

'Of course,' the waitress replied. 'It won't be a jiffy.'

'Sorry,' Hattie sighed as the waitress walked back towards the counter.

'There's no need to apologise,' Patty insisted firmly. 'You look like you need something warm and comforting inside you.'

'Thank you. I must admit I do feel a bit lightheaded.'

'I'm not surprised if you aren't sleeping well, on top of working all day at the factory.'

'I'll be okay. At least we're not back to work until Monday. You don't mind if I don't come out tonight, do you? I just really haven't got the energy and I don't want to leave Mum by herself.'

'You don't have to explain. I just hate seeing you looking so worn out.'

'I'll be all right.'

Desperate to say something to cheer Hattie up, she asked, 'Have you heard from John recently?'

'I have actually,' Hattie replied, a small smile emerging. 'I got a letter yesterday. He's still on Salisbury Plain but he's been promoted to corporal. It sounds like he's now involved in training up other soldiers.'

'That's great news. You must be so proud. Do you think he will get back to Sheffield again anytime soon?'

'I am. He works so hard. But I'm not sure when he will next get home. A bit like William, I don't think they ever really know when their next leave will be. It would be lovely to see him, but I don't want to get my hopes up.'

Patty nodded, once again feeling grateful, despite how much she worried about the air raids, that her Archie was close by.

'You will get through this,' she said, with as much confidence as she could muster, but if the truth be known, Patty had no idea how her friend was coping as it was, and there didn't seem to be any light at the end of the tunnel.

Patty's thoughts were interrupted when the young waitress returned balancing a tray. 'Here we go.' She smiled as she carefully placed on the table two steaming bowls of soup, a large pot of tea, accompanied by two cups and saucers and a jug of milk.

'Thank you,' Hattie said, gratefully. 'This looks wonderful.'

'Get tucked in,' Patty encouraged as soon as the waitress had deposited their lunch. 'It will perk you up.'

Fifteen minutes later, after the two women had finished their last spoonful and managed to squeeze two cups of tea out of the pot, Patty asked for the bill. 'This is on me,' she said when the waitress popped the slip of white paper on the table.

'No! You don't have to do that,' Hattie protested.

'I know, but I would like to. Besides which, it is hardly breaking the bank and I'd only spend it on make-up, which, even by my standards, I've got more than enough of.'

'Patty Andrews!' Hattie gasped, with a slight giggle. 'I never thought I'd hear the day you would admit to having too many lippies or pots of rouge.'

'Just don't tell Archie!' Patty said, placing a finger to her lips. 'I don't want him to think there's any reason for him to stop treating me.'

'You are a one,' said Hattie, shaking her head in mock horror. 'But seriously, I'm happy to split the bill. I'm not quite on my uppers yet.'

'I know you're not, but I would like to. You have treated me plenty of times in the past. And it's hardly lunch at the Ritz!'

'It doesn't have to be,' Hattie replied. 'I'm very grateful regardless.'

After Patty left enough change on the table to cover the bill, the two women pulled on their coats, picked up their gas masks and bags and headed towards the door. As they got outside, the cold air instantly assaulted them. Patty quickly took her gloves from her pockets. 'Chuffin' 'eck. I wasn't lying when I said it really is chilly. It's going to be another long winter.'

'You will have to get knitting some more woollies,' Hattie teased.

'Don't! Betty has already started telling us all she wants to send another care package off to the troops. I'm not sure what poor sod would want anything I manage to make. The number of stitches I drop, I can't imagine they last very long.'

'Your scarves weren't so bad.'

'Mmm. Maybe if you don't look too closely. Anyway, it's too cold to stand still here. What are you doing for the rest of the afternoon?'

'Nothing very exciting. I'm going to nip out and get some meat from Oliver's for Mum, then go home and give her a helping hand with some cleaning.'

'Please try and have a rest, too, if you can,' Patty said, giving her friend a hug. 'That soup has helped but you still do look a little peaky.'

'I will,' Hattie promised, more out of reflex than conviction. 'And I hope you all have fun at the City Hall tonight. I can't wait to hear all about it on Monday.'

'Thank you. I'm sure it will be a giggle, but please take care, won't you, Hatts?'

'I will.' Her friend nodded, trying to sound buoyant, despite the sinking feeling that was beginning to consume her at the thought of what a weekend with her dad would bring.

* * *

Just after seven thirty, Daisy and Patty, who had struggled to shake off her worries about Hattie, were stood on the corner of Barker's Pool, as they waited for Betty to join them.

'I really wish nylons were easier to get hold of.' Patty shivered. 'Gravy browning and kohl might look the part, but it certainly ain't any good for keeping m' legs warm.'

'You're not wrong there!' Daisy said, having also used the same trick to give her normally long, slender, milky legs a bit of colour.

'At least we look good!' Patty grinned, suddenly deciding her appearance was far more important than combatting the cool November air.

'You are a one.' Daisy laughed.

'You're only young once,' Patty trilled. 'And despite this blasted war, I'm determined to make the most of it.'

Before Daisy could answer, their conversation was interrupted by Betty. 'Sorry! You haven't been waiting long, have you? The trams were running late.'

'No,' Daisy reassured her friend. 'We've literally only just got here.'

'Oh good. Shall we get inside?' Betty asked. 'It's nippy, isn't it?'

'We've just been saying exactly the same,' Daisy affirmed as the three women joined the queue and made their way inside the City Hall.

'Let's go downstairs?' Patty asked. 'I think the music

will be a bit livelier down there and I'm ready for a good dance. It's ages since I've been here.'

'Yes, let's,' Betty enthused, as the memory of William appearing in the exact same venue flashed before her, the weekend he had proposed. The war had only just really started, and no one could have predicted how only months later Hitler would be bombing the country, and William would one day, possibly sooner rather than later, be taking to the skies to fight off the Luftwaffe. 'Not tonight,' Betty whispered to herself, discreetly biting down on her lip as she fought off the worries that had been niggling away at her for months.

'Come on,' Daisy said, bringing Betty back to the moment. 'Let's go and have some fun.'

The three women made their way down the majestic mahogany winding staircase, following the beat of the fast-paced swing music which was emanating from the lower floor dance hall. After leaving their coats in the cloakroom, Betty, Daisy and Patty all linked arms as they trotted onto the dance floor, their hips already swinging to Benny Goodman's 'Sing, Sing, Sing'.

'Come on, girls,' Patty cheered over the high tempo music, which was reverberating around the room. She led the way and found a gap on the already busy dance floor. Clicking her fingers and grinning from ear to ear, Patty's exuberance was contagious. Packing away her fears, determined to have a good night, just as she knew William would want, Betty allowed the rhythmic music to consume her and soon she too was swaying away alongside Patty and Daisy.

It was over half an hour, and at least another five songs later, before the trio emerged from the dance floor, their faces rosy pink and their toes still tapping. 'That was so much fun, but I'm gasping for a drink,' Patty said, putting her hand to her throat. 'Shall we go to the bar?'

'Yes,' her two friends replied in unison. 'I'll get these,' Betty added.

'You don't have to do that,' Daisy argued.

'I know, but I would like to. Class it as a little thank you for dragging me out and pulling me out of the doldrums.'

'Don't be daft. That's what friends are for, and we all need a few distractions, especially at the moment.'

'We do and tonight was exactly what I needed, so thank you.'

Patty's mind quickly flitted to Hattie. She knew her oldest friend's heart wouldn't have been in it, but she did so wish Hattie could have made it and allowed herself a bit of fun to take her mind off things at home. 'Maybe next time,' Patty said to herself optimistically, determined to be a good ally to Hattie, in the hope she could help ease the load her friend was being forced to deal with.

'Right, let's get to that bar before it's six deep and we don't stand a chance of getting a drink in the next hour,' Betty said, piercing Patty's thoughts.

As luck would have it, a gap in the crowds gave the women a direct line to the long wooden bar and ten minutes later, each of them was holding a much-needed chilled glass of port and lemon. 'Cheers,' Patty toasted, before quickly emptying her glass in a few large mouthfuls.

'My goodness. You really were thirsty!' Daisy laughed, slightly astonished.

'I did tell yer! And besides which, there's dancing to be done.' Patty grinned, taking hold of her floaty deep-blue skirt and performing a twirl.

'I think that's our cue.' Betty laughed, quickly sipping the last of her drink, the sudden intake of alcohol having the desired effect of relaxing her. 'I'm ready if you are.' She giggled, looking at Daisy.

'Absolutely!' came the animated response.

With that the women nimbly tottered back onto the dance floor, their heels fervently clicking, just in time for Ella Fitzgerald's peppy 'A-Tisket, A-Tasket'.

Chapter 10

'Right, ladies, how do we all feel about firing up the Victory Knitters again?' Betty asked enthusiastically, walking back from the clothing Swap Box, which she had set up to help her fellow factory workers, and back towards the dining-room table where all her friends were tucking into their sandwiches.

'Errrr,' Patty groaned, visibly deflating at the thought of having to once again master her knit and purl.

'Now, come on. It's for a good cause,' Betty cajoled. 'We managed to produce dozens of hats, scarves, jumpers and socks last winter. It really was quite the feat! Daisy and I were talking to Mrs Rafferty, the manager at the WVS depot, and she said she can arrange for some more care packages to be sent to our troops.'

'I agree it's a good idea. I just know I'll drop more stitches than I knit,' Patty sighed.

'I can help you,' Nancy encouraged. 'You did start to get the hang of it last winter.'

'Only because you rescued everything I attempted.'

'Patience is a virtue,' Nancy teased playfully. 'We will make a knitter of you yet.'

'I wouldn't risk yer last shilling on it yet.'

'Anyway, apart from Patty,' Betty interrupted, shaking her head in mock jest, 'are we all up for it?'

'Count me in,' Nancy agreed. 'Now Bert's home, it means I'm not as busy of an evening, so it's no bother. I'm sure I've still got a few balls of wool left at home and Doris hands me any old jumpers she's given from her laundry business to unpick.'

'They get quite a few donations at the depot too, so I can bring in some extra balls as well.'

'Me and Mum can also help,' Hattie offered.

'That would be lovely,' Betty replied gratefully. 'If I remember rightly, you produced bag loads last year.'

'I do find it quite therapeutic. I can do some when I get home of an evening.' What Hattie didn't say was, it would help keep her mind off John and distract her when her dad was stomping around the house like a bear with a sore head. She knew it helped her mum too, whose nerves were shattered.

'You can count me in,' Daisy added. Ever since she started volunteering at the Women's Voluntary Service with Betty, she'd felt like she was doing something worthwhile, alongside working at Vickers, to help the war effort, despite how worrying the work felt. She and Betty had been charged with making bandages for hospitals and the demand wasn't showing any signs of slowing down.

'I didn't doubt it.' Betty nodded.

'And I'm sure my mum will help too,' Daisy enthused. 'She used to knit all my jumpers, hats and scarves when I was little.'

'That's brilliant. I've just been chatting to a few women at the Swap Box who are also happy to contribute, so we should end up with another huge haul.'

'I'm sure it will all be greatly appreciated,' Nancy commented, taking a sip of her steaming mug of tea. 'Bert was very grateful for the socks last year. It must be perishing for them when they are—' Nancy stopped, checking herself.

'Sorry,' she said, turning to Hattie. 'That wasn't very thoughtful of me.'

'It's okay, I know exactly what you mean. Let's hope nothing is as bad as Dunkirk. At least John is only on Salisbury Plain, although I can imagine it gets pretty nippy there, especially at this time of year. I think he does quite a few overnight and early morning exercises.'

'Do you think he may be able to stay in England for a bit longer yet?' Daisy asked.

'I'd love to think he can, but I really don't know. He's certainly not told me anything different yet, but I suppose he might not know either.'

'I'll keep everything crossed for him,' Daisy said.

Hattie had quietly hoped John might get home for Christmas, their first as a married couple, but hadn't dared vocalize her thoughts, not wanting to tempt fate.

'Let's hope he can.' Nancy smiled kindly, not wishing the worry she had so recently endured, while Bert had been away at war, on anyone.

'Thank you,' Hattie replied. She had missed John terribly since their wedding, and especially since her dad's drinking had caused him to become even more volatile. She was exhausted by his behaviour and desperately longed for her husband to come home and whisk her away from the drudgery and fear of her home life, hoping he would also have a magical answer on how she could help her mum escape too. There were nights when she cried herself to sleep, leaving her pillow sodden with tears, before slowly falling into a restless slumber. She would dream that John was by her side and that they were living together as man and wife, but the harmonious and contented doze was always cruelly cut short when she woke up and the harsh reality of her life kicked in.

The news across Europe wasn't filling her with any hope either that her husband would return home any time soon. Allied troops had bombed Germany and Italian forces had attacked Greece, indicating this war was far from over.

'Can I get you a top-up?' Nancy asked, cutting into Hattie's thoughts, sensing her friend was having a pretty miserable time of it right now.

'Er' – Hattie looked down at her empty mug – 'yes. Sorry. That would be lovely, but I can get them.'

'You stay where you are,' Nancy insisted, already on her feet. 'I wouldn't mind a top-up anyway. I'll get them.'

Then turning to the rest of the tale, she added, 'Anyone else for another cuppa?'

'I wouldn't say no, duck,' Frank replied.

'Yes, please,' Patty parroted. 'I'll never say no to another brew.'

A few minutes later, mugs refreshed, Nancy sat back down next to Hattie. 'Are you getting enough sleep, luv?'

'Not really,' Hattie confessed.

'Things still tough at home?'

Hattie nodded in resignation. 'Afraid so.'

'I'm sorry,' Nancy sympathized. 'Is there anything I can do.'

'I really don't think there is, well, not unless you know how on earth I can stop my dad drinking.'

Nancy bit back her anger towards Vinny, knowing it wouldn't help Hattie, who looked as though she had the world on her shoulders.

'I'm afraid I'm not much use on that front, but I'm always happy to chat, if it helps.'

'Thanks, Nancy. I don't mean to sound so miserable. I'm just worn out,' Hattie replied, putting it down to how on edge she constantly felt.

'You don't at all,' Nancy insisted. 'But I'm not surprised you're tired. This job alone can leave you exhausted, without any extra worries and not being able to sleep. It's not easy.'

'I'll be okay,' Hattie replied, but with little gumption.

'And how's your mum?'

'I think she's just so used to my dad's behaviour; she just does what she can to keep the peace. I don't think she knows any other way.'

'That's hard, for both of you.'

Hattie couldn't think of anything to say to try and counter Nancy's point. 'It's certainly getting that way,' she finally agreed.

'I hope you don't think I was eavesdropping; I really wasn't, but I overheard Dolly chatting to you last week about your mum coming to work in the canteen. Do you think she would?'

Nancy remembered how much working with Dolly and Josie had helped her when she was consumed by her own worries after Bert had been declared 'missing in action'. Those two women had been a godsend, keeping her upright when she'd reached rock bottom, and for the life of her couldn't see the light at the end of the tunnel.

'To be honest, I haven't found the right moment to ask her. I need to try and catch her at a time when she is feeling a little calmer. My dad has left her a nervous wreck and she's frightened of doing anything to upset him.'

'Will he not like the idea of your mum working at Vickers?'

'It's hard to say. He'll definitely not turn down the extra money she brings home, but he won't like her surrounded by other women.'

Hattie noted Nancy's look of confusion and added: 'He

doesn't want her to have friends. He says they are a bad influence on her.'

'What do you mean, luv?' Nancy was desperately trying to get her head around how Vinny's twisted mind worked. Bert had been delighted when she had told him she was starting at the factory, pleased Nancy would be keeping herself busy, a distraction from the worries of war.

'It's hard to explain, but my dad likes to control her, even though half the time he's not even conscious of what he's doing, let alone anyone else. I think he's probably sacred that if she has any friends they will convince Mum to leave him, then he'll have no one to cook his dinners and fund his drinking habit.'

Nancy did her hardest to blink back her shock. Hattie had hinted in the past, and slowly told her work mates, that things were difficult at home, but Nancy hadn't realized quite how toxic and manipulative Vinny really was. 'Has he always been like this?' she asked, tentatively, horrified Hattie and her mum were trapped in such a horrible life. She knew Hattie was an adult, but in that moment, she looked so small and vulnerable, and Nancy had a maternal urge to wrap the younger woman in her arms.

'No.' Hattie shook her head. 'At least I don't think so. Mum said they were happy once and Dad wasn't a drinker when they first met, but he came home from the Great War a different man. She says he's never spoken about it, but instead drowns his sorrows in the bottom of a pint glass.'

Nancy instinctively bit down on her bottom lip. When Bert had returned home after Dunkirk, he too had been closed and distant, a stranger whom she barely recognized. Nancy had been frightened she'd lost the loving and caring man she'd married, that the war had cruelly stolen him from her, Billy and Linda. For weeks she couldn't penetrate the hard exterior that had formed around her husband, no matter how hard she'd tried. He'd barely spoken and when he did, he'd been snappy and defensive; even the kids, whom Bert had always loved with all his heart, had been wary. It was only after Frank had taken him to the pub, and had a man-to-man chat with Bert, that he'd gradually started to soften, and his affectionate and kind personality began to reappear. He'd finally confessed to Nancy that he'd felt lost in life after being shot in his right leg, and no longer able to go off and fight the war with the rest of his platoon. Joining the Home Guard had given him the purpose and focus he needed to feel worthwhile again. As Nancy listened to Hattie, she felt a mixture of overwhelming gratitude Bert had found his way back to her, but also tremendous sadness that Hattie's dad hadn't been able to find his route back to happiness.

'I'm sorry,' Nancy finally said, in response to her friend's heart-breaking revelations. 'I can't even begin to imagine how hard this has been for you and your mum.'

'Thank you, but there's no need to be sorry, it's not your fault. I just hope I can find a way to help Mum.'

'I hope so too,' Nancy replied. 'You both deserve better than this. Please say if I can do anything to help.'

'I will. Just talking about it helps. I kept it all in for so long, only really telling John, but now he's away, it feels so much harder. I'm so sorry. I didn't mean to moan on.'

'You aren't at all,' Nancy firmly insisted. 'Take it from me, it's better to talk about these things. No good comes from keeping everything bottled inside. If it wasn't for all of you, I would have gone mad with worry when Bert was away.'

Hattie managed a weak nod, recalling the months of angst Nancy had endured. 'Even so, I am still very grateful to be able to confide in you. I've told Patty, and Dolly guessed a while ago – she's been so kind.'

'That woman is a true saint,' Nancy agreed. 'I have a lot to thank her for.'

'She really is.' Hattie nodded.

'I'll keep everything crossed you can somehow find a way for your mum to come and work here. I'm sure it would do her the world of good.'

'Thank you. I'm sure it would help her too. I just need to find my moment to ask her.'

And with that, Frank's usual announcement that it was time to get back to work put an end to their chat.

'Try and keep strong,' Nancy added, as the women

made their way through the canteen and back to the factory floor for the afternoon shift. 'And don't forget, I'm always here if you need someone to talk to.'

Hattie returned the kind offer with a weak smile, grateful she was surrounded by such a caring group of friends, who, despite not knowing her that long, had taken her under their wing.

Chapter 11

Betty couldn't miss the huge grin appearing on William's face as she walked towards him at the bus station.

'Are you ready?' he asked, as his fiancée got closer.

'Yes!' Betty grinned.

William had surprised her by turning up at her house on Thursday night, announcing that he'd been given a few days leave and had booked for them a night away. Flabbergasted, Betty had asked where they were going, but William had refused to tell her, insisting it was a surprise. She was simply to meet him at the bus station at eight o'clock this morning. 'But what about work?' Betty had asked, realizing it would mean getting Saturday morning off.

'I'm sure Frank won't begrudge you one morning off,' William had said, hoping he was right and hadn't jumped the gun. Thankfully he'd been right, and Frank had told her not to think twice about taking the time, insisting it was the very least the gaffers could do after how hard she worked. So here she was, wrapped up in her brown tweed coat, excited about the weekend ahead.

'Let me take that,' William insisted, reaching for Betty's small black holdall, before giving her a kiss on the cheek.

'Thank you,' Betty said, her cheeks flushed. 'Now are you going to tell me where you are taking me?'

'Patience,' William teased, playfully. 'Follow me and all will be revealed.'

As much as Betty normally liked to be fully in control, she felt a fissure of delight that William was taking the lead and insisting she didn't have to think about a thing.

She allowed William to lead her through the station until they came to a stop next to a bus, where the odd passenger was already boarding.

'Last call for Blackpool,' a conductor who was stood next to the vehicle called.

'Blackpool!' Betty exclaimed, in complete surprise.

'That's right.' William grinned, then quickly added, 'Is that all right?' a moment of panic coursing through him, suddenly worried Betty would hate the idea. 'I know it's hardly the height of luxury, but it was the best I could do with such short notice.'

'Of course,' Betty replied. 'I just had absolutely no idea where we were going. It's a wonderful surprise.'

'In that case, your carriage awaits,' William said, lifting an arm into the air, indicating for Betty to climb aboard.

A couple of minutes later, the couple were cosily tucked up together, sat side by side on the bus, their bags safely stored in the luggage compartment. 'Our adventure begins,' William said, giving Betty's hand a gentle squeeze.

'I think the last time we had a little holiday was when we went to Cleethorpes,' Betty commented, a wave of nostalgia seeping over her as she recalled their weekend away the summer before war broke out. She had a black-and-white photo of them – strolling hand in hand along the promenade – on her bedside, an identical copy of the one William told Betty he always kept in his shirt pocket while he was away, so he always felt close to her.

'It was,' William agreed, interrupting Betty's thoughts. 'I know it's not the middle of summer and I doubt we will be paddling our feet in the sea. I should imagine the North Sea is a bit nippy at this time of year, but I'm sure we will have a lovely time regardless.'

'We will,' Betty replied, smiling. 'I really don't mind where we are going or what time of year it is. It's just so nice to have a little bit of time together, just the two of us. I've missed you so much while you have been away.'

'I've missed you too. I promise once this war is over, we will spend every spare minute we have together.'

Comforted by William's affectionate words, Betty rested her head on her fiancé's shoulder, the motion of the bus making her feel sleepy after a week at work and another early start.

A few hours later, the driver pulled into Blackpool bus station and the couple disembarked, Betty wrapping her scarf a little tighter around her neck to ward off the late autumn chill, while William, once again, insisted on carrying both bags.

'It's not far to the guest house,' he assured Betty. 'A ten-minute walk at the most.'

William had memorized the directions to the quaint Victorian bed and breakfast, overlooking the seafront. 'Here we are!' he announced proudly as he directed Betty up the pavement to the deep-blue-painted front door.

'It looks lovely.' Betty smiled as she took in the hand-painted sign, which hung from a nail in the front door. 'Welcome to Sea View' had been inscribed on the wooden plaque in cheery yellow letters.

Before William even had a chance to knock on the door, it swung open to reveal a wholesome-looking woman, wearing a bright-pink headscarf, tied at the front of a crown of black hair set in large rollers. 'You must be Mr and Mrs Smith,' she said, her victory-red lips forming into a huge smile.

'That's right,' William replied quickly, before Betty could contradict the woman she assumed must be the owner.

'I'm Lily, it's lovely to meet you. Come on in, it's freezing out there. I have just popped the kettle on, I'll get you settled in the resident's lounge and then bring you a nice fresh cuppa and a couple of sandwiches. I expect you'll be hungry after your journey.'

'That would be wonderful,' William thanked the owner,

before glancing at Betty and throwing her a conspiratorial wink.

Too stunned, and slightly horrified, to argue, Betty followed the landlady, who was dressed in a heavy black skirt and a loud pink blouse to match her headscarf.

'Take yer coats off and get warm by the fire,' she insisted, directing William and Betty into a cosy front room, where two flowery couches, adorned with a multitude of matching cushions, sat adjacent to the roaring fire. A glass coffee table sat in between the sofas, and in the centre was a cream vase, holding a bunch of pink-and-white chrysanthemums. Next to it was a well-thumbed, large, square visitors' book, and an array of black-and-white postcards, with scenes of the famous Blackpool Tower, donkeys parading along the beach and the North Pier.

As soon as Lily was out of sight, Betty caught William's arm. 'Why on earth did you say we were married?'

'Why do you think?' William grinned.

'What?' Betty gasped, taken aback by what she assumed was a hint at what William was expecting of her this weekend. 'I hope . . .'

'Oh, Bet.' William laughed. 'I don't mean that.'

'Well, what do you mean?'

'I just wanted us to share a room tonight.'

'William!' Betty whispered, trying to keep the landlady from overhearing William's clandestine untruth, but the sharp inflection in her tone made it clear how horrified she was. She had been brought up with more morals than that!

Struggling to contain his laughter, but sensing his fiancée was on the verge of telling him to take her home immediately, William checked himself.

'What's so funny?' Betty hissed, starting to feel hot and flustered, but too tense to take off her heavy coat.

'Just the look on your face,' William said, a playful grin emerging.

'William!' Betty gasped, exasperated, starting to question what her fiancé was playing at.

'Sorry,' William said quickly. 'What I meant is, I didn't want us to be apart. We get so little time together; I didn't want to waste a minute.'

Betty looked even more perturbed. *Surely, he doesn't think we can share a bed*, she silently fumed.

'I'm not doing very well here, am I,' William stated more than asked.

Betty didn't respond, wondering if being in the RAF and surrounded by scores of what she assumed to be rowdy men had turned William from a sweet and caring man to someone who just wanted to, well . . . She couldn't even think the words, let alone say them, her cheeks flushing at the very thought.

'I'll try and explain,' William said, breaking into Betty's thoughts. 'There was only a twin room or single rooms available, so I asked for the twin. What I'm trying to say is I wanted us to be together, but we have our own beds.'

Betty's blushes went from pink to crimson, the heat rising through her neck, as she realized how she had put two and two together and got five, her lips forming an astonished 'O' shape.

'You daft thing.' William chuckled, lifting Betty's left hand, and planting a kiss on exactly where her engagement ring sat, underneath her black leather glove. 'You should know me better than that by now.'

Feeling a little sheepish and slightly cross at herself for assuming her sweet-natured William would be anything but a true gentleman, Betty bit down on her lip. 'I'm sorry,' she said. 'I've been rather foolish, haven't I? I think I was just a bit shocked by the fact you had announced we were married.'

'I didn't want to spoil your reputation,' William explained. 'Something I have no intention of doing either!'

Relief soaring through her, Betty shook her head, as if she was trying to shake her own misguided thoughts away. 'I feel a bit silly,' she confessed.

'Don't! I just want us to have a lovely weekend away and enjoy the precious time we have together.'

'Thank you,' Betty replied, grateful William hadn't mercilessly teased her any further for her 'Patty-style' faux pas.

Beginning to relax but feeling stuffy, Betty finally took off her coat, but as she looked at her gloved hands, she realized it wouldn't take a genius to see they weren't actually married.

'I really don't think she'll give it a second thought,' William said, noting with amusement the new look of concern on his fiancée's face. 'We won't be the first to tell a white lie and I'm fairly sure we won't be the last either.'

'I know,' Betty muttered, 'but I just can't let her . . .'

'Sit on your hand,' William said, determined to stop Betty getting into another fluster.

'What?'

'When Lily comes back just pop your hand under your leg, not that I think she will even notice.'

'William!' Betty exclaimed, half giggling, starting to see the funny side of his little indiscretion.

'I bet you she doesn't even look. She'll be used to couples turning up claiming to be married.'

But Betty wasn't prepared to take any chances, so when Lily reappeared holding a tray laden with sandwiches, a teapot, milk jug, cups and saucers, she instinctively tucked her now ungloved hand slightly under her thigh, praying her cheeks hadn't reddened again.

'Here you are,' Lily announced, popping the welcoming lunch on the table. 'Get this down you. And tell me, what plans have you got for while you are here?'

As William began listing their plans, Betty lifted the two side plates off the tray, taking care only to use her right hand, then divided out the array of sandwiches, filled with what she took to be thin slices of tinned Spam.

'I thought we'd have a walk along the pier and maybe get some fish and chips for tea, before going dancing or maybe to the theatre. Can you recommend anywhere?'

'Well, you can't do wrong at the Tower Ballroom.' Lily smiled. 'It's where all the young 'uns go, and actually some of us old timers too.'

'Have you brought a pretty frock with you?' Lily added, turning to Betty, who was still sitting on her hand, hoping she didn't look too conspicuous.

'I have.' Betty nodded. 'I wasn't sure what to expect but popped one in just in case.'

'Good girl. We can't let Hitler spoil our fun, can we? He might think he can trample through Europe, but he will have a job on destroying the British bulldog spirit.'

'Exactly,' William agreed.

Betty smiled politely. The last thing she wanted to do this weekend was think about the war.

Lily must have picked up Betty's resistance to dwell on the state of the world around them and added: 'We are the resort that never stops, yer know. The winter might be drawing in and the beach deserted, but there will always be dancing, places to eat and the theatre. I've got a couple of leaflets, including one for the Grand, if you'd like to see what's going on?'

'That would be wonderful,' Betty replied, happy the conversation had moved on.

'You have your lunch and I'll dig one out for yer,' Lily said, already backing out of the lounge. 'Oh, and your room is ready if you want to take your luggage up after you've eaten.'

'Thank you,' William replied, knowing Betty would either end up stuttering over her words or blushing if she had to enter any discussion over their *shared* room.

Half an hour later, William did the gentlemanly honours and carried their two holdalls upstairs to room two, which Lily had given them the key for when she'd nipped back into the lounge with the promised leaflet, which due to wartime paper shortages had been shrunk so much, it easily fitted in the palm of Betty's hand.

Opening the door, William smiled at his fiancée. 'I promise your reputation will remain intact.'

'William!' Betty admonished, half in jest, still not quite sure how to take her fiancé's innuendos.

'I'm just teasing you,' he replied, his reassuring manner returning, sensing Betty's uncertainty. The last thing he wanted her to think was that he'd turned into some sort of cad, with only one thing on his mind. He was desperate for this weekend to be as special as possible.

'Well, this is really lovely,' Betty commented, looking around at what would be their abode for the next twenty-four hours. The homely atmosphere of the room replicated that of the front room, with matching pastel-coloured patchwork eiderdowns covering both single beds, complemented by cream-and-pink wallpaper and a small glass jam jar of flowers on the windowsill.

'I'm glad you like it,' William enthused. 'Shall we

quickly unpack and go and see what Blackpool has to offer?'

'That sounds perfect.'

An hour later, the couple were walking arm in arm, along one of the town's piers, marvelling at the huge waves crashing against the deserted beach, the silhouette of the famous Blackpool Tower dominating the skyline. Despite the bracing sea breeze making the temperature feel even lower than it already was, the pier was full; mums were gripping their excited children's hands as they too watched the dramatic waves, and servicemen, in varying blue and grey uniforms, held hands with young girls, colourful scarves protecting their fancy hair-dos from the ever-dominant North Sea wind.

'Is there a military base here?' Betty enquired.

'I believe so, and more than one,' William replied. 'The RAF have a station here, and the Polish too. A lot of pilots train here. I think that's one of the main reasons the theatres have stayed open, as a form of entertainment for the crews.'

'Could you end up here?' Blackpool felt like a promising alternative to the south coast, which had borne the brunt of the Luftwaffe's raids over the last few months.

'I suppose there's every chance.' William nodded. He was keen to avoid the subject of where he would be posted to next but had known it was inevitable.

Despite her initial question, Betty also didn't want to spoil their trip worrying about what was still to come, so she quickly diverted their conversation, as she pointed farther down the pier to two children who were desperately clinging on to their knitted bobble hats, trying to prevent them from flying off. A woman they assumed to be the little girl and boy's mum was watching, smiling at their excited giggles.

'I hope that's us one day,' William said, equally as taken by the innocent scene.

Betty turned to face her fiancé. 'Me too.' She smiled, the vision of a perfect future flashing before her eyes. The couple had talked in the past about getting married and spending the rest of their lives together, but they hadn't discussed it since William had returned from Canada. But as she envisaged a time when they could become a family, without the threat of war disrupting their lives, it strengthened Betty's hope for the future.

'I want our little girl to be as strong and determined as you,' William confirmed.

'And our son to be as brave as you,' Betty replied, returning the compliment. Despite how much she'd hoped beyond hope, when William had first suggested joining the RAF, he wouldn't go through with it, she had nothing but admiration for his courage and unflappable spirit. They were the very traits which had caused her endless worry, but Betty knew they were also the precise reasons she loved her fiancé and wanted to spend the rest of her life with him.

After the contented couple had whiled away the rest

of the afternoon, wandering up and down the piers and watching the world go by, William suggested they find something to eat. 'Fish and chips?'

'Oooh yes,' Betty agreed, enthusiastically. 'We can't come to the seaside and not have fish and chips, and all this sea air has made me quite peckish – I keep getting a tempting whiff of salt and vinegar.'

'In that case, your wish is my command.' William grinned. 'And it's not like we are short of spots to choose from.'

Twenty minutes later, William and Betty were sitting opposite the seafront, mesmerized by the vastness of the sea, as they ate their tea out of yesterday's newspaper, and sipped on a bottle of shandy.

'Today really has been quite the tonic,' Betty mused, as she used the mini wooden fork to pick up one of her chips.

'I absolutely agree,' came William's muffled response as he quickly took a bite of a rather large chip. Then finishing his mouthful, he added, 'And it's not over yet. The night is still young. What do you fancy doing tonight?'

'Gosh. I'm not sure. All this fresh air has made me feel rather sleepy. What are our choices?'

'Well, we could go to the theatre and watch a play, or go dancing, or just go to see a picture. I really don't mind what we do, so I'll do whatever you want.'

Betty took a moment to think about the options. Although going to watch a play sounded like quite the treat, she wasn't sure she would be able to keep her eyes open in a darkened theatre and going to the pictures didn't feel special enough somehow.

'Well, I've brought a nice dress and we haven't been out together for such a long time, so how about we go dancing?'

'I was hoping you would say that,' William enthused. 'It's been quite a while since I last led you around a dance floor.'

Betty smiled fondly as she reminisced about how she and William would often make a date of meeting up on Lover's Corner near Barker's Pool on a Saturday night before heading to Sheffield's City Hall.

'And we can't miss an opportunity to go the famous Blackpool Tower Ballroom!'

'No,' William affirmed. 'We certainly can't.'

Back at the guesthouse, the couple made their way back to their room. 'I'll nip to the bathroom and get myself ready, so you can use this room,' William offered, forever the gentleman.

'Thank you,' Betty replied gratefully, glad William had proved, yet again, he really did only have honourable intentions.

Not wanting to waste a moment of their evening, within the hour, the pair, dressed in their finest glad rags, joined the queue outside the ballroom. Once inside the majestic hall, after placing their winter coats in the cloakroom, William swept Betty onto the sprung wooden dance floor to the sounds of Francis Collins and his ensemble.

Their feet tingling to the infectious beat, Betty couldn't help but giggle as William positioned them over one of the illuminated glass panels, which in turn reflected their swaying silhouettes.

'This is so much fun,' she said, laughing, as William spun her around, her satin navy skirt rising slightly to form a perfect circle around her knees.

The rest of the evening passed in a whirl as Betty allowed her fiancé to lead her from one dance to another, only stopping for a quick drink once, the upbeat, cheery music too infectious to resist. Only when the clock struck eleven o'clock did the deliriously happy couple retire to the sidelines.

'I haven't had that much fun since before the war,' William exclaimed, his smile the size of the moon.

'I agree.' Betty giggled, touching her flushed cheeks. 'I'm so glad we did this. It really has been a wonderful evening.'

Once back in their coats, with scarves wrapped around their necks to protect them against the decidedly chilly winter evening, William took Betty's hand.

'You really do make me feel like the happiest man alive,' he said, pulling Betty closer.

'Good,' Betty replied. 'Because you have exactly the same effect on me.'

True to his word, when the pair returned to the room for the night, William nipped to the bathroom while Betty slipped into her lilac flannelette nightdress and climbed under the eiderdown of the single bed she had opted for. Part of her would have loved nothing more than to fall asleep in her fiancé's arms but, however tempting, her good, moral upbringing wouldn't allow it. Instead, when William came back into the cosy lamplit room, she savoured the gentle kiss he tenderly placed on her lips.

'Good night, my lovely, sweet Bet,' he whispered, forcing himself to pull away. 'I really will remember tonight for a long time to come, and it will help me through the next few months until we see one another again.'

As William tucked himself under the adjacent bed, only a narrow set of drawers separating them, he reached his hand from under the eiderdown and reached for Betty, who instantly reciprocated the affectionate gesture.

'I love you, Betty,' William breathed, quietly.

'I love you too,' came Betty's warm reply.

And with that, their hands tightly entwined, the couple fell into a heavy sleep, the memories of the special day they'd shared infiltrating their dreams.

Chapter 12

Monday, 11 November 1940

'Well!' Patty trilled, expectantly, as she plonked herself down on the canteen chair next to Betty. Eyes wide, she added, 'Are you going to tell us all about your cheeky little weekend away?'

Nancy glanced across the table, amused. Poor Betty had only just sat down herself and Patty was already giving her the third degree. She knew there was no point telling their younger friend to at least let Betty open her pack-up and have a drink, knowing it would only fuel Patty's persistent and insatiable need to hear every detail about Betty's little sojourn to Blackpool.

'I'll grab you a cuppa, Betty.' Daisy chuckled, popping her snap down and making her way to the tea urn, which Dolly had as always freshly filled, ready for the lunchtime rush.

Knowing she wouldn't get a moment's peace until she'd repeated every detail of her thirty-six hours away with William, but also more than happy to relive the magical weekend, Betty said, 'It really was quite lovely.'

'Was it terribly romantic?' Patty probed.

'Yes. I can't lie. It really was perfect in every way.' Betty would have given her right arm, in that moment, to be back in William's arms, dancing the night away, or walking down the pier, hand in hand, chatting about their future.

'Have you heard this, Archie?' Patty said, playfully nudging her boyfriend in the ribs.

Archie raised his eyebrows, as the rest of the group chuckled at Patty's remark, all of them used to her pointed, but innocent, comments.

'I don't think I do too bad,' he replied, patiently.

'I s'ppose not,' Patty conceded, as she recalled the huge effort Archie had gone to arrange a surprise eighteenth birthday party for her.

'Anyway, enough about that,' she added, accepting her argument wasn't going to hold much water. Then turning back to Betty, blind to the fact she was the one who had changed the subject, Patty said: 'What did you do? We want to hear every single detail. Did you have fish and chips on the seafront and go up the Tower?'

'Yes, to your first question but no, to your second. I'm afraid we couldn't go up the Tower. Apparently, the RAF had to take the top part down for fixing. It's being used as a radar.'

'Is there anything this chuffin' war isn't ruining? Patty sighed.

'Oh, it was fine. We still had a truly lovely time.'

And with that, as Patty finally stopped talking, and

sipped on the flask of vegetable soup her mum had prepared for her, Betty was able to repeat the events of her trip away, reminiscing about the dreamy couple of days.

'That really does sound very special,' Nancy enthused, after her friend had finished, delighted for Betty.

'It was,' Betty mused, the memories fresh in her mid.

'You deserve it,' Nancy added. 'You work so hard. It's nice you have been spoilt and had a little break. Do you feel refreshed?'

'I do, yes. I think just having Saturday off made a big difference.'

'Oh. I bet. No less than you deserve. It will have done you the power of good.'

'It really was a very special treat.'

Nancy grinned, delighted to see her friend flushing with happiness. Betty worked so hard and was always helping others out. Being swept off her feet, even if it was just for a weekend, was the very least she deserved. 'Has William gone back to Harrogate now?'

'Yes.' Betty nodded, taking a bite of her thinly sliced beef sandwich, determined not to allow her disappointment show. 'He got an early train this morning.'

'Is he going to be there for a while, still?' Daisy tentatively enquired, hoping her friend would manage to see her fiancé a little more if he was stationed in Yorkshire.

Despite her resolve, Betty's expression ever so slightly faltered. She had vowed she wouldn't allow herself to feel too disheartened, buoyed by the couple of days she and

William had been lucky enough to share, knowing so many women sat in the canteen would have given their right arm for the same. But as she recalled their bus journey home, with William explaining he would soon be sent to Scotland, a spontaneous cold shiver shot down her spine.

'I'm not sure to be honest. There's a chance he could be posted somewhere else soon.'

'In this country?' Daisy gently probed, knowing how anxious Betty had been about William's future as an RAF pilot, especially after the aerial attacks from the Luftwaffe during the summer.

'I'm hoping so. He hasn't finished his training yet, so I'm keeping everything crossed it's just to another base to master his skills, and not too far away.'

What Betty didn't vocalize was she was secretly praying it would take quite some time yet before her fiancé finally got his wings, in the hope this blasted war would be over in the meantime, but she knew in her heart of hearts that was wishful thinking on her part. She'd caught a glimpse of Frank's *Daily Mirror*, and the news that a British armed merchant cruiser HMS *Jervis Bay* had been sunk. Thankfully most of the convoy had survived, but it was another sign Hitler was still hellbent on his mission to take over Europe.

'We'll all keep everything crossed,' Daisy replied, bringing Betty back to the moment.

'Thank you.' She nodded, gratefully, silently shaking her worries from her mind. Then mindful Hattie must also be concerned about how the war was progressing, she looked across and asked, 'How about John? Is he still at Salisbury Plain?'

As Hattie feebly nodded to indicate her husband was still at the military training base, Betty couldn't help but notice how deathly pale she was. 'Gosh are you okay?' she added, taken aback by how pasty she looked. 'I hope you don't mind me saying but you don't look so clever.'

'Oh sorry.' Hattie sighed wearily, then covered her mouth to shield a yawn. 'I'm okay. I'm just a bit tired, I think. I've not slept well this weekend.'

'Can I get you another cuppa?' Patty asked instinctively as she simultaneously kicked herself for not noticing, until now, how ghastly Hattie looked.

Hattie glanced down at her still half-full mug. 'No. It's all right. I haven't finished this one yet.'

'Are you sure you should be here?' Patty asked. She couldn't remember seeing Hattie ever looking so wrung out.

'Absolutely. Don't worry. I'm sure it will pass. I'm not ill. I just need a bit more sleep.'

Patty couldn't help but worry that Hattie's dad was responsible for how drained she looked and obviously felt.

'Are things tricky at home?' she said, lowering her voice, so as not to involve the whole table in the conversation. Patty assumed Vinny must be coming in at all hours, resulting in Hattie barely getting much shuteye at all.

'Yes. I don't think there's any chance of things changing now,' Hattie replied, resigning herself to the fact that the kind and considerate dad of her childhood was long gone.

'Please do tell me if I can do anything,' Patty insisted, feeling a little useless.

'Thank you. I will.' Hattie didn't have the energy to explain that there was nothing anyone could really do. Her dad wasn't going to listen to anyone. Instead, he had been falling in at all hours, drunk as a lord and making a racket. If he wasn't tripping over his own feet, he was cursing at Hattie's mum, calling her all the names under the sun, constantly telling her how useless she was. Whenever Hattie tried to calm her dad down, he would turn his anger onto her, claiming he would throw her out on the street if she backchatted him. Was it any surprise she felt so tired?

'What's this?' Dolly asked, approaching the table, giving the tea urn a shake as she went past.

'Poor Hattie is shattered,' Patty said sympathetically.

'Really, duck?' Dolly asked, looking at Hattie, who she had to admit did appear a little worse for wear.

'It's nothing a good night's sleep won't cure.'

Like the rest of Hattie's friends, Dolly wasn't convinced, but she was also astute enough to know Hattie wouldn't want anyone making a fuss.

'Well, take it steady,' she said kindly. 'Working here is exhausting enough when you feel shipshape, let alone when you aren't feeling one hundred per cent.'

'I will,' Hattie promised. In all honesty, she thought, coming to work was the escapism she needed from the torrid atmosphere at home.

Changing the subject, Dolly added, 'I don't suppose

you have managed to speak to your mum, have yer, duck? We seem to be busier than ever.'

'I'm so sorry,' Hattie apologized. 'I haven't managed to find the right time yet, but I promise I will. Things have just been a little hectic.'

Daisy's mum, Josie, joined the group of women then. 'Do let her know we would make her feel very welcome,' she said. 'It really is the best thing I ever did, coming to work here.'

'Thank you. I will,' Hattie replied gratefully. 'I know you would both look after my mum.'

Dolly didn't press, sensing that things were as tough as ever at home for Hattie. 'You know where I am if you need a chat,' she offered.

'I do and it is appreciated.' Hattie nodded, genuinely touched, knowing how thoughtful Dolly was.

'How about a drink on Friday night at The Welly?'

'That sounds nice.' Hattie said, but instantly worried if her mum would be okay at home by herself. 'Can I let you know?'

'Of course, duck. Or we could maybe go for a cuppa at Browns on Saturday after work?'

'Actually, that would be nice,' Hattie replied. 'Maybe I could bring my mum too.'

'Yes. Why don't we do that? If it's easier I could mention the job in the canteen? Josie could join us too.'

Hattie took a minute to think about Dolly's offer. She had no doubt the job would do her mum the power of good, that wasn't the issue. It was getting the idea past her dad that would be the stumbling block, but maybe Dolly and Josie were just the pair to give her mum the confidence to at least think about the job. She still wasn't sure what Dolly had endured in the past, but Hattie sensed whatever she would say may resonate with her mum. And Josie had endured her own share of worries. Hattie was sure they would be empathetic.

'Okay,' she finally agreed. 'If nothing else, it will do my mum good to get out of the house for an hour or so.'

'That's a date then,' Dolly confirmed. 'Josie, does that work for you?'

'It certainly does. I'm sure Alf won't mind me nipping out for an hour or so.'

'Right, we better get back behind that counter. There'll be another load of workers any minute, all claiming they're starvin'. Now you look after yerself, duck, and we'll see you in the week.'

'Thank you and you most certainly will,' Hattie said, although, going on how exhausted she felt right now, she had no idea how she was going to get through the rest of the day, let alone the week.

Chapter 13

'I'm so glad you could make it,' Dolly enthused as she and Hattie made their way out of gate three, navigating their way through the sea of overall-clad workers who had also clocked off for the weekend.

'Are you feeling any better?'

'I'm okay,' Hattie answered.

'Really?' Dolly raised her left eyebrow.

'Just a bit sleepy, but I'll be fine,' Hattie replied. She really was quite tired and it wasn't like her to feel so lacklustre, but yet again her dad had come home last night after a heavy drinking session, making a racket as he fell into the kitchen. The only saving grace was he was so drunk he'd fallen asleep at the table before he found a reason to start on her mum.

'Well, let's go and get you a bite to eat and a nice warming cuppa and see if that helps.'

'Sounds good,' Hattie agreed, as the two women made their way up the cobbled paving stones of Brightside

Lane; a heavy fog, tinged with a heavy chemical smell, enveloping them.

'Is your mum still joining us?' Dolly asked.

'Yes. At least she said she was this morning, and my dad is on days at the pit today, so hopefully there is no reason she wouldn't. Her cleaning shift finished about eleven thirty, so she's coming straight from there.'

'I am pleased, duck. I'm sure it will do her good. Josie is coming along too.'

'Me too. She really doesn't get out much.'

'Would you still like me to mention the job?'

Hattie hadn't had the energy to give it much thought, but in her heart of hearts, she knew if her mum could be surrounded by well-meaning women all day, it could only be a good thing, despite how much her dad was likely to turn his nose up at the idea and argue that his wife was getting ideas above her station.

'I think so.' Hattie nodded. Her mum needed something to uplift her. It might only be chopping veg, washing dishes and serving dinner to ravenous workers, but it was everything else the job would bring her. She could natter to Dolly and Josie, make new friends and earn a damn sight more than she did now scrubbing offices and pub toilets for little reward. Hattie hoped, more than anything, a job at Vickers might inject her mum with a good dose of self-worth, something she was severely lacking due to years of her dad relentlessly pecking away at her confidence.

To Hattie's relief, when the two women arrived outside Browns, Diane was already waiting, wrapped up in her worn brown Mackintosh, her brown hair tied up in an equally tired and dowdy-looking scarf. Josie was stood next to her, and it looked like the two women had already had a natter.

'I took a wild guess this was your mum and introduced myself,' Josie said.

'Aw, that's good,' Hattie enthused, pleased her mum hadn't immediately clammed up; a habit that had started after Vinny began ostracizing Diane from all her friends.

'Mum, this is Dolly,' Hattie said.

'Lovely to meet you. Call me Diane,' she replied shyly, her gentle voice barely audible above the noise of shoppers rushing up and down Attercliffe Road.

As the canteen manager returned the smile, memories of her own earlier life flashed through Dolly's mind as she took in Diane's browbeaten demeanour. It felt like looking into the past as she saw the image of the person she had once been. But Dolly also knew the last thing Diane needed was pity so in her cheeriest voice, said, 'Lovely to meet you too, at long last.'

'Shall we get inside?' Dolly added. 'The weather really isn't pleasant at all. This fog is suffocating.'

'You're not wrong there,' Diane agreed. 'It's like pea soup.'

A few minutes later the four women had positioned themselves around a square table in the warm café.

'This really is quite pleasant, isn't it?' Josie enthused. 'I'd normally be at home with a list of jobs to sort out.'

When Diane didn't respond, Hattie knew it was because her mum had programmed herself not to complain about her mundane, humdrum life, terrified if she slipped up in front of her dad, the consequences didn't bear thinking about.

'It is,' Hattie chipped in.

'What do we all fancy?' Dolly asked encouragingly, keen to keep the conversation upbeat.

'A hot cuppa would be just the tonic.' Diane smiled.

'How about a sandwich and a cake?' Dolly added. 'You must be famished after working all morning?'

'I'm not too bad,' Diane replied.

But Hattie knew the real reason was her mum would be worried about spending a penny more than she needed to.

'Today's my treat,' she said firmly, placing her hand on top of her mum's. And before her mum could argue, as Hattie knew she would, she added, 'Think of it as a thank you for making my pack-ups most mornings.'

'You really don't have to,' Diane quietly protested.

'I would like to,' Hattie countered.

'Shall we have a look at the menu?' Josie tactfully interjected. 'I seem to recall they do a nice soup – not that I get out very often.'

'That's a grand idea,' Dolly said, recalling how she had scrimped and saved every week to balance her once-meagre family budget and would never have dreamt of a lunch out in a café, knowing it would pay towards a bill or buying her sons a much-needed pair of shoes.

'Yes. Let's do that,' Hattie affirmed, despite the fact she wasn't sure she could face anything to eat but adamant her mum enjoyed a rare lunch that someone else had made for her.

By the time the waitress arrived, dressed in her perfectly pressed black-and-white uniform, it had been agreed the four women would each enjoy a bowl of homemade leek and potato soup and share a huge pot of tea.

'That will warm our cockles,' Dolly cheered, after their lunch had been ordered. 'And I should imagine it will be more potatoes than leek, so it will fill us up too.'

'I do like a nice bowl of soup,' Diane replied, keen to show Hattie she was grateful for her daughter's kind and thoughtful gesture to take her out for lunch.

'Me too,' Josie said. 'In fact, Dolly and I were thinking of putting it on at the canteen, as an alternative over the winter.'

'I should imagine that would go down well,' Diane commented.

'I reckon so,' Dolly agreed. 'I'm just not sure I have the manpower to prep it all.'

'Hattie was saying you had Nancy working with you for a while.'

'Ay, she did, luv, and she was great too, but since she went back onto the cranes we are a pair of hands down, so it's been a bit frantic, to say the least.'

'You can say that again,' Josie reiterated.

'Are Vickers still recruiting more women too?' Diane asked.

'They are. From what I hear, they can't get enough.'

Diane turned to her daughter, her eyes full of pride. 'You are all doing such a marvellous job.'

'I don't know about Hattie,' Josie replied, 'but as much as we never stop, and it's all-hands on deck, it doesn't always feel like work.'

'I'll second that.' Dolly nodded.

'What do you mean?' Diane quizzed.

'I suppose, because we all get on so well, it makes the job really enjoyable, for the most part at any rate. In fact, I'd go as far to say, I think I'd be quite lost in life without it. I class a lot of my workmates as friends. I might be knee deep in veggies and pies, but I also have a good old natter with a lot of the women working here. It helps me forget about what's going on outside the factory's walls for a few hours every day. And then when times do get tough, my pals here are always there to pull me through.'

Diane nodded, the words striking a chord, as memories of happier times came flooding back. Before Vinny had started drinking as much and making her life a living hell, she'd always enjoyed spending time with her friends, catching up over a cuppa as well as the odd night out. They had gone dancing, enjoyed trips to the pictures and spent Saturday afternoons shopping in town. After Hattie had been born, her friends had been on hand to help when her exhaustion levels had set in, taking her tiny daughter for a walk while she grabbed a much-needed nap or prepared an evening meal. Diane had never undervalued their friendship, but the irony was, now when she desperately needed their support and advice the most, Vinny's volatile temper had pushed them away.

'Friends are the greatest gift,' Diane mused sadly, only partially aware she was saying the words out loud.

Dolly quickly glanced at Hattie, who sensed her mum's mind had drifted to a happier time.

I need to help this poor woman, Dolly thought, the unforgettable raw pain of her own destructive marriage coursing through her. She knew first-hand how impossibly hard life felt when you couldn't see the wood for the trees, especially when you felt so desperately alone in the world, your self-esteem completely destroyed and your shattered confidence in a heap on the floor.

'They certainly are,' Dolly agreed. 'Worth their weight in gold. I'm sure your Hattie has told you how we've all pulled together for one another, especially when Nancy was at her wit's end fretting about her Bert.'

'And they all did the same for me and Daisy when I had that blasted stomach ulcer,' Josie commented.

'Oh, yes, she did,' Diane replied. 'And I'm also very grateful for all the support you gave Hattie when she was worrying about John.'

Hattie nodded gratefully in appreciation. She hadn't mentioned to her mum what a tower of strength Dolly had also been when it came to her dad, just by listening when she'd vocalized her frustration about her dad's incessant drinking habits. But now Hattie was wondering if she should tell her mum. Hattie worried, though, it would cause her mum more upset, thinking that she too was fed up with her dad's selfish behaviour.

'It's no problem, duck. We're all struggling in our own ways with this godforsaken war, but as I said, being surrounded by so many women with the biggest of hearts is a massive help.'

Diane turned to Hattie. 'I'm glad you have so many friends at Vickers, luv.' She hated the fact her daughter was forced to not only deal with her husband being away, but she was also having to put up with Vinny making their lives an absolutely misery. For years she had tried to protect Hattie from her husband's abhorrent ways, but as his drinking, and spending, had increased, Diane could no longer hide his increasingly violent behaviour.

'Why don't you come and join us, duck?' Josie said, seizing the opportunity to try to persuade Diane to take the role in the canteen.

'Now, that sounds like a grand plan.' Dolly grinned.

But before Diane could answer, the waitress appeared balancing a tray in her arms. 'Four bowls of soup and a large pot of tea,' she proffered.

'That's us,' Dolly replied.

Once their lunch was carefully placed before them, and Hattie was pouring them all a cup of tea, Dolly, who was on a mission to encourage Diane to come and work at Vickers, repeated, 'What do you think, duck? Would you like to come and work with me and Josie in the canteen?'

'I promise we're a friendly pair,' Josie said.

Hattie looked at her mum, praying Dolly and Josie's straightforward approach didn't scare her mum off, knowing how much she fretted about anything that her dad might not approve of.

Diane bit her lip and started nervously pulling at her thin, bony fingers.

'It would be nice for you to see more people, Mum,' Hattie put in, tactfully. 'And you would be great in the canteen. You've always been a dab hand in the kitchen.'

'And you get yer snap for free,' Dolly added. 'I don't know about you, but juggling these chuffin' rations is always a battle, but I have a cooked meal every dinnertime, so it means my rations go a damn sight further.'

'It means I can let my girls have a bit more meat of an evening,' Josie interjected. 'And my Alf, who is a proper meat-and-two-veg man, isn't complaining either.'

Hattie could have hugged Dolly for her last point. Not only might her mum put some meat on her bones, she could use this as an incentive, when she spoke to her dad. If he knew there was going to be more food on the table for him, and the fact she would be earning more money, it might just be enough to topple the scales in her favour. It grated on Hattie that her dad would benefit, yet again, from her mum's sheer hard work, but she also knew working at Vickers would help her mum no end.

'I haven't got any experience working in a canteen,' Diane said, instinctively assuming she wouldn't be suitable, but also unsure if she had the strength to ask Vinny if she could start working in the same factory as her daughter, because, let's face it, she *would* have to ask him.

'Neither did I before I started,' Josie explained.

'None needed, duck,' Dolly insisted, lifting a spoonful of the steaming soup to her lips. 'If you can make pastry, a good gravy and mash some potatoes, then you are ready to go.'

'That's something I've never struggled with,' Diane said, a smile emerging on her weary face.

'There you go then. All I need is someone who doesn't mind a bit of hard graft and can help me feed the hundreds of workers who claim their throats have been slashed, they are that hungry.'

'What do you think, Mum?' Hattie tentatively asked.

'I am very grateful,' Diane answered politely. 'And I agree it really would help. When do you need to know by? Would I be able to have a little think about it?'

What Diane didn't say, embarrassed that she didn't have the courage to make her own decision, is that she would have to somehow convince Vinny first, knowing if she accepted the job without his approval, her life wouldn't be worth living.

'Of course, you can, duck,' Dolly said kindly, dabbing

her lips with the brilliantly white starched napkin. 'If you could just let me know in the next week or so that would be grand. Does that sound doable?'

'It does.. Thank you.' If the truth be known, Diane really had no idea when she would find the right moment to speak to Vinny, but she didn't want to mess Hattie's friends about. If the worst came to the worst, she could simply decline the offer and wouldn't be any worse off than she was now, but the more Diane thought about the job, the more appealing it sounded; she just didn't want to get her hopes up for them to be dashed under her controlling husband's wrath.

Chapter 14

Wednesday, 20 November 1940

'Tea's ready,' Diane said, keeping her tone as neutral as possible, as she popped her head around the door to the front room, where Vinny was half asleep on the couch, the *Sheffield Star*, open on his knees.

'What is it?' he demanded, without a word of thanks.

'Stew and mash.'

'Any meat in it?'

'I managed to get a bit of brisket from Oliver's,' Diane replied, hoping that would at least appease her husband. 'There's some bread to mop up the gravy too.'

'Pff,' Vinny grunted.

A few minutes later the whole family were sitting around the kitchen table, tucking into the warming meal Diane had prepared, which should have acted as a balm to the soul, combatting the increasingly winter weather, but unfortunately was doing little to melt the icy atmosphere inside the house.

'This is lovely, Mum,' Hattie said, breaking the silence, in a bid to put her mum at ease and let her know she, at least, appreciated the effort she had gone to.

'Thanks, luv. How was your day?'

'Busy as ever, but at least it makes the day go quicker, even with the extra overtime.'

'Does that mean you will be bringing home more money this week?' Vinny snapped.

'Yes,' Hattie replied, determined to keep her tone neutral and prevent another explosion.

'Good. I reckon it's time we put up yer keep. If yer earning more, you should be paying us more for putting a roof over yer head and for putting meals in front of yer.'

Hattie bit her lip, in silent fury. She already tipped up most of her wages to her mum, so she could try to keep the wolves from the door, after her dad spent most of the household income in the local boozer. It meant she was barely putting a penny away in her bottom drawer to save up for all the things she and John were bound to need when they moved into a house of their own.

'Hattie does her best . . .' Diane began, her protective maternal instinct kicking in, as she jumped in to defend her selfless, hard-working daughter.

'Well, why is there never enough money to get us through the week?' Vinny stormed, his already bloodshot cheeks turning a deeper crimson.

'I do what I can,' Diane replied, resigned to the fact whatever she said or did wouldn't be good enough for her selfish husband.

'That's a bloody joke!' Vinny shouted, heavily banging

the knife and fork onto the table, causing all their plates to shake.

Diane bowed her head, knowing there was no point arguing with her husband when he was vying for a row.

'You put in a few hours a week cleaning and claim you are *doing what you can*! Well, you need to pull yer chuffin' finger out and do more. I'm working all the hours God sends down the pit, risking life and bloody limb, and you tell me washing a few floors is enough! Yer a bloody waste of space and don't know how flamin' lucky you are.'

It took all Hattie's willpower to stop herself from saying anything. It wasn't that she didn't want to defend her mum – there was nothing she wanted more – but Hattie knew if she retaliated, the outcome would be much worse and would no doubt end with her volatile dad resorting to his fists. The best thing she could endeavour to do was to defuse the situation, which was now on the precipice of erupting.

'There's never a bloody penny to rub together.' Her dad's uncalled-for rant continued. 'I have no flamin' idea what you do with all the money I bring into this house.'

Hattie looked at her dad in disbelief. If his angry outbursts weren't so terrifying, they would feel like some sort of ill-timed satirical joke. Was he really so unaware as to not know that it was *his* actions which left her nervous wreck of a mum robbing Peter to pay Paul and keep the debt collector from the door, or was he simply trying to deflect his inexcusable behaviour to justify his mood swings?

'I mean it, Diane. You are going to have to start pulling yer finger out!'

Hattie knew from how much her mum's hands were shaking and how red her eyes were that she was desperately trying to dam the river of tears. Seizing the moment, and not sure if she would ever pluck up the courage again, Hattie gently placed her cutlery either side of her plate. The calm and measured moment caught her dad's attention and was enough to momentarily stop his incessant diatribe.

'Is yer tea not good enough?' Vinny spat, looking at his daughter's barely touched meal.

'It's fine,' Hattie replied, quietly.

'Then what is it? Are you not hungry, yer ungrateful little bitch!'

Stunned, Hattie froze. Although her dad wasn't shy of effing and jeffing, he'd never actually referred to her in a shocking manner, or with such venom. Taken aback, Hattie was momentarily unable to speak, wondering if her intended suggestion would be better off left until another time.

'Vinny!' Diane gasped, unable to stop herself. Her husband might have called her all the names under the sun over the last few years, but it struck her like a punch to the heart to hear him being so horrible to their daughter.

'It's okay, Mum,' Hattie said, finding her voice.

'Oh. What's this? United front against me?' Vinny

spluttered, furiously waving his fork, his eyes darting manically from his daughter to wife.

Hattie knew it was now or never. Her dad was like a pressure pot and Hattie knew if she didn't do something quickly to release his valve, he would literally explode.

'Actually,' she said, summing up all the courage she could muster, 'I might have a solution.'

'Do yer now?' Vinny smirked, patronizingly. 'This will be worth hearing.' The sarcastic tone in his voice chipped away at Hattie's mettle.

'Well, come on then, clever clogs, spit it out.'

Hattie quietly prayed she wasn't about to make a huge mistake that would cause her exhausted mum to suffer even more at the hands of her dad. Then, without turning to glance at her mum, even for a split second, in case the expression on her face warned Hattie against saying anything, she took a deep breath. She just hoped her mum played along with the risky game she was about to play.

'I heard while I was having my dinner the other day, there's a job going in the canteen, and I thought . . .' Hattie took another deep breath, determined not to falter, then added, 'Well, I wondered if it might be something Mum could do.'

Hattie couldn't work out if the stunned look on her mum's pale and weary face was due to the fact she had brought up the idea, or that Hattie was trying to make out Diane had no idea about Dolly's offer. Either way Hattie was sure her dad would feel like he was in control and that any decision made would be his and his alone. In some ways, it wasn't too far from the truth, because both Hattie and her mum knew if Vinny refused to consider the idea, then there would be no persuading him.

'What sort of job?' Vinny demanded, shovelling a mouthful of now tepid stew into his snarling mouth.

'Just cooking in the canteen and serving up dinners,' Hattie explained, keeping her tone neutral, in a bid to prevent her dad from working out her intentions.

'Nancy, one of the crane drivers was working in there for a while, but she's now back on the shop floor and it sounds like they are short-staffed.'

'How many hours a week is it?'

'I don't know exactly, but I think it's full time, so Mum would be earning more than she is now.'

With that, Vinny looked up from his tea, the thought of extra cash piquing his interest. 'And who's gonna cook my tea and keep on top of the house?'

Hattie had known her dad would be thinking of himself and had her answer prepared.

'I could help Mum with the housework of a weekend and I'm sure we could prepare meals the night before, but I think Dolly and Josie, who work in the canteen, finish at four o'clock anyway.'

What Hattie didn't say was she hoped this job would somehow restore some of her mum's self-worth, and be the first step in improving her downtrodden life.

Vinny greedily shovelled more food into his mouth as he contemplated Hattie's unexpected suggestion, before glaring at his wife, growling, 'As I've already said, you could do with pulling yer weight a bit more and bringing in more than the paltry amount yer do at the moment.'

Diane had the good sense not to argue with Vinny or point out that if he didn't spend all their money in the pub, they would have more than enough to go round. Without even consulting Diane or asking his wife what her thoughts would be on taking on the role, Vinny turned to his daughter. 'Why don't you find a bit more out about this job and tell 'em yer mum would be up for it.'

'Okay,' Hattie obliged obediently, allowing her dad to think he was the one in control and making all the decisions.

Then, to reiterate his position in the household, Vinny added, 'But if I find out you give one of those blokes in that filthy factory even a sideways glance, yer life won't be worth bloody living.'

Humiliated, Diane's cheeks flushed. *How had her life become this bad?* But swallowing back how degraded she felt, Diane nodded obediently, hopeful this threat, no matter how despicable, meant her husband was at least contemplating the suggestion.

Chapter 15

'Is anyone up for a drink in The Welly tonight?' Patty asked, in between mouthfuls of Dolly's Friday special of mince and onion pie.

'I'm probably going to have to pass,' Nancy said. 'Bert has been busy with the Home Guard all week, and he said, as a treat, he will pick up a fish and chip supper for us all tonight.'

'That will be lovely,' Patty said. Like the rest of their friends, she was delighted Nancy's homelife had taken an upturn since Bert had found a new role after being medically discharged from the Army.

'Your Billy and Linda will love that.'

'They will!' Nancy nodded. 'You know what our Billy is like; always thinking of his stomach. Anyway, I promise I will try to make the next one.'

'Don't worry,' Patty replied. 'Anyone else up for it?'

'Oh, I could be,' Daisy replied. 'As long as my mum doesn't need m' for anything, I'll be there.'

'Count me in too.' Betty nodded, as she took a sip of her steaming mug of tea.

'How about you, Hatts?' Patty asked her friend, who, as opposed to eating her dinner, was absent-mindedly pushing it around her plate.

'Sorry. What did you say?'

Patty looked at her quizzically. 'Are you okay?'

'Sorry. I was in a world of my own. Did you ask me something?'

'I just wondered if you fancied coming for a drink tonight. Daisy and Betty are coming.'

'Actually, I could come for an hour,' Hattie replied. She knew her dad would already be in the boozer, so as long as she got home before he did, her mum wouldn't be by herself with him.

'Brilliant.' Patty beamed, delighted her friend was feeling a little more chipper.

'What's this?' Dolly asked, as she appeared at the table. 'Did I hear someone mention a trip to the pub?'

'I was just asking who fancied a quick one in The Welly tonight, but Nancy has a better offer. Do you fancy it?'

'I could be. Shall I ask Josie too?'

'Absolutely,' Patty trilled. 'The more the merrier.'

'You say that,' Frank interjected, moving his empty plate to one side and picking up his *Daily Mirror*, 'but I don't recall getting an invite.' He winked conspiratorially at Archie as he glanced at the headlines and quickly folded up his paper again, keen to avoid panicking his friends and colleagues. The paper was full of news about the previous week's bombing on Coventry and the more recent air raid on Birmingham that had left over fifty workers dead after a factory took a direct hit

'You would be very welcome,' Patty chirped, 'but Archie won't be there. He's on air-raid duty and I can't imagine you would want to sit and listen to us lot gassing.'

'Oh, I don't know,' Frank chuckled, 'I might learn a thing or two.'

'And what would Ivy say about you going out with a bunch of younger women?'

'I think she would be quite bemused! Anyway, I'm only teasing, duck. I've promised Ivy I will be home sharpish tonight. With all the overtime this week, I've barely seen her.'

As the rest of the group carried on chatting, Dolly popped herself down next to Hattie.

'Are you feeling better, duck? I hope you don't mind me saying but you didn't look so clever for a few days.'

'I am. I think it was a bug or lack of sleep. It just left me a bit lethargic.' Then looking at her still very full plate, not wanting Dolly to be offended by how little of her dinner she had eaten, Hattie continued, 'And, sorry, it seems to have drained my appetite. I promise, I love your dinners, I just don't feel very hungry.'

'Don't worry. No offence taken. I've got some soup in the kitchen. Would you rather have that?'

'No. It's okay. I really don't feel like anything.'

'You really must try and keep your strength up. You need all the energy you can working in this place.'

'I'm sure I'll be back starving again in another few days,' Hattie insisted.

'Cheers, girls.' Patty grinned, raising her glass of port and lemon. 'Thank God, it's nearly the weekend.'

'I'll drink to that,' Dolly replied. 'It's been a beast of a week in that canteen. Josie and I have been run off our feet, haven't we, duck?'

'We certainly have.' Josie nodded, stifling a yawn. 'Sorry. It's almost worse when you stop, isn't it?'

'It is. Yer adrenalin keeps yer going when you are stood up. Anyway, cheers!'

'Cheers,' Betty, Daisy and her mum, Josie, said in unison.

'Right, enough about work. What have you all got planned for the weekend?' Dolly asked.

'Not much. Archie won't be around much.'

'Has that left you at a loose end?' Betty asked Patty.

'A bit, but I'll probably take m' sisters to The Skates and give m' mom a hand in the house. She never stops, so I'm sure she would appreciate it.'

'Is Archie on air-raid duty all weekend?' Dolly enquired. Although the women hadn't spoken much about it in the last few weeks, since the air raids during the summer there was definitely an increased sense of fear of what Hitler was planning, especially after Jerry had launched countless, indomitable attacks over the Midlands. Dolly had heard the workers at Vickers talking about how over five hundred people had been killed in Coventry alone after tens of thousands of incendiary bombs had been dropped across the city. Even the medieval cathedral had been razed to the ground, alongside the countless houses that had been destroyed, leaving thousands unable to go back to their homes. And now Birmingham had been targeted by Hitler's Luftwaffe. Was Sheffield next on his list?

'Yes, tonight and tomorrow night, but he's coming round for Sunday dinner,' Patty replied, bringing Dolly back to the present.

'That will be nice,' Dolly replied, while praying Archie wouldn't be left in the thick of things if the Germans moved their assault northwards. 'How about the rest of you?' she added, blinking away the intrusive thoughts. 'Have you got any nice plans?'

'Daisy and I are nipping over to the WVS tomorrow afternoon,' Betty remarked. 'And then I promised Ivy I would help make the Christmas puddings and a Christmas cake on Sunday. Apparently if we don't do it soon, we will have left it too late for the brandy to soak in! I owe William a letter too, so I need to sit down and reply before Monday comes round again and I don't have a minute.'

'How's he getting on, duck?' Dolly asked. 'Is he still in Harrogate?'

'I'm afraid not. I got a letter earlier this week. He's now in Perth.'

'Where's Perth?' Patty quizzed, completely oblivious. 'Isn't that in Australia or somewhere?'

'Scotland.' Betty grinned, bemused by Patty's innocent naivety.

'What's he doing up there, duck?' Dolly probed, bringing her half-pint glass of pale ale to her lips.

'From what I can gather, just more training. He's flying in something called a Tiger Moth. I think he might have piloted one while he was in Canada, but I suppose he needs more practice. He said he was doing some cross-country flying too.'

'Will he be there long?' Daisy asked, knowing how much her friend would miss William not being as close by.

'No, I don't think so. He said about a month but then I think he's off to Oxford. I'm not sure what for. They have to be careful what they say in their letters, don't they?'

'They do that,' Dolly agreed. 'I've had a few off our Michael and Johnny, and there's been lines drawn through some of their writing because they've obviously said something they shouldn't have. To be honest, there are times I have no idea where they are, let alone what they are doing.'

'That's hard,' Betty said. 'You must miss them so much.'

'I do that, duck, but as long as I get regular letters, I can sleep a little easier knowing they are all right. Knowing they are still together brings me a lot of comfort. Despite their bickering as kids, they have always been close.'

'I can understand that,' Betty replied. 'And you have your lovely little granddaughters to make you smile.'

'That I do.' Dolly nodded, the corners of her lips

turning upwards. 'They really are little treasures and both of them look like their daddies, or at least I think they do. It sounds daft but whenever I look at our Lucy and Milly, it's as though their dads are with me.'

'Not at all,' Betty said. 'If it helps you, that's all that matters. We all must do what we can to get through.'

'We do that, duck. Anyway, I don't want to start getting all maudlin-like, especially on a Friday night. That's no good for anybody. I'll keep my fingers crossed your William will get some time off at Christmas.'

'That would be lovely.'

Betty was also determined to stay positive, outwardly at least. She knew how lucky she was to have seen William so recently, especially as Dolly hadn't seen her two sons since war had been declared over a year earlier. But the thought of what the future held still filled her with dread. Frank had the wireless on the night before when she'd nipped into the kitchen to make herself a cup of tea before going to bed, and she too had overheard how badly other cities had suffered under the most recent raids. She had no idea how long it would be before William was fully qualified and was sent to defend the skies against Hitler's planes. If that wasn't enough of a worry, if Jerry was targeting cities like Birmingham and Coventry, how long would it be before Sheffield came under attack again? Like Dolly, she hadn't voiced her concerns, not wanting to scare her friends, but equally wasn't naive enough to think Hitler wouldn't strike again.

'It will soon come round,' Josie said, breaking Betty's thoughts.

'Yes, it will,' Betty agreed, keeping her tone upbeat. 'Only another week or so and we will be in December.'

'I'm determined to make this one really special for Alf and the girls.' Josie smiled, looking at her eldest daughter, Daisy. Nobody needed to be reminded how the previous Christmas Josie had been convinced she was dying and had spent the day barely able to move off the couch in the front room, thinking it would be the last festive period she had with her family.

'I'm sure it will be wonderful,' Betty said tactfully and discreetly gave Daisy's arm a little pat, knowing the events of a year ago still upset her friend.

'We should organize a little party,' Patty piped up. 'I reckon we all deserve it.'

'That's a great idea, duck,' Dolly agreed.

As Patty, Betty and Daisy chatted about how they could arrange a little party, Dolly turned her attention to Hattie, who was sat to her right.

'Did your mum manage to speak to your dad about the job? I don't want to pressure her; I was just wondering.'

'Actually,' Hattie started, picking up her mug of tea and nursing it in between her hands hoping it would somehow magically make her feel better, 'Mum didn't, but I did.'

'Really?'

'Yes. I knew my mum would struggle to find the right moment or pluck up the courage. She's terrified of saying anything that will set my dad off on another one of his rages. Anyway, he was moaning about lack of money on Wednesday night – the irony of it, considering he is the one spending all our hard-earned wages. Anyway, I could see he was vying for a row, so I took my opportunity to bring up the job.'

'Well done, duck. I don't doubt that took some guts. Dare I ask what he said?'

'It was typical really. The main thing he cared about was how much money Mum would earn and who was going to cook his tea every night.'

'Sounds familiar,' Dolly muttered, shaking her head, cross on Hattie and her mum's behalf. The memories of her own former controlling and selfish husband never too far away.

Determined to focus her energy on helping Hattie and her mum, she said: 'Well. The gaffers pay three pounds a week and I'm sure we could pack up the odd extra meal for your mum to take home if it stops your dad having a go at her.'

'Thank you, Dolly. I know the job would do her the power of good. She's just so worried about doing anything to upset my dad.'

'Don't worry, duck. I get it, but I guess if we can play on the fact she will be taking home some extra cash, that might be enough to keep your dad happy.'

'And the fact your mum will have a hot meal every lunchtime, so she won't need to use as much of her rations, that might help too,' Josie, who was sat the other side of Hattie, added.

'I think it will help,' Hattie sighed, part of her happy they had found a solution, but another part of her couldn't help feeling angry.

'What is it, luv?' Josie asked, sensing Hattie's frustration. 'Is there something still bothering you?'

'I'm sorry. I don't mean to sound ungrateful. I really do appreciate the job offer and how kind you are both being.'

'But?' Dolly prompted kindly.

'It just upsets me to think that my dad will simply squander away all the extra money she earns down the pub. Despite the fact Mum is prepared to work longer hours, which, by the way, will be so good for her to be with you both, she won't benefit at all financially. She will just be paying even more towards Dad's beer money.'

'I can understand why you are frustrated. It does feel very unfair,' Josie said.

'I guess she can't squirrel any away without him realizing?' Dolly asked.

'We've tried, but he always finds it. We've even put money under the floorboards but it's never there by the end of the week.'

'I'm sorry,' Josie sighed, horrified. Her Alf had never been anything but loving and generous – she couldn't imagine the rotten time Hattie and her mum had to endure.

'I agree. It's not fair, duck,' Dolly added.

'It's okay. I am trying to focus on the fact that Mum will be much happier just being here. She doesn't really see anyone in her cleaning jobs and, I think I told you, Dad has scared all her friends off.'

'You did, duck, but don't you worry, Josie and I will take good care of her.'

'We will that,' Josie echoed.

'I know you will, and I really am ever so grateful. You have both been so kind.'

'So, do you think she will accept the job?' Dolly asked hopefully.

'I think so. I'm going to try and speak to Mum and Dad again this weekend but I'm pretty sure my dad will agree to anything for the extra money.'

'Okay, duck. Just let me know. I'm more than happy for your mum to start as soon as she's ready. Josie and I definitely won't turn down an extra pair of hands.'

Chapter 16

Monday, 2 December 1940

'Make sure you don't make a chuffin pig's ear of it,' Vinny grunted, in his normal derogatory manner, as he pulled on his heavy black coat and grabbed the bag holding his gas mask and his pack, which Diane had just carefully finished making for him.

Charming, Hattie silently fumed. It was the first day of her mum's new job and that was all her dad could manage.

'I'll do my best,' Diane whispered obediently, before Vinny slammed the back door as he left, sending a wave of cold air through the kitchen.

'Don't let him get to you, Mum,' Hattie said. 'You are going to be brilliant and remember you aren't doing this for Dad.'

'What do you mean, luv?'

Hattie bit her lip in frustration. She hated seeing how little self-esteem her mum had in herself, after years of being put down and insulted by her dad. The constant nit-picking and unjustified sly digs about her not being able to do anything right had left Diane believing what her cruel and manipulative husband said.

'Mum, I didn't want you to take this job simply to earn extra money to compensate for dad's spending,' Hattie explained, in a mixture of sadness and exasperation.

'Well. I've got to do something, otherwise we'll be in real trouble. I'm barely making ends meet.'

Hattie bit her lip. What she really wanted to say was her dad shouldn't be so selfish and spend all the household income on booze, but Hattie didn't want her mum's first day to start on a negative note. She needed to bolster her mum and remind her of what a good opportunity this was for her.

Pouring her mum a much-needed cuppa, Hattie said, 'You are going to really enjoy working with Dolly and Josie. They are such lovely women, and you will all get on so well.'

'But what if I really do make a pig's ear of it?'

Hattie knew her mum's confidence levels were at rock bottom, and she was terrified of not only making a fool of herself, but also giving Vinny the ammunition to say 'I told you so'.

'You won't, Mum. I promise. You'll be cooking dinners and serving them up. What can possibly go wrong? Let's face it, if I can operate those great dangerous machines and not make a mess of it, I'm quite sure you can do something you have been doing for years, albeit on a slightly bigger scale.'

'I just feel so nervous,' Diane confessed, her hands shaking as she wrapped them around the mug of hot tea.

'That's completely normal. Everyone does on their first day. Remember how anxious I was. I was terrified of making a mistake, and if I'm honest I probably made the odd one but nothing too serious, and you will be exactly the same. I can guarantee by the end of the week, you'll be well into the swing of it and loving your new job.'

'Do you really think so, luv?'

'I don't just think it; I know it,' Hattie confirmed authoritatively, as she swallowed back the unexpected nausea that had left her feeling a bit off-kilter since she'd got up. She knew she should eat something, but the thought of it made her feel worse.

Maybe, I'll just have a slice of dry toast, she thought to herself, hoping it would help.

'Thanks, luv,' Diane said, distracting Hattie and bringing her back to the moment. 'I do appreciate what you have done to get me this job.'

'You don't have to thank me. It will be lovely that we are working together. I'll get to see more of you, but most importantly it will be good for you.'

As Hattie carved a thin slice of bread from the loaf her mum had baked the night before, a new set of thoughts penetrated her mind. She wasn't sure exactly how yet, but this job couldn't just be an extra wage packet for her dad. Apart from making new friends and boosting her self-worth, some long-term good had to come out of this for her mum. She didn't know how yet, but Hattie was hoping by some miracle it could be a new beginning for her.

'How's she doing?' Hattie asked Josie as she approached the canteen serving counter. Diane was a few steps away dishing up dinners to hungry workers, politely smiling as she handed over one plate after another.

'Not bad, luv. Not bad at all.'

'Are you sure?' *Not bad* wasn't *good* or *grand*.

'Yes. Your mum's just a bit quiet, but it's her first day. I wouldn't expect anything else. It can feel quite overwhelming dealing with this lot.' Josie nodded towards the line of burly workers, all of them covered in muck and talking loudly to compete with the constant chatter that reverberated around the high-ceilinged canteen. 'They can be an uncouth bunch at times. It took me by surprise too when I first started. Even with more women around, they don't hold back with what they are thinking.'

Hattie nodded as she recalled what a culture shock it had been moving from the safe and calm environment of the make-up counter at Woolies to Vickers, which was like nothing she had ever experienced. The cacophony of ear-splitting noise, the dust, the heat, as well as getting used to the coarse, and often unfiltered, banter of her male colleagues. Although some of them would try to rein it in a bit around their female counterparts, there were still plenty of them who effed and jeffed and didn't think twice about talking about their Saturday night conquests, no matter who was listening.

'Apart from my dad, my mum hasn't been around big groups of men in her jobs as a cleaner,' Hattie explained.

Josie nodded. 'It can feel very intimidating when you aren't used to it.'

Hattie knew her mum wouldn't know how to react around the blokes and would struggle to join in with their banter after Vinny had ebbed away at her confidence leaving her a nervous wreck, not to mention warning her not to even look at another bloke sideways.

'Don't worry, duck. I'm keeping an eye out for her,' Dolly put in, after handing over a hot dinner to a dust-covered older man. 'The blokes can get a bit lairy every now and 'gain, but I only have to give them one of my killer glares and they soon shut up. That or they know they are risking not getting their snap! I won't serve anyone who gives me any lip.'

Hattie grinned. She knew the factory workers respected Dolly and it wasn't just the fact that she was filling their stomachs every day, but also she had a heart of gold and would always do what she could to help someone out if they were in trouble or needed anything. They all confided in Dolly and sought her advice. She was well and truly the matriarch of her canteen.

'Thank you,' Hattie replied gratefully, certain Dolly and Josie were just the women to take her mum under their wings. She was also hoping that her mum might eventually confide in them and in return receive some sound advice on what to do about her dad. Heaven knows Diane needed someone to help her cope. Hattie was all too aware that her mum felt she shouldn't always tell her everything, her protective maternal role kicking in, not to mention she probably felt worn out by her husband's obnoxious actions.

'I just hope my mum will start to come out of her shell a bit and realize she is allowed to enjoy life a little too.'

'I'll do what I can to make her feel comfortable,' Dolly said.

'I do appreciate it and I know I keep saying it, but I really am very grateful to you for giving my mum this chance.'

'You don't have to thank me, duck. Don't forget yer mum is doing us a favour too. We have been rushed off our feet since Nancy went back on the cranes. It's a blessing to have another pair of hands to help us out.'

'And she's a dab hand at making a good gravy,' Josie enthused. 'And I don't think I've ever seen anyone peel potatoes as quickly.'

'Exactly what we needed,' Dolly affirmed.

But Hattie knew Dolly could have filled the role ten times over and had deliberately held out, giving her mum time to pluck up the courage to agree to come and work at Vickers.

'Well. I better let you get back to it before this queue ends up trailing halfway around the canteen,' Hattie said. 'I won't interrupt my mum. I don't want to put her off but tell her, from me, it looks like she is doing a great job and that I'll see her when I get home. We've been asked to do a couple of hours' overtime, so she will finish before me.'

'I will do, duck. And as soon as the lunchtime rush is over, I'm going to make sure she sits down with a cup of tea and a hot meal. Speaking of which, have you had your snap yet?'

'No,' Hattie replied honestly.

'Well, go and grab it while you can.'

'Okay,' Hattie agreed.

But as she turned to walk to the table she and her friends shared, Hattie spotted her mum facing her and giving a discreet wave. Hattie felt overwhelmingly grateful. For so long she had been the only one looking out for her mum, trying to get her to eat regularly and look after herself. It wasn't that she minded, but it was a huge comfort knowing Dolly and Josie also had her mum's best interests at heart. Between them, they might just be able to show Diane she had a life worth living and, despite how inadequate Vinny made her feel, that people genuinely cared for her.

Chapter 17

Saturday, 7 December 1940

'Does anyone else fancy joining Daisy and me for a spot of Christmas shopping?' Betty asked as the group of friends piled out of Vickers towards gate three, the cold air biting at their ruddy cheeks.

'Oooh, yes, please,' Patty replied, wrapping her scarf tighter around her neck. 'I need to find something for Archie. Maybe we could grab a cuppa too. I'm parched after being stuck up in that crane for the last four hours.'

'I think we could manage that.' Betty chuckled, pulling her gloves on. 'Does anyone else fancy it?'

'I'd love to,' Hattie said. 'But I'm pretty tired, and I have promised my mum I will help her catch up with all the jobs. I think she feels she needs to get everything done now of a weekend after working all week.'

'Bless her. She must be shattered,' said Nancy. 'Has she enjoyed it?'

'I think so,' Hattie said. 'She's still getting used to it, but I know she's loved working with Dolly and Josie. They have made her feel so welcome and really took my mum under their wings.'

Daisy smiled in response. 'My mum has said she is doing a grand job.'

'Aw, that's lovely to hear,' Hattie said. 'I'm hoping it will give her a little boost.'

'I'm sure it will,' Nancy said. 'I was so shy when I first started here.'

'And look at you now,' Patty said, giving Nancy a friendly nudge.

'I'm certainly grateful for all the friends I've made. I don't think I'd have coped without you all over the last year or so.'

'We make a good bunch,' Betty confirmed. 'Now, would you like to come into Attercliffe with us?'

'I would have loved to,' Nancy replied. 'But Bert is on duty with the Home Guard today and Doris has had our Billy and Linda all morning. I'd feel terrible not getting back.'

'Don't worry at all,' Betty said. 'I'm sure you're desperate to go and spend some quality time with those little ones.'

'I am.' Nancy smiled. 'I've promised Linda we can make some paper bunting and Christmas cards.'

'That sounds lovely,' Betty commented. 'And it will get you in the Christmas spirit. It will be here before we know it.'

'I have to say, I am really looking forward to Christmas

this year with Bert being at home.' But as soon as the words had left Nancy's lips, guilt coursed through her. She knew how much Betty and Hattie would love to have William and John with them over the festive period.

'I'm sorry,' she apologized quickly, Nancy's cheeks reddening. 'That was thoughtless of me. I didn't mean to be so tactless.'

'Don't be daft!' Betty admonished. 'Of course, you're looking forward to Christmas, which is exactly how it should be. You, Billy and Linda deserve to have a truly happy Christmas.'

'Thank you,' Nancy replied, gratefully. 'We all do. I do hope William and John can get some leave.' Then turning to Daisy, she added, 'It will be lovely for your family too after how difficult last year was.'

'Yes,' Daisy enthused, memories flooding in of her mum lying on the couch, barely able to swallow a mouthful of food, until Nancy had managed to persuade her to seek medical help.

'She is planning to cook a big roast and invite lots of family over. She's already made a Christmas cake and keeps pouring more brandy into it. She's talking about having a Boxing Day party too, so you will all be invited.'

'Yes, please!' Patty trilled excitedly.

'That sounds perfect,' Nancy added, delighted to see how happily things had turned out for Josie. 'You all deserve a big celebration.'

'It should be lovely,' Daisy agreed. 'My sisters are very excited.'

'If they are anything like Billy and Linda, they will be counting down the days already.'

'They are! They have got a calendar on the wall and put a big cross over each day at bedtime.'

'I am pleased,' Nancy commented. 'Right, I better get off. Poor Doris will have had her hands full this morning, so I better go and give her a break.'

'Have a good weekend!' Betty waved as Nancy made her way down Brightside Lane, joining the sea of workers who were all heading home after a week's hard labour.

Twenty minutes later Betty, Daisy and Patty were all sitting in Browns, each nursing a warming cup of tea and sharing a saucer of shortbread biscuits.

'Do you think these air raids that have been happening all over the country will affect us?' Patty asked, as she eyed a couple of wardens who were sitting at a nearby table. 'I don't like to ask Archie. It doesn't seem right, somehow, but I keep hearing snippets when m' dad has the wireless on.'

Betty had been thinking exactly the same. She hadn't said a word in her letters to William, either, terrified he might announce that he would be taking to the skies to defend Blighty from Jerry.

'I don't know, if I'm honest,' she said solemnly. 'So many cities have been attacked now. I heard Frank and Ivy talking about Bristol. It sounds like a lot of buildings, including churches and almshouses, were destroyed.'

'I wish someone would just put an end to Hitler,' Patty exclaimed.

'I don't think you're alone there,' Betty agreed.

'And London has taken a real hammering,' Daisy added. 'It feels like every day there's another headline in Frank's paper about the East End and how many people's houses have been destroyed.'

What Daisy didn't vocalize was how many lives were being lost too, not wanting to add to the angst her friends were already feeling, but she didn't have to. The thoughts that they were all trying to lock away in the back of their minds momentarily silenced the women. It was almost impossible to imagine their homes being obliterated. Sheffield had suffered some minor damage during the summer, but nothing on the scale that other cities had experienced.

'What plans have you got for Christmas?' Daisy asked, turning to Patty, conscious their little sojourn to the café was meant to be fun, as opposed to worrying about something out of their control. 'Will you and Archie spend it together?'

'I think we will do the same as last year. We'll both spend the morning with our own families, then Archie will come to my house in the afternoon and then I'll go to see his parents and nannan in the evening.'

'That sounds perfect!'

'I'm just praying Hitler doesn't have any plans to ruin the day.' The thought of the German dictator's next move still played heavily on her mind. 'My dad has been glued to the wireless this week. I didn't know about Bristol, but I heard them talking about what a battering Liverpool and Southampton took. Apparently, hundreds of bombs were dropped, and in Southampton it went on for six hours!'

'Crikey,' Daisy whispered. 'That does sound terrifying. You can't imagine how scared all those poor people must have felt.'

'No,' Betty agreed, shaking her head.

'Do you think he will ever stop?' Patty asked.

'That's anybody's guess, but we must stay positive,' she replied, also conscious their afternoon out wasn't going as planned. 'He hasn't conquered England, far from it, in fact.'

But even as Betty said the words, the worries she'd desperately tried to bat away sent a shiver down her spine. The RAF had their work cut out defending Blighty and the need for pilots had never been greater. She knew, in her heart of hearts, those in command of the Allied military operation would be keen to get trainee pilots, like her William, fully ready to take to the skies against the Luftwaffe.

'Surely it will never come to that?' Patty exclaimed, interrupting Betty's thoughts. The idea of the Germans taking over their country was incomprehensible.

'I'm sure it won't,' Betty said, taking a deep breath,

determined to keep their afternoon together upbeat. She couldn't dwell on the ifs and maybes. Betty knew it wouldn't do her any good whatsoever. Nobody knew what was around the corner, so as she had repeatedly told herself recently, there was absolutely no point fretting about what might happen.

'Let's not worry about that, especially not today,' Betty added encouragingly. 'We are supposed to be getting into the festive spirit!'

'You're right,' Daisy enthused, also keen to move away from the subject of war, and to help her family make this Christmas especially special.

'Why don't we all order a little slice of Christmas cake each to keep us going and then go shopping?'

'That sounds like a marvellous idea,' Betty replied. 'Now you mention it, I am rather peckish, and I do love Christmas cake. Ivy is adamant we can't touch hers until at least Christmas Eve.'

'My mom is the same,' Patty commented, rolling her eyes, in mock rebuff. 'And I chuffin' love it too.'

The atmosphere lifted, the three women spent the next half an hour enjoying numerous restorative cups of tea, accompanied by rather more generous slices of the rich fruit cake than they'd dared hope for.

'Right,' Patty said, after every single crumb had been consumed and their dainty cups emptied. 'Shall we go to Banners?'

'I think we should,' Betty affirmed, knowing a couple of

hours choosing gifts for all the people she loved and cared for would be just the tonic to stop her mind wandering down a road she didn't care to travel.

A couple of miles away, Diane had just finished frying three rashers of streaky bacon and carved two slices of homemade bread.

'Here you go,' she said, placing the sandwich in front of a gruff-looking Vinny, who had just got home from a morning shift at Tinsley pit.

'Thanks,' he begrudgingly acknowledged, not even looking up.

'What would you like for your lunch, luv?' Diane asked, as Hattie came in through the back door, a cold draught accompanying her.

'Don't you worry about me, Mum. I'll heat up some of that soup you made last night.'

'I can do it,' Diane said instinctively. 'You have had a busy morning. Sit yourself down. I've just made a fresh pot of tea too.'

Knowing it made her mum happy to fuss over her, Hattie perched herself opposite her dad, who was greedily eating his bacon sandwich, as he absent-mindedly flicked through the *Sheffield Star* at the kitchen table.

After he had stuffed the last corner into his mouth, Vinny shoved the plate forwards and out of his way, and roughly closed the paper.

'How much did you bring home this week in yer fancy

new job, then?' he barked at Diane, who was heating a pan of vegetable soup on the range.

Diane stiffened. She had been waiting for this. The only reason he hadn't demanded to see her wage packet the night before was down to the fact he'd gone straight to the pub after work. By the time he rolled in, Vinny had been incapable of asking anything. Too drunk to even get upstairs, he'd collapsed onto the front-room sofa, where he'd stayed until Diane had woken him, with a strong brew, to get him to go to work, knowing her life wouldn't be worth living if she let him oversleep.

Biting down on her now dry lip and clenching her hands into a ball to give her some courage, Diane took a deep breath. She was astute to know the only reason Vinny had permitted her to start working at Vickers was so he could benefit from the extra cash she earned.

'Just short of three pounds,' she said, keeping her tone matter of fact, silently praying her husband wouldn't pick up on her lie.

'Is that it?' he grunted, unappreciatively. 'All those hours for that. Hardly seems worth it.'

'It's a lot more than I was bringing home from my cleaning jobs.'

Vinny grunted, momentarily stumped. Noisily standing up, he banged his hands on the table, causing the tea in Hattie's mug to spill over.

'So where is it then?' he demanded.

Diane had been prepared for this, too. 'I paid the rent

man last night and I have been to the butcher's and grocer's this morning. There's some put aside for the bills and the rest is here.' Diane took the little brown envelope out of her pale-green gingham apron pocket.

Vinny snatched it without even looking inside. Normally, there wasn't a single penny left after everything had been paid for. 'I've put my share in the jar, but I'll take this,' he charged, scraping his chair backwards as he stood up. 'I'll be back later.'

Without another word, Vinny strode across the kitchen, grabbed his coat, leaving his gas mask on the hook, arrogantly believing he was immortal, and left the house through the same door Hattie had come in through a few minutes earlier.

Waiting a minute to be sure her dad was out of earshot, or didn't come back, Hattie just looked at her mum, her eyes a mix of pride and affection. As soon as she was confident the coast was clear, Hattie asked, 'That wasn't really all you got paid, was it?'

Diane slowly shook her head, full of nervous trepidation, silently revealing her indiscretion. 'Do you think he'll know?' she asked.

Hattie didn't know whether to laugh or hug her mum. She'd hoped the job would give her some much-needed confidence but hadn't dared to hope she would do something so daring.

'I can't let him drink it all away.'

'I completely agree but you don't have to explain

yourself to me, Mum. You've worked hard for that money.'

'I just thought if I could put a little bit away every week, it would . . .' But Diane's words trailed off. She wasn't sure where it would lead; maybe a nicer Christmas, the chance to treat her daughter to something special or have enough money to splash out on a slightly bigger chicken, instead of scrimping and saving to buy the smallest cut of meat the butcher would give her at a knock-down price. The one thing Diane was sure of, though, was that she couldn't just be a piggy bank to fund her husband's destructive drinking habits.

Hattie stood up and wrapped her arms around her mum. 'I am so proud of you. I know how much you worried about taking the job at Vickers.'

'You shouldn't be,' Diane countered. 'I feel like I've failed you as a mum. I should have found a way to escape your dad years ago. I just didn't want you to come from a broken home.'

'No, Mum. You haven't. We've been through this before. All you have ever done is try and protect me from Dad. You aren't responsible for his actions or selfish ways.'

'Thank you, luv, but I should have been stronger,' Diane whispered, as Hattie released her from her grip.

'And where would you have gone, Mum? It's not like you have family to rely on, or someone who could have taken us both in.'

Once again, Diane was grateful for how understanding her daughter was. Like Hattie, she had been an only child and her parents had long since passed, after the Spanish Flu, along with the hundreds of thousands of others across the world.

'I'm so glad I have you, even if I do wish I'd been able to give you a better life.'

'Enough of that,' Hattie admonished kindly. 'Life is what it is and there's nothing we can do to change the past, but we can influence the present and what we really need to talk about is where you are putting the money you didn't tell Dad about.'

'I know.' Diane nodded. No matter where she had tried to hide any spare cash in the past, Vinny had an infallible skill of hunting it out.

'I'm sort of hoping because I've given your dad more money than I ever have, he won't go looking.'

Hattie agreed her mum had a point, but she also knew how the consuming need for her dad to have a drink would mean if he got the slightest sniff there was extra money in the house, he would be like a man possessed until he found it.

'I think we need to be a little more cautious than that,' Hattie warned. 'We can't take the risk.'

And Hattie also knew, as she was sure her mum did, if her dad found out Diane had been lying to her, the consequences wouldn't bear thinking about.

Diane grimaced. The unspoken words had haunted her

since she'd made the decision to squirrel away some of her wages.

'Why don't you let me hide it?' Hattie finally suggested.

'No!' Diane replied immediately. 'I'm not risking your dad taking his temper out on you. I would never forgive myself if he as much as laid a finger on you.'

'But . . .'

'No,' Diane repeated firmly. 'It's not up for discussion, luv. It's bad enough you've had to see his foul temper. I won't let you bear the brunt of it as well.'

Hattie knew there was no point protesting but at the same time it pained her knowing her mum could end up being on the receiving end of her dad's increasingly violent temper. They were both battling to protect the other.

'There is one place that might work,' Diane started, as she poured the steaming soup into two bowls.

Hattie, who was arranging two placemats on the table, raised her eyebrows quizzically.

As Diane carefully placed their lunch in the designated spots, accompanied by a spoon for each, she explained, 'When I was sweeping the front room this morning, I spotted a loose floorboard under the sofa.'

'Mum, you shouldn't have lifted that couch by yourself. I told you I would help with all the cleaning this afternoon.'

'I had time, and you were working. I just thought I'd get ahead. Anyway, I can't imagine your dad would ever move that sofa. All the other spots I've hidden money in have been a bit more obvious.'

To a certain extent, this was true. Diane had stuffed the odd note and few coins in socks at the back of drawers, under her mattress, and behind the few glasses Vinny hadn't smashed in the kitchen cupboard.

Hattie thought about her mum's suggestion. It wasn't a bad idea and probably the best option they had if Diane wouldn't let her take care of the money.

Sensing her daughter was assessing the viability of the hiding place, Diane added, 'Your dad generally goes to the pub on a Friday night and works Saturday mornings so I could hide it then and he would never be any the wiser.'

Hattie tentatively lifted a spoon of the thin soup to her lips, hoping it wouldn't be yet another assault to her still fragile stomach. It didn't take her long to weigh up the pros and cons. This was the first step her mum had taken in years to stand up to her dad, to defy the tyrannical rule he'd upheld with his fists and threats for years. She needed to support her mum or risk Diane living under her dad's heavy-handed thumb for the rest of her life.

'Okay,' Hattie finally acquiesced, despite how jittery she still felt. 'But only until we think of a better idea.'

Chapter 18

'Did anyone else hear about London?' Patty asked, opening her snap bag to reveal a thinly sliced beef sandwich, made from the Sunday roast leftovers. 'M' dad had the wireless on while we were having breakfast and it sounds like they took another battering.'

'Ay, I did, duck.' Frank nodded, as he dug into his own lunch. 'Too many lost lives. That flamin' man is hell bent on causing as much destruction as possible.'

'Is it selfish to say, I just hope he sends his chuffin' planes away from Sheffield.'

'Patty!' Archie admonished.

'You know what I mean, though. I don't want any of us to go through all that horror. And . . .' she added turning to her sweetheart, 'I'm thinking of you too, patrolling those streets of a night.'

'I know. I just wouldn't wish it on anyone, that's all.'

'Fair do's,' Patty reluctantly conceded.

'I know what you are saying,' Nancy interjected, understanding what her friend meant. 'I want us all to stay safe. It's just horrible thinking about anyone who has been affected by this war.'

'I'll second that,' Josie said, as she checked the tea urn. 'It feels like every day there's some bad news.'

'It can't last forever,' Betty said, forever optimistic, catching Hattie's eye and noticing her forehead creased with worry lines. She knew that her friend would be as worried about John, as she was William.

'Nothing ever does,' Josie reiterated, sensing the tense atmosphere.

'I hope so,' Hattie whispered, accidentally saying out loud what she continually prayed for.

'It will end eventually, luv. I know it's hard, but I promise you everything comes to an end eventually.'

'Sorry, I don't mean to sound so gloomy,' Hattie said.

'You have nothing to apologise for,' Josie replied kindly. 'Have you heard from John recently?'

'Yes. I had a letter at the end of last week. He's still on Salisbury Plain but I don't know how long they will keep him there. He keeps telling me there's still work for him there, but I suppose it depends on what happens.'

'I'll keep everything crossed for him,' Josie replied.

'Thank you.'

For the next twenty minutes, the group tried to distract themselves, talking about Christmas plans, and avoiding talk of the war, but no matter how much they discussed who was doing what over the festive season, the thought of Hitler's latest barbaric actions couldn't escape their minds.

'Right,' Frank announced when the thirty minutes came to an end. 'I'm afraid it's time to get back to it.'

'I suppose the one good thing about being busy is it will go fast,' Betty commented.

'There is that,' Nancy affirmed. 'Fingers crossed it passes without any hiccups.'

Betty's proclamation seemed to be going as predicted, but as the end of the day felt within touching distance, the dreaded wail of the air raids pierced the sound of machinery.

'Chuffin' 'eck,' Patty said in a mixture of frustration and anger, as the high-pitched screech assaulted her senses and brought her to a grinding halt. Shattered from a non-stop day in the crane, like the majority of the factory workers, she'd been hoping, once her shift ended in a couple of hours, for a hot tea and an early night. 'Well, that's paid short shrift to that,' she mumbled through gritted teeth, pulling the crane hook back into a safe position as she prepared to make her way down the steep ladder.

At the bottom, Frank was instructing the hoard of workers, who had put down their tools and started gathering on the shop floor, to get a move on. 'Come on. Quick sharp,' he bellowed, over the chatter.

'Where's Archie?' Patty asked, her eyes darting across the vast room, as workers made their way to the huge double doors.

'I don't want you to panic, duck,' Frank started. 'He's just . . .'

'What?' Patty demanded, cutting the foreman off, panic rising in her chest.

Frank had no time to beat around the bush, conscious he needed to get his battery of workers to safety and fast. Cities across the country had taken a hammering over the last few weeks and he was sure it was only a matter of time before Sheffield was targeted.

'I don't want you to worry, but he's nipped up to the roof to give the fire watchers a hand. They're a bit short.'

Horrified, Patty tried but failed to swallow back the fear, which was surging through her. 'But. But . . .'

'Come on, duck,' Frank said, placing a reassuring hand on her shoulders. 'I promise there's no need to get into a pickle about it. It's no worse than what he does most weekends.'

'Isn't it?' Patty muttered. Frank ushered her out of the shop floor, and they began navigating their way through the maze of corridors. She wanted to believe her foreman, but surely being stood on the roof of the monstrous factory, exposed to all the elements, and ever worse, a prime target for the Luftwaffe, was a damn sight worse than being on the ground, with the protection of a shelter to keep him safe.

Betty who had heard the back end of the conversation was now at Patty's side.

'Frank's right,' she said gently. 'Your Archie isn't daft. He knows how to keep himself safe.'

'I don't know. It doesn't feel right,' Patty exclaimed as

she allowed herself to be guided towards the underground shelter in the bowels of the factory.

As the hundreds of workers filed into the cavernous shelter, Nancy, who had only been a few yards behind, caught up with her friends. Like Patty, she looked terrified.

'After what we were chatting about while we had our snap, I don't like the feel of this,' Nancy sighed.

'It's going to be okay. I promise,' Betty said, squeezing her hand, with more bravado and conviction than she felt.

'It's Billy and Linda,' Nancy gasped. 'They will still be in school. I should be with them. I can't bear to think of them being scared, especially when I'm not there to comfort them. Our Linda will be terrified. She hates the sirens.'

Betty tightened her grip. 'The teachers will know exactly what to do to keep them all calm and will take good care of them.' But even as she said the words, Betty knew her optimism would do little to alleviate Nancy's understandable anxiety.

'Let's just hope it's over quickly,' Patty said, as the three women found a spare bench to perch on.

'I'm sure it will be,' Betty replied, praying her prediction was accurate, for all their sakes. She didn't like the feel of the afternoon air raid more than anyone else.

'Can we squeeze on?'

Her thoughts broken, Betty looked up. Daisy and Hattie had zigzagged their way through the crowd to find them.

'Of course,' Betty said, squidging along the bench, which was now filling up with anxious workers, to make extra room. 'Come and sit down.'

'Hattie, are you okay?' Betty added, taken aback by how pale she looked. 'I hope you don't mind me saying but you look shattered.'

'I think it was the shock of the siren and rushing here,' Hattie replied, exhausted. If the truth be known she hadn't felt too good all day. Yet again, her dad had drunk himself into a stupor the night before and made a racket as he attempted to make himself a sandwich at midnight, knocking jars and bottles over, leaving her unable to sleep.

'Come and take a minute,' Betty encouraged. 'The shock of these sirens is enough to knock the stuffing out of anyone, especially when you're not feeling right.'

'Did I hear someone isn't feeling so good?' came Dolly's voice over the cacophony of chatter that was echoing through the now dank and crowded room.

'I'm just a bit tired,' Hattie explained.

Dolly glanced at the group of women, instantly spotting the terrified expression on Nancy and Patty's faces, and how grey Hattie looked.

'It's a good job I collared a handful of blokes, then. They very kindly lifted me a few urns of tea down.'

'My goodness, Dolly. You really are a saint!' Betty replied appreciatively, hoping a restorative cuppa would act as a much-needed balm to the soul for her friends.

'Consider it done!'

Betty was grateful for Dolly's unfaltering cheery demeanour. It would be no use if they all fell to bits now.

'Is my mum, okay, Dolly?' Hattie asked, unable to spot her tiny frame through the sea of people.

'Yes, she's fine, duck. She and Josie are just serving up endless brews. I'll get them to bring you all one over.'

'Thank you,' Hattie said, partially relieved. Although she hated the air-raid warnings, at least they were together, another reason to be grateful they were both now employed at Vickers.

As voices filled the subterranean shelter, Betty caught snippets of the animated conversations.

'Bloody Hitler. I bet he knew we were in the middle of a big order,' one disgruntled-sounding bloke commented.

'I think that's the whole point,' another quipped. 'He probably knows what we're doing in here and wants to put an end to it.'

'For the love of God, shut up, will yer, Stan. That's hardly going to put everyone's minds at rest.'

'No need to get narky. I'm just saying it how it is. We're bound to a prime target. Like a sitting timebomb, and now we're trapped in here. Next to a flamin' river too. If we do get hit, we'll either be blasted to death or drowned.'

'Stan!' someone else protested. 'Will yer put a chuffin' sock in it or I'll have to gag yer m'self.'

'I'm just saying!'

'Well don't!' came the curt reply. 'No one needs to hear that sort of scare-mongering, especially right now. And let's face it, you haven't got a crystal ball, so maybe keep yer bloody useless thoughts to yerself.'

'Hear. Hear,' came a chorus of responses.

'Thank goodness,' Betty whispered. Those sorts of fatalistic predictions were the last thing Patty, Nancy, Hattie or anyone else for that matter needed to hear right now.

Unfortunately, the doom-mongering comments hadn't been lost on the women.

'Do you think he's right?' Patty asked, her voice, trembling, revealing how utterly terrified she felt.

Betty had always gone by the motto 'honesty is the best policy', and although she knew the burly worker, who clearly loved the sound of his own voice, had a point, there was absolutely no need to add to her friend's fear, especially when no one could say with any certainty what was going to happen.

'We've had plenty of false alarms of late,' Betty proffered. 'There's nothing to say this one won't be any different.'

'I really hope so,' Patty sighed.

'Me too, luv,' Nancy added.

Daisy and Betty swapped a concerned glance. Neither of them felt at ease in the factory's underground cavern, but they appreciated why Patty and Nancy's fears were even further heightened.

'Do you think we would hear the planes?' Patty asked.

'What do you mean?' Betty replied.

'It's just when we are in the communal shelter, you know it's a false alarm if you can't hear Jerry overhead, but would we hear anything down here?'

Oh gosh, Betty thought. Patty had a point, and she was struggling to think about how she could put her friend's mind at rest.

'I reckon we need to assume silence is golden,' Dolly tactfully interjected as she and Diane approached carrying a tray each, holding several mugs of tea. 'Get one of these down yer, duck. It will help calm your nerves.'

Patty didn't argue, willingly accepting one of the freshly made brews, hoping Dolly's prediction was accurate.

'I'd just feel better if I was with our Billy and Linda,' Nancy muttered, her hands trembling as she took a mug of tea.

'That's understandable, duck,' Dolly acknowledged. 'Is your Bert at home?'

'No. He's doing a shift with the Home Guard today. At least he'll be able to get to a shelter and he'll have someone with him if his nerves take over. He's still a right old wreck when the bangs start, but he seems to get on well with the fellas he's working with.'

'That's good news, luv.'

'It is and I know how lucky I am that he's back in Sheffield. I just wish we were all together.'

'Of course you do. But hopefully this will be over soon,' Dolly replied, trying to keep up morale.

Every one of the women was battling her own fears.

Like Nancy, Daisy and Josie were worrying about her younger sisters, Annie and Polly, who would be at school. Dolly was quietly praying both her daughters-in-law and granddaughters had got to a shelter, and Betty was hoping her brother and dad, who would be at the pit, were safe, and that Ivy was with one of her friends, knowing how much she hated being alone when the sirens started.

Hattie looked at her mum. 'Are you okay?' she mouthed.

'I think so.' She nodded, but Hattie knew, despite the hell her dad put them both through, her mum still worried about him; her parents had been married for over twenty years after all. She also knew, though, the air-raid sirens, whether they turned out to be false alarms or not, would be the catalyst for yet another drinking spree.

'He'll be okay,' Hattie said.

Diane smiled weakly.

'I know it's easier said than done, but try not to worry, luv,' Josie said. 'Hopefully this will be over before we know it.'

'And there's a good chance he'll be underground,' Hattie added, in a bid to reassure her mum. It was normal procedure to keep miners below ground when the sirens started, deeming it safer than bringing them up.

'How about a sing-song to pass the time?' a woman further along the shelter suggested.

'As long as you promise not to deafen us all with your dulcet tones,' someone trilled.

'Cheeky beggar!' the first woman shot back. 'Reyt then. Here we go.'

And with that, she began a joyful rendition of 'Pack Up Your Troubles'. As more of the women joined in, the warm, nostalgic words filled the underground chamber, a much-needed antidote to ease the tension.

To pass the time, in another corner, a few women had also started knitting, their needles clacking along in time to the upbeat tune, under the dim gaslights.

But despite the effort everyone was making to keep the mood from descending into one of apocalyptic terror, Betty and her friends were all lost in their own thoughts, every minute feeling like an hour.

'Why don't we plan something nice?' Daisy said, finally breaking their numbed silence.

'Hey?' Patty asked, missing most of what had been said.

'Shall we arrange a night out?' Daisy asked. 'It's always good to have something to look forward to.'

Her attention caught for a few moments, Patty stopped dwelling on what was going on outside the confines of the claustrophobic shelter they were gathered in.

'What are you thinking?'

'Some of the women were saying this morning the Henry Hall band are playing at The Empire on Thursday night. Does anyone fancy it?'

'Ooh! That does sound fun. I haven't been into the city for a night out for a while,' Patty replied excitedly, momentarily forgetting about the predicament they were all in.

'Anyone else fancy it?' Daisy asked.

'I would be keen,' Betty replied, also eager to distract her friends. 'It would be nice to have a reason to get dressed up.'

'How about you, Hattie?' Daisy asked. 'Would you like to come?'

Hattie's gut instinct was to say no. She still didn't feel right, and she hated leaving her mum if she didn't have to. 'Can I let you know?'

'Oh, come on, Hatts,' Patty pleaded. 'It would be fun. Let's face it we all need something to make us smile right now.'

Diane, who was still handing out mugs of tea a few steps away, had caught the back end of the conversation.

'You should go, luv,' she encouraged. 'You don't do much for yourself. It will do you the power of good to have a night out with yer pals.'

'I'll have a think about it,' Hattie promised.

'Okay,' Daisy said. 'No rush. You can even tell us on Thursday.'

Patty looked at her friend, unsure what to think. She knew Hattie had been exhausted lately, but she seemed to decline nearly all their suggestions for a night out or was one of the first to leave if they went to The Welly. Patty really hoped her friend wasn't going to turn into a boring old housewife now she was married.

'Anyone else fancy it?' Daisy asked.

'If you don't mind, I'll say no,' Nancy replied. 'I

don't like to leave Billy and Linda for any longer than I have to.'

'Of course,' Daisy said. 'I just didn't want you to think you wouldn't be welcome.'

'That's very kind of you. And I'll do my best to make sure I get to the pub next time you all go.'

'And I think I'll leave you young 'uns to it,' Dolly proffered. 'I'm sure you will all have a lovely night, though. I've seen the Henry Hall band before, and they are good. You will have a great time.'

'If you change your mind, you would be very welcome,' Daisy said, pleased that she had at least managed to move the attention away from the air-raid sirens. 'We could all meet up and get the tram together,' she added. 'And depending on what time we get away from work, we might be able to stop off and have a drink first.'

'That sounds like a plan!' Patty enthused; her attention diverted from Hattie back to the thought of having an excuse to get dressed up. 'We may as well make a night of it.'

'Betty, if it's easier you could come to my house straight after work, instead of going all the way home,' Daisy suggested.

'If you are sure your mum won't mind, that would save me a lot of time.'

'Of course she won't! In fact, why don't you bring an overnight bag to work and stay at mine. That way you won't be traipsing home by yourself.'

'Why not! That would be lovely.'

'Brilliant. Sounds like we have a plan, then?' Daisy smiled. 'And I'm sure it will be lots of fun.'

And with that, as if fate had lent a helping hand, the all-clear sounded.

'Thank the chuffin' lord for that,' Patty exclaimed, already on her feet, now desperate to check Archie was okay.

'Nowt to worry about folks,' came the reassurance from a foreman, who had opened the doors of the underground cavern. 'Looks like Jerry didn't have Sheffield in his sights after all. I'm afraid that does mean it's back to work until the end of yer shifts.'

'Don't s'ppose yer can have everything,' a gruff male voice replied.

'Let's be grateful this is the result, though,' someone else commented.

'Aye, yer right there, Mick,' the first bloke said.

As the scores of workers started making their way out of the shelter, the relief was palpable, rigid shoulders relaxed and frowns reversed. Hattie caught her mum's eyes, and they exchanged a relieved glance, while Nancy momentarily closed her eyes, once again counting her blessings that they had all survived another day.

A couple of nights later, as arranged, Daisy, Betty and Patty all gathered at Daisy's house after work, perfecting their hair and make-up and putting on their glad rags, each one of them looking as pretty as a picture.

'You girls have a good night.' Josie grinned, as she waved off the three girls. Daisy had set their hair in rollers, while Patty had insisted on applying extra rouge to her cheeks and a second lick of luscious, bright-red lipstick.

'It is nearly Christmas,' she chortled, noting the amused grins of her friends. 'If we can't wear red now, when can we wear it?'

'We wouldn't expect anything less.' Betty laughed. 'Now come on, or we'll miss the start.'

After making their way into Attercliffe, they climbed aboard the tram. The three women couldn't stop chattering, excited about the evening ahead. Frank had agreed they didn't have to do any overtime, knowing a night out would do them all the power of good, determined to keep up morale with all the horror stories from air raids causing untold deaths and destruction across the country.

'It's a shame Hattie couldn't make it,' Daisy said, as they took their seats, each one of them taking a couple of coins from their purse to pay the clippie their fare.

'I was really hoping she would,' Patty sighed. 'She doesn't seem to want to do much at the moment.'

'I think she was still feeling a bit off, and I got the impression she was worried about her mum being at home alone with her dad,' Daisy offered empathetically.

A pang of guilt surged through Patty. She knew there was every chance Vinny would have gone on another one of his drinking binges and Diane would bear the brunt of his drunken stupor.

'They really don't have it easy,' Betty commented. 'I'm just glad we can keep an eye on Hattie and her mum now they are both at the factory.'

'Me too.' Patty nodded, making a mental note to think before she spoke.

Twenty minutes later the trio of women disembarked from the tram and instinctively linked arms. Betty had already taken her little torch with its lens cover out of her bag.

'Just in case,' she said, directing the dimmed light at the ground, as they made their way towards The Moor, the huge, bright moon also helping to light up the city's streets.

'Oooh, it's making me feel all festive,' Patty said, admiring the shop windows, adorned with red and silver tinsel, and paper chains of bunting. 'I must finish my Christmas shopping this weekend. I still haven't got Archie a present.'

'You've got a couple of weeks yet,' Betty encouraged.

'I think I'll go shopping again this Saturday. I've seen a winter jacket in Banners that he might like. Have you got your William anything yet?'

'Yes. I've bought him a new watch. He somehow managed to crack the face of his old one.'

'That's a good idea. I'm sure he will appreciate that,' Daisy added. 'Do you think he will get home for Christmas?'

'I'm still not sure. He didn't mention it in his last letter.

I'm assuming he won't, as I think he's still in Scotland, but I can't really complain, as I only saw him last month.'

'Here we are!' Patty exclaimed, as the women came to a halt outside the grand, ornamental, arched entrance of The Empire theatre, where a queue was already forming around the outside of the building.

'Let's hope it doesn't take too long to get inside. I'm chuffin' freezing now,' Patty said, rubbing her gloved hands together.

Thankfully as soon as the doors were opened, the line of people quickly made their way indoors.

'I'm so looking forward to this,' Betty said, as she Patty and Daisy made their way into the auditorium, joining the sea of excited music fans.

'I've never seen a live band before,' Patty commented, as she looked at the huge stage, which was already set up with music stands, instruments and microphones.

'You are in for a treat,' Daisy said. They all took their coats off and folded them under their seats, keeping their evening bags on their knees.

A couple of minutes later, as Henry Hall himself, followed by his ensemble of musicians made their way onto the stage, Patty, who was sitting between Daisy and Betty, squeezed both their hands in delight.

'This is so exciting,' she whispered.

The band burst into life with their opening piece, encouraging a chorus of 'oohs' and 'ahs' from the jubilant audience.

'I can't wait!' A woman behind her applauded, clapping her hands together in glee.

'Me neither,' her friend replied. 'It's been ages since I've had a night out. This is just what the doctor ordered. It makes a change from working in that chuffin' factory all day long. I'm just glad to be out of those filthy overalls.'

'Here's to a night of fun!' the first woman replied. 'And you never know, there might be the odd available fella to have a drink with later!'

'Now you're talking.'

But the band had only been playing a few minutes at the most when the musicians came to an abrupt and unexpected halt, causing a fissure of whispers through the bewildered theatregoers. Henry Hall, his face no longer adorned with a huge smile, but instead replaced with a serious expression, calmly announced, 'The air raids have started, and the red alert is ringing.'

Chapter 19

Thursday, 12 December 1940

Stunned, Patty looked to her friends, unsure what to think. *Please let it be another false alarm.* After the one two nights earlier, she really didn't know what to think.

The whispers from the crowds echoed around the room.

'Not again,' one person sighed.

'It's bound to be another panic over nothing!' came another disgruntled voice.

In a bid to ease the frustrated and befuddled crowd, Henry Hall added, 'You can go if you want to, or you can stay. We will continue to play.'

But as soon as the words left his lips, a huge explosion echoed through the concert hall, followed by shrieks of shock and horror.

'Betty! Daisy!' Patty instinctively yelled.

Before either of them had a chance to answer, the flustered-looking manager, Fred Neate, dressed in a smart, dark-coloured suit and tie, emerged from behind the stage. Worry etched across his face, he began dashing up and down the aisles. 'You must leave if you want to find shelter,' he lamented. 'Go as quickly as possible. Get to safety. Stay safe. This isn't a false alarm.'

The music-hall goers got to their feet, but undeterred the band sparked back to life. Betty looked towards her friends. The thought of staying put was not even a consideration. She would never be able to enjoy the concert now, worrying about all the commotion going on outside. Betty quickly tried to gather her thoughts and think of a logical plan of action, but before she could make sense of what was going on around her, Patty tugged at her sleeve.

'Come on,' she said urgently, her fear suddenly replaced by a nervous excitement. 'We must go and see this. We will never see anything like this again.'

'Pardon?' Feeling somewhat discombobulated, Betty didn't know what to think, but before she knew it, Patty was pulling her to her feet.

'Let's go now,' she repeated, as if she were about to go and watch the latest Clark Gable picture.

Betty looked at Daisy, who looked equally befuddled. *At least we could get to safety if we leave*, Betty silently rationalized.

The three women quickly pulled on their coats and squeezed past the half a dozen people who, accommodatingly, pulled in their legs but stayed firmly sat in their seats, determined their night wouldn't be ruined by whatever was going on outside.

With Patty leading the way, the three women hurried

to the exit, following at least twenty others who had opted to leave Henry Hall and his determined band behind.

But as the women passed through the doors and went out into the street, an incomprehensible scene stopped them in their tracks. In whatever direction they looked, the earlier crystal-clear winter sky was now lit up with crimson-red fires, while screeching firework-like explosions echoed around them.

'It's like something out of a film!' Patty naively exclaimed, as a cascade of exploding and blinding lights shot through the air in all directions.

Stunned, Betty froze to the spot, as she took in the landscape before her. The once-stylish shops that had proudly lined The Moor, displaying their splendid array of clothes, gifts and selection of festive treats, were now a corridor of flames. The buildings were crumbling to the ground, like a deck of cards, as windows were blown out and their wares catapulted across the road.

'Oh, my goodness,' Betty gasped as the enormity of the situation enveloped her. She instinctively reached for her friends' hands, but the constant drone of aircraft drowned out her desperate comments that they find shelter, as the Luftwaffe dropped one incendiary bomb after another. The night air was now thick with dust and the pungent, chemical smell of fire was intoxicating.

'Betty!' Patty whimpered, now stock-still, her initial excitement extinguished and replaced with an all-consuming terror. 'I'm scared.'

Just able to hear the fear in Patty's voice, Betty came to her senses.

'Don't worry,' she said, mustering up as much courage as she could. But even as she said the words, Betty knew if they didn't get to safety and fast, they might not live to see the night out. In all directions terrified men and women, their faces contorted in shock, were running across the road, desperately trying to escape Jerry's firing line. Blinding flashes and deafening explosions were punctuated by piercing screams for help. For the first time in her life, Betty really had no idea what to do for the best. They could go back inside The Empire, but she knew it was as likely to be hit as all the buildings that were collapsing around her and she had absolutely no idea where the nearest community shelter was.

'We need to get away from here,' Daisy gasped, but she too was at a loss on how to escape the burning inferno which was surrounding them.

'Girls. Come on!'

Betty, Patty and Daisy all looked towards the stranger who had delivered the confident and firm command. It was an air-raid warden, his blue uniform and face covered in dust.

'Archie,' Patty whispered, the man in front of them reminding her that her beloved was also on air-raid duty in Darnall tonight.

'Come on, girls, there's no time to waste. We need to get you all to safety.'

'The bombs,' Patty muttered, almost dumbstruck by the catastrophe playing out around her. 'Are they dropping everywhere?'

'I don't know, luv. I just know, right now, the sky is full of planes targeting our city. Now, come on. I need to get you out of here.'

Terror-struck, the three friends did as they were instructed and quickly followed the man, who was almost running, down The Moor. As they did so their little group began to grow as more frightened people followed them, all of them relieved to be guided by someone in authority.

As they reached the corner of Surrey Street, the warden turned to face them all.

'The door to the vaults of the Yorkshire Bank have been opened. You all need to go in there and, whatever you do, don't come out until the all-clear sounds. Be quick. There's no time to waste.'

They didn't have to be asked twice. Betty, Daisy and Patty hurried down the steep, dusty steps of the bank, in single file, into the bowels of the building. Deep inside the underground chamber, the three women, overcome with fright, crouched closely together on the stone floor.

'I just never thought we would actually get caught up in an air raid,' Patty muttered, in a state of bewilderment.

'No, me neither,' Daisy admitted.

'I'm scared,' Patty said, tears seeping from the corner of her eyes. 'What if we don't . . .'

'Now, come on,' Betty said, finding some courage. 'We can't think like that. Besides which, I can't imagine there's a much safer place to be. This is where they hide the city's money.' Whether she believed her own words or not, Betty had to hope and pray she was right. The alternative didn't bear thinking about.

'But the bombs,' Patty choked. 'What if one hits the bank? We would be buried alive.'

No sooner had Patty finished her sentence than another loud whoosh echoed through the cavernous bolthole.

'No!' the youngest of the three steelworkers gasped, as she gripped Betty's arm.

An audible intake of breath reverberated off the vault's walls, followed a few seconds later, after no visible destruction was caused, by a chorus of 'Thank God' and 'Please let this be over' from the twenty-five or so people who had been guided into the make-do shelter.

'It's okay,' Betty reiterated as Patty, who was now shaking with fear, clung to her. 'It's passed.'

But Betty's words came too soon. A minute later a cloud of thick black soot and dirt dropped from the ceilings and walls, peppering the temporary inhabitants, as more explosions erupted in the streets above them.

'It's never going to end,' Patty sobbed, folding herself into Betty's chest, too afraid to even open her eyes.

'It will,' Betty said, hoping her reassuring words hid how terrified she was truly feeling, as she wrapped one arm tightly around Patty, and her other hand interlinked with Daisy's.

'What about Archie?' Patty quivered. 'What if he's above ground?' This was the whole reason she hadn't wanted him to take the job in the first place; not because he wasn't capable, simply because Patty was terrified he would get hurt, or something even worse.

'Remember how sensible he is,' Betty replied. 'He knows how to stay safe.'

But just like a couple of nights earlier, as the minutes passed, each of the women's thoughts drifted to their own loved ones. Had the Luftwaffe attacked the whole of Sheffield? Were other parts of the city suffering too from their damnable bombs? What havoc were they wreaking?

Once again, Patty, like Daisy, prayed her parents and siblings had made it to the communal shelter. Betty took some comfort in knowing Frank was at home with Ivy, so she wouldn't be alone, and hoped her dad and brother were together, wherever they were, unsure if they were on a day or night shift at the pit. A mixture of guilt and relief flashed through her mind as she thanked God William still wasn't qualified to go into battle with Hitler's air force.

Daisy silently hoped her little sister, Polly, who hated the shelters since she'd fallen in a scrum to get into one earlier that year, wasn't too scared. She hated being separated from her family during an air raid, her imagination playing havoc, taunting Daisy with all sorts of terrifying scenarios.

The minutes turned into hours, the time interspersed with vibrations and frequent thuds from the explosions going on outside.

'Please let it end soon,' Patty muttered intermittently, as she continually fretted about Archie, terrified he was above ground and trying to help extinguish fires and usher people to safety. How on earth could individual wardens, with nothing but a poxy tin hat to protect them, combat the killer missiles falling from the sky?

Every now and again, the three women would overhear some of the other conversations. Husbands cursing themselves for having a night out, leaving their wives and children at home, young men swearing our RAF pilots would bomb the *bloody Nazi swains* out of the sky and other tearful young women biting down on their lips every time the aftershock from another menacing bang pulsated through the sunken, dark shelter.

When the tension got too much, an older man, with a calming and reassuring tone, would interject. 'They will run out of steam soon,' he said authoritatively, in a bid to calm everyone's nerves, or 'We're as safe as can be down here. Try not to worry.' But no matter how ataractic he attempted to be, his soothing tones did little to slow down the racing heart rates of Betty, Patty and Daisy.

'I'm so sorry,' Daisy said at some point in the dead of night.

'What on earth for?' Betty quizzed.

'It was my idea to come out tonight. I thought it would be a way to cheer us up after the last raid but look how that's turned out. I feel terrible.'

'Don't be daft!' Betty retorted firmly. 'You can't blame yourself for Jerry deciding to make another appearance tonight. You mustn't think like that.'

'I just wish I'd never mentioned it.'

'Look, there's nothing we can do about it. No one can predict what Hitler has planned. At least we are all together.'

'I know. I just wish we were all at home, as I'm sure you both do too.'

'Of course we do. That goes without saying, but that's not your fault, so you have to stop feeling guilty.'

'Betty's right,' Patty added. 'There's only one person responsible for this and it definitely isn't you.'

With that the three women huddled even closer together, their arms interlinked as they leant on each other's shoulders, squeezing one another tighter with each unwelcome blast. At some point, the two dozen or so strangers who were all encased in the dark and damp cellar all silently joined hands, their grips tightening with each terrifying explosion.

Then, just when they thought their interminable imprisonment or the night would never end the sound of footsteps pierced the fretful chatter, bringing the conversations to a stunned halt.

'It's over,' announced the young lad, who was covered in muck, only the whites of his eyes visible as he entered the dimly lit vault.

'Thank God for that!' someone exclaimed over the audible sigh of relief.

'I thought I'd never hear those words,' an older woman cried.

'How bad is it, son?' someone else asked.

'I'll not lie, gaffer. It's not great. The bloody Germans have obliterated the city.'

Anxious, Betty, Patty and Daisy all looked at one another in simultaneous consternation.

'Come on. Let's get home,' Betty said encouragingly. 'We all need to get out of here.'

Despite how desperate everyone was to escape, in a typically British manner, the temporary inhabitants of the underground cavern formed an orderly line to carefully ascend into the early morning, but as the three women emerged, the arresting sight before them stopped them in their tracks. The city they had left behind ten hours earlier was completely unrecognizable. The once-familiar shops and buildings had been annihilated, reduced to smouldering rubble, pavements were peppered with gaping craters, vehicles turned on their sides, windows smashed, signposts flattened. Firemen were gathered around tumbling buildings. The tongues of red flames had been replaced by flumes of dirt and soot. There was an eerie silence to the city. Wardens were rushing about, guiding the stunned inhabitants from underground shelters, most of whom were shocked into silence. Barrage balloons hovered limply in the early morning sky, with a hint of silver, a reflection of the now dim moon.

'Oh gosh,' Betty gasped in shock, horrified to see the city centre she had grown up in destroyed.

'I've never seen . . .' But Daisy didn't even know how to finish her sentence.

'How could they?' Patty exclaimed.

All around them people were emerging from makeshift shelters, in a state of utter bewilderment, brushing off the layers of soot and dirt that had covered them from the earth-trembling vibrations. As their eyes slowly adjusted to the dawn light, they were confronted with a city they no longer recognized.

Betty, Patty and Daisy attempted to take a few tentative steps away from the corner of Surrey Street, but they stumbled on the piles of crumbling bricks, shards of metal and shattered glass that were scattered across the pavements. Shaking their heads in disbelief; shock rendering them unable to speak.

Silently they started to walk again, terror catching in their throats, but they hadn't gone more than a handful of steps, when something stopped them in their tracks. The heart-wrenching shape was unmistakable, the remains of a charred, blackened body. Next to it was another, and then another; a whole line of lifeless bodies lying, abandoned, before them. Gasping in horror, the friends struggled to process the incomprehensible sight.

'Oh God,' Patty whispered. She'd never seen a dead body before, let alone one that was so badly charred even their own mother wouldn't recognize them.

'Come on,' Betty said, gripping Patty's arm tighter, desperate to avert their collective gaze from the disfigured corpses. The friends attempted to get their bearings, so they could make their way home, knowing their families would be out of their minds with worry, but with all the familiar landmarks either gone or smouldering, there was nothing to guide them. The trams, their normal mode of transport, had stopped running, carriages now on their side, the once-straight tracks now twisted like molten snakes. Alongside countless others, the women, now exhausted as well as in shock, began aimlessly trampling through the carpet of debris, which was interspersed by a layer of lacy frost. But with each tentative step they became increasingly confused, unable to work out a route home.

'This is hopeless,' Patty sighed tearfully, exhausted, and traumatized.

'Are you all right, luv?' a bloke, his face black and thick with dirt, asked.

'I'm afraid we're a bit lost,' Betty explained wearily.

'Where do you need to get to?'

'Attercliffe and Darnall,' Betty answered.

'Follow us,' the friendly man offered, tilting his head to a bigger group. 'We are all heading that way too.'

'Thank goodness,' Patty whispered gratefully, part of her desperate to get home but equally as frightened at what she might be forced to face when she got there.

As they headed out of the broken city, the group grew in size, as more and more people who had hidden in basements, under tables and in underground shelters, joined the exodus out of the city centre, all desperate to reach the safety of their homes. United in a fretful confusion, a camaraderie emerged. Compassionate strangers kindly asked each other if they were okay. Relief, guilt and immeasurable sorrow intermixed; after all they were the lucky ones – they were going home.

Chapter 20

Friday, 13 December 1940

'Thank God, you're home,' Archie cried, running towards Patty as she stumbled up Thompson Street, barely able to put one leg in front of the other.

'Are you okay? Where have you been? Did you find a shelter?'

'Oh, Archie,' Patty sobbed, letting the dam of tears behind her eyes overflow and spill down her cheeks. 'It was awful. I was so scared. I didn't think we were going to get out.'

'Come on,' Archie comforted, wrapping Patty in his arms. 'Let's get you a cup of strong tea. Your mom and dad will be so relieved to see you. They have been out of their minds.'

He wasn't wrong. As soon as Bill and Angie caught sight of their ashen-faced daughter, they tightly cocooned her into a loving embrace. Only then did Angie insist Patty sit down at the kitchen table and pour her a hot, sweet and much-needed restorative cup of tea.

After recounting the night's horrifying events, Angie took her daughter's hand.

'I'm just so glad you got home,' she said. 'We were so worried. I don't think a night has ever lasted so long.'

'Were you in the communal shelter?' Patty asked.

'Yes. Daisy's parents and sisters were there too. Your dad and Alf were biting at the bit to come and find you girls.'

'I'm sorry,' Patty said, knowing how frantic they must have all been.

'Don't be daft, luv,' Bill said. 'This isn't your fault. We just wanted to know you were okay.'

'I am now.' Patty nodded. 'But what was it like here? Did the planes come over?'

'If they did it was only to get to the centre. Me and Alf kept popping our heads out of the shelter. All we could see was explosions coming from the city. It looked like the whole place was ablaze.'

'I think it was, Dad. All the shops, everything, they've gone. There's nowt left, but it was worse than that.'

'What do you mean, luv?' Angie asked.

'Bodies. The people who didn't make it. It was horrible,' Patty whispered, her eyes filling with tears again.

'Come here,' said Archie, who was sat next to Patty, gently pulling her to his chest.

'And I was so worried about you too,' she sobbed. 'I kept thinking about you trying to get people to safety, and was terrified that bombs would be dropping, and you wouldn't be in the shelter.'

'But I'm all right,' Archie soothed, stroking Patty's mass

of dusty hair, which had looked so pristine just twelve hours earlier.

'I know. I know. I was just so scared.'

'It's over now,' Archie reassured. 'Why don't you get yourself to bed. You must be exhausted.'

'No!' Patty quickly protested, sitting up again. 'If you and my dad are going to work, then I am too.'

'Really? Are you sure, luv?' Angie asked, slightly taken aback by her daughter's announcement. 'You'll be exhausted. Are you sure you should be operating one of those great cranes today?'

'After what Hitler did to Sheffield last night, it's exactly what I need to do. If we don't carry on making the parts our troops need, that chuffin' man will end up destroying the whole country.'

Bill and Angie swapped an astonished glance. Although their daughter was far from work shy, she was normally the first to take advantage of an extra few hours in bed. Whatever she'd witnessed had clearly had a profound effect on her. *Maybe she really is growing up*, Angie thought to herself, simultaneously saddened that Patty's innocence was eroding away due to this blasted war.

An hour later, Patty and Archie were walking up Brightside Lane with Betty, Daisy, Hattie and Nancy.

'That sounds utterly terrifying, but thank God you are all okay,' Nancy said, after her friends had relived the events of the night.

'It was terrifying,' Betty admitted, her face grey with exhaustion. 'But at least we are here to tell the tale.'

'Was your Bert okay?' Daisy asked Nancy, recalling how much he hated the air raids.

'He tried to keep it together for the kids, but he struggled while he was in the shelter. I think he was angry at himself too, as in his heart of hearts he just wanted to be out there helping, but at the same time he just wanted it to end.'

'How is he now?'

'Well, like the rest of us, he hasn't slept and left when I did so he could go and see what he could do to help.'

'He'll feel better for doing something,' Betty said.

'He will.'

'And how were you, Hatts?' Patty asked, turning to her equally as weary-looking friend.

'I think I had it a lot easier than you three,' she replied.

'Was your dad at home? Did you manage to get to the shelter?'

'He was,' Hattie sighed. 'And no. He refused to go, so I persuaded mum to sit under the stairs with me.'

'Oh Hatts!' Patty silently fumed at the thought of her best friend and her mum only having a poxy cupboard to protect them against the monstrous bombs the Luftwaffe had dropped.

'It's okay. We're fine.' But what Hattie didn't say was her dad had spent the night getting slowly inebriated; his usual way of blocking out the sirens, without a single thought to how his selfish actions would impact anyone else. By the time the all-clear had sounded, he was so drunk he'd collapsed into a stupor on the front-room sofa. Her mum had desperately tried to wake Vinny for work but whenever he lifted his eyelids, instead of fully waking up, he lashed out at her, his fists flailing in all directions, Diane only avoiding as many blows as she did because she knew what was coming.

'Let him take the flack at work,' Hattie had told her mum, as she tried to pull her away. But as Diane took a step backwards, Vinny swung out and caught her cheek, leaving an angry red welt down the right side of her face.

'Dad!' Hattie had cried, but his eyelids had already closed and his breathing heavy, indicative that he was virtually unconscious.

'Maybe I should try and wake him again,' Diane had said, holding her hand to cheek, which was now stinging sharply.

'No, Mum,' Hattie protested protectively, not prepared to let her mum become a punchbag for her dad, but she knew he was likely to explode when they got home from work later. It would be her poor mum who would yet again pay the price, not only financially, as his wages would be docked for missing a shift, but also he was bound to take his temper out on her.

'Thank goodness you are all okay,' came Frank's voice, his relief palpable. 'Ivy and I have been worried sick,' he added as the group moved closer to the clocking-in machine, interrupting Hattie's thoughts.

'I'm sorry,' Betty said. 'I had no way of letting you know and didn't have enough time to get home.'

'Don't be daft, duck. I'm just so pleased you are all right. And the fact you have all come into work today is just incredible.'

'You didn't really expect anything different, did you?' Betty smiled.

'Well, I'm very grateful regardless. You must all be exhausted. It goes without saying, you won't be expected to do any overtime tonight.'

'Thank chuff for that,' Patty said, as she took her timecard out of the metal rack and pushed it into the machine.

'Let's get through the morning and I'm sure Dolly will have a warming dinner ready for you all.'

The morning passed slowly, everyone determined to keep going despite how exhausted they felt, each of them recalling the horrific events of the night before. By the time they arrived in the canteen for their usual dinner of mince, pie and mash, stories had begun circulating about how much the city had suffered.

'They reckon dozens were trapped underneath,' Archie was telling Frank. 'I think they are still searching for survivors.'

'What's that?' Patty asked, as she put her plate down on the table.

'The Marples,' Archie said sombrely. 'Yer know, the hotel in town.'

'The one on the corner of Fitzalan Square and High Street?'

Archie nodded. 'Some of the lads were telling me this morning it took a direct hit last night. A couple of their mates have stayed off work, to join the rescue operation as they knew people who were inside.'

'That's awful!' Patty gasped. 'Do they know how bad?' She couldn't bring herself to say the exact words.

'All I heard was that all seven storeys collapsed into the cellar where guests were taking shelter. Apparently, the rescue team had to abandon their search during the night as it got so dark, but they were back there at first light this morning.'

'I hope they can get those poor people out,' Patty said, moving her steaming dinner further into the table, her appetite suddenly vanished. It was sinking in what a lucky escape she, Patty and Daisy had had.

'Me too.' Archie nodded, unable to envisage the horrifying scene his fellow air-raid wardens must have faced. Thankfully Coleford Road, where he was based, had been unscathed.

As Betty and Daisy joined their friends, Nancy and Hattie were deep in conversation.

'Did Billy and Linda's school get any damage?' Hattie asked. 'I heard from some of the women this morning, their kids' schools had been hit.'

'Gosh, I hope so, but I don't know to be sure. Bert left early with me as he wanted to go and help with any clean-up operations, so Doris offered to take my two to school.'

'I'll keep everything crossed,' Hattie said.

'Thank you.' Nancy smiled, praying Huntsman Garden School where her own children, along with Doris's, attended, was still in one piece. Nancy had no idea how on earth she would cope if she had to juggle schoolwork in the day too, but as soon as the thought passed over her, she filled with guilt. She and her family were alive, unlike so many others.

'Just checking the tea urn is full,' Dolly said interrupting her thoughts. 'I thought you might need more than one cuppa each today.'

'You are a good 'un,' Frank said. 'I think we're all in need of a couple of extra brews today.'

'You deserve it, all of yer, coming in to work today after last night.'

'Have you heard much more,' Frank asked, 'while you've been serving up?'

'Probably similar to you. Did you hear the hospitals were hit?'

'No!' Nancy gasped. 'How could they do that?'

'Someone was telling me Nether Edge Hospital took a hit and Jessops, the women's hospital, is in a reyt mess.'

'Do you think anyone died?' Patty asked, still unable

to touch her dinner, overwhelmed by the reports of the bombings.

'I'm not sure, luv,' Dolly said tactfully. Rumours were already circling that several patients had died, but she knew there was no good bringing the mood down any further. Although Hitler had been dropping bombs all over the country in the last few weeks, last night's catastrophic events had stunned them all, none of them ever really believing their city would take such a hammering.

'Listen,' Frank said, his tone slightly more upbeat. 'Ivy said this morning, she would like to cook up a big stew tomorrow afternoon for anyone who fancies it. She thought you might all appreciate a hearty meal.'

'Count me in!' Patty quickly replied. 'Our gas was flickering this morning. I think the pipes must have been hit and after last night, I could do with something to look forward to.' Then turning to Archie, she asked, 'Can you make it?'

'I don't think so, I'm afraid,' he said, shaking his head as he took a mouthful of his dinner. 'I need to go and help with the clean-up operation and then I'll be back on air-raid duty.'

'I understand, son.' Frank smiled. 'But if you get a break and want a bite to eat, you know where we are.'

'Thanks, I'll be there if I do.' Archie nodded gratefully. 'Anyone else?'

'I'd love to,' Nancy replied. 'But do you think we will be all right? I don't mean to be such a worrier but what if the Luftwaffe strikes again?'

'You're right, duck. Why don't we play it by ear and see how things go tonight?'

'Okay, but are you sure? You both must be exhausted. I bet neither of you slept a wink last night, especially as Betty wasn't home.'

'Well, you know what Ivy's like. She's adamant she wants to do something to help, knowing you will all be shattered after coming in to work today.'

'If you're sure she doesn't mind, and things are calmer tonight, I'd love to come along with Billy and Linda. I'm not sure what Bert is doing yet. He might be busy with the Home Guard, but I'm sure he will be there if he's home. Can I bring anything?'

'I'll check, but my guess is Ivy will insist you just bring yourselves,' Frank replied.

'That's all well and good, but she can't be feeding us all. I'll rustle up some jam tarts tonight if we still have gas. Linda will enjoy helping me.'

'Does anyone else fancy coming along?' Frank asked. 'Hattie? Would you and your mum like to come over?'

'I can ask her. Thank you.' There was nothing Hattie would like more, but she knew there was a good chance her dad would kick off if they disappeared for the afternoon. He'd accuse her mum of *neglecting her duties* in the house after being out at work all week. But at the same time, Hattie knew an afternoon with friends would do her mum the power of good.

'Betty and I were going to put a couple of hours in at the WVS straight after work on Saturday,' Daisy interjected. 'I assume they will want as many volunteers as possible this weekend.'

'Of course,' Frank said. 'Don't worry. There will be plenty of food for when you get back.'

'What's this?' Dolly said, interjecting, as she gave the nearby tea urn a shake. 'Did I hear the mention of food? Are you all still hungry? I can try and rustle up some extra . . .' But as Dolly looked round, more plates than not still had nearly full portions of her normally much-sought-after mince pie and mash left on them.

'Sorry, Dolly,' Patty said. 'It was just hearing about all those people in the hotel.'

'Don't worry, duck. I know exactly what you mean. Everyone in the queue for their snap has had a different story. All of them chuffin' horrific.'

'I was just saying, Ivy has invited you all for a bit of tea tomorrow if you fancy it?' Frank said.

'Well, as long as flamin' Hitler doesn't strike again, that would be grand. I haven't got my granddaughters until Sunday, so it will keep me out of mischief and my mind busy.'

'Lovely. Ivy will be pleased.'

'Tell her I'll bring something. Maybe a pan of soup. She can't be feeding all of us – besides which her rations won't stretch that far.'

'I'm sure Ivy will be very grateful.'

'Reyt, count me in then. Now, I better get back to work. The next lot of workers will be here in a minute.'

'I'm afraid it's time we got moving too,' Frank said.

As the group stood up, they stifled yawns, each of them already counting the hours until the end-of-the-day hooter sounded. Exhausted, they trundled back to their post, the events of the night before playing heavily on their minds.

Chapter 21

'We're here to help,' Ivy said, as she and her friend Winnie found the woman they assumed was the manager of the city centre WVS. It had taken some doing to find where the depot had moved to, after they discovered the Church Street centre had moved to the Town Hall following the destruction of the city the night before.

'The more hands the better,' the kindly younger woman said thankfully. 'It's chaos here.'

Ivy looked around. She wasn't wrong. Among the cacophony of noise, volunteers were shifting countless boxes, bags and cases of clothes. Another woman was filling a giant tea urn, while a couple of others were making scores of Spam sandwiches on a long wooden table. And among the volunteers were dozens of bewildered and ashen-faced women, their exhaustion evident in how grey they looked, some clinging on to equally confused small children, others nursing babies in their arms. Queues were forming at every table, the humdrum of chatter revealing the extent of the overnight air raid.

'All of them left homeless,' the WVS official said. 'And this is just a fraction of them.'

'Dear me,' Ivy sighed. 'Do you know how many were affected?'

After she and Frank had emerged from their Anderson shelter in the back garden and spoken to a few neighbours, the extent of the bombing had started to become apparent. They'd heard the planes overhead and the bangs of explosions, but apparently some of the bombs had been dropped not too far away. Men and women had emerged on the street, keen to understand what 'he', as Hitler was commonly referred to, had done to their city. Those who had been trapped in shelters in the city centre gradually returned, exhausted and browbeaten as they saw the extent of the damage.

'It's like hell was let loose,' one said.

'Fires everywhere,' another commented. 'Flames like the red tongues of serpents, from every building.'

'It went on for hours. The noise was horrific. The cracking of gun fire, the roar of buildings collapsing and windows smashing.'

The vision of what their neighbours had seen was being vociferated over and over again, as if articulating the atrocities they'd witnessed would somehow help them come to terms with what had happened.

'Wardens were covering the bodies after firemen pulled them from under the rubble,' an exhausted-looking woman, with a baby on her hip, exclaimed.

'Some of them were completely unrecognizable!'

Thank God Betty is all right, Ivy thought, unable to bring herself to ask if there had been many casualties. She'd lost one person she'd loved to war, the mere thought of losing a second had been too much to bear.

Frank had wrapped his arm around Ivy's shoulders that morning as they had heard about the heinous events of the night before. When he'd eventually rang her from Vickers to say Betty was okay, tears of relief had poured down her cheeks.

It was only then Ivy had found the strength to pull on her coat and gloves, walk to Winnie's house and tell her they had to go and do something to help. After arriving at the WVS depot in Fulwood, Mrs Rafferty had explained they would be more urgently needed at the city centre depot.

They didn't have to be asked twice. Ivy and Winnie had managed to catch a bus so far into town, before walking the rest of the way, avoiding the mammoth craters in the pavements and roads, and taking in the devastation Jerry had caused. As they'd headed down Surrey Street, the empty and destroyed remains of shops had brought to life the scenes which had been spoken of all morning. Workers were trying to repair water leaks and patch up exposed gas pipes. The steps at the front of the City Hall were crumbled and a cloud of dust hung heavily in the air.

When Ivy and Winnie glanced down The Moor, they'd recoiled at seeing the rows of once-immaculate shops now unrecognizable, most of them completely gone. They had so recently been adorned with Christmas decorations, tinsel hanging in their windows, a reminder the festive period was just around the corner, but now their contents were spilling out onto the pavements. Some of the owners were busily trying to salvage what they could, others were nowhere in sight.

'Look at that,' Winnie said, pointing to one of the tumbled-down shops. An elderly man, dressed in his coat and hat, with a canvas apron over the top, was using a pile of crates to create makeshift tables, and on the top, he'd placed more of the same, only these held potatoes, carrots, turnips and swede.

'True Yorkshire grit,' Ivy commended, admiring the sheer determination.

Now as the two women were directed to help sort out the boxes of clothes that were being donated and delivered as quickly as those in need were arriving, they began to get an even greater sense of the determined spirit which was emerging from a city that had been tested but was far from defeated.

'Any kiddies' jumpers in there, luv?' a bedraggled and tired woman asked Ivy, as she began piling the stacks of garments into categories.

'Oh, I'm sure there are,' Ivy replied. 'What sort of sizes are you after?'

'I've got a girl of six and a lad just turned eight.'

'I'm sorry,' Ivy replied. 'Was your home hit?'

'Aye. It was that, luv. Nowt left of it apart from a pile of bricks and wood.'

'What will you do?' Ivy asked, trying to keep her voice level, sensing the last thing this poor woman needed was pity.

'I'm going to have to take m' kids and bunk down at m' mams. M' sister and her kids still live there, but we'll make do. At least we'll have a roof over our heads tonight. There are plenty of folk worse off than me and m' bairns.'

'Will these work?' Ivy asked, producing a red cable-knitted jumper and a similar, slightly bigger navy one.

'That's grand, luv. Thank you.'

'I wish you all the very best,' Ivy said, handing over the woollies.

'That's kind of yer. I'll be reyt. There's one thing for sure, after hearing those bombs fall last night, I'll never be afraid again.'

'God love them,' Ivy said to Winnie, after she handed over another bag of clothes to a newly destitute woman, who had appealed for anything the WVS could offer, holding a baby in one arm, and two preschool children gripping the side of her legs.

'Where on earth will they all go?'

'Rest centres are being opened up all over the city,' the manager, whom Ivy and Winnie had reported to a few hours earlier, answered, as she handed them each a strong mug of tea.

'At least that's something,' Ivy said, but she still couldn't help feeling utterly bereft by all the stories of devastation she'd heard. She knew no matter what time of year it was, losing your home would be heart-breaking, but somehow, the fact it was just a couple of weeks before Christmas amplified how devastating it was.

As Ivy handed out woollies and basic items of clothing, she wondered how she too could do more to help those who had been left with just their clothes on their back. She made a mental note to talk to Frank about opening up her spare rooms to help a few folk, who through no fault of their own had been left homeless.

Chapter 22

Saturday, 14 December 1940

'Come in. Come,' Ivy said, as she welcomed Nancy, Bert, Billy and Linda into the house. 'Josie, Alf, the girls and Patty are already in the kitchen and the kettle is on. You must be freezing.'

'It is a bit nippy,' Nancy admitted, stepping into the warm hall, a sharp and welcome contrast to the bitter chill outside. 'I swear it feels like it's going to snow.'

'It was reyt icy playing out this morning,' Billy chipped in. 'I thought m' fingers were going to drop off.'

'I told you to put your gloves on.' Nancy laughed.

'Well, if you nip into the kitchen, Frank will warm you up some milk.' Ivy grinned.

'This is very good of you,' Nancy said, handing Ivy a biscuit tin.

'What's this?'

'It's not a lot. Just some jam tarts Linda and I made last night as a thank you for inviting us. Thankfully our gas hasn't been affected, but from what I gather quite a few folk haven't got any power.'

'I heard the same,' Ivy replied, graciously accepting the gift. 'This really is lovely of you. You didn't need to but thank you. I'm sure they will go down a treat. Now come in and let me get you a nice, hot cup of tea. You look chilled to the bone.'

'Bert! Lovely to see you,' Frank said, as the family walked into the homely kitchen. 'I was hoping you would make it. Nancy wasn't sure if you would be busy with the Home Guard.'

'I have been,' Bert said, as he popped his walking stick next to a chair and sat himself down. 'I put a few hours in this morning, but my gaffer insisted I came home after lunch.'

'Archie is still hard at it, according to Patty,' Frank said. 'I'm guessing they will be clearing up for quite some time to come?'

As the women started their own conversation, Bert explained he'd been helping delegate volunteers to clean-up operations. 'There was so much damage, we had men all over the shop. It will take weeks before some of the tram lines can be fixed and all the rubble from the destroyed buildings and houses can be cleared.'

'I've heard bits at work this morning. Sounds like Attercliffe and Darnall got a lucky escape,' Frank commented.

'They certainly did,' Bert replied. 'There's great craters in the road at Neepsend, part of Nether Edge Hospital took a hit and a public shelter on Manor Estate was damaged, but thankfully everyone got out in one piece.'

'Thank goodness,' Frank sighed.

'We did lose a member of the Home Guard up at the Electricity Department, though, along with a fireman, who was trying to put out the flames when the chimney collapsed.'

'I'm sorry, pal. That's bloody rotten.'

'I won't lie. It's been a rough few days. I worked virtually through the night last night, hence why m' gaffer sent me home today.'

'Cup of tea?' Ivy said, interrupting Bert and Frank's conversation.

'That would be grand. Thank you,' Bert replied gratefully.

'I'll never say no,' Frank added, giving Ivy a loving smile. After what he'd just heard, a good brew was just what he needed.

Then turning back to Bert, he added, 'And how are you finding the Home Guard?'

'Despite what I've seen and heard the last couple of days, I'm really enjoying it. I owe you a massive thank you for that.'

And he meant it. The Home Guard had been just the thing to help Bert, after he'd dropped into the depths of despair upon coming home from war.

'Not at all, pal. I'm just glad it worked out for you.'

'It really has. You were right, I just needed something

new to focus on. I really thought after I was shot, I was no use to anyone, but what you said was true; after years of training with the Territorial Army and nine months at war, I could still do something to help. I'm not as physical as I used to be. I'm not sure I ever will be. My leg still gives me some gip, but I can get around, with my stick, and help with training. It feels important, especially right now.'

'Good for you,' Frank encouraged. 'I knew they'd snap you up.'

'Well, thank you again. You probably saved my marriage too. I was a flamin' misery to live with. I drove our Nancy half mad.'

'All in the past, pal. I'm just glad you are doing something you enjoy, as I'm sure Nancy is.'

At the other side of the kitchen, Ivy, Josie and Nancy had been joined by Dolly, Hattie and her mum, Diane.

'I'm so glad you could all make it,' Ivy enthused.

'Thank you for the invite. It was very generous of you,' Diane replied.

Hattie was more than pleased she'd managed to get her mum out of the house too. Diane had worked like a Trojan since the crack of dawn, scrubbing floors, black-leading the range, cleaning windows and washing the bedding. Her dad had come home from an early shift down the pit and announced he was going straight to the pub.

'There's no reason for you to stay at home,' Hattie had reasoned. 'And an afternoon relaxing will do you the power of good.'

Diane had succumbed after Hattie had promised she would help tomorrow with any chores that still needed to be done.

'What's the point in staying here, waiting for Dad to come home drunk as a lord?' Hattie had pointed out.

'Okay, luv,' she'd said. 'But what about this?' Diane added, touching the nasty red welt down the right side of her face. 'I've put some Pan-Cake on, but I can't fully hide it.'

'You will be among friends,' Hattie had reassured her. 'Besides which, you have been with Dolly and Josie all week.'

It was true. Diane was convinced they had seen the angry mark, the result of Vinny's temper two mornings earlier, but no one had said a word.

Now as she stood in Ivy's warm and welcoming kitchen, Diane instinctively lifted her hand to her cheek, conscious of how obvious the wheal looked.

Dolly touched her friend's arm. 'Are you okay, duck?'

Diane instantly blushed, blood rushing to her cheeks, turning them crimson.

'It's all right, Mum,' Hattie added.

'I'm sorry,' Dolly said instantly, silently chastising herself. 'I didn't mean to embarrass you, duck. I just wanted to make sure you are as well as can be.'

'Thank you.' Diane nodded, her words barely more than a whisper. 'It was just an accident.'

'They happen, luv,' Josie interjected.

But Dolly wasn't daft. Wasn't that the same excuse she had used time and time again when her own brutal husband had used his fists to take out his anger on her? To begin with, the bruises, small cuts and swellings on her arms, back and legs had been easy enough to hide, but as her vicious husband had got freer and easier with his attacks, she'd been left using more and more make-up to cover up the injuries.

'Why don't we sit down?' Ivy suggested, lifting up the floral teapot, and tilting her head in the direction of the now abandoned kitchen table. 'It looks like Frank, Bert and Alf have disappeared off somewhere with the kids.'

As the group pulled up a chair each, Diane resigned herself to the fact, no matter how hard she tried, it was becoming increasingly difficult to hide Vinny's actions.

'It's only when he's had a drink,' she attempted to reason.

'Listen, duck, tell me if I'm speaking out of place,' Dolly started. 'But take it from someone who knows, once they start getting handy, they rarely stop.'

Diane quickly turned to her daughter. 'I'm sorry, luv. You should never have had to witness all this.'

'Please don't worry about that, Mum,' Hattie said kindly. 'All I care about is making sure you are all right.'

'But I'm the parent. That's my job.'

'Listen, duck,' Dolly interjected. 'Sometimes we all need a helping hand. Your Hattie is a good girl, you don't need me to tell you that.'

'I know I haven't known you that long,' Josie added, 'but I've got to know Hattie these last few months, and she's a grand girl. You have obviously done a brilliant job to have such a lovely daughter. All that said, is there anything else we can do to help? Anything at all?'

'Thank you,' Diane replied graciously. 'But you have all been so kind already. Just going to work every day feels like a blessing. It's a relief to get out of the house and earn some extra money.'

'And it's been wonderful to have you in the canteen,' Josie replied, gently patting Diane's arm.

'Are you managing to put some away for yourself, duck?' Dolly asked.

'A bit but Vinny has a good way of spending every penny that comes in.'

'Well, listen. I don't want to harp on at you but please let me know if I can do anything else to help.' Dolly did have an idea, but she didn't know Diane well enough yet and wanted to run it past Hattie first.

Before anything more could be said, the kitchen door swung open.

'I think this little tyke is hungry,' Frank announced, a grinning Billy at his side.

'There's a surprise.' Nancy laughed, shaking her head. 'Anyone would think I never fed him.'

'Well, it's a good job tea is ready,' Ivy said, standing up. 'I was just waiting for Betty and Daisy to get home.'

'I've just seen them walking up the road,' Frank said.

Right on cue, the back door opened and the two women, wrapped in winter coats, hats and gloves, entered.

'We were just talking about you.' Ivy smiled, as she lifted the ginormous casserole dish out of the oven. 'You must be cold and hungry.'

'It is quite nippy out there.' Betty nodded, devesting herself as the warmth of the kitchen hit her.

'Get yourself sorted and I'll serve dinner. This needs to cool down a bit first, anyway.'

For the next five minutes, everyone did their bit to help Ivy. Nancy made a fresh pot of tea, while Diane laid the table and Josie rounded up all the kids, making sure they'd washed their hands before sitting down at the table. Frank mashed the potatoes and Nancy poured soft drinks for the kids and a glass of beer for the men, as Bert and Alf carried pots and pans across the kitchen. Dolly sliced up the loaf of homemade bread she brought with her to go with the pan of vegetable soup, while Hattie and Patty carried the bowls into the dining room.

'Thank you so much for this,' Nancy said, as everyone took their places round the oblong mahogany table.

'It's my pleasure,' Ivy said. 'And the very least I can do. I wanted to do something, especially after listening to all the tales of people being left homeless yesterday but still rallying round.'

'You do plenty,' Frank commented affectionately, placing his hand on Ivy's. 'You were at the WVS all day yesterday, helping all those poor folk who have been left homeless, and you went back this morning.'

'I'll second that,' Betty enthused. 'Oh, and I've managed to bring some baby clothes from the Swap Box at work. Although, that's going to need replenishing as well. Lots of women were looking through it. Everyone seems to know someone who was affected by Thursday night's raid.'

'Dear me,' Ivy sighed, reminding herself once again to talk to Frank about taking in a family or two. She just hadn't had a minute to find the time to talk to him.

'Anyway, please tuck in, everyone, before Dolly's soup gets cold. It looks too delicious to waste.'

'Cheers,' Frank said, raising his glass of pale ale. 'Let's hope the days ahead are better than the ones which have just passed.'

Chapter 23

Sunday, 15 December 1940

'That looks lovely, girls,' Josie's husband, Alf, said to his two youngest daughters, Polly and Annie, as they finished their latest Christmas decoration – a long red-and-green paper chain.

'Can we hang it up in the living room?' Polly asked. 'Please?'

'You know how your mum doesn't like to trim up until Christmas Eve. She likes to give the whole house a going-over first.'

'Just this one, Dad,' Annie begged. 'We can pin it to the ceiling. Surely, she won't be washing that!'

As Alf looked at the two pairs of pleading eyes, he didn't have the heart to refuse, especially after he and Josie had promised their girls an extra-special Christmas to make up for the year before, when their mum had been ill.

'Can we, Dad? Please say yes,' Polly said. 'It took us ages to make.'

'You two will get me into no end of trouble but go on then.'

'Thank you,' the delighted girls cheered in unison.

'Let me get the stepladder.' Alf laughed, secretly cherishing the moment.

A few minutes later, on the top rung of the ladder, Alf stood with the bunting in one hand and a couple of brass drawing pins in the other.

'Here?' he asked, indicating to above the window.

'Yes,' Annie said. 'But make sure it's in the middle.'

'Okay, bossy britches,' Alf teased, while ensuring the carefully made Christmas decoration was arranged perfectly symmetrical. 'What do you think?' he asked, as he stepped down.

'They look lovely.' Annie beamed. 'I can't wait for Christmas Day and for Father Christmas to come.'

'Do you think you have both been good girls?'

'Yes!' came the excited response.

'I've done all my homework and cleaned my teeth twice a day,' Polly exclaimed.

'Oh, well in that case, I'm sure you will be on the nice list.'

Polly's eyes lit up in excitement at the thought of what was to come.

Alf had always loved the festive season. After he finished work on Christmas Eve he would nip into Attercliffe and pick up a bag of hot roasted chestnuts for them all to share and once his daughters were in bed, he would take great pleasure in filling their pillowcases with little treats and hanging them on the end of their beds. There was no better wake-up call than the sound of his daughters' cries of delight the following morning when they realized Father Christmas had paid them a visit. It was utterly magical.

And this year, now Josie was back to full health, was going to be just wonderful. As a surprise, Alf had secretly been putting some money aside with the Banners saving scheme all year and last week had used it to buy his wife a silver necklace, and his three girls a bracelet each as an extra-special surprise. He couldn't wait to see all their faces when they opened the beautifully gift-wrapped presents on Christmas morning. It was going to be a day to remember.

'What's this?' Josie said, coming into the house and interrupting Alf's thoughts.

'Guilty as charged!' Alf said, lifting his hands into the surrender position.

'Don't tell him off, Mummy. We begged him,' Polly confessed, unable to bear the thought of her beloved daddy getting into trouble.

'It's okay.' Josie grinned as she admired the paper bunting. 'I think it looks rather pretty and will get us all in the mood for Christmas.'

'You aren't cross?' Annie tentatively enquired.

'No, sweetheart. I'm definitely not mad.' She smiled,

gently popping a loving kiss on each of her daughters' heads. 'I'm as excited as you are about Christmas.'

'It's going to be perfect,' Alf affirmed, wrapping his arm around his wife's slender waist.

But just as he was about to steal a kiss, the tender moment was crudely interrupted by the high-pitched wail of the air-raid sirens.

Chapter 24

We could be in for a long night, Josie thought. *Please, God, don't let this be a repeat of Thursday.*

'I'll grab the flask of tea, Mum,' Daisy called from the kitchen, where she had been sat reading *Gone with the Wind*, and had only just put the kettle on to make a cuppa. 'I've grabbed some biscuits too.'

'Let's be quick,' Alf said, hurrying his wife and daughters into the hallway. The events of three nights earlier made him feel extra cautious. 'Let's get down to the public shelter as fast as we can.'

Within three minutes the second siren was shrieking out across the city, and the family were already at the back door.

'Quick, put your hats and gloves on, girls,' Josie fussed. 'It's bitingly cold out. There's a frost settling already.'

Seconds later, Alf was guiding his family onto the street, where at least a dozen or so other neighbours were already marching towards the communal shelter, bags holding snacks, hot drinks and insurance documents.

Whereas in the past there had been a lack of urgency to make their way to a place of safety, tonight, with just the silvery moonlight to guide them, the residents of Darnall had picked up pace, all of them desperate to make sure they weren't left to the elements if Jerry decided to make another appearance across their beloved city.

'Are we going to be all right?' Polly asked, her little hand trembling inside her dad's.

'Of course we are,' said Alf, his voice steady and unfaltering, as they reached the public shelter on Coleford Road, and in true British spirit, joined the queue to enter.

'Look, there's Archie,' Josie said, as she kept her arm firmly around Polly's shoulder. 'Hiya, luv,' she added, as Archie caught her eye.

'Evening all.' He smiled in return, as he made a written note on his clipboard of everyone entering the cavernous shelter. 'Go and grab a spot on one of the benches, while there's still space.'

'Thanks, Archie,' Daisy replied gratefully, making a mental note to tell Patty how efficient and calm Archie was; a much-needed antidote to the palpable, rising tension of the early evening.

'Right, let's get you all inside,' he added, as the stream of anxious neighbours made their way inside, using their dimly lit torches to guide them.

As Josie directed her daughters to a free spot, Alf held back.

'If you need a hand tonight, mate,' he said to Archie. 'I'd like to help, if I can.'

'Thanks, Alf. We've got a lot of wardens on duty tonight, but I'll definitely let you know. To be honest, I'm just hoping it will be over soon and we can all get home.'

'I'll not argue with you there, son,' Alf said, before joining his family on one of the long wooden benches that ran down one side of the subterranean cavern.

'Right, girls, let's get some books out,' Josie said, opening the bag that she hadn't emptied since the last raid, three nights earlier.

'I'll read you both a story,' Daisy offered, knowing it would calm her own nerves, as well as keep her little sisters at ease.

'I know this is flamin' awful, but we are lucky,' Josie said, touching her husband's hand, as they both watched their three girls huddle together, Daisy with one arm wrapped around Polly, and the other pulling Annie close as she opened *Wind in the Willows*, under the warm glow of the gaslights.

'We are that, luv,' Alf replied, grateful after Josie's ill health a year ago that they were still all together.

All around the shelter, parents entertained their children, women began knitting and a few blokes had started a game of seven-card rummy, while others had found a corner of space to pull out a box of dominoes. The residents of Coleford Road and the nearby streets were well-versed in how to pass the time of the interminable air raids.

For the next hour, time passed without any interruptions, a tentative calm gradually taking over the initial panic.

'You never know, we might get home soon,' Josie said hopefully.

But no sooner had the words passed her lips than the reverberations of an explosion sent shockwaves through the shelter.

'Mummy!' Polly screeched, jumping up, the terror in her voice instantly echoed by the desperate cries of countless other children.

'I'm scared,' she sobbed, as both Josie and Daisy tightened their grip on Polly, who was shaking with fear.

'It's okay, sweetheart,' Josie said with all the maternal courage she could muster, despite the surge of panic that coursed through her.

Suddenly, the atmosphere of the shelter changed from one of measured calm to that of instant terror.

'Bloody Jerry,' someone proclaimed.

'He needs to bugger off back to Germany,' someone else admonished.

'Take it steady, fellas. There are kids in here,' Alf said, protectively.

But before the understandably frustrated men could comment further, another ear-splitting bang left the occupants of the shelter shrieking in shock.

'That was chuffin' close,' someone gasped.

'Too close,' another gulped.

'I don't like this,' Josie whispered to her husband.

'It will pass,' Alf said, trying his best to reassure her, but the lack of confidence in his voice betrayed his own fears.

Just then the shelter door swung open. 'In you go, ladies,' Archie said, ushering in two older women. 'Go and grab a spot on one of the benches. I'm sure everyone will move up and make room for you both.'

'We can squidge up,' Josie offered, pulling Polly onto her knee, as Daisy did the same with Annie. The two elderly women, who must have been twins, perched on the edge of the bench, all colour drained from them.

Alf looked at Archie quizzically. 'I found them wandering down the street. I think the last explosion forced them out of their house.'

'We'll keep an eye on them,' Josie offered. 'I've got a big flask of tea too.'

But before Archie could reply, the vibrations of another explosion sent him catapulting, head over heels, into the shelter, while a terrified chorus of cries bounced off the concrete and metal walls.

'Archie, lad!' Alf was on his feet before Archie'd even had chance to raise his head.

'I'm all right,' Archie said, pulling himself up. 'No damage done, but I better get back out there and see if anyone else needs help. The bombs are dropping thick and fast.'

'I'm coming with you,' Alf insisted.

'No. You don't have to do that,' Archie countered, wiping himself down, and repositioning his tin hat.

'I can't sit here and do nothing while there's folk out there in danger,' Alf protested.

'Alf!' Josie called. Her instinct screaming to tell him to stop, that he must stay with her and their girls, but the pleas got lost in her throat. How could she ask him to stay while Archie, at least half his age, was doing his bit to keep their friends and neighbours safe? Besides which, she knew in that split second, her brave husband would not be stopped.

'I'll be back,' Alf said, reading his wife's mind. He quickly stepped back to the bench where his family were huddled together. Kissing them all in turn, his daughters on their foreheads and Josie on her lips, Alf told his wife and three daughters how much he loved them before following Archie to the heavy metal door, the only protection from the barbaric bombs that were raining down on their city.

'I'm coming too,' another bloke announced.

'Me too,' came a second voice.

Within seconds at least half a dozen men were on their feet and following Archie out of the shelter.

'Please be careful,' Josie whispered.

'Come back soon,' Polly called after her daddy, a dam of frightened tears welling in her eyes.

'I will,' Alf promised, turning back to give his family a final glance before he made his way out.

'It'll be okay,' Josie said with conviction, holding her youngest daughter tight. 'Daddy will be back before we know it.'

But as the metal door slammed shut, the last of the men leaving the safety and confines of the shelter, the already tense atmosphere intensified.

Daisy squeezed her mum's arm with her free hand, both of them doing their best to stem the fear that had made them freeze in terror. Their silence was short-lived as another alarming explosion sent ripples of fear down the spines of each and every man, woman and child who were huddled together in the purpose-built chamber, which now felt woefully inadequate.

'Mummy!' Annie and Polly shrieked in unison, their shaking arms tightening around Josie and Daisy, their desperate cries replicated by a chorus of others.

'It's okay,' Josie whispered, the words catching in her throat, as she attempted to comfort her children, despite the fact she was just as frightened.

Like many other residents of Darnall, the ripples from the bombs were completely alien to her. During the spate of air raids in the summer none had felt so dangerously close. Streets had been damaged, houses destroyed, but the bombs had been in other parts of the city. Her children, her husband had been safe.

Even when Jerry had attacked Sheffield three nights earlier, the bombs which had annihilated the city centre hadn't come near the east end. Josie realized now she had been lulled into a false sense of security. It wasn't that she hadn't taken the bombings seriously or been devastated by the horrifying news of those whose lives had been lost, it was just that Josie had thought *her* family would somehow escape the devastation.

But now as one deafening bomb after another exploded, in what felt like yards from where they were sitting, Josie realized with terrifying reality, how naive she had been.

Chapter 25

Outside, hell was raging as bombs rained from the sky indiscriminately along Coleford Road. As Archie and Alf momentarily took shelter in the air-raid warden's office, they listened to the instructions from the senior wardens.

'There's no need for me to tell you this is the real thing,' Mr Wilson said. 'We are going to need our wits about us. Our priority is to get anyone who is outside to safety as quickly as possible. If this raid carries on, there will be folk trapped in their own houses. Our job, if it's safe to do so, is to help them. The fire brigade and ambulances will be trying to get to us. They know we are under attack, so back-up will be on the way, but if we can put out any incendiary fires, then let's do our best to. Good luck, men!'

With that, the group of wardens, and the added volunteers, backed out of the cramped office, just as the skies darkened once again, peppered with German planes.

'Take cover!' someone called, as another cluster of bombs rained down. Archie threw himself on the floor, taking Alf with him, as a cacophony of explosions erupted, temporarily deafening the pair of them. It was a few seconds before the piercing ringing in their ears eased and they tentatively lifted their heads.

'Good Lord!' Alf whispered, as his eyes adjusted to the brightness of the flames which had now taken the place of the darkness from minutes earlier.

As he looked down the street, at least a dozen houses were ablaze, fire shooting out of windows, the violent combination of reds and oranges illuminating the usual blackness of the December night. As more incendiary bombs exploded, the sounds of windows smashing mixed with the crashing of masonry, bricks and timber filled the now smoke-infused air.

'What do we do first?' Alf asked Archie, as he rose to his feet, aghast at seeing his neighbours' houses crumbling before his very eyes.

'We need to make sure no one is in those houses,' Archie replied, now stood up, instinctively shaking off the layers of dust that had covered him.

'Be careful!' Mr Wilson called, above the whirring of the German bombers. 'I doubt they've finished yet.'

The street was in utter chaos. The latest attack had not only obliterated houses, but the bombs had left craters wider than most people's kitchens in the road.

'The fire brigade are going to have a reyt job on getting down here,' Archie said, as he and Alf ran towards the burning properties, stretching their arms across their foreheads to shield their faces from the flying debris that was being spat out from windows and roofs, some of it still ablaze.

'Over here,' another warden called, from the opposite side of the road.

Archie and Alf instinctively ran towards him, circumnavigating one of the giant holes.

'I can hear voices,' the warden, Peter, said. 'Listen,' he insisted, putting his hand to his ear.

Beyond the bangs and firework-like crackling, there was something else. Archie and Alf heard it too; the faint pleas for help from below the rubble, which only an hour earlier had been the brickwork of a house.

'Dear God! There are people down there,' Archie exclaimed incredulously, as he looked in horror at the mountain of debris trapping the occupants.

'We've got to get them out,' Alf said, already frantically moving stones with his bare hands.

'Hang on,' Peter said. 'We might be quicker going through the crater.'

'Really?' Alf asked.

The three men peered into the dark hole, a gas pipe at one end on fire, but Alf noted how close it was to the remains of the tumbled-down terrace.

'I think you're right. If we can shift some of the stones, we should be able to get into the cellar, which is probably where they are.'

'Typical,' Peter sighed, already jumping into the gaping

hole in the ground. 'I bet they thought they were safer there. Chuffin' Hitler.'

Archie and Alf climbed down next to Peter, and the three men started moving the loose stones, desperately trying to ignore the flames just feet away from them. Within minutes, using nothing but their bare hands, they started shifting the stones.

'Let's just pray the whole thing doesn't cave in,' Peter said. 'We're going to have to take it really steady.'

The tension in the heavy fog of smoke, infiltrated by the acrid smell of fire, was palpable. The thought of not saving the poor souls who were encased in the potentially underground tomb was inconceivable. Determined, the three men worked perfectly in sync, lifting the dirty rubble onto the road above them, careful to prevent further travesty.

'Please save us,' came the cry of a clearly terrified older woman. 'There's a baby in here.'

'We're coming,' Alf called. 'Stay calm and we will get to you.'

Almost immediately came the muffled whimper of what could only be a newborn, sending a shiver of paternal horror through Alf. Visions of his own three daughters as tiny babies flashed before him. He'd have moved heaven and earth to save them from danger. Alf couldn't let this tiny child die. He had to get them out and fast.

'We're coming,' Alf called, trying to keep his tone calm, a contrast to how anxious he felt.

The three men gradually eased out one brick at a time, aware one wrong move could cause the rest of the building to collapse in on the underground prisoners. Although their attention was fully focused on the job in hand, the streaks of red flames which shot out of nearby houses acted as a terrifying reminder of what a perilous situation they were in.

'Do you need a hand?' a voice from above asked.

Archie glanced upwards at the concerned-looking police officer peering down into the crater.

'We wouldn't say no. We don't know how many, but there's folk stuck in the cellar. We need to get them out before this whole building gives way.'

'What can I do?'

'Maybe take some of this rubble off us as we pass it up and see if there's any ambulances free. I don't know what state they are in.'

'There's one on the way, but God knows how long they will be. There are bombs going off all over the shop. I hate to say it, but I reckon we are facing a much worse night than Thursday.'

'Dear God,' Archie sighed, but he couldn't allow his mind to wander. If he started thinking about where else the Luftwaffe were dropping their heinous bombs of destruction, he would be no use to anyone, but he quickly prayed Patty and his own family were safe. There was no time to chat, instead the policeman dropped to his knees and took the stones, wood and bricks, which Alf, Peter and Archie passed to him. He only had his helmet to protect him from whatever rained down from the skies above or flying debris.

'That should do it,' Peter called over the ear-splitting cacophony of noise, as a hole just big enough for an adult to crawl through was opened up. 'Right,' he called into the dark gap. 'How many are in there? Is anyone hurt?'

'There's six of us,' the woman who had initially called for help replied.

'How many children?'

'Four, including a week-old baby, two toddlers and a seven-year-old.'

'Anyone hurt?' Peter asked again.

'The eldest. I think it's her leg.'

'Can she stand up or crawl?'

'I don't think so, but me and her mum can lift her.'

'Okay, let's give it a go,' Peter instructed calmly. 'I'll be here to take her.'

'Thank God they are all alive,' Alf said.

A minute later, the face of a bewildered little girl appeared through the void, her long, curly hair tumbling around her face. Initially the hair looked black, but as the police officer directed the light of his torch onto the frightened youngster, Peter realized it was impossible to decipher the colour, as she was covered in a filthy layer of dirt and dust.

'Easy does it,' Peter said gently, putting his arms under her shoulders, guiding her body into the night air.

'Mummy,' the little girl whimpered.

'It's okay,' Alf said. Standing alongside Peter, he supported the girl's back, as the full length of her body emerged. But as her legs came into view, Alf had to swallow back the gasp which was threatening to escape from his mouth. Her right leg was twisted at an ugly angle, bone visible just below her knee, blood dripping down the now crimson makeshift bandage, which had been made from what looked like the sleeve of a jumper.

'Is my mummy coming?' the girl asked, in between sobs, streaks of tears creating smudged lines down her mucky cheeks.

'She'll be here soon,' Alf promised. 'My name is Alf. I'm going to find someone to make you feel a little bit better first, if that's okay with you?'

Dazed, the injured girl nodded hesitantly.

'Can you tell me your name?' Alf asked, hoping if he kept her talking, it would help divert her attention to the relentless explosions that erupted every few seconds all around them.

'Patricia,' she whispered.

'Okay, Patricia. We are going to lift you up onto the road, where me and this policeman are going to look after you, until we get your mummy out. Is that all right with you?'

Patricia nodded, biting down on her lip. 'My leg really hurts.'

'I know, sweetheart,' Alf said kindly. 'We are going to find a doctor who can help you feel better.'

'Okay, fellas,' Peter said, addressing Alf and Archie. 'Let's lift her upwards.' Then looking up at the bobby, he said: 'Can you be ready to take her?'

'Hang on a minute,' Alf said. 'If you and Archie can hold her now, I'll climb up and take her from above.'

A couple of minutes later, after Alf had climbed out of the crater, Patricia was hoisted into the air and delivered into his waiting arms.

'Any sign of an ambulance?' Alf asked, looking up and down the smoke-filled road.

'I think I've just spotted one down the bottom,' the officer said.

'Okay.' Alf nodded. 'I'll carry her. Will you let her family know where I've taken her?'

'Of course. Now go.'

With one arm tucked under Patricia's back and the other firmly under her legs, trying to keep them still, Alf rushed down the road, the frightened little girl gripping his jacket.

Careful to avoid the craters and potholes which were increasing in number by the minute, Alf whispered kind words of reassurance to Patricia, continually promising it would all be over soon.

Stepping over pieces of wood and panes of shattered glass, which had been spewed out of the broken, tumbling buildings, Alf prayed the Luftwaffe would spare them both for the minute or so it would take him to get Patricia to safety.

'This way,' a woman's voice called over the deafening noise. Alf looked up and through the smog of acrid smoke and dust saw a female ambulance driver, beckoning him towards them.

'It's her leg,' Alf announced, as he reached her. 'We might need a stretcher.'

'No problem! There's one in the back of the ambulance. Is anyone else injured?'

'Not from this young lass's house, but half the houses on the road are destroyed. I don't know if any of the wardens have found anybody ese who needs help.'

'Okay, well, let's get this one in the ambulance and I'll try to find out if anyone else needs help.'

Alf gently lifted the girl, who was wincing in pain, into the back of the war-battered vehicle, which had clearly seen better days.

'Where's my mummy?' Patricia whimpered.

'She's coming,' Alf said as reassuringly as possibly, hoping and praying the rest of the little girl's family had been rescued in one piece before the Germans did any more damage.

'Will my baby brother be okay? He's only a week old.'

'I'm sure he will be just fine.' But as the words left his mouth, the sound of glass smashing caused Alf to stiffen and Patricia to burst into tears. By the sounds of it, the window of a nearby house had been blown out.

'Don't worry,' Alf said, keeping his voice as calm as possible.

'I don't like all the bangs and my leg really hurts,' came the little girl's sorrowful whimper.

'Come on,' Alf said. 'Let's get you on this stretcher.'

'I just want my mummy,' Patricia cried, her eyes flooded with tears of fear.

'I know, sweetheart,' Alf replied, as he thought of his own three girls entrapped in the public shelter, who he knew must have been equally as terrified as they listened to the bombs drop down just yards from where they were sitting. 'Please God, let them all be all right,' Alf quietly prayed, unable to bear the thought of anything happening to them.

'Is she coming?' Patricia whispered, bringing Alf back to the moment.

'I'm here, Patricia!' came the relieved voice of a woman from behind Alf.

'Mummy!'

Alf carefully finished lifting the shaking little girl onto the stretcher, before stepping out of the way for the anxious mother and daughter to be reunited, their arms firmly encasing one another.

'Thank God you are okay,' the woman, grey from ash, said, kissing her daughter's face over and over again.

'Where's Johnny?' Patricia asked.

'He's with your nannan and sisters. The warden took them to the shelter.'

'Right,' Alf said. 'I'm going to leave you with the ambulance driver now. She is going to take good care of you. I just need to check on my own family and if anyone else needs help.'

'God bless your soul,' the woman said, standing up and gratefully throwing her arms around Alf. 'I can't thank you enough for rescuing my family tonight. You saved our lives.'

'There's no need,' Alf replied. 'I'm just glad we were able to help.'

'Where do you live? I'd like to come and thank you properly after this one is right.'

'There's no need,' Alf said.

'Please,' the woman pleaded, 'I'd like to.'

Alf told the kindly woman his address, before adding, 'You just look after yourselves. That's one very brave little girl you have there.'

'Thank you. I will. I'm Margaret, by that way.'

'Take care, Margaret,' Alf said, jumping out of the ambulance just as the driver returned, supporting an elderly man whose left arm hung limply at the side of his body.

'We need to make room for another one,' the driver instructed, helping the elderly chap aboard. 'I've got one more coming too, and then I'll get us out of here.'

Alf waved with a quick flick of his hand, as he made his way back down Coleford Road. He'd just go and check in at the warden's office about what he could do next to help, before popping his head around the shelter to make sure Josie and the girls were okay.

As Alf made his way back up the barely recognisable, horribly annihilated street, all he could think about was getting to see his own wife and daughters. Rescuing Margaret and her family had brought home to him how fragile life was. He couldn't bear to think of anything so barbaric happening to his family. Just the idea of it caused Alf to audibly gasp. He'd been terrified, a year earlier, when he thought he was going to lose Josie to some awful illness. Now all he wanted was to wrap Josie and his three daughters in his arms, and keep them safe from all the atrocities this sickening war was throwing at them. Determined to get to his family as quickly as possible, Alf picked up his pace and rushed inside the warden's office. A quick check-in, then he would get back to his precious girls.

'Ah, there you are, Alf,' Peter said as he shut the door behind him.

'Sorry. I just wanted to make sure the little girl was in safe hands before I left her.'

But before Peter could reply, a vacuous whooshing sensation flooded the cramped room, and everything went black.

Chapter 26

The vibrations of another bomb threw Archie against the shattered remains of an already near-ravaged house, the side of his face cracking against the rough bricks. Collapsing onto the rubble-ridden ground, he gasped, red-hot pain coursing through him. For a few seconds Archie was paralyzed, unable to move a single limb. When he did scramble to his feet, the ringing in his ears and the fog in front of his eyes meant he struggled to comprehend what was happening. Plumes of soot and ash meant he couldn't see further than the length of his own hand. His head throbbing, Archie rubbed his eyes as he tried to make sense of the world around him. As the dust settled enough for the disorientated air-raid warden to see further than his own hand, he gradually processed the scenes of utter devastation. Houses that had escaped the earlier onslaughts were now razed to the ground, completely unrecognizable. The high-pitched screeching of sirens pierced the backdrop of tumbling houses, bombs detonating, the violent hiss of fire taking hold, but it was the sound of harrowing cries for help that finally brought Archie to his senses.

His thoughts clarifying, Archie took in the trail of destruction Hitler's bombers had left behind. Instincts kicking in, he knew there was no time to waste. Archie's brain went into auto-pilot. The mental list came in staccato-like points. Assess the damage. Establish if anyone is trapped. Guide people to safety. Administer basic first aid where possible. Direct the wounded to the ambulances as soon as they arrive.

Despite the commotion all around him, the well-versed plan was cemented. Archie knew what was expected of him. But first, he needed to check in with his manager and the rest of the wardens so they could coordinate who was doing what. Trying to get his bearings Archie looked around, but as he turned in one direction and then the other, he couldn't work out where on the street he was. 'Come on, Archie,' he furiously reproached himself, assuming he was still slightly confused after the blast had temporarily knocked him out. 'Get a grip now. People need you.'

Archie was sure he had been on the opposite side of the road to the air-raid warden's office when the bombs had dropped, but now as he peered around everything looked different and unfamiliar.

'Archie!' a younger warden called. 'Bleedin' hell. I thought you'd gone too.'

'What are you talking about, Lewis?' Archie asked, disconcerted.

'The office. It's gone. Chuffin' Hitler. He has killed them all.'

'What? What are you on about?' The words had come too quickly. Archie couldn't make sense of what Lewis was saying.

'Look!' Lewis exclaimed, his face black, smeared in thick soot, as he pointed across the road.

It only took less than a second for Archie to register what Lewis was telling him, and just as quickly the unimaginable pierced the smog in his brain.

'No!' Archie gasped, the sickening truth dawning on him.

'Not the office!' This time the unbidden, guttural remonstration screeched out of him, in protest to the utter horror that lay before him. Without stopping to consider his own safety, Archie ran across the road, towards the entrance of what had been the air-raid warden's office.

'Where's Alf?' he shouted to Lewis as he dashed across the road.

'Your friend who helped rescue the family out of the cellar?' It was a question more than a statement.

'Yes. He was wearing a brown overcoat.'

'I'm sorry, Archie,' Lewis sighed heavily, catching him up, forcing his friend to face him. 'He headed into the office seconds before the bomb fell.'

'No!' Archie cried for the second time. 'Are you sure? Lewis, are you sure?'

Lewis looked at his friend, the horror in his eyes revealing everything Archie needed to know.

The revelation hit Archie like a punch to the stomach. Not Alf as well. He wasn't even supposed to be in the air-raid warden's office. He wasn't even meant to be outside. He'd just wanted to help. He'd saved a family, who surely would have died without his determination. In the same moment Archie's thoughts turned to Josie, Daisy, Polly and Annie. How on earth could he tell them their husband and dad had been killed? *Soddin' Hitler!*

'We've got to try and save them,' Archie cried in desperation, moving closer to the wreck of the building, ignoring the fact it was ablaze, glass and wood being catapulted indiscriminately across the road. But he couldn't just watch as his friends were buried alive. 'We can't let them die in there. Lewis, come on, help me.'

Despite his young age, Lewis knew it would be beyond miraculous if anyone survived the cataclysmic bombing, and if he didn't stop Archie, he too would end up risking his life.

'Stop!' Lewis shouted, trying to pull at Archie's arm. 'It's not safe. We have to move away. The whole building is going to go up.'

Shock and desperation rendering Archie blind, he brusquely shrugged Lewis off, his own safety not even a consideration. All he could think about was the men inside the collapsing building. The men he classed as friends. The men he had grown close to since becoming an air-raid warden. Each one of them, including Alf, who had families of their own, but had been willing to risk life and limb to protect their city.

'This isn't how they should die,' Archie gasped, grappling with the scene in front of him.

Lewis pulled at Archie's arms again, this time managing to usher him a few steps backwards, away from the blistering heat of the flames.

'Water. We need to get water,' Archie pleaded.

'I'm not sure where from, gaffer. It looks like there's been another mains burst.'

Archie looked at the ground; water was pumping out of manholes. *How could this be happening?*

'The fire engine will be here soon,' Lewis said, more out of hope, as he attempted, once again, to guide Archie away from the burning inferno.

This time Archie didn't fight. Despite his desperation to save his friends, he knew nobody inside stood a chance. The top floor of the two-storey building had already caved in, encasing anyone inside the deathly tomb. The flames that were burning inside began sprouting into the air, turning the blackness a deathly red.

'Were all the wardens in there too?'

'I think so,' Lewis whispered. 'They were quickly regrouping to check in.'

The irony was cruel. Archie looked up towards the sky, which for the first time in two hours was clear. *Hitler's parting shot.* Dropping to the floor, which was quickly turning into a pool of mud, water mixing with dirt and rubble, Archie put his head in hands, the desperate reality sinking in. So many of his friends were dead. *Dead.* In one cruel moment of time, they had been taken. They didn't stand a chance and now their families would have to pick up the pieces and try to find a way to carry on.

'Archie,' Lewis prompted, his hand reaching out towards him. 'Let me help you up.'

Bewildered, Archie looked up at the young lad. He didn't want to move. He wanted to remain perfectly still, seal his eyes shut, and pray when he next opened them, this would have all been a terrible nightmare. He didn't want to believe the unthinkable had happened.

'Why don't I take you somewhere further down the street?' Lewis suggested, assuming the sight of the smouldering building would only make feel Archie worse.

Please let the bomb have killed them instantly, Archie silently prayed, anger at this godforsaken war now infusing with the gut-wrenching heartache that sucked all the air out of his chest. It was only the sound of sirens that made Archie look round.

'Reinforcements are coming,' Lewis said.

'But it's too late for Alf,' Archie muttered.

Chapter 27

'Archie, where's Alf?' Josie asked as soon as Archie opened the doors to the public, the sound of the all-clear reverberating around the cavernous shelter.

'All the other fellas came back, but Alf didn't.'

The desperation in Josie's tone rendered Archie speechless.

'Is he okay?'

Josie looked at Alfie, waiting for an answer, but even in the dimly lit cavern, she could see his face was grey.

'Let me just get everyone outside,' he eventually said, but Josie didn't miss the tremor in his voice.

Before Josie could question him any further, a voice from the back of the long rectangular temporary hideout interrupted Archie.

'What the chuffin' hell has bloody Hitler done now?'

'I need to explain,' Archie started, obviously trying to keep his voice strong. 'I'm afraid it's not good news.'

'Some of the blokes told us Hitler had a bloody good

go at us this time and by the sounds of those explosions, I'm guessing they weren't wrong,' a woman said. 'How bad is it?'

Josie watched as Archie took a deep breath.

'I'm sorry,' he began, 'but many of your homes have been destroyed tonight. Half the street has been wiped out by Jerry.'

'Oh, dear God!' an older woman gasped.

'Soddin' Hitler,' someone else bemoaned angrily.

'Which half?' asked a younger woman, with a fractious baby in one arm, and a sleepy-looking toddler gripping her legs.

'The upper half,' Archie replied solemnly.

'Oh no,' the deflated-looking mum said, tears instantly filling her already exhausted eyes. 'That's my end. What am I going to do?'

'I'm sorry,' Archie repeated for the second time in as many minutes. 'There are police officers outside who can help with advice on where to go if you have no nearby family. I believe some of the local churches and community halls have opened their doors to offer some temporary accommodation.'

'That godforsaken man,' another woman retorted.

'Ten days before Christmas too,' someone else admonished. 'I hope he rots in hell.'

'Well, we better go and see the damage, and if we still have a house to call a home,' said one of the blokes who had done his best to help at the start of the raid, putting his arm around a terrified-looking woman, whom Archie assumed to be his wife.

Archie nodded. 'Please, all of you, stay safe,' he said, opening the shelter doors. 'If your house has taken a hit, but is still partially standing, don't go inside unless it's deemed safe.'

Josie couldn't help but notice how anxious Archie sounded. *Poor lad, he's clearly been through the mill tonight*, she quietly thought. *But where is Alf?*

As all the exhausted occupants of the shelter made their way outside, Josie was keen to join them. As much as she would rather not know if her precious family home had fallen victim to Hitler's latest tirade, she wanted Alf by her side, so they could face whatever damage had been caused together, but then she had a thought . . .

'Archie,' Josie prompted, after everyone else had left, trying to keep her voice calm, for the sake of her girls. 'Where's Alf? Is he surveying the damage at our house? I'm assuming it was hit and that's why he isn't here.'

Josie watched attentively, as Archie momentarily closed his eyes and took a deep breath.

'Archie,' Josie repeated, starting to feel increasingly anxious.

'Let's sit down,' Archie finally said, tilting his head to the now-empty benches.

Daisy, now alert to the fact something was wrong,

took Polly and Annie, guiding them back, deeper into the shelter. 'Mummy just needs to speak to Archie,' she said gently, keeping her tone even despite the unnerving feeling of dread that was now accelerating through her.

Josie took a seat and Archie sat down next to her.

'Is everything okay?' she asked, hoping her fears were just a result of paranoia rather than anything more concrete.

'I'm so sorry,' he began, gripping one shaking hand in the other, clearly working up to something.

Josie's heart began to race. 'Please, Archie. Tell me,' she pleaded.

'Oh, Josie. I'm sorry,' he started again. 'Alf was in the air-raid warden's office . . .'

'Go on,' Josie replied, her voice faltering.

She watched as Archie bit down on his already trembling lips, sending a cold shiver down her spine.

'Josie. I'm sorry,' he repeated for the third time, as he looked straight at her, his eyes beginning to glisten. 'It took a direct hit.'

For the next few seconds, time stood still and Josie didn't say a word; the silence hanging heavily in the air.

Then, almost without thinking, she finally asked: 'Are you telling me, he couldn't be rescued?'

'Yes.' Archie nodded, his face grave. 'No one could. All the other wardens were in there too.'

'No,' Josie whispered, her words barely audible, shock rippling through every fibre of her being, as the awful enormity of what Archie had just told her started to seep through and take hold.

'Are you sure? Not my Alf. Please no. Not Alf.'

'I'm sorry.'

Josie gasped, tears falling unbidden down her cheeks. Conscious her daughters were just a few feet away she pulled her quivering hands up to her face, in a bid to muffle her sobbing.

But despite her efforts, the agonizing sound of Josie's heartache echoed around the shelter.

'Mum!' Daisy said, already on her feet. 'What is it?'

Josie's eyes widened. Her daughters. Her three precious daughters. Their lives were about to be ripped apart. How on earth could she tell them they would never see their father ever again?

'Oh luv,' Josie wept, pulling Daisy and her younger two daughters towards her. 'Come here. All of you.'

Bewildered, Polly and Annie did exactly as their mum asked, confusion at seeing their mum so upset causing them to cry too. Daisy looked from her mum to Archie.

'What's happened?' she asked, a sense of fear draining the colour from her cheeks.

Josie took her eldest daughter's hand, as Daisy sat down next to her mum. With Polly on her knee and Annie the other side of her, Josie took a deep breath. Despite the overwhelming sense of shock which was consuming her, her maternal sense of duty kicked in. Josie had to be strong. That was her job as their now only remaining parent.

'Girls,' Josie started, her voice broken and distorted as she fought against the excruciating agony which was threatening to paralyze her. 'I need to tell you something. Something very sad.'

Daisy stiffened. She had never seen her mum look so fractured. Her eyes pleading, she looked at her mum. 'What is it? What's happened?' But even as Daisy muttered the words, she didn't want her mum to answer her. Instead, Daisy willed the answer not to come, because she instinctively knew once her mum started to speak, her life would never be the same again.

'I need you all to be brave for me,' Josie continued, one arm pulling Annie closer and her other hand gripping Daisy's slender fingers.

Archie looked on silently, admiration for Josie's unimaginable strength, spiked with anguish.

'Girls, when your dad went to help Archie and the other air-raid wardens tonight, something happened. Something very sad.'

Daisy shuddered, her foreboding sense of dread proliferating exponentially. *No*, she wanted to shout. *Don't say it, Mum. Don't say it and it won't be real!*

'What happened, Mummy?' Annie asked. 'Where's Daddy now? When is he coming to take us home?'

The innocent words hit Josie like a thunderbolt. She bit down hard onto her bottom lip, quickly blinking back the next flood of tears which were gathering like a well behind her eyes.

'There's no easy way of telling you this, my lovely, sweet, girls, but your dad won't be coming home.'

An icy cold shiver shot up Daisy's spine, but at the same time her whole body started to overheat. 'Mum,' was all she could whisper, unspoken words lodging in her throat, which suddenly tightened, preventing her from asking the question she didn't want the answer to.

'Is he still helping Archie's friends?' Polly asked.

'No, sweetheart,' Josie answered, her heart aching with what she was about to say, because, like Daisy, she knew once the words were spoken she had to accept the terrible reality of their new lives.

'Your daddy,' she began again, wondering how on earth she hadn't crumpled into a heap on the floor. 'Well, your daddy did something very brave tonight and he got badly hurt. Very badly.'

Instead of asking any more questions, as they normally would, something about the sombre tone of their mum's voice silenced Polly and Annie.

'I'm so sorry, girls, but . . .' Josie took another deep intake of breath. 'The angels. The angels have taken him to heaven.'

Nobody said a word, the shelter now eerily quiet, until a heart-rending sob filled the cavernous chamber. 'Mummy,' Polly cried, her cheeks flushing with colour and her little body shaking. 'I don't want the angels to have Daddy. He's my daddy, not theirs. I want him to come back. We still need to finish putting the Christmas decorations up.' And with that the devastated little girl buried her face into her Josie's chest, wrapping her tiny arms around her mum's back.

'Has he really gone to heaven?' Annie whispered, her tear-filled eyes pleading with her mum to tell her she'd not heard her properly.

'Oh, my lovely girls.' Josie exhaled, pulling all three of them closer. 'He has, but we're going to be okay. We'll find a way. I promise.' But even as the words passed Josie's lips, she had no idea how on earth they would survive the next hour, let alone the rest of their lives.

'Mum,' Daisy said, unable to elevate her voice more than a whisper. The single word was loaded with questions that Daisy didn't have the strength to voice. *How has this happened? What are we going to do now? How will we survive without Dad?* But Josie, despite her own state of shock, instinctively knew what her eldest daughter was asking.

'We'll find a way. We have to be strong.'

Daisy understood. No matter how broken she and her mum felt right now, they had to galvanize themselves, armour their fragile souls, and shelter Polly and Annie as much as they could from the inevitable misery and despair ahead.

'Archie,' Josie asked, aware she needed to get her daughters out of this shelter to somewhere they could all try and make sense of how cruelly their day had ended. 'Our house. Is it . . . is it still in one piece?'

Archie, who had remained quiet, hating the fact he was intruding on Josie and her family's most agonizing and private of moments, now looked up, his heart pounding at revealing yet more devastating news.

'It's standing,' he offered, 'but I'm afraid it's not safe to live in.' Archie had caught a glimpse of the once immaculately kept family home, which now resembled a doll's house; upright but the wall which separated Josie's house from their neighbour's completely gone.

'The houses next to yours suffered a direct hit and I'm afraid there isn't much left. Yours escaped the worst of it, but the wall which adjoined your next-door neighbour has completely gone.'

Josie and Daisy looked at each other, both quietly questioning how God had dealt them such an inexplicably inhumane blow.

'Does that mean we have nowhere to live?' Polly asked, bewildered.

'No,' Archie interjected, unable to just sit there. 'You will all come home with me. My mum will make you up a bed.'

'Oh, Archie. You can't do that. You haven't got space for us all.'

'We will find it,' Archie said adamantly. 'It's the least I can do.' *After all*, he told himself, *I shouldn't be here. I shouldn't have survived!*

'Thank you,' Josie replied, too weak to argue, and without any alternative option, what choice did she have?

'Okay,' Archie said, in a bid to take some form of control. 'Do you think you can all walk?'

'We can.' Josie nodded, gently lifting Polly off her knee. 'Come on, girls. We have to go now.'

Chapter 28

Monday, 16 December 1940

'Archie!' Patty gasped, as she opened the back door to find her very pale and drawn sweetheart facing her. 'Thank goodness you are okay. I've been worried sick.'

'Can I come in?'

'Yes. Of course. You look awful. Let me get you a cup of tea.'

Archie stepped in, out of the perishingly cold early morning air into the warm kitchen, where Patty's dad, Bill, and little brother, Tom Tom, were sitting at the table, and Angie was ladling porridge out of the pan into bowls.

'Archie,' Bill said. 'Sit down. You look exhausted, son. Dare I ask how bad it was?'

Bill had ushered his family to their nearest public shelter when the sirens had screeched the previous afternoon, and listened in horror to the sounds of bombs exploding, praying Hitler's Luftwaffe would spare them. When the all-clear had finally reverberated around the concrete temporary building, everyone inside there had breathed an audible sigh of relief, but as they had emerged onto

Thompson Street it was obvious their city had taken another battering. Fumes of smoke could be seen in all directions, the smell of burning attacked the senses of those who stood on the pavements, and the nearby sirens of fire engines and ambulances competed with the all-clear.

'I don't know where to start,' Archie conceded, his puffy red eyes glistening.

'Oh, Archie. What happened?' Patty asked, sitting down in the chair next to Archie, her anxious tone revealing the concern she felt at seeing her sweetheart look so distraught.

'It's Alf and the other wardens,' Archie said, shaking his head.

'What do you mean?' Patty asked.

'They've gone. All of them. Just gone.'

'What do you mean, luv?' Angie asked, pouring Archie a strong mug of tea, and adding in a spoonful of sugar for good measure. The poor lad obviously needed it.

'They . . . they didn't make it.' As soon as Archie had said the horrifying words, he dropped his head to his hand. 'It should have been me. Not Alf.'

Patty glanced at her parents, trying to process what Archie was telling them, as she put her arm over Archie's shoulder. It was a few seconds before he sat upright again, his eyes glazed over and his face ashen.

'Do you want to talk about it, son?' Bill asked, tentatively.

'The bombs. They just didn't stop. I tried to get to Alf and the others but the whole building was collapsing. I promise I tried.'

'It's okay,' Patty whispered.

'It's not,' Archie retorted, shaking his head. 'Alf insisted on helping. I tried to tell him not to. I should have stopped him.'

As Archie carried on talking, Bill, Angie and Patty listened in silence as he slowly repeated the horrifying events of the night before.

'Alf shouldn't even have been outside,' Archie said. 'It's not fair. He shouldn't have died. It was my job, not Alf's.'

'Now, son,' Bill said, 'no matter what's happened, you can't think like that. From what you've said Alf wanted to help. You didn't force him.'

'But he wasn't a warden. I am. It was my job to protect everyone.'

'Archie,' Patty said kindly. 'It sounds like you did everything you could. There's no way you could predict the warden's office would take a hit.'

'But I should have said no when Alf offered to help. It's my fault he's dead.'

'No, no, it's not, son. None of this is your fault. You couldn't have stopped Alf, no matter how hard you tried,' Bill said firmly. 'I'd have done exactly the same if Thompson Street had been targeted.'

Archie just shook his head, his eyes grey, a mixture of sorrow and incomprehension.

'But he's gone. How will Josie, Daisy and the girls ever get over this?'

The words hit the family. How on earth would they cope? This was the first time Hitler's despicable actions had taken the life of someone they knew and loved.

'I don't think you should go in to work today,' Patty said tentatively, unsure what else to say, not wanting to heighten how awful Archie was already feeling. 'You don't look as though you have had a wink of sleep.'

'I'm going,' Archie snapped, more harshly that he'd intended.

Again, Patty glanced at her parents. Angie gently shook her head, silently warning her daughter to go easy.

'Okay,' Patty conceded. 'Have you eaten anything? There's plenty of porridge in the pan.'

'I'm not hungry. Shouldn't we get going?' Archie's words were staccato-like, impulsive, functionary. Then he added, 'How will I tell everyone? Alf's dead because of me.'

'No,' Patty protested, taking Archie's hand. 'None of this is your fault. None of it. Everyone knows what a brave job you do. I promise you no one will think this is your fault.'

'But I do,' Archie muttered.

'Are you sure you should be going to work?' Patty asked again, convinced it was the last place Archie should be.

'Yes,' he replied firmly, already standing up. 'I can't let anyone else down.'

Realizing there was no point in arguing, Bill looked at his watch. 'It is just before seven thirty. I guess we should get going, otherwise Nancy will be thinking we aren't coming.'

'Give her my love,' Angie said, as Patty, Archie and Bill all stood up. 'I hope Bert is okay this morning.' Yet again, the sound of the bombs had left their friend's husband in a trancelike state for the duration of the raid.

'Will do,' Bill said, pecking his wife on the cheek, before ruffling Tom Tom's mop of blonde hair, as he wolfed down his jammy porridge.

The walk to work was overshadowed by the terrible events of the night before. Patty stayed close to Archie, as Bill told Nancy about Bert. By the time they reached Vickers, the sombre atmosphere had increased. Instead of the usual animated chatter among the female workers, the conversations were more subdued, tinged with an overwhelming sense of disbelief.

Archie wandered off to find Frank, and as Patty and Nancy stood in line, they looked around, checking for familiar faces, praying no one was missing.

'Thank goodness you are both here,' Betty said, finding her friends in the queue. 'We've been worried sick. Have you seen Hattie and Daisy yet?'

'I'm here,' Hattie said, joining the women. 'What a horrible night that was.'

'I'm so glad you are okay,' Patty exclaimed, her eyes

glistening as she hugged her friend, who looked as though she hadn't slept a wink. 'I assume you didn't get to the shelter again?'

'No. Dad refused. He drank himself into a stupor while me and Mum hid under the stairs. It was terrifying. The bombs sounded so close, and Darnall is such a mess. There're craters everywhere and burst water mains. Our street was okay, but I heard people say as I was walking here that loads of houses have been destroyed. Those poor people. You just can't imagine it, can you?'

'No,' Betty replied. 'You can't.'

'Where's Daisy? I've just heard a few people say Coleford Road was hit,' Hattie asked, looking around.

Patty looked at Nancy, a rock of sadness forming in her stomach.

'Has something happened?' Betty asked, a sense of foreboding coursing through her.

'It's her dad,' Patty said quietly. 'He was helping the wardens when their office took a direct hit.'

'Is he badly hurt?' Hattie asked. 'Will he be okay?'

The tears Patty had been battling to hold back for Archie's sake now burst from her eyes.

'Oh, Patty. What's happened?' Hattie gasped, placing her hand on her friend's arm.

At the sight of Patty crying, a few other women had turned to look around.

'Patty,' Betty mirrored Hattie.

'He didn't make it,' Patty whispered, her voice

trembling. 'They were all killed. Only Archie and another young warden survived.'

'Oh, my goodness,' Betty exclaimed, her heart suddenly lurching as she digested what Patty has just told them. Visions of Daisy and the heartache she must be suffering filled her mind, and she felt sick thinking about what they must be going through.

'Where's Daisy, Josie and the girls now? Are they at home?' Hattie asked.

'No.' Patty shook her head, using the heel of her hand to ebb the flow of tears. 'They went to Archie's house last night after their house was too badly damaged to go back to.'

'Goodness,' Betty whispered.

'I know. It's hard to take it in, isn't it?' Nancy said, more than asked, as the group moved closer to the clocking-in machine.

'I'll go and see Daisy after work. They must all be in so much shock,' Betty said, sadness consuming her as the news sunk in. This war had tested them all in so many ways but this was definitely the hardest news they'd had to shoulder. Betty couldn't begin to imagine how Daisy and her family were feeling right now. Their whole world had been turned upside down in just a few hours.

'Would you tell her we are all thinking about her?' Nancy said. 'And tell her if there's anything we can do, to please say.'

'Yes, please do,' Hattie reinforced. 'If there is anything Mum or I can do, just let me know.'

'Of course.' Betty nodded, as she lifted her timecard from the left-hand rack and slotted it into the time machine.

'How's Archie?' Hattie asked. 'He must be in a lot of shock?'

'He's not good,' Patty replied, taking a deep breath. 'I've never seen him so upset. He could barely speak this morning. I'm not sure he should be at work, but he insisted he had to be here. I'm going to ask Frank to keep an eye on him.'

'Dear me,' Nancy said. 'I agree, he should have stayed at home.'

'I don't think he could face Josie, Daisy and the girls. He's blaming himself.'

'But this isn't his fault,' Hattie gasped.

'I know but he's really not thinking straight.'

Subdued and hushed, the women made their way to their designated parts of the factory. Hattie felt oddly alone as she made her way to the turner's yard without Daisy; they had become rather close over the last few months. Betty wished she could be with her friend and somehow help ease the pain she was suffering. Nancy couldn't even start to envisage the immeasurable loss Josie must have been enduring, alongside trying to remain strong for her daughters, and Patty was overwhelmed with sadness for Daisy, alongside worrying about Archie, who she knew was torturing himself with a guilt he shouldn't be feeling.

All of them lost in their own thoughts, the morning passed in a haze of instructions; the whole workforce in a state of shock at how their city had been obliterated for the second time in three days. When the hooter for lunch sounded, Patty sped down her crane ladder, hoping to catch Archie before they got to the canteen. She found him next to one of the furnaces, sitting on a metal stool, looking vacantly into the middle distance.

'How are you feeling?' she asked, awakening him from his thoughts.

Archie looked up blankly, his face ghastly white despite the immense heat of the shop floor. 'Sorry. Did you say something?'

'I was just asking if you're okay?'

Archie didn't answer. His mind hadn't stopped going round in circles for hours. If only he'd insisted on telling Alf to stay inside the shelter. If only he'd checked on him after they'd saved that family. If he had done either of those things, Archie had convinced himself Alf would still be alive. It had been his job to keep people safe, not allow them to walk into danger. He'd failed at the one thing he'd hoped to be good at and now Daisy and her sisters had lost their dad, and Josie would never see her husband again. It was his fault. Alf was dead because of him.

'Are you coming for something to eat?' Patty asked, once again, interrupting his thoughts.

Archie shook his head. Food was the last thing he needed. Besides which, Daisy and Josie's friends would all be in the canteen. How could he look them in the eye, knowing he was responsible for the immeasurable pain they must be suffering?

'Shall I stay here with you?' Patty popped herself down on an empty stool next to Archie.

'You don't have to,' he muttered.

'I want to,' Patty said, reaching out and putting one of her hands onto his.

Archie turned to face Patty. How could she be so kind after he'd let her friend's dad die?

'This isn't your fault,' she said gently, as if reading his mind. 'You must not blame yourself.'

'I should have made Alf stay in the shelter. I shouldn't have let him come and help.'

'You couldn't have stopped him,' Patty reasoned. 'He wanted to help, to try and protect his, our, city.'

Archie dropped his head into his hands. No matter how many times he heard that statement repeated, it didn't ease the fact Alf should still be alive.

'Would you like some tea? Mum made me a flask this morning.'

Archie shook his head.

'Have you eaten anything at all?'

'I can't face it,' came his muffled response.

Patty didn't want to push Archie, but he looked terrible. 'I'm just worried about you,' she said gently.

Archie didn't respond, his silence lingering between them.

Unsure what to do, Patty stayed put. Hoping she could tempt Archie with some lunch, she opened her bag and pulled out the small biscuit tin that held her Spam sandwich and a slice of vinegar cake.

'We could share?'

'No,' Archie muttered, then shook his head to reinforce the point.

Despite how worried she was, Patty didn't push Archie, knowing there was a good chance he would pull even further away. So instead, she sat quietly by his side, nibbling on her own dinner, her thoughts alternating between how she could help the man she loved with all her heart, and then to Daisy and the unimaginable pain she must be feeling.

For everyone, the end of the day couldn't come soon enough and as the gang of workers departed through gate three, which they'd entered through eight hours earlier, they hoped and prayed their city would not fall victim to a third night of raids.

'Can I walk with you?' Betty asked Archie as she pulled on her black leather gloves, to protect herself from the sharp December air. 'I thought I would go and see Daisy.'

'No problem.' Archie nodded, absently.

After waving goodbye to Hattie, who looked as exhausted as the rest of them, Nancy, Betty, Archie and Patty all set off in the opposite direction along Brightside Lane.

'Frank has just been telling me a couple of the factories

were damaged,' Betty said, in a bid to break the heavy atmosphere.

'Badly?' Nancy asked.

'Thankfully not. And it sounds like even the ones that suffered the most will be up and running again in the next couple of days,' Betty explained.

'That's good,' Nancy said. 'Do you think Hitler was deliberately targeting the factories?'

'There's every chance.' Betty nodded. 'He's bound to know the steelworks are making parts for planes and tanks.'

The thought sent a shudder down Nancy's spine. She'd always known they were doing important war work but had never really thought that they were at risk. Had they just been lucky this time, unlike poor Alf?

Chapter 29

'Ah, you're home, luv,' Archie's mum said. 'And, sorry. I didn't realize you were bringing a friend back too.'

'Please, don't apologise,' Betty interjected. 'I'm Betty. I work at Vickers. Daisy and I are good friends and I just wanted to come and see how she and her mum and sisters are.'

'That's kind of you, luv,' Gracie said. 'They aren't doing so well, as you can imagine. They are all in the front room. Why don't you nip through, and I'll bring in a fresh pot of tea.'

'Thank you. I won't stay long. I just wanted them to know we are all thinking of them.'

'I'm sure they will appreciate that.'

Betty carefully placed her bag holding her gas mask by the back door, then made her way down the hall. The door to the living room was slightly ajar, but Betty still knocked, conscious of disturbing a private moment.

'Come in,' Josie said, her voice barely audible.

Betty slowly opened the door. The room was dimly

lit, the curtains were drawn over a blackout blind, only a lamp on an occasional table, offering a hazy light. Josie and Daisy were sat on either end of the couch, Annie and Polly were curled up, fast asleep in the middle of them.

'Betty,' Daisy whispered, slowly lifting herself from the couch, so as not to wake her sisters. 'Thank you for coming.'

'I'm so sorry,' Betty replied, wrapping her arms around her friend. 'I really am. Your dad was such a lovely man. One of the best.'

'He was,' Daisy agreed, her slender body now quivering. 'I just can't believe he's not here.'

For the next couple of minutes Betty hugged her friend, allowing the flow of tears to soak into her coat, wishing more than anything else in the world she could take her pain away.

Daisy only lifted her head up when Gracie gently nudged the door open, carrying a tray in her arms, with a teapot, three cups and a jug of milk.

'I do apologize. I didn't mean to disturb you,' she said.

'Please. Don't be,' Josie said quietly, placing the tray of drinks on the rectangular coffee table in the centre of the room. 'I don't think I will ever be able to thank you enough.'

'Not at all. Now, I've made a big stew. Whenever you are all ready, please come and let me know, and I'll serve some up.'

'That's very kind of you.' Josie smiled in return. 'I'll just let the girls sleep a bit longer, if that's okay. They didn't get a wink last night.'

'Of course. I'll leave you in peace, but please just give me a call if you need anything at all.'

As Gracie quietly slipped from the room, Daisy sat back down on the couch, and Betty poured all three women a warm drink.

'Everyone at the factory asked me to send their love,' Betty said.

'Thank you,' Josie replied. 'People are very kind. Will you tell Dolly I'll get back to work as soon as I can, but I just need to be at home for Annie and Polly at the moment.'

'Oh, please don't worry about that,' Betty insisted, keeping her voice low. 'No one expects you to be in work. Nor you, Daisy.'

'I know. Sorry. I just can't think straight,' Josie said. 'None of this feels real and I really don't know what I'm going to do. Alf held us all together. I just can't imagine. I don't even want to say the words.'

'Mum,' Daisy choked, reaching her arm across the couch, to her mum's. 'We'll find a way. I promise.'

Betty thought her heart would break in two, painful memories of losing her own mum at just ten years old piercing her thoughts.

'Is there anything at all I can do to help?' Betty asked.

'Oh luv, you are busy enough between Vickers and the WVS.'

'It's okay. I can always find time. Please say if there's something that needs doing.'

'I just need to find us somewhere to live,' Josie sighed. 'Although our house is still standing, it's in no fit state to live in. I can't face going yet but Archie's mum nipped down earlier. She said the street is a reyt mess. Loads of houses have completely gone. Gracie spoke to some of our neighbours. Those who can't go to family are in rest centres. I think I'll have to take the girls to one of them. We can't stay here indefinitely. It's not fair on Archie's family. As much as Gracie and Don are insisting we can, there isn't enough room.'

'Come and stay at Ivy's,' Betty said, the words springing from her lips instinctively.

'We can't do that,' Josie answered.

'Why not? I know Ivy would be happy for you to. The whole top floor is empty. Her last lodgers left not long after war was declared, and she's never filled the rooms. It would be perfect for you all. There are two rooms, so you could have your own room, Annie and Polly could share and there's a spare bed that we could put in my room for you, Daisy.'

'But what if Ivy wants to take in more lodgers? I don't want her to feel like she has to take us in,' Josie asked, not daring to hope Betty's idea could turn into a reality.

'Ivy would never think like that. I know she will want to help you. How about I ask her tonight and send a message back with Archie tomorrow?'

Josie glanced at Daisy, and then at the sleeping forms of her younger daughters. None of them had more than the clothes on their back, although a fireman had told Gracie they would be able to go into their house and collect some of their belongings as soon as the property had been deemed safe. They had no family nearby who could take them in, and she was sure the waiting list for a new house would be as long as her arm, after Hitler's latest heinous attack. And to top it all off, it was Christmas in nine days. God knows how they would get through the day without Alf. Josie couldn't allow her mind to think about it, but if they didn't find somewhere more permanent to live, she had no idea what they would do.

'Why don't we let Betty ask, Mum?' Daisy prompted, gently stroking Polly's long, auburn hair. 'It doesn't have to be forever. Just until we get ourselves back on our feet.'

Gracie and Don had given up their bed for all four of them to share and had insisted on doing the same tonight, Archie's mum bunking in with his nannan and his dad sleeping on the sofa. Josie's conscience wouldn't allow the family to put themselves out indefinitely, besides which, she knew Archie was struggling and needed his space.

'Okay,' Josie conceded. 'But please let Ivy know

she doesn't have to take us. We will find somewhere. I was going to go and work out how to apply for new accommodation tomorrow.'

But Betty already knew Ivy, and Frank, would welcome Josie and her daughters with open arms. They both had hearts as big as the moon and wouldn't hesitate to give the family a roof over their heads.

Chapter 30

Tuesday, 17 December 1940

'That poor family,' Ivy said, as she buttered Frank two slices of toast from the homemade loaf she'd baked the night before. 'I barely slept thinking about Josie and the girls last night.'

'I know,' Frank agreed, packing his snap Ivy had prepared into his rucksack. 'I wish we could do something to help. There's going to be so many in the same boat.'

'There is,' Ivy said, placing Frank's breakfast in front of him on the kitchen table. Ivy had spent the day before helping out with the WVS. As well as sorting clothing donations, she had spent several hours in a mobile canteen, serving up bowls of steaming soup and hot drinks.

'I never thought I'd see so many people looking destitute and desperate. Whole families with nowhere to go and women telling me about relatives who were killed. And I have no doubt I will hear more terrible stories today.'

Frank took a bite of his breakfast, then asked, 'What time are you going over?'

'I thought I'd go and see Josie first and bring her and the girls back here, if they agree, then I might see if I can put in a couple of hours this afternoon with Winnie.'

'You are so kind,' Frank said affectionately. 'The world needs more people like you.'

'I can't just sit here and do nothing when so many people are suffering.'

'I know you can't, luv. And that's the reason I love you.'

'Oh, Frank. I love you too.' Ivy smiled, giving him a peck on the cheek. The last few days had reminded Ivy of how precious life was and the fact you never knew when those closest to you could be taken away.

'Morning.' Betty yawned as she walked into the kitchen dressed and ready for another day at Vickers, inadvertently interrupting the tender moment.

'I'm guessing you didn't get the best night's sleep?' Ivy asked, before quickly turning back to the worktop to pour Betty a cup of tea, her cheeks flushing.

'It could have been better. I couldn't stop thinking about Daisy and her family,' Betty answered, taking a seat at the wooden table.

'I'm sure, dear. I was the same. I was just telling Frank, I'm going to see Josie this morning and tell her she is welcome here.'

'This really is ever so kind of you,' Betty said, appreciatively. 'I know we can't take the pain away that they are all feeling right now, but if they have somewhere to live, and know we are all here for them, it might help a little.'

'We can only try,' Ivy said, popping a freshly boiled egg, courtesy of their still very productive battery of hens, on a plate, with a slice of toast, for Betty.

'Thank you, and you're right. We have just got to do what we can and hope that somehow, Daisy, her mum and sisters can find a way through this horrible, horrible time.'

A few hours later, after a much shorter tram ride than usual, due to how many damaged tracks were out of use, followed by a thirty-minute walk, Ivy finally arrived at Howard Street.

'This is good of you to come all this way,' Gracie said, inviting Ivy in after she'd introduced herself at the front door.

'It's no bother. I'm hoping I might be able to offer a potential living solution to Josie and the girls.'

'Oh, yes.' Gracie nodded, leading Ivy into the warm and welcoming kitchen, which smelt of freshly baked fruit cake, no doubt in preparation for upcoming festivities.

'Please sit down and I'll get you something warm to drink. It's perishing out there.'

'Thank you,' Ivy replied, gratefully. Then in a hushed whisper, she added, 'I just keep thinking of all those poor souls who have been made homeless. I don't know why, but somehow it seems even worse in this weather and downright cruel with Christmas around the corner.'

'It really does,' Gracie agreed, in an equally sombre tone. 'I heard Josie come down in the night and found her sobbing at the table. I thought my heart would break in two.'

'Dear me. That poor woman and those poor girls. Nobody deserves the pain they are being forced to endure right now.'

As the words passed Ivy's lips, her mind flashed back to years earlier during the Great War, to when she discovered her fiancé, Lewin, had been killed, and a cold shiver shot down her spine. At the time, Ivy thought she would never recover from the paralyzing pain which had consumed her, or get through a day without spending most of it in floods of tears.

'They certainly don't,' Gracie said, pulling Ivy back to the moment. 'It really is very kind of you to offer them somewhere to live until their own house is repaired. Daisy mentioned it last night. Obviously, they are welcome to stay here, but it's a little bit cramped for them and they could do with some privacy.'

'It's no trouble at all. I've got a couple of spare rooms which I used to rent out to lodgers, but since this awful war started, I've not bothered, so they are just sat empty, collecting dust.'

'Well, I'm sure Josie and the girls are ever so grateful. Now, would you like to go in and see her?'

'If that's okay, that would be lovely.'

'Of course. I'll fetch you both a cup of tea once you're settled.'

Ivy took off her thick winter coat, hanging it over the back of the kitchen chair and popped her navy leather gloves into her handbag, before making her way into the living room.

'I'm not interrupting, am I?' Ivy gently asked, as she slowly opened the door into the dimly lit room, the blackout blinds still attached to the windows.

'Oh, hello, luv,' Josie, who was sitting on the couch, said, lifting her head from her hands. Her eyes were bloodshot red, a sharp contrast to her pale, washed-out cheeks.

'May I sit down?' Ivy asked.

'Of course. Sorry. I thought I was doing so well, but I didn't sleep and I'm struggling to think straight.'

'There's no need to explain,' Ivy replied, as she sat down next to Josie on the couch and placed her hand over the top of Josie's, which were clasped together on her knees.

The tender act of kindness caused Josie to crumble, her shoulders involuntarily caving in as they began to shake, and her whole body fell in on itself.

'You poor dear,' Ivy said, tightly enveloping Josie in her arms, as her tears flowed down her sallow cheeks. The two women stayed in the same position for the next few minutes, as Josie, who had been desperately trying to hold herself together for her daughter's sake since they had woken up, allowed her sadness, anger and frustration to pour from her.

'I'm sorry,' she gasped when she finally released herself from Ivy's arms. 'I didn't mean to get so upset.'

'Please don't apologise. My dear woman, after what you have had to deal with in the past couple of days, you would be forgiven for never lifting your head ever again.'

'I've got to think of my girls,' Josie said, taking a deep intake of breath, as she accepted the clean and neatly pressed handkerchief Ivy had produced from her pocket.

'You do' – Ivy nodded – 'but you are also allowed to have a moment to yourself. You've been through an awful lot. It's okay to succumb to tears.'

'Thank you,' Josie replied, grateful for someone to lean on.

'That's okay. I remember the pain of losing a loved one all too well.'

'You do?'

'I do, but that's a story for another day. I just wanted you to know I understand and that if you need to talk or cry, I'm happy to listen. And I also wanted to let you know, Betty's offer from last night stands. Frank and I would love to offer you and your daughters somewhere to live until your own house is repaired.'

'I don't know what to say,' Josie sighed, her voice trembling. 'Are you sure? It's so generous of you. Christmas is just around the corner. Are you sure you want us with you? We might not be much fun right now.'

'I am certain,' Ivy insisted. 'I have several empty rooms which you can put to good use. I wouldn't dream of suggesting I can ease the pain you are all suffering right now, but I can offer you a roof over your heads, and time and space you need to try and find a way through the weeks ahead.'

'I will obviously pay you rent,' Josie said, but not sure how on earth she was going to juggle the family budget without Alf's wages. It hadn't even occurred to her until that very second.

'That's not something we need to even think about at the moment,' Ivy answered, politely waving the offer away, but also acutely aware of the fierce Yorkshire pride that was intrinsic in so many Sheffield folk. 'As I said, those rooms are standing empty. They aren't costing me a penny.'

'Are you sure we won't be putting you out?' Josie repeated.

'I'm certain,' Ivy responded, with just the right balance of authority and kindness. 'Now, why don't I take you back now, and let you and the girls get settled.'

'Thank you. Daisy is just getting the girls dressed. One of Gracie's friends brought round a couple of sets of clothes for them, which was a godsend, as they only had the dresses and coats they were wearing on Sunday.'

'I might be able to collect some bits from the WVS later,

too. We have been inundated with donations. I can try and find you and Daisy some bits and bobs as well.'

'You really are very kind,' Josie said. 'I can't thank you enough.'

'There's no need. If we can't help friends and neighbours at a time like this, then there's something very wrong.'

'Well, it really does mean the world.'

'Now, that's settled, would you like me to take you all over to my house?'

'Would it be okay to go in an hour or so? Daisy has said she wants to go down to the house and try to salvage some of our belongings. I've told her she doesn't have to, but she's insisting.'

'That's incredibly brave of her,' Ivy said, worried that if Daisy saw the site where her dad had died it might be too much.

'I would rather she didn't, but I think she is assuming it will help me if she can get some of our clothes and some toys for the girls.'

'Will the authorities even let Daisy in the house? It could be dangerous.' Ivy was avoiding saying what she was really concerned about, not wanting to say the words out loud and upset Josie any further, but she didn't have to.

'I don't know if I'm honest, but I'm also worried about her seeing the remains of the bombing. It's too soon,' Josie said, her chest physically heaving at the thought.

Ivy didn't even have to think about what she said next. 'How about Frank, Betty and I go and see what we can retrieve for you? We could try and go one night this week or at the weekend. Do you think Daisy might agree to that?'

But before Josie could answer, the front-room door opened.

'Did I hear someone say my name?' Daisy asked, as she stepped inside, looking as washed out and as exhausted as her mum. 'Oh hello, Ivy. I'm sorry, I didn't realize you were here.'

'That's okay, dear,' Ivy answered, already on her feet, ready to embrace Daisy, whom she had grown rather fond of since she and Betty had built up a close friendship.

'Thank you for coming,' Daisy said, allowing Ivy to wrap her in her arms.

'I'm so very sorry,' Ivy repeated for the second time that morning.

Daisy didn't answer, not because she didn't want to. She simply couldn't find the words to express how utterly bereft she was feeling. Instead, she slowly moved her head up and down against Ivy's shoulder, tears soaking into Ivy's emerald-green cardigan.

'My poor dear girl,' Ivy responded, stroking Daisy's slender back. 'This world is far too cruel at times.'

'It really is,' Daisy whispered, lifting her head, using the back of her hand to dab her sodden cheeks. 'And I don't even think it's really sunk in yet.'

'I'm sure it hasn't,' Ivy replied. 'It's going to take time.'

'I just wish I could turn back the clock and stop Dad leaving that shelter. I know he just wanted to help, but if he'd stayed with us, he would still be here now.'

'Of course, you do,' Ivy sympathized. 'This isn't how it should be.'

'It hurts so much,' Daisy said, her voice breaking.

'Come here, luv,' Josie said, holding out her hand to her daughter, who willingly accepted her mum's offer of comfort.

'We'll find a way through this. I promise you,' Josie said, mustering up as much maternal courage as she could.

Daisy nodded, allowing her mum to wrap a protective arm around her back, as she let her head fall onto Josie's shoulder.

'Listen, luv,' Josie said kindly. 'I know you wanted to try to get some things out of the house, but I'm worried it's a bit too much.'

Daisy sat up and turned to face her mum. 'But we need some of our things. Some clothes and I think it will help Polly and Annie if they've got some toys.'

'I know. I'm not disagreeing with you, but maybe it shouldn't be you that goes. It will upset you and the last couple of days have been hard enough.'

'You can't go, Mum,' Daisy protested, as protective of Josie, as she was of her daughter.

'I know that, luv. I can't face it yet either.'

'Then, who?'

Sensing Daisy's panic, Ivy explained, 'I've offered to go. If you tell me what sort of things you would like me to collect, I'll ask Frank and Betty to help me.'

Daisy looked from her mum to Ivy. 'Are you sure? I don't want to put you out.'

'Absolutely. It's no trouble and I agree with your mum. It's too soon for you to try and go back. You need time to rest and come to terms with what's happened.'

'Thank you.' Daisy nodded appreciatively. 'I didn't want to go, but didn't want Mum to face it.'

'Well, neither of you has to. Don't give it another thought. Now, shall we gather up your sisters and make our way to my house?'

Chapter 31

Wednesday, 18 December 1940

'There's Ivy,' Frank said, as he and Betty waited outside gate three, the sharpness in the air biting at their already rosy cheeks.

'Sorry, you haven't been waiting long, have you?' Ivy asked, as Frank bent down to give her a kiss on the cheek.

'Not at all.' Betty smiled. 'Less than a minute. How have Josie, Daisy and the girls been today?'

'As you would expect. I heard Annie and Polly getting upset, asking why the angels had taken Alf. It's heart-breaking to hear.'

'Daisy woke up in her sleep a few times last night crying,' Betty said. 'I ended up getting in next to her and giving her a hug until she dropped off again.'

'Those girls are lucky to have you two,' Frank said proudly.

'And you!' Ivy praised. 'It was you who moved the spare bed into Betty's room and played several games of snakes and ladders with Polly and Annie last night, to help keep their minds busy.'

'It was nothing,' Frank replied, in his typical modest manner. 'Anyway, shall we see if we can retrieve anything from their house before it gets any darker?' It was only four o'clock but already the light was fading. 'I've borrowed a few torches from the factory.'

'Yes. Let's go and see what we can find,' Ivy said stoically, despite how anxious she felt about the job ahead.

Ten minutes later the group of three were making their way down Coleford Road, and just as Archie had warned, initially the street looked completely untarnished by the air raid, which had caused tens of thousands of people across the city to lose their homes. But with each step they took, the destruction Hitler's Luftwaffe had caused started to become evident.

'Watch that hole,' Frank said, protectively, putting his arm in front of Ivy and Betty, as the dim light of his torch revealed a giant crater spanning the pavement and half the width of the road.

'Dear me,' Ivy gasped, as they sidestepped around it.

But that was just the start. As the trio walked on and looked around them, the sight before them stopped them in their tracks. Frank had explained whole streets had been torn apart, houses demolished, and communities destroyed, but as Ivy and Betty took in the remains of the street Daisy and her family had once called home, they were utterly aghast. Instinctively, the two women reached out for one another's hands, as the piles of rubble, shards of glass and pools of stagnant water caused their chests to tighten. Farther along the obliterated road, the once-neat terraced houses, which had stood proudly shoulder to shoulder, had fallen like dominoes, and in their place left rows of oddly shaped, lopsided remains.

'I didn't know what to expect,' Ivy whispered, 'but this is far worse.'

'It is,' Betty agreed, barely able to vocalize her thoughts, overwhelmed by the sheer level of needless destruction surrounding her.

'Can you make out Daisy's house?' Frank asked, unsure how anyone would recognize their home among the wreckage.

'It's that one.' Betty pointed across the road at the still erect brick house. Most of the windows had been blown out and in front of the house were piles of stones.

'It doesn't look as bad as I was expecting,' Betty said. 'At least it's still standing.'

But as the group zigzagged across the road, avoiding an exposed gas pipe, they saw the real damage. Although the front of Daisy's home looked relatively unscathed, apart from the missing windows, the left-hand adjoining wall was completely missing, now reduced to a mountain of debris, mixed with what could only be the remains of the house next door. As Frank directed his torch to the pile, chairs, mixed with clothes, pans and what looked like a mattress, were all piled high.

'Goodness me,' Ivy sighed. 'This was someone's home a few days ago.'

'All of them,' Betty commented as she looked at the toothless street. 'Where will all these people go?'

'Rest centres or to family,' Ivy responded sadly. 'I dread to think how long it will be before their homes can be repaired or rebuilt.'

'If ever,' Frank said, shaking his head. He'd heard so many of his men tell him how their homes had been ripped apart in the last day or so. Darnall had taken a battering and with it so many lives were irrevocably changed.

As the three of them peered into Daisy's home, now resembling a doll's house, where the wall had previously stood, they could see into every room. Downstairs, in the front room, apart from the missing mantelpiece, which had come away with the wall, everything else was intact. The blue fabric sofa adorned with matching cushions, a small occasional table, holding a lamp, and even one of Annie or Polly's dollies was sitting, untouched, on the floor, next to Saturday night's paper.

'Look,' Betty said, pointing to the ceiling, where a chain of paper bunting, dust disguising its true colour, still hung.

'Dear me,' Ivy responded, shaking her head.

The kitchen revealed a similar picture. The table was still full of leftover craft paper, next to it was a teapot and two cups and saucers. On the stove sat a single pan, a lid protectively covering its contents.

The everyday image caused Ivy's eyes to glisten. 'They were just enjoying their afternoon and getting ready for

Christmas,' she whispered, her voice shaking, emotion threatening to consume her. 'Why did that awful man have to do this?'

'Come on, luv.' Frank comforted Ivy, putting his free arm around the waist of her thick winter coat. 'Let's see what we can do to make their lives a little easier.'

'Okay.' Ivy nodded, despite the fact she thought her heart would crumble, as she thought about what a terrible hand Josie and her daughters had been dealt. 'Do you think it's safe to go in?' she asked, taking a deep breath as she stared at the house.

'I'm not sure,' Frank replied cautiously. 'It might not be safe, but I could try.'

'Can I help you?' A fireman, dressed in his tell-tale navy uniform, interrupted the group.

'Hello,' Frank responded, turning to face the weary-looking man. 'This is our friend's house. We were wondering if we could retrieve a few of their belongings. They are staying with us and desperately need some clothes and a few personal items.'

'I don't mean to doubt you, pal, but how do I know you really are friends with the poor souls who live here.'

'Maybe I can help there,' Betty interjected, pulling something shiny from her bag. 'These are the keys. One of the girls who lived here is my best friend and she and her mum and sisters are staying with us until their house can be repaired.'

'You look like a trustworthy bunch, but would you

mind if I try the keys? I just need to be careful. As you can imagine, not everyone is completely honest.'

'Of course,' Betty obliged, handing over the keyring Daisy had given her before she and Frank had left for work.

'Thank you.'

The four of them made their way to the front door. Using his own torch to guide him, the fireman tried one of the keys. It fitted perfectly but as he tried to turn it, he realized he didn't have to. The door was unlocked.

'I'm not sure why folk have locks. I don't think anyone uses them, or maybe they were just in a rush to get to safety.'

'Fat lot of good that did,' Ivy retorted, uncharacteristically.

'Sorry?' the fireman asked.

'No. It's me that should be apologizing,' Ivy responded, immediately regretting her curt remark. 'It's just. Well. Dear me. I can't actually say it.'

The fireman's expression changed from confusion to sympathy, at Ivy's obvious angst.

'Our friend,' Frank took over, 'her husband didn't survive the bombing.'

'I'm so sorry,' the fireman said. 'This war has taken far too many. The sights I've seen over the last four or five days will haunt me forever.'

'Ay. I'll second that. Anyway, we should let you get

home to your own family and have a rest. Are we okay to go into the house if we're very careful?'

'Yes, we've checked it over. Take it steady and you should be fine. I'm sure you don't need me to tell you to stay away from the edges where the wall is missing.'

'We'll take extra good care,' Ivy agreed. 'We just want to collect a few personal items to help our friend, Josie, and her daughters.'

'No problem.' The firefighter nodded, before turning on his heels and raising his hand to say goodbye.

Frank opened the front door, then followed by Ivy and Betty, the three of them carefully stepped inside the eerily quiet house. The front-room door was open, the sight of the homemade, but now weather-beaten Christmas bunting making them all shudder.

'Dear me,' Ivy whispered, recalling how Josie had explained the family had decided to put up Polly and Annie's colourful paper chain early, in a bid to make this year extra special. Life really could be unbearably cruel.

'Is it mainly clothes we should take?' Frank gently asked, the enormity of the situation momentarily consuming him, as he walked through the house where only days earlier, Alf had been enjoying time with his wife and daughters.

'Yes. I think so,' Betty replied. 'Shall Ivy and I pick some things out?'

'That sounds like a plan,' Frank answered. 'But I'll

come upstairs with you. I don't want either of you falling and doing yourselves an injury.'

A minute or so later, they entered Annie and Polly's room. The heads of each of their single beds, which had once leant against a wall, were now exposed to the elements, their normally pink bedding was sodden wet from all the recent rain and covered in a thick layer of dirty black dust.

'Let's come back again this week,' Ivy said. 'We can strip these beds and I'll see if I can get those eiderdowns clean.'

'Of course,' Frank obliged, smiling, knowing Ivy wouldn't be able to rest until she had done what she could to clean up the house.

Fortunately, the girls' drawers were on the opposite of the room to the missing wall. Betty began looking through and picking out jumpers, a couple of pairs of trousers, two pinafores and several pairs of woolly tights, underwear and nightdresses. Then she spotted, on top of each bed, a rather mucky-looking dolly.

'I'll take those too,' she said, about to walk deeper into the exposed room.

'Oh no you don't,' Frank said, instinctively. 'You stay where you are. I'll get them.'

Betty and Ivy looked at one another and smiled knowingly at the protective gesture.

'Thank you,' Betty said graciously.

After leaving the girls' room, they all started towards

Josie and Alf's bedroom. Frank held back. 'It doesn't feel right, somehow,' he said, quietly, hesitant to intrude on what should have been a private space, which felt even more poignant now.

'Don't worry,' Ivy replied, already pulling open a drawer, understanding Frank's trepidation. 'Betty and I will just get a few bits for Josie.'

After filling a bag full of clothes, the three of them then ventured into Daisy's attic bedroom, where Betty repeated the task, knowing exactly what her friend would need. Just as they were about to leave, Betty noticed a framed photo at Daisy's bedside table. The black-and-white picture was of the whole family on a promenade, maybe at Cleethorpes or Blackpool. It must have been from a couple of years earlier, as Polly and Annie looked more baby-faced.

'Maybe I'll take this too. It might bring them all a bit of comfort,' Betty suggested. Then, as if doubting herself, she asked, 'Or do you think it might be too painful for them to look at?'

'Bring it, dear,' Ivy insisted. 'Take it from me, they will want it.'

Betty didn't need to ask why, instead she carefully slipped the precious memento into the cloth bag, among Daisy's clothes.

'I think that should be enough for now,' Ivy said. 'We can come back again and get anything else they need.'

With that, Frank, Ivy and Betty made their way down

the two flights of stairs, and back out the front door into the bitterly cold evening air.

'I know it won't take away their pain, but it might make things a little easier,' Ivy said, as they made their way back along Coleford Road, the devastation and destruction a painful reminder of the horror and heartache the war had inflicted on their friend and her family.

Chapter 32

'Luv, you must try and eat something,' Diane said, protesting her daughter's reluctance to touch her bowl of freshly made porridge.

'I just can't stomach it,' Hattie said, a wave of nausea making her feel woozy.

'You ungrateful little witch,' Vinny snarled, as he scraped his chair back from the table. 'Is your mother's food not good enough for you now you are married?'

Hattie glanced at her mum. Her dad had been on another one of his drunken benders the night before after the sirens started up again, and she knew it wouldn't take much for his bad mood to escalate into a full-blown explosion.

'It's . . .' But before Diane could finish her sentence, Hattie interrupted her.

'Sorry. Of course, I'll eat it,' she said, forcing a smile, keen to dissolve the situation. She lifted a spoon of the steaming breakfast to her lips, fighting back the urge to run to the outside toilet and vomit.

'I should bloody well think so too,' Vinny snapped back, pulling his coat off the hook and reluctantly picking up his gas mask, which more often than not he refused to take with him. 'I don't go out to work for you to turn down the food we put in front of yer.'

Hattie bit her lip, as Diane discreetly shook her head, forcing her daughter to swallow her mounting fury at Vinny's brazen audacity. Virtually every penny of his wages went on booze. If her mum hadn't taken the job at Vickers and Hattie wasn't contributing as much as she was, they would have all been evicted long ago. She and her mum were just grateful he hadn't found their hiding place for the extra money they put aside for bills, under a floorboard in the front room.

'Reyt,' Vinny growled. 'I'll be home later. I don't know what time, but I'll be starvin' so make sure m' tea is ready.' And with that he swung open the back door, stomped out and made sure to slam it shut.

'No doubt he's going straight to the pub again after his shift,' Hattie fumed as soon as she was sure her obnoxious dad was out of earshot.

'Don't let him upset you,' Diane said. 'It won't change anything. Now, do you think you can maybe eat a bit of something? You've got a long day ahead of you. You need something to keep you going.'

But as Hattie attempted to bring another spoonful to her lips, her mouth filled with water, and she knew she wasn't going to be able to stop the urge to be sick.

'I'm sorry,' she mumbled, jumping up and dashing to the back door. Hattie only just reached the outside loo before she dropped to her knees and vomited profusely into the basin.

Standing up, she gripped the wall, feeling shaky and lightheaded. This was the third morning in a row she'd been violently ill.

'Are you all right, luv?' Diane asked, as her daughter walked back into the kitchen.

'Just feeling a bit off. I'll be okay after another cup of tea.'

'I've just poured you a fresh one and done you a flask in case you get a chance to have a quick break at work.'

'Thanks, Mum,' Hattie replied, gratefully. 'I'm sure I'll feel better in an hour or two.'

But as much as the feeling of nausea passed by the time Hattie made her way into the canteen at dinnertime, she was still feeling out of sorts.

'I hope you don't mind me saying, duck, but you really do look rather peaky,' Dolly said, as she handed Hattie her Friday special mince pie and mash.

'It will pass. I've just been a bit off it the last couple of days.'

'Your mum said you haven't been right. Do you think you've caught a bug?'

'Probably,' Hattie sighed, taking the plate, the aroma of the cooked meal alerting her senses, and making her realize how hungry she was.

'Do you think you might need to see a doctor?'

'Maybe. If I don't feel better in a few days, I'll maybe see if I can.'

'Might not be a bad idea, duck.'

Hattie nodded as she paid for her heavily subsidized meal before making her way over to the shared table, taking a seat just as Patty was asking Betty about Daisy.

'She's done ever so well considering the circumstances and she's doing her best to keep Annie and Polly entertained. Not that they would have gone back to school just yet, what with them all being closed after the air raids, but she's trying to keep them busy.'

'If you think a change of scenery would help, I'm sure my mom would be happy to have them for a day or two,' Patty commented. 'My brother and sisters are at home too. Their school is being used as a rest centre, so the teachers are helping with that.'

'That's very kind. I'll mention it. It might do the girls good to see some other children. In between shifts at different rest centres, Ivy is playing endless games of snakes and ladders, draughts and doing jigsaws with them, but maybe a little playdate would be nice.'

'They would be welcome to come to me of a weekend too,' Nancy interjected, as she placed her knife and fork down, while she spoke. 'I can't really help in the week. Doris is already looking after my two while Bert is busy with the Home Guard, and their school is also being used as a rest centre.'

'How's he getting on?' Betty asked.

'Not too bad, like the rest of us he's tired. The sirens didn't help last night, but at least it was short-lived, and no more bombs were dropped.'

'Archie said it was just gunfire,' Patty added, taking a big gulp of her tea.

'Is he feeing any better?' Nancy asked.

'Not really,' Patty replied, shaking her head. 'He seems to have gone in on himself. Keeps saying he shouldn't have lived and that it's not fair.'

'Oh dear,' Betty sympathized. 'That's not good at all.'

'Where is he now?' Nancy asked.

'On the shop floor. He said he wants to be by himself so is having his snap up there. Frank said he would stay up there with him and have a chat, but I really don't think it will help. He doesn't seem to want to listen to anyone.'

'Poor Archie. He's always worn his heart on his sleeve,' Nancy commented. 'I know you will have told him this countless times, but no one could have predicted where those awful bombs fell.'

'I have, but I think the main thing that's upsetting him is the fact he agreed to Alf leaving the shelter.'

'I'm sure, but I doubt he could have stopped him.'

'I know. I keep telling him that but nothing I say seems to make the slightest bit of difference. I think I've just got to give him time. This chuffin' war has got a lot to answer for.'

'It has that, luv,' Nancy agreed. Then turning to Betty,

she added, 'How on earth are Josie, Daisy and those two little girls going to get through Christmas? Somehow it all feels so much worse at this time of the year.'

'I really don't know. Ivy, Frank and I had a chat last night and said we would keep it as low key as possible, but at the same time try to make it special for Polly and Annie. I'm going to go shopping tomorrow afternoon to buy them a few extra little bits. A couple of books and maybe a new doll each. I know it won't make up for what's happened, but I just want to give them a reason to smile again.'

'That's very thoughtful of you,' Nancy replied. 'I'll bring the girls a little gift too next weekend if they are up for it. I know we talked about arranging a party before the air raids, but it doesn't feel right now. I'd be very happy to have them over at some point, though.'

'I think it's just comforting for them to know we are all there for them. Now, if you will just excuse me for a minute or two, I'm going to have a word with those women at the Swap Box and check they are okay, and see if there are any clothes I can take which can be donated to the rest centres. Ivy was telling me over forty thousand people have been left homeless.'

'Before you go,' Hattie interjected, lifting her bag up, 'my mum has finished a load of knitting. She thought it might be useful for some of the poor souls whose homes have been destroyed. She asked if you could pass it all on to Ivy.'

'That's grand! Thank you. Ivy said they are crying out for donations. She will be delighted.'

'No problem and do give Daisy and Josie my love. They are constantly in my thoughts.'

'Of course, I will. You must miss Daisy in the turner's yard?'

'I do. I just hope they can all find a way through.'

'I'm sure they will, eventually.' Then turning to Nancy and Patty, Betty asked: 'I don't suppose either of you have managed to do any more knitting, have you?'

Patty shook her head sheepishly. 'Sorry. That last scarf I attempted was full of holes.'

'Don't worry.' Betty chuckled. 'Nancy?'

'I have actually. I'm just finishing a hat and I've got a few pairs of socks too. Can I bring them in tomorrow for you?'

'Of course, and thank you. We were going to send them all off to the troops but Mrs Rafferty at the WVS also suggested it would be a good idea to offer them to the people of Sheffield first. Everyone who has registered at a rest centre has been promised at least one full set of clothes each. Right, on that note, I'll be back in a jiffy.'

Betty stood up and walked the few yards to the corner of the canteen where a small group of women were chatting and looking through the box.

'Carol. How are you?' Betty asked one of the women. A year earlier Carol had been one of Betty's prolific knitters in the build-up to her winter woollies event and had constantly finished hand-made hats and socks for the troops.

'Oh. Not s' bad, luv. I can't moan after m' lucky escape last week on The Moor, but m' sister, our Vera, has had a pretty rough time of it.'

'I'm sorry to hear that,' Betty responded. 'Dare I ask why?'

'Her house was blown to flamin' bits on Sunday night.'

'Dear me,' Betty said, shaking her head. 'Has she got little ones?'

'Yes. Three bairns. They went to that rest centre at Fir Vale but I told her she couldn't stay there, especially with Christmas just around the corner, so they all moved in with me a couple of days ago. It's a bit tight with my own little blighters but we'll make do. Got no choice, have we?'

'I really am very sorry,' Betty answered. 'I know it's not much, but if there's anything that can be of some use, please take anything you need from the Swap Box.'

'Thanks, luv. I've just picked out a few jumpers for them all and a pair of trousers for our nephew, Stanley. Poor lad was in his pyjamas when they rushed to the shelter.'

'Bless them,' Betty said. 'They must feel like their lives have been turned upside down.'

'Ay. They do that, but it could have been a lot worse. At least they didn't decide to take cover at home. I can't imagine they would have made it out alive. Their house took a direct hit. It was blown to smithereens. We've got to count our blessings, haven't we?'

'Yes. We have.'

'And no matter what. We'll make Christmas special for them. One thing's for sure, I won't have to put the fire on as much. We are like sardines in my little terrace. Body heat alone is keeping us all warm.'

'That's one way of looking at it I guess.' Betty smiled.

'It's the only way. We can't let Hitler win. He might be able to knock down our houses, but he won't crush our spirit. Anyway, luv, I better get back to m' scran before it goes cold, but thanks ever so much for keeping up this Swap Box. It's been a godsend.'

And with that, Carol threw Betty an enormous smile and made her way back to her table.

Well, I never, Betty silently thought, in quiet admiration for her fellow worker. The strength of character of those faced by the most testing of circumstances never ceased to amaze her.

Chapter 33

'Thanks for meeting me,' Daisy said, as she stood up from the table at Browns to hug Betty and Hattie. 'I don't think I could have done this by myself.'

'Don't be daft,' Betty replied, wrapping her arms around her. 'This is exactly what friends are for.'

When Daisy had mentioned the night before she wanted to do a bit of Christmas shopping for her mum and sisters, but didn't think she would be able to cope alone, Betty had immediately offered to come with her as soon as she'd finished her last shift of the week. When she'd mentioned it to Hattie, she'd agreed to come along too, desperate to see how Daisy was coping.

'It's good to see you,' Hattie said, giving Daisy a hug. 'I really am so sorry about your dad. He sounded like such a wonderful man.'

'Thank you.' Daisy nodded. 'He was the best dad I could have hoped for.'

'Of course he was,' Hattie said, releasing Daisy from

her arms. 'Please just let me know if I can help with anything at all.'

'Thank you. Just being here today is a great help. I just couldn't face it alone. My mum had already done all her shopping before . . . well, you know, before.'

'It's okay.' Betty nodded, as she slipped out of her brown tweed winter coat and hung it on the back of the chair. 'We wouldn't leave you to do this by yourself.'

'Thank you. I don't know what I would do without everyone's support. You have all been so kind. I'm so grateful to you, Ivy and Frank for going to retrieve our things from the house. I really thought I'd be able to go and get them myself, but just the thought of walking down our street makes me feel sick.'

'There's absolutely no need for you to put yourself under that pressure. We were happy to nip back. I can go as many times as you need me to as well, if there's anything else you would like me to collect.'

'And I can go with Betty,' Hattie offered.

'Thank you. I do appreciate it. Maybe just a few extra clothes but that's about it. Mum said the authorities would be putting up some sort of cover to stop everything inside getting damaged.'

'That's good news. The weather is awful, so the sooner the better. And how is your mum today?' Hattie asked.

'Not great if I'm honest. I nearly didn't come but she

insisted. I found her in bed sobbing into her pillow this morning. She promised to meet me at the church later on this afternoon, though, so we can speak to the vicar about Dad's funeral.'

'Are you going to be all right?'

'I don't know, if I'm honest, but we can't put it off any longer. As much as it's the last thing I want to do, we need to arrange the funeral. I'm worried Mum might really fall to pieces. She's really not coping that well.'

'I'm so sorry.' Betty empathized. 'It's going to take time and the offer still stands. If you need me to come with you, I will.' What she didn't say was not a single night had passed without Betty waking up to hear Daisy crying in her sleep. Each time, she had quietly reached her hand over to her friend's bed, and gently placed it on Daisy's arm, until her breathing had settled, and the heart-breaking whimpers had gradually stopped.

'Thank you. I know you would, and I appreciate it. It just doesn't feel real,' Daisy added. 'I can't really believe we have got to sort out a funeral. I keep expecting to wake up and it's all been a bad dream or for Dad to walk through the door at any moment.'

'I'm sure,' Betty said. 'It's still very raw and very early days. You are all still in shock.'

'You mustn't put too much pressure on yourself,' Hattie explained.

'You're probably right, but we have to sort things out. I have no idea when we will even be able to bury Dad. I don't know how long these things take. But I have made one decision.'

'What's that?' Hattie asked.

'I spoke to Mum, and I think I'm going to come back to work straight after Christmas.'

'Really? You know how intensive the turner's yard can be. Are you sure you will feel up to it?'

'Yes. I wasn't sure at first, but it was Mum who told me I should think about it. She thinks it will do me good if I have some sort of routine and something to keep my mind busy.'

'Okay,' Betty tentatively interjected. 'But how do you feel?' Betty hoped she had managed to mask the apprehension she and Hattie were feeling. It hadn't even been a week since Alf had died. There was still a funeral to arrange, Christmas to contend with, not to mention Annie and Polly to look after.

But just as Daisy was about to answer, the smartly attired waitress appeared, holding a tray adorned with a large teapot, a milk jug, three cups and saucers and a couple of scones.

'I added an extra cup,' the waitress said. 'When I saw there are three of you.'

'Thank you,' Daisy acknowledged. 'I do appreciate it. We might order another scone, but we'll see how we get on.'

'No problem. Just call me over if you need me.'

'I didn't realize you had already ordered,' Betty said.

'I thought you might be ready for it after working all morning.'

'I definitely am. Thank you.'

Betty waited for the waitress to place everything on the table, before asking, 'Are you sure you won't find it too difficult? I would just hate you to do too much too soon.'

'I think I need to do something normal. I know I'm hardly sat with nothing to do looking after Annie and Polly, but it's not quite the same and Ivy has been so good. She insists on entertaining the girls when she isn't helping with the WVS at the rest centres. And if I'm brutally honest, money is going to be tight without Dad's wage coming in, so my pay packet will come in handy.'

Betty was momentarily stumped. She had no idea if Josie would be entitled to a widow's pension but the fact they even had to think about money at such a harrowing time felt unbelievably cruel.

'Daisy, I'm sorry,' she eventually said.

'Please, don't be. It's not your fault. I just want to do something useful. I'm hoping we can get a lot of the funeral arrangements sorted out today and I can't keep sitting around crying constantly. I'm sending myself mad. I think Mum is going to wait for the girls to go back to school before starting work again but maybe she's right, it might do me good to come back.'

'You know I'll be there for you,' Hattie said. 'And at dinnertime, you would be surrounded by friends.'

'Thank you. I do appreciate it. I'm not sure I'd be quite as strong if there wasn't a friendly face a few steps away.'

'That's what friends are for.' Hattie smiled.

Betty, who had comforted Daisy virtually every night, took a few seconds to collect her thoughts. She remembered how after her mum died, her dad had been keen to send Betty back to school in a bid to keep her routine. It had helped. It meant she wasn't sitting in a house all day under a suffocating cloud of sadness. Betty could play with her friends and although she didn't forget about her mum, she could find some relief from the overwhelming loss she felt. Then she thought about Nancy, who had reiterated, more than once, work had been her salvation when she'd been out of her mind with worry after Bert was declared missing in action.

'If things got a bit tough, we would all be there for you and if it really did feel too hard, I'm pretty sure your foreman would understand and let you go home.'

Then realizing her accidental faux pas, Betty corrected herself. 'Sorry, that was very tactless. I meant to Ivy's house.'

'Oh, Betty. You have nothing to be sorry for. Ivy has made us feel so welcome and it's probably for the best. Going back to our house, even if it wasn't so badly damaged, would be so hard. I'm pretty sure I would see Dad's image in every room, and right now, I just don't think I could cope with that.'

Daisy picked up her white napkin and raised it to her

face as her eyes began to glisten. 'Oh gosh. Here I go again. I'm afraid it doesn't seem to take much.'

'It's okay and perfectly understandable,' Betty said affectionately, pouring Daisy a cup of tea.

'I just miss him so much. He was the best dad, you know. I know everyone says that, but he was just always there. Do you know what I mean?' The words caught in Daisy's throat, preventing her from carrying on.

'I do.' Betty nodded. Although over ten years had passed, there wasn't a single day when she didn't think about her mum and wished she could feel her arms wrapped around her just once more.

'Does it get any easier?' Daisy asked, as if reading her friend's mind.

Betty took a sip from her tea before placing the delicate china cup back on its matching floral blue saucer. 'It does,' she replied kindly. 'I won't lie. It takes time but eventually instead of feeling just sadness, you start to smile at all the happy memories you shared, and they eventually become a comfort.'

'That's good to know.' Daisy nodded appreciatively, the tears which had been threatening to erupt were now receding slightly.

'Don't get me wrong, there are times I still shed many a tear for my mum. I think I always will, especially on special days, but it doesn't hurt as much. And I'm also able to smile when I remember certain moments, like when she used to place a buttercup under my chin to see if my skin turned yellow, or how she used to climb under my eiderdown with me and I'd fall asleep in the crook of her arm. Every time I smell someone wearing Lily of the Valley perfume it takes me right back to the days when Mum would dab a tiny bit on her wrists and neck and let me have a little spray too.'

'She sounded like a wonderful mum.'

'She was,' Betty agreed. 'And your dad was a truly wonderful man. I promise you, one day, so many of the memories that are making you cry now will make you smile.'

'Oh. I do hope so, because right now, every time I think of Dad, I just want to burst into tears.'

'Of course you do,' Betty said, empathetically. 'You wouldn't be human if you didn't. Besides which, as my sister used to say when I thought I would never stop crying, tears are nature's way of taking away all the pain in your chest.'

'Aw. What a wise woman. She's so right. It does hurt at first, but it helps afterwards.'

'And, eventually, you will cry less too.'

'That's good to hear. I wonder how many tears I can possibly have left.'

'Maybe coming back to work might help you a little,' Hattie suggested. 'It's not that you will forget about your dad, but you will have other things to think about too. And, as we have both said, we will be there if you need a shoulder to lean on.'

'Thank you. You really are the best of friends.' Then turning to Betty, Daisy added, 'I don't think I could have got through this last week without you.'

'And you would do exactly the same for me,' Betty replied, knowing if she was ever in need, she wouldn't have to think twice about who to turn to.

Across town, Ivy was gently directing Polly and Annie on how to put just enough homemade mincemeat into each carefully rolled-out pastry case.

'Just a teaspoonful in each one,' Ivy said. 'And then pop a pastry star on top.'

'Like this?' Annie asked, distributing a small amount of the glossy, brandy-infused mixture into one of the delicate little compartments.

'Perfect,' Ivy praised. 'And once they have cooked you can both have one each and be my official tasters.'

The girls' eyes lit up at the thought of each receiving a delicious treat.

'And then I need a new angel for the top of the Christmas tree. If I bring out my craft box, do you think you could have a go at making one for me?'

Annie and Polly looked at one another, as if to check the other agreed, before nodding enthusiastically.

'They will like that,' Josie said, as she joined Ivy and her daughters in the warm kitchen, which emanated a plethora of Christmas-imbued scents, from cinnamon to nutmeg to the comforting smell of freshly baked biscuits.

'Well, I'm grateful to have such willing assistants. They have been so helpful. I've managed to get through far more than I would have done normally.'

Josie wasn't daft. She knew Ivy was being kind, but she truly appreciated the thoughtful sentiments, especially when she considered the unimaginable task she had to face in a few hours' time. She still wasn't sure how she was going to sit and talk to a vicar about the type of church service she wanted for her husband, who a week ago had still been alive and looking forward to a family Christmas. How on earth was she supposed to protect her children from the heart-wrenching task of saying goodbye to the man they had all loved with every fibre of their souls? Her daughters might have shown far more resilience and courage than she'd been able to muster, but there had still been plenty of tears, particularly at bedtime, when Alf would have normally tucked Annie and Polly under their eiderdowns, kissing each one of them in turn on their foreheads, never failing to say, 'Sweet dreams. I love you to the moon and back.'

'Is there anything I can do to help?' Josie asked, feeling guilty that she had spent most of the morning in her newly adopted bedroom, desperately trying to stem her flow of tears.

'Would you be happy to slice up some of that bread? It should have cooled down enough by now,' Ivy asked, implicitly understanding Josie wanted to be useful and keep herself busy.

'Of course.' And as Josie started the task, she added: 'I meant to say, I can nip to the shops this afternoon on my way to the church. I haven't used any of our rations since we've been here, and I can't expect you to keep feeding us all. We'll eat you out of house and home at this rate.'

Leaving Polly and Annie to continue making the festive treats, Ivy joined Josie at the other side of the kitchen.

'If you feel up to shopping, then that would be grand, but please don't feel you have to. Our autumn harvest from the garden means we have a pantry full of chutneys and I have enough potatoes to keep me going for months yet. And the hens are still producing plenty of eggs too, so we won't go hungry just yet.'

'But there are four of us,' Josie highlighted.

'There are,' Ivy replied, 'but you and Daisy have barely eaten a thing since you've been here, and the girls eat such small portions. Besides which,' Ivy continued, quickly glancing over to her youngest house guests, 'they are more than earning their keep.' She was keen to avoid the topic of money and food, knowing Josie had more than enough to contend with. If she couldn't help out a friend in need at the most testing time of her life, there was something very wrong.

'I must admit I'm struggling to eat. My appetite has completely vanished and even when I try to have something, I can't actually swallow it.'

Despite the decades that had passed, Ivy remembered

all too well how grief caused your body to shut down, responding physically as well as emotionally to the shock.

'Do you think you could manage a small bowl of soup?' Ivy asked gently. 'It might feel a little gentler on your tummy.'

'Thank you.' Josie nodded gratefully. She wasn't hungry, but Josie knew she had to try to keep up her strength for her daughters' sakes. They needed her more than ever and she couldn't let them down. As Josie watched Polly and Annie smile at one another as they diligently filled the pastry cases, she wished she had even an ounce of their strength. They had been a million times braver than she had, getting up each morning and facing the day ahead. It took all Josie's determination just to open her eyes, as she prayed the last week had been nothing more than a cruel nightmare.

'I've got some broth left over from yesterday. I'll heat some up.' It might have been thinner than what she made before the war, and had substantially less meat in, but it was still full of goodness, courtesy of the generous portion of vegetables she had finely chopped and added into the mixture, and might just give Josie a little bit of much-needed energy.

'That sounds lovely,' Josie said, as she smeared a thin layer of jam onto two slices of bread, before turning them into sandwiches.

'Finished,' Polly announced proudly, showing off the baking tin.

'Perfect.' Ivy applauded. 'They look wonderful. You have made a much better job of them than I would have. Why don't you have your lunch, which your mum has just finished making, then I will get the craft box out. And then if we have time while your mum nips out, we can have another go at knitting.'

'Yes, please.' Annie beamed. 'Do you think I could get mine done in time?'

'I'm sure,' Ivy replied, then discreetly raised her finger to her lips.

Josie looked at her youngest daughter quizzically but sensing this was something she wasn't meant to ask questions about, she simply placed the sandwiches, which she had cut into neat triangles, on two side plates and encouraged the girls to come and sit at the kitchen table.

Determined not to let them see her struggle, Josie waited for Annie and Polly to be finished, and had gone off to start making a Christmas angel in the dining room, before she attempted to start her own dinner.

'I hate them seeing me like this,' Josie sighed, as she sat down in front of small bowl of warm soup. 'Losing their dad is hard enough without seeing their mum fall to bits too.'

'You must try not to be so hard on yourself,' Ivy said. 'You are doing just fine, and the girls are doing wonderfully under the circumstances. They don't expect you to be acting as if nothing's happened. That would seem very odd to them too.'

'Do you really think so?'

'Yes. I do. I'm not saying they should see you when you are feeling at your most anguished, but they also know you are very sad, and that's okay. They have to know it's all right to cry, otherwise they won't feel able to release their emotions either.'

'Thanks, Ivy. I hadn't thought about it like that. I just want them to know I'm here for them. I've got to be their mum and dad now.'

'They know that,' Ivy encouraged. 'You will always be their mum. It's you they want to cuddle when they get upset and as for being their dad too, there's no rules. Things will just happen naturally. And don't forget, as Frank and I keep saying, you don't have to do any of this alone. We will be here for you every step of the way.'

'Thank you. You are both so kind. I don't know what we'd have done without you.'

'You don't have to thank me, dear. I have no doubt you would do the same if the shoe was on the other foot. Now, I hate to bring it up, but is there anything I can do to help you with your appointment with the vicar or the funeral arrangements?'

Josie's eyes glistened once again, the reality of the impending task consuming her. 'I don't know, if I'm honest. I've let Alf's brother know and said I would be in touch again this weekend. I suppose it depends on what date the vicar says we can have the service. I don't know whether it's better or worse to have it before Christmas.'

'I don't think there's a right or wrong, but whatever he says, please know we will be there for you.'

'Thank you. It just doesn't seem real. We should be planning Christmas with the girls, but instead I've got to arrange Alf's funeral.'

The words acted as a catalyst and Josie couldn't hold back the flood of tears any longer. Dropping her hand into shaking hands, she sobbed.

Ivy was immediately on her feet. 'It's okay,' she soothed, wrapping her arms around Josie's shaking body, and letting her cry into her chest, knowing there weren't any words that would alleviate Josie's pain. The two women stayed in the same position for the next ten minutes; Ivy stroking her friend's back while rivulets of tears fell down Josie's sodden pink cheeks.

'I'm sorry,' she whispered, finally lifting herself up. 'I vowed I wasn't going to cry again today.'

'Well, take it from me, there is no point making promises like that. You cry as much as you need to. Keeping it all locked in will do you no good at all.'

'Will it get easier?'

'Yes. I assure you it does, but it takes times. Love is the greatest gift, but it comes at a price and sadly is the hardest loss too.'

'You're not wrong there,' Josie replied, lifting a handkerchief from her pocket, and dabbing her cheeks. 'No one ever tells you it's going to be this hard, do they?'

'No. But I guess even if they did, we would never fully

appreciate it. And, as I learnt to understand, no matter how hard it feels right now, it's better to have loved and lost, than never loved at all.'

'I wouldn't change my life with Alf for the world.'

'I'm sure you wouldn't, and remember, no one can ever take those memories away from you.'

'Thank you, Ivy. I needed to hear that.'

'As I keep saying, you have nothing to thank me for.'

'I suppose I better go and wash my face and go and meet Daisy,' Josie said, as she stood up. 'I promised her I wouldn't be late, and I can't let her speak to the vicar alone.'

'Of course. And don't worry about Annie and Polly. I will keep them entertained all afternoon. We have lots of little jobs to get through.'

Chapter 34

Two days after going to see the vicar, Josie gripped her youngest daughters' hands as they stood either side of her, each of them dressed in black, and turned to Daisy, who was bravely fighting back her emotions, desperately trying to remain stoic and firm for her mum and sisters.

'We're going to be okay,' Josie whispered as they passed through the gates into the grounds of Darnall Parish Church.

Not daring to speak in case her fortitude faltered, Daisy simply nodded. She clasped Polly's hand, and followed her mum and Annie up the steps, which had been cleared of the snow that had fallen heavily through the night, and into the old stone-built building. As they slowly walked down the central aisle, avoiding the buckets which were collecting water from the melting snow dripping from the holes in the roof, another casualty of the Luftwaffe's indiscriminate air raids, Josie and Daisy were only semi-aware of the dozens of sympathetic eyes watching them. Taking their places on a cold wooden pew at the front of the church, Josie still couldn't comprehend how she was supposed to say her final goodbye to the only man she had ever truly loved. But there in front of her, on a stand, was Alf's coffin. It took every ounce of restraint to stop herself running over to the oblong box and ripping off the lid, just so she could hold her husband in her arms once more.

The vicar, Father David, began talking, but despite his strong, clear voice, Josie and Daisy only managed to take in snippets of what he was saying.

'We are here today to celebrate the life of Alf Smith, who was sadly taken from us . . .'

Josie, Daisy, Annie and Polly all squeezed each other's hands a little bit tighter as the vicar continued his thoughtfully prepared eulogy. In between poignant anecdotes about the wonderful father and husband Alf had been, they joined the congregation in prayers and hymns, all of which had been chosen by Josie and Daisy, in a haze of overwhelming grief. Neither of them could have said how long the service lasted, but after what could have been twenty minutes or an hour, they were being ushered into the churchyard. A fresh scattering of snow gently fluttered from the sky, as Josie and Alf's immediate family gathered around the grave, each of them weeping as the coffin was carefully lowered into the ground.

'Mummy,' Annie cried.

'It's okay, sweetheart,' Josie said, protectively pulling her daughter closer towards her. 'The angels are looking after Daddy now.'

Consumed with grief, the family allowed themselves to be ushered into the church hall, where most of the people who had attended the service were waiting.

'Thank you for coming,' Josie repeatedly said, almost robotically, to the scores of mourners, made up of close family, friends and work colleagues from Tinsley pit.

'How are you, dear?' Ivy said, handing Josie a small glass of brandy.

'I don't really know. Numb, I suppose. It feels like I'm not really here, as though I'm watching the whole thing from above. Does that make sense?'

'It does, but be very proud. You held yourself and those girls together with such dignity and strength.'

'I couldn't fall apart. Not today. They needed me to stay strong.'

'Remember you are allowed to feel sad too,' Ivy said gently.

'I know. I do and I'm sure I will fall apart later when Annie and Polly are tucked up in bed.'

'Just do what you have to do.'

'Thank you and thank you for sorting all of this,' Josie said, glancing around the room at the tables adorned with an array of simple sandwiches and scones.

'Well, I can't take all the credit. Dolly and Diane, along with my friend Winnie, all helped.'

'Hello, luv,' interrupted a familiar voice.

'How are you?' asked another.

'Dolly. Diane. Thank you both so much for coming

and for helping with the food. I really am very grateful. How on earth did you all get the day off work?'

'Not at all, duck,' Dolly replied, wrapping Josie in her arms. 'And don't you mention it. Frank pulled some strings. As for the food, it was the very least we could do. I'm just so sorry. Your Alf was one of life's good 'uns.'

'He was,' Josie agreed, tears threatening to emerge as her voice showed the first hint of breaking. 'I always knew I was lucky to have him. I just never really realized how much, yer know?'

'I do, duck.'

'No one can ever take those memories away from you,' Diane reassured Josie. 'They will always be yours to cherish.'

'Thanks, luv. You're right.'

Across the room, Daisy was also surrounded by her friends from Vickers.

'How are you?' Hattie asked tentatively. The last time she had been in the same church was just over two months earlier when she and John had married.

'I'm getting there. I think we needed to get today done. The last few days have been horrible just imagining what the funeral would be like.'

'It was a lovely service,' Betty commented. 'The vicar said some wonderful things about your dad.'

'Did he? I hardly took in a word. I was trying so hard to stay strong for Mum and my sisters.'

'It was very fitting,' Betty assured her friend.

'I know it sounds awful, I'm just glad it's over. I've been dreading it and it's probably better it was before Christmas. Not that it makes losing Dad any easier, it's just, I don't know, one less thing to worry about. I'm not explaining myself very well, am I?'

'You are and I know exactly what you mean,' Betty replied, handing Daisy a steaming cup of tea. 'There is something a little stronger if you'd prefer?'

'No, this is perfect. I'm so tired and it was freezing outside. I feel chilled to the bone.'

Over the next half an hour, Daisy was besieged with friends and distant relatives, offering their heartfelt condolences.

'Are you coping okay?' Patty asked, when she finally got a chance to talk to Daisy. 'I really am so sorry. I've been thinking about you so much.'

'Thank you. I'm doing as well as can be expected. How's Archie? Betty explained he's been struggling.'

'Not so great if I'm honest,' Patty answered, slightly turning her head to indicate where Archie was sitting on a chair, pale faced, his head laying heavily in his hands. 'He's not so good. He keeps blaming himself.'

'No, he mustn't do that,' Daisy sighed. 'None of this is Archie's fault. He is not responsible for the actions of that godforsaken man.'

'I know. I've told him the same, but he won't listen.'

'What's that?' Josie asked, approaching the group.

'Oh. It's nothing,' Patty quickly responded, not wanting

to add to Josie's worries and suddenly feeling guilty for mentioning Archie at all.

'It didn't sound like nothing to me.'

Patty looked at Daisy, unsure what to say next.

Sensing how uncertain her friend felt, Daisy told her mum, 'Archie is blaming himself for Dad.'

'He really shouldn't do that,' Josie sighed. 'Alf was his own man and knew his own mind.'

'I think he just feels as the warden on duty he should have protected Alf. I really am so sorry, Josie. Your husband was a wonderful man.'

'He was,' Josie replied, thanking Patty, the smallest hint of a smile appearing on her drawn face, as she acknowledged what a tremendous man Alf had been. Those thoughts, instead of paralyzing her, gave Josie the smallest hint of strength. 'And he would be so upset, let alone cross, if he knew Archie was blaming himself. There's been enough sadness over the last ten days.'

'I'll try to speak to him again,' Patty offered.

'Actually, luv. Do you think I could have a chat with Archie? I know he tried his best to rescue Alf and I would like to thank him.'

Patty was momentarily stuck for words. The last thing she'd intended to do on the day of Alf's funeral was to give Josie something else to contend with.

Sensing Patty's trepidation, Josie added, 'I really would like to, and it seems fitting I do it today. It's what Alf would want me to do.'

'Only if you're sure?' Patty said, truly hoping she wasn't about to cause Daisy's mum any further anguish.

With the first sense of purpose she had felt since losing her husband, Josie made her way over to where Archie was and sat down on the chair next to him.

'Mrs Smith,' Archie said, surprised to see Josie joining him.

'It's Josie, you should know that by now.'

'I wanted to say how very sorry I was about Alf. And . . .'

'You don't have to say another thing,' Josie said, stopping him.

'But I should have told Alf to stay in the shelter. It was my job to protect him.'

This time, Josie allowed Archie to finish, seeing how much he needed to say the words which were clearly ripping him apart.

'I should have insisted he stay with you and the girls. That way, well, you wouldn't. I mean, he would still be with us. I really am so sorry.' Archie looked at Josie, then pulled his hands to his face, unable to cope with seeing the pain he'd caused, as well as trying to hide the fact his eyes were brimming with heavy, guilt-ridden tears.

'Archie, luv,' Josie said softly, placing one of her hands on Archie's knee, hoping the well-intentioned gesture would help him realize she felt no malice or anger towards him. 'Do you really think you could have stopped my Alf?'

Archie dropped his fingers from his eyes and turned to face Josie.

'I should have tried. I should have found a way.'

'And how do you think you could have managed that?'

'What do you mean? I should have just said no.'

'Archie,' Josie said kindly, but firmly. 'My husband was forty-five years old. He was the kindest man I knew and with that came a fierce and unyielding determination to help people. He felt bad enough that he couldn't go off to war like so many of his friends. There was no way he was going to sit in that shelter when bombs were going off around him and not do a single thing. I didn't want him to do what he did either, and believe me, I've asked myself a million times since that night, why I didn't try and put up a bigger fight to stop him. But the truth of the matter is, I couldn't have stopped him, and neither could you.'

Taken aback, Archie looked at Josie, dumbfounded. He'd assumed she would be angry at him, would blame him for her husband's death, but instead, despite the utterly harrowing loss she and her daughters had suffered, Josie was being kind to him. Telling him he wasn't responsible.

'I could have insisted he went back when the other men did.'

'Maybe you could have,' Josie conceded. 'But he was a grown man, old enough to make his own decisions. From what I've been told, he went back to the warden's shelter to check what else he could do to help. As I've already said, you couldn't have stopped him doing that. I know my husband, and he would have felt that was the least he could do.'

'He was so brave,' Archie said. 'The way he helped that trapped family was amazing. He was so calm and logical. I don't know if we would have got them out without him.'

Josie's eyes glistened at the thought of her husband selflessly risking his own life to save that of someone else, knowing this was one of the many reasons she had loved him with all her heart.

'I guess all his years down the pit taught him a lot,' Josie acknowledged.

'He was a hero that night,' Archie said, swallowing back the pain of watching the air-raid warden's building ignite into flames and crumble.

'He was,' Josie agreed, pinching her eyes together to fight back the tears, conscious her youngest daughters weren't far away. 'I'm sorry you had to witness what you did,' she added. 'I know you tried to go into that burning building, which was very brave, but for what it's worth, I'm glad you didn't.'

'But, I might have been able to . . .'

'No,' Josie said authoritatively. 'From what I've been told, you wouldn't have been able to save anyone, and there's a good chance that it wouldn't just be Alf's funeral we would have all been attending. And no matter what you think, it was not worth sacrificing your life for.'

Archie was once again left lost for words. How could Josie be so forgiving?

'This war is creating enough sadness. Nothing good will come of adding to that. I'm glad you didn't go into that building. And as much as I would do anything at all to have Alf back, I know in my heart, that he died being the man he'd always been.'

'Okay,' was all Archie could manage.

'Now, I'm not saying it takes away the pain. I'm not sure I will ever stop hurting and it will take you a long time to recover from the events of that night, but promise me, you will stop blaming yourself.'

'I'll try,' Archie whispered, overwhelmed by Josie's kindness and astonishing fortitude.

'Good,' Josie replied, and before Archie could respond, she wrapped her arms around him. 'And thank you for doing everything you possibly could. Like Alf, you are a very brave and courageous man.'

Chapter 35

'Mummy,' Annie whispered, gently rubbing Josie's arm. 'Wake up. It's Christmas Day.'

Josie forced her eyes open. She'd barely slept a wink. She and Daisy had spent the night before filling Annie and Polly's pillowcase stockings and placing their main gift under the tree in Ivy's front room. Once Daisy had gone up to bed, Josie had done exactly the same for her eldest daughter, before bringing a cup of cocoa up to bed. But no matter how hard she'd tried, sleep evaded her. Josie had seen every hour as she'd remembered Christmases past with Alf and wished with all her heart he was by her side to celebrate this year too. It didn't seem conceivable that two days earlier Josie had said her final goodbyes and buried her husband.

'Are you awake?' Polly asked quietly.

'I am, sweetheart.' Josie lifted herself up on the bed, painting on her bravest smile, knowing Alf would want her to try and make the day as special as possible for the girls.

'Come here,' she said, gesturing for her youngest daughters to climb into bed with her.

'We brought our stockings,' Annie said, lifting up the white pillowcase Ivy had donated for the occasion.

'I said we couldn't open them until you and Daisy were awake,' Polly said.

It had always been a family tradition to open their stockings as a family all snuggled up in bed together on Christmas morning.

Josie looked at the little clock next to her bed. It was half past seven. 'I'm sure Daisy will join us very soon.'

'Did I hear my name?'

All three faces turned towards the bedroom door, where Daisy was peeking her head around.

'Daisy! Come and get into bed with us,' Annie said, beckoning enthusiastically.

'Okay,' Daisy replied, stifling a yawn, as she discreetly glanced at her mum. Like Josie, she'd struggled to drop off. The idea of Christmas Day without her dad felt inconceivable. But before she and her mum had kissed goodnight, they had promised to try and remain strong for her little sisters. They'd suffered so much already and although they were expecting tears from Annie and Polly at some point throughout the day, they were going to do their best to make Christmas as nice as possible under the circumstances.

With all four of them tucked under the eiderdown, Josie encouraged her youngest daughters to open their stockings. As always, each one contained a couple of pennies, a handful of nuts and a small gift each.

'I got a new book,' Annie cheered, as she unwrapped the copy of *Swallows and Amazons*.

'Me too.' Polly grinned, as she held up her copy of *Thimble Summer*.

'Father Christmas knows you both well,' Josie said, taking pleasure in seeing how happy her little girls looked.

'What did he bring you, Daisy?' Polly asked.

Daisy lifted her gift out of the makeshift stocking and gently peeled away the brown paper which had been tied with string, to reveal a beautiful blue satin neck scarf.

'It looks like Father Christmas knows me very well too,' Daisy commented, throwing her mum a grateful smile.

'And what about you, Mummy?' Annie asked.

As Josie lifted out her gift, Daisy silently prayed she'd made the right decision when she, Betty and Hattie had gone shopping at the weekend.

'Oh,' Josie gasped as she looked at the gift, her eyes ever so slightly glistening at the sight of her and Alf on their wedding day.

'It's the photo from our living room,' Polly said.

'Yes. In a lovely new frame.' Josie put her free hand under the bed covers and squeezed that of her eldest daughter's. 'Father Christmas must have realized how much I was missing this picture. I have always treasured it.'

All their gifts open, Josie pulled her three daughters closer towards her. 'Happy Christmas, girls,' she said.

'Merry Christmas, Mummy,' Annie and Polly said in unison.

'Now, girls,' Josie said, taking a deep breath. 'I know today is going to feel a bit strange. We aren't in our own house and your daddy isn't here, but he would want us all to try and have a nice day. Do you think we can do that?'

'Do you think Daddy will get his presents in heaven?' Annie asked, full of concern and sadness.

Josie had suspected there would be questions. 'Yes. And he will get to have chicken and vegetables and I'm sure there will be mince pies too.'

'What about the presents me and Polly made for him and left under the Christmas tree? We drew him some pictures and Ivy helped us wrap them up.'

'I'm sure Father Christmas will have delivered them,' Josie said confidently. After Ivy had told Josie about the presents, she and Daisy had spotted the gifts after the girls had gone to bed and retrieved them. They had carefully opened them to discover two colourful pictures of four of them. Both Josie and Daisy had thought their hearts would break as they looked at Annie's pencil drawing of them all in front of a Christmas tree, while Polly's showed them all making a snowman.

'He can put them next to his bed.' Annie smiled, happy in the knowledge the gifts had been safely delivered.

Twenty minutes later, dressed and hair brushed, Josie

led her daughters downstairs and into the kitchen which was emanating a mixture of tempting smells.

'Good morning,' Ivy warmly greeted her guests.

'You must have smelt the bacon.' Frank grinned, taking it in turns to hug Josie and Daisy, before gently ruffling Annie's and Polly's hair.

'Oh, you didn't have to do that for us,' Josie said.

'Nonsense! If we can't have a cooked breakfast on Christmas morning, then there's something very wrong.'

'Thank you,' Josie said appreciatively. 'At least let me make a pot of tea.'

Ivy joined Josie at the range, while the girls sat at the table, where Daisy was pouring them each a glass of milk from the jug.

'Are you okay?' Ivy whispered.

Josie nodded, more on auto-pilot than out of conviction. 'I will be. I just need to get through today for the girls' sake.'

'And you will. But if it all gets a bit tough, you know where I am.'

'I do. Thank you.'

The rest of the morning passed in a flurry of activity. After a hearty breakfast, which she barely touched, Josie truly appreciated the effort Ivy and Frank had made and took comfort in seeing her youngest daughters' enjoyment. Afterwards the now extended household all moved into the front room and opened the array of presents under the beautifully adorned Christmas tree.

Frank insisted on playing Father Christmas, handing out the neatly wrapped packages. Annie and Polly's eyes lit up when they discovered they had both received a new doll each, and hugged Ivy when she presented them with identical navy-blue dresses, entwined with intricate red stitching around the Peter Pan collar and buttoned cuffs.

'That was very kind of you,' Josie thanked Ivy, knowing how delighted her daughters would be with new outfits.

'And these are off me,' Frank said, handing over two rectangular boxes. 'But I confess, I may have received a little bit of help.'

When the girls carefully opened their boxes wrapped in brown paper and red ribbon, they grinned and picked out the navy patent leather Mary Jane–style shoes.

'Oh girls,' Josie gasped. 'You will both look a picture.'

'And this is for you, dear,' Ivy said, passing Josie a soft parcel.

As Josie opened the gift, she smiled gratefully at the chunky cable-knit cardigan.

'It's just a little something to keep you warm.'

'It's so kind. Thank you. It's so bitter at the moment, this is ideal,' Josie said, thankful for Ivy's thoughtfulness.

'I'm just happy you like it.' Then turning to Daisy, she passed an equally neatly wrapped gift.

'Oh, thank you.' Daisy smiled, as she held up the beautiful black leather gloves. 'They are perfect.'

'Now,' Frank said, 'I've got something a little special for you all.'

'You've given us enough,' Josie protested.

'These aren't from myself or Ivy,' Frank explained, picking up four wrapped gifts. 'They are from Alf,' he added softy.

A look of understandable confusion came over Josie.

'He bought them a few weeks ago,' Ivy explained. What she didn't expand on was Frank had found them when he'd nipped back to the house to collect more of the family's belongings.

Daisy instinctively gripped her mum's hand, as Frank placed the quartet of presents down in front of them.

'Isn't your daddy very clever,' Josie managed to whisper, turning to Polly and Annie, who looked equally as puzzled.

Carefully the family each opened their labelled presents.

'Oh, Alf,' Josie choked, as she opened the lid of a square jewellery box to reveal a delicate silver chain.

'Mummy,' Polly said, as she and Annie discovered a matching bangle, and Daisy's eyes filled with tears, as she carefully fingered the elegant silver bracelet her dad had chosen for her.

Biting down on her lip, Daisy pulled her three daughters close. 'Now when we wear our lovely presents, we know your daddy is always with us.'

'I will treasure my bracelet forever,' Annie answered, her gentle voice breaking.

'Me too,' Polly echoed, as she held the shiny, polished silver bangle in her hands. 'I'm going to call it Daddy's bracelet.'

'Your daddy would love that.' Josie nodded, swallowing back the overwhelming grief that was coursing through her, as she imagined Alf secretly saving up to buy them all something special.

'Thank you,' Josie mouthed to Frank, once again eternally grateful for the thoughtfulness he and Ivy had bestowed upon her family.

In return Frank nodded, thankful the gifts he'd found at the back of Alf's bedside drawers had brought the comfort Ivy had assured him they would.

After a fresh cup of tea, the exchanging of presents continued, until there were only a couple of presents left under the tree, labelled to Betty's dad and brother, who for the second year would be joining them for Christmas lunch.

Betty had bought Daisy some new rouge and a lipstick, and in return Daisy had given her friend a pair of pearl-effect hair slides. Ivy had treated Frank to a new smart shirt and some much-needed gardening gloves, while Daisy had bought her mum a pot of face cream and treated her little sisters to a craft set each, as well as a new headband that would perfectly complement their new outfits. William had sent Betty a delicate pair of beautiful gold loop earrings, with a note saying he was sorry he couldn't be there for Christmas but hoped he would get some leave very soon. She would have loved to have seen her fiancé but knew how lucky she was to be surrounded by people who loved her. The fact

William was alive and for the moment still safe was the greatest gift.

The rest of the day passed in a haze for Josie, as she went through the motions knowing her daughters needed her to be strong. What she really wanted to do was go and hide under her eiderdown, but she knew there would be plenty of time for that once the day's celebrations finally came to an end. So instead, she watched Annie and Polly laugh and play, their remarkable resilience galvanizing her, giving her just enough strength to be the strong one when her daughters had their quiet moments, spurring them on with a reassuring cuddle. As ever, Frank was on constant alert, keeping Polly and Annie's spirits high, insisting on playing games, serving up an extra portion of sherry trifle and going on an egg hunt, to make sure they had breakfast tomorrow.

At nine o'clock, after Betty's brother and dad had gone home, and Annie and Polly were snugly tucked up into bed, their brand-new dollies next to them, Josie announced she would turn in too.

'I think I will too.' Daisy yawned, emotionally exhausted.

'Actually, I'll come up too,' Betty added. What she didn't say, not wanting to upset Daisy or Josie, is that she would write William a letter, thanking him for her lovely gift.

As Josie and Daisy went to part on the landing, they hugged tightly.

'Would you like me to snuggle in with you for a bit?' Daisy asked.

'Oh, luv, you don't have to do that.'

'I'd like to.' Daisy knew how hard her mum had worked to keep it together all day and sensed more than anything, like herself, she just wanted to be close to someone she loved.

'That would be lovely,' Josie conceded. 'Thank you.'

Betty quietly tiptoed off to her bedroom, as Daisy made her way into her mum's room, their arms tightly wrapped around one another.

Please let them find some peace in sleep, Betty silently thought, suspecting she wouldn't see her best friend until the morning.

After getting changed into her nightdress, Betty climbed into bed, her writing pad and pen in hand. There was only one person she would rather be with right now.

My Dearest William,
Merry Christmas! I hope you have managed to enjoy your day, although I realize it's not quite the same when you are away. Did you get a dinner and manage some downtime? I do hope so. I should imagine you won't be very happy if you haven't had a hearty meal and a mince pie.

Thank you so much for my beautiful earrings. They are just perfect, and I will treasure them forever. I have had them on all day and every time I touched them, it was as though you were here next to me. I hope my gift got to you on time.

Today has gone as well as it possibly could do, under the circumstances. Josie and Daisy have been ever so strong, but I could tell they were just putting on a brave face for Annie and Polly. I wish I could take their pain away and bring Alf back, but I know that's not possible. Despite their young age, the girls are so resilient. Their strength astounds me. I'm just glad they managed to enjoy the day.

Now, I know you don't like me to fret, but please stay safe, William. I know you will take care, but this war seems to be stepping up a level and I can't help but worry about you. Just promise me, you will look after yourself.

I can't wait to see you again. I miss you so much and you are forever in my thoughts. I hope it's not too long before we can see one another again.

Okay, I will sign off now, as it's late and my eyes are starting to close.

I love you so much, now and forever.

Betty xxx

As Betty placed the missive in an envelope, she held it to her chest as she fell into a deep sleep, hoping beyond hope this war wouldn't cause any of them any more pain.

Downstairs, Frank poured himself and Ivy a small spooner of brandy each and came and sat next to her on the couch, the last of the fire offering a warm glow to the room.

'What a day,' Ivy sighed, taking a grateful sip of her nightcap. 'Josie did so well. Today must have felt like torture for her. It just shows the inner strength we all have when we need it, and those girls are a credit to her. They have been so brave.'

'They certainly have,' Frank agreed. 'It can't have been easy for any of them, but I reckon Alf would have been proud of each one of his girls today.'

Ivy rested her head on Frank's shoulder. 'I think you're right. I just wish I could make the agony they are feeling go away, but I know it's going to take time. I just hope one day they can smile instead of cry at all the happy memories they shared with Alf.'

'I think they will. It might not be tomorrow or next week, or even next month, but it will come with time.' Frank knew first-hand what a long and complex thing grief could be. 'But they are lucky to have you. You have helped them all so much.'

'As have you,' Ivy said, reciprocating the compliment. 'You are a natural with Annie and Polly. They clearly adore you and I can see how Daisy looks upon you as someone she can rely on.'

'Ah well. I'm just happy to help. Anyway, I'm sorry. I didn't mean to bring the mood down. There is actually something I'd like to ask you.'

'Fire away,' Ivy replied, intrigued.

Frank fidgeted slightly and took another sip of his brandy. 'This war and particularly the last few weeks have made me realize how fragile life is.'

Ivy lifted her head from Frank's shoulder and turned to face him. She'd never seen him look so serious.

'Are you okay?' she asked tenderly.

'Yes. Yes. It's just, well, I suppose it's just made me realize how much you mean to me, and the fact I want to spend the rest of our years together.'

'Oh, Frank. I promise I'm not going anywhere. We make rather a good team, don't we?'

'That's what I'm trying to say. I want us always to be together.'

Ivy looked at Frank, not entirely certain what he was hinting at, but felt a strange sensation tingle through her.

'What I'm asking,' Frank continued, placing his glass on the coffee table, before reaching into his trousers pocket and pulling out a small red velvet box, and flicking it open, 'is, will you marry me?'

Ivy was momentarily speechless as she gazed down at the gold and emerald ring. A proposal was the last thing she'd been expecting.

'Frank,' she finally whispered, her eyes shining.

'Just tell me you would do me the honour of being my wife, Ivy. I love you with all my heart and don't want to spend the rest of my life without you by my side.'

With that, the tears which had been forming in the corner of Ivy's eyes now slowly trickled down her cheeks.

'Yes. Yes, Frank. Nothing would make me happier.'

'Thank the Lord for that. I had a horrible feeling for a second then you were going to turn me down.'

'No. Of course not. You just took me by surprise, that's all. I promise, the thought of becoming your wife really is the most perfect Christmas present. The time we have spent together has been some of the happiest of my life. You really have given me something to smile about again.'

'I feel the same. For a long time, I never thought I would be happy again, but, Ivy, you have made life feel worthwhile.'

'Oh, Frank.' Ivy dabbed her eyes with a pristine white handkerchief, which she pulled out from under her sleeve. 'You'll set me off again, but I promise they are tears of joy.'

'Thank goodness for that!' Frank teased, before adding, 'I have been holding out to ask you all day. It didn't seem appropriate this morning, so I was waiting for a quiet moment just the two of us.'

'I couldn't wish for a more perfect ending to the day.'

With that Frank removed the ring from the box, and placed it onto Ivy's finger with ease, before gently pulling her close and tenderly kissing her on the lips, the pair melting into one another. After they pulled apart several seconds later, Frank lifted up both their glasses from the table. 'I think this deserves a toast, don't you?'

'Yes.' Ivy beamed, still a little shocked.

'To us,' Frank said, gently clinking the crystal glass with Ivy's.

'To us,' Ivy mirrored, barely able to believe at the grand old age of fifty she was about to get married for the first time.

'And another thing,' Frank added. 'I think we shouldn't waste any time in making this official.'

Chapter 36

Saturday, 4 January 1941

'Oh, Ivy,' gasped Betty. 'You look truly beautiful.'

'Thank you, dear,' Ivy replied as she slipped into a pair of elegant green leather shoes. 'That's all down to you and Daisy pampering me.'

The last ten days had passed in a whirl of excitement after Ivy and Frank had announced their engagement. And to top it off, Frank had stuck to his word and insisted they tie the knot as soon as possible. He'd been to see the local priest who had managed to fit them in after a cancellation. 'You're lucky,' he said. 'What with all these special licences being issued, I'm performing up to eight weddings a day, but I think the poor soul who was supposed to be getting married didn't survive the second night of the bombings.'

'For heaven's sake, don't tell Ivy that!' Frank had retorted. 'She'll see it as a bad omen.'

After the date had been confirmed it was all systems go. Ivy's friend Winnie had sprung into action, organizing everything from the food and the flowers, to helping Ivy choose her outfit. They had settled on a deep-forest-green skirt and matching jacket with a cream blouse, adorned with a lace collar. 'I'm far too old for a white wedding,' Ivy had insisted.

And now, as Ivy stood in the hallway of her home, Betty, Josie, Daisy and Winnie by her side, she turned to Annie and Polly who were in the prettiest pale-green dresses, with a delicate cream rose attached to a silk band on their wrists.

'Well, I think it's these two who steal the show.' Ivy smiled at the two beaming little girls who she'd asked to be her flower girls. Of course, it meant a shopping trip to Marks & Spencer in town, which had managed to keep its doors open despite the Blitz, for yet another new outfit. But, Ivy had insisted if she couldn't spend her savings on her wedding day, then there really wasn't any point in putting away every spare penny for years on end.

'Are you ready?' asked Winnie, who was giving Ivy away in absence of her late father.

'I think so,' Ivy replied, a tremor of nerves emanating from her normally stoic voice.

'Just enjoy every minute,' her lifelong friend replied, opening the front door to the crisp January air.

Due to the church only being a couple of minutes' walk away, Ivy had insisted on not wasting anyone's petrol rations and walking.

'The fresh air will calm my nerves,' she said, taking a deep breath, as she stepped over the doorstep onto the frosty path that led to the pavement.

The small procession headed towards the Fulwood church, led by Ivy and Winnie, with Annie and Polly closely behind, wrapped in mock fur cream shawls, then Daisy, Josie and Betty at the rear. Ivy had also been insistent on not having bridesmaids, not wanting the attention to be taken away from Annie and Polly, but had asked the three women she now shared her home with to follow her into the church as an official part of her wedding party.

As they arrived at the gated entrance, Winnie squeezed her friend's hand. 'You deserve this,' she whispered. 'Cherish every moment.'

'Thank you. I'm still pinching myself that it's really happening.'

At the large wooden doors was Frank's smartly dressed younger brother, all suited and booted in his Sunday finest, acting as an usher. With a nod of his head, the elderly female organ player sprung into life and Wagner's 'Bridal Chorus' echoed around the lofty old building. As heads in the congregation turned to welcome and smile at the bride, the group slowly walked forwards. It was only as Betty stepped inside the traditional church did she feel someone link her left arm.

'May I accompany you to your pew, madam?'

Stunned, Betty quickly turned her head, the familiar voice alerting her senses, barely able to imagine the whispered voice was who she thought it was, but as she took in the handsome man in his blue pilot's uniform, her face burst into the biggest smile.

'William!' she whispered. 'What on earth are you doing here?'

But before he could answer, Josie gently nudged her. The procession had begun walking.

At the altar, Winnie delivered Ivy to a delighted Frank, who was stood with his best man, his older brother, Albert. As the group all took their seats at the front of the church. Betty looked to William again, just to be sure she hadn't actually imagined his surprise appearance, but his solid hand resting on her knee indicated her fiancé wasn't some sort of trick of her mind.

'Ladies and gentlemen, we are gathered here today to celebrate the marriage of Frank Brown and Ivy Wallis,' the vicar began, pulling Betty back to the moment. The happiness in the air was almost palpable as the wedding guests smiled with pure joy at the occasion. Nancy, who was sitting a few rows back, squeezed Bert's hand, grateful her husband had survived the last year, and Archie linked his little finger through Patty's, the smallest sign that his old self was emerging, even if he was still haunted by the dreadful images of that fateful night three weeks previously. Determined to stay strong, Josie managed a weak smile, pleased to see some happiness come out of this terrible war, even if she wished with all her heart that Alf was by her side to share the moment.

'In sickness and in health . . .' As the vicar's words echoed around the chamber-like building, Hattie instinctively put her hand to her heart, as she recalled her own wedding day from nearly three months earlier.

'To love and to cherish, till death do us part.'

Josie clenched her eyes shut and took a deep breath, her whole body tensing. When she and Alf had tied the knot, she didn't envisage their marriage would be so cruelly cut short.

Seeing the physical reaction to the vicar's words, Diane, who was sat behind Josie, gently placed a hand on her friend's shoulder, giving it a gentle squeeze, unable to imagine the pain Josie must be feeling. Although Josie kept her eyes firmly focused on the altar, she gave a little nod of appreciation, to let Diane know she was grateful.

'Now,' the vicar added, ever so slightly speeding up his ceremony, aware another couple, who had been granted a special licence, would be arriving at the church at any moment. 'Do you, Frank, take Ivy to be your lawful wedded wife?'

'I do,' Frank said, a huge smile appearing across his face.

'And do you, Ivy,' the religious man of the church asked, 'take Frank to be your lawful wedded husband?'

'I do,' Ivy whispered, her eyes glimmering with pure happiness.

'I thereby pronounce you man and wife.'

As the newlyweds came together in a tender kiss, whispers of 'oohs' and 'ahs' could be heard through the church.

'That will be us one day,' William whispered to Betty, adding to how enthralled she already felt.

The congregation stood up and made their way back out of the church, forming two lines, all holding little handfuls of rice which Winnie had distributed in bags to use as confetti. Then just as the happily married newlyweds appeared in the doorway, the lightest fluttering of snow began, framing the pair in what looked like the most perfect winter scene.

'Congratulations!' the guests cheered at the beaming couple.

Archie ushered Patty towards the church hall, which Ivy's friends had spent the morning decorating. The walls were adorned with homemade bunting in the shape of horseshoes, and a banner with the words 'Ivy and Frank' had been pinned above a table, where a beautifully iced cake had been placed. On the adjacent tables were platters of egg sandwiches, courtesy of Ivy's hens, plates of mini sausage rolls and an array of jam tarts and scones.

'My goodness,' Ivy gasped when she took in the celebratory sight.

'You're worth it,' Winnie said, waiting with a champagne flute in each hand for Ivy and Frank. Within a couple of minutes every guest was also armed with a drink of something fizzy.

'To the bride and groom,' Winnie said first.

'Ivy and Frank,' the guests reciprocated.

As the couple circulated, thanking their guests for

coming, gratefully accepting gifts, and exchanging hugs and handshakes, conversations throughout the room were ignited.

Seizing the opportunity to quietly sneak off to the loo while she hoped no one would notice, Hattie quickly dashed out of the hall to the outside lavatory, clenching her tummy. All morning, the feeling of nausea, which had plagued her continually over the last week or so, had suddenly become overbearing. Only just making it on time, she vomited into the basin.

'Oh gosh,' she gasped, standing up, dabbing her mouth with a handkerchief, hoping she didn't look as wretched as she felt. The last thing she would want to do is take the attention away from Frank and Ivy. But a few seconds later, water rising in her throat, Hattie was sick again. When she was finally able to stand up, she leant her back against the cool wall, a welcome contrast to how clammy and sick she felt. *What on earth is wrong with me?* Hattie patted her cheeks and took a deep breath. 'I'll be okay in a minute,' she told herself, but just as she was attempting to suppress how ill she felt, Hattie heard footsteps approaching. 'Okay, you need to pull yourself together now,' she quietly asserted.

'Hattie. Are you okay, luv?'

'Mum?'

'Yes, it's me. I saw you dash out. Is everything all right?'

Hattie slowly opened the door, quickly checking no one else was around.

'What is it?' Diane asked, taking in how ghostly pale her daughter looked.

'Oh, Mum,' Hattie sighed, relieved to see the one person she always turned to when she was under the weather. 'I don't know. I've felt queasy every morning for what feels like forever, and now I've just been really quite ill.'

A smile emerged across Diane's face.

'Mum,' Hattie gasped, confused by her mum's unexpected and somewhat perplexing reaction. 'Why are you grinning? I've been sick!'

'I'm sorry, luv. It's just, I think I know the reason you have been feeling so poorly the last few weeks.'

'You do? Then please tell me, because I would like it to go away, especially today.'

'Luv, have you really not put two and two together?'

'What do you mean? I have no idea what you are talking about.'

Taking Hattie's slightly trembling hand, Diane whispered, 'When did you last have your monthlies?'

It took a couple of seconds for the penny to drop, but as she did the calculations in her head, Hattie's look of confusion turned to one of utter astonishment.

'Oh. Mum, do you really think so?'

'You tell me, luv,' Diane replied. 'Do you think you could be pregnant? Your symptoms would certainly indicate that you are.'

Hattie's eyes began to shine. 'My goodness. Why didn't

I realize sooner? It makes perfect sense. Of course, that's what is wrong with me.'

'This is wonderful,' Diane said, wrapping her arms around her daughter. 'You're going to be a mum and I'm going to be a grandma.'

'Gosh,' Hattie gasped. 'I can't believe it.'

'Well, you probably need to.' Diane laughed. 'This baby will be here before we know it.'

A flood of emotions soared through Hattie. Suddenly everything made sense, the nausea, lack of appetite and general feeling of exhaustion. She'd put it down to not getting enough sleep, but all along a tiny baby had been starting to grow inside her.

'I can't wait to tell John.' She giggled jubilantly.

'He will make a great father,' Diane affirmed.

Then suddenly, a myriad of thoughts threatened to dampen Hattie's excitement. When would she next see John? And her dad's behaviour – would he ruin everything?

'Stop it,' Diane said firmly, reading her daughter's mind. Then taking Hattie's hand, she added, 'Everything will turn out fine. We will make sure of it.' The words came more from a deep-rooted maternal instinct than the power to know if they were true, but for today at least, Diane was unflinchingly resolute that her daughter was going to enjoy her special moment.

'Thank you,' Hattie replied, appreciatively. 'And just one thing, Mum.'

'Yes, luv?'

'Can we keep this a secret, just between me and you. I don't want to take the moment away from Frank and Ivy, and I'd also like to tell John before anyone else.'

'Of course. Now pop on a bit of lippy and spray some scent and let's go back and enjoy this wedding.'

Doing exactly as her mum instructed, Hattie forget about how sick she had been, a tingle of elation enveloping her.

Back inside the church hall, the guests were all chatting happily.

'Why didn't you warn me you were coming?' Betty asked William, who had his arm firmly around her waist, as if making up for all the months they had been apart.

'I wasn't sure I'd be granted the leave. I didn't want to get your hopes up, but when the forty-eight-hour pass was granted, I jumped on the first train, praying I would get here in time for the wedding.'

'Well, I'm so glad you did.' Betty grinned with a smile as big as the moon. 'It's the icing on the cake.' And with that, she stood on her tiptoes and gave William an affectionate kiss on the cheek.

Patty caught up with Hattie as Diane handed her a glass. 'Are you not having a glass of bubbly?' Patty asked her friend, as she sipped on the barley water.

'No. I still don't feel right.' Hattie shook her head, resisting the urge to rest her hand on her tummy, the internal flutters, which she had mistaken for a tummy bug, now a source of comfort.

Patty threw her a concerned glance. 'Maybe you should see a doctor?'

'You're probably right,' Hattie replied, more mysteriously than Patty could possibly realize. 'How's Archie?'

Patty glanced to where her sweetheart was stood congratulating Frank. 'Good days and bad days. Just when I think he's turning a corner, he gets all down again. But I'm determined to keep him bolstered today for Frank and Ivy's sake.'

'That's the spirit, luv,' Diane commented. 'Time is a great healer. Things will ease. I promise you. Right, I will let you girls have a natter, I'm just going to see how Josie is.'

Diane made her way to where Josie was standing with her three daughters, and Dolly and her two granddaughters, who looked as pretty as a picture in their red velvet dresses and their matching patent leather shoes.

'I've just been told you girls can all go and have one of those jam tarts I made,' Dolly said.

The thought of something sweet was all the encouragement they needed, the four pairs of legs dashing over to the food table.

'How are you both holding up?' Diane asked kindly, looking at Josie and Daisy.

'It still doesn't seem real,' Josie confessed. 'It's like I've lost my best friend.'

Daisy instinctively put her hand on her mum's arm.

'I'm sure, luv. Please say if I can do anything at all. Even if it's just a natter over a cuppa.'

'Thank you. I will. And I think once the schools open, I'm going to come back to work. It will do me no good just sat at home, sorry at Ivy's, all day long.'

'Well, you know we will all be there waiting for you.'

'I do and it means a lot. Daisy and I would be lost without all our friends right now.'

'That's what we are here for. Please don't forget that.'

'We won't,' Josie said, as Daisy nodded appreciatively.

'Excuse me!' came Winnie's voice, as she clinked a spoon against a glass. 'It's time for the speeches. I'm not going to say much apart from thanking everyone who made today possible at short notice. I'm not sure I could have cooked, baked and decorated without all the help so many of you provided. I'm sure you will all agree, it's wonderful to see Frank and Ivy so happy.'

'Here, here!' replied Frank's brother, Albert.

'So now, I shall pass you over to the man himself,' Winnie concluded.

'Thank you.' Frank smiled, taking centre stage. 'Well, as you know I'm a man of few words,' he said, chuckling, the irony not lost on any of the guests. 'But I would like to take this opportunity to also say thank you to everyone who has come here today to celebrate with myself and Ivy. It means so much. This war has tested us all in so many ways.'

Josie took a deep intake of breath and squeezed Daisy's

hand, determined not to let her emotions overtake her for the next few hours at least.

'But,' Frank continued, turning to face his new wife, 'there are many good things that we can be thankful for. Good friends, support and a determination to survive whatever we are dealt.'

Daisy nodded. She might still feel utterly broken inside but she was grateful for her friends who had helped pull herself and her family through.

'So, I would like to raise a toast,' Frank added. 'To my beautiful wife who has shown me how to be happy, something I never thought I would ever feel again, and to all of you for being the kindest of family and friends we could wish for.'

'To friends and family,' Albert parroted, lifting his glass in the air, and the sentiment was quickly mirrored by all the guests.

'And now it's time for the first dance,' Winnie announced, as right on cue the gramophone that had been heaved into the church hall came to life, and Irving Berlin's 'Cheek to Cheek' emanated from the polished mahogany music box.

'Please all join us,' Frank said, as he led a glowing Ivy into the middle of the hall, where a space had been made for them to sway along to the music. 'I love you, Mrs Brown,' Frank whispered in Ivy's ear.

'I love you too,' she replied, somewhat amazed how life had turned out.

One by one, more couples joined them. Bert, who gave his walking stick to Billy to hold, took Nancy's hand, while William didn't need any encouragement to escort Betty onto the now appropriated dance floor. Even Archie managed to take the hint after an expectant glance from Patty, and the groups of little girls all joined hands in a circle to enjoy the special moment.

As Frank spun Ivy around, she glanced around at her guests, taking in the scene before her. William had come home, and her younger house guests were managing to still smile despite the unimaginable loss they had endured. Ivy was grateful their tender age also armoured them with a steely resilience to carry on. She knew it would take a long time for Josie and her daughters' hearts to heal, but as she contemplated how life had turned out for her, she was hopeful, with time, love and support, they too would one day smile again.

Author's Note

I started the Steel Girls series after spending two years researching the true-life stories of the women who worked in the factories which lined the River Don during World War Two. Their tales of hardship, strength and resilience left me humbled and in complete admiration of what this tremendous generation endured.

Many were mums or young girls, with no experience of what it was like to be employed in one of the ginormous windowless factories, which were described on more than one occasion as entering 'hell on earth.' The deafening, ear-splitting cacophony of noise mixed with the perilously dangerous but accepted working conditions, alongside the relentless and exhaustingly long shifts, was a huge culture shock for so many of the women who walked through those factory doors for the first time.

Those who had young children had no choice but to hand their precious sons and daughters over to grandparents or leave them in the care of older siblings, some of them only just out of school themselves, but were expected to grow up fast and also do their bit to help.

What struck me in the course of my research, though, was how little resistance was offered to this new arduous, strangely unfamiliar and frequently quite terrifying way of life. 'We were just doing what was needed,' was an all-too-common answer when I asked the women I had the pleasure of talking to why they so eagerly took on the somewhat risky roles they volunteered for. 'We had no choice. It was what was needed to keep the factories going.' This is true, the foundries desperately needed workers, with so many of the opposite sex signing up to begin a 'new adventure.'

It soon became clear to me that this band of formidable, proud and hard-working Yorkshire women were not going to just stand by and let Hitler and his troops wreak havoc across Europe and beyond, without them doing what they could to aid their husbands, bothers, sons and uncles, who were off fighting someone else's war.

Over and over again, I was left in complete awe of how much the women of Sheffield sacrificed, day in and day out, for six long years. It's hard for most of us to comprehend now what a difficult and seemingly never-ending length of time this was. As well as working night and day as crane drivers, turners, making camouflage netting or working next to a red-hot and at times a fatal Bessemer Converter, they were also terrified by the very realistic fear they may never see their loved ones ever again.

One lady, Kathleen Roberts, told me whenever a shooting star was seen going over a factory, it was a sign another soldier had fallen and a telegram bearing the bad news would be delivered soon afterwards. To live with that level of sheer terror, let alone cope with the ominous air-raid sirens, which indicated the Luftwaffe could be on their way, is truly unimaginable. But this is the harsh and constant reality which thousands of women lived with across Sheffield.

It wasn't all doom and gloom though. The one thing that struck a chord with me while talking to the women and their families was the way in which they counteracted the harshness life had thrown at them. They created unbreakable bonds with their new female fellow workmates and a camaraderie which even Hitler himself couldn't break. In a determined bid to 'keep up morale', our feisty factory sisters focused on safeguarding a warm community spirit to keep them all going when times got hard. Friendships were created in the most unlikely of circumstances, often among women who would never normally mix. Lipsticks were snapped in half and divided between colleagues, and a single wedding dress could be worn a dozen times to ensure a Sheffield bride didn't walk down the aisle without looking her absolute best. It really was the era of sharing what you had with your neighbour and never letting someone in need go without.

Of course, it would be easy to romanticise this period, or hale it as 'the good old days', but the reality is it wasn't that either. It was simply a case of facing head-on the atrocities life was dealing and getting on with it as best you could. Some had it easier than others but no matter what, all these women woke up in September 1939 to a new life and somehow managed to take it in their stride, but they really didn't have much choice. With no savings to fall back on to tide them over, or a welfare state to lighten the load, it was a case of 'cracking on' and doing what was needed.

In 2009, Kathleen Roberts rang the *Sheffield Star* and asked why she and others like her, who had sacrificed so much of their lives had never been thanked, after watching a TV show on the Land Girls. What started as a frustrated phone call developed into a campaign by the local paper to ensure the women of the city who had worked day and night in the steel works, were finally recognised. Kathleen, alongside Kit Sollitt, Dorothy Slingsby and Ruby Gascoigne, representing this whole generation of women, were whisked down to London to be personally thanked by the then Prime Minister, Gordon Brown. Afterwards a grassroots campaign was launched by the *Sheffield Star* to fundraise for a statue representing the female steelworkers to be commissioned and erected in Barker's Pool, in the city centre, directly outside the dance they would often visit on a Saturday, to escape the drudgery of their lives.

In June 2016, the larger-than-life bronze statue, paid for entirely by the people of Sheffield, was unveiled to the sheer and rapturous delight of the still-surviving women of steel, their contribution to the war effort now eternally immortalised.

Although the characters in this book are entirely fictional, their experiences a result of my creative imagination having a bit of fun with itself, the truth is every page is based on the interviews I conducted, the factual books I've read from the period and the ongoing research I'm still undertaking. Any factual errors made are my own.

I hope within my books I can also help keep this generation's memory alive. I interviewed women who flew up crane ladders, others who were scared witless and many who remember only too clearly what it was like to live in absolute poverty, the talisman a regular visitor to their door. So, despite the poetic creation of Betty, Nancy and Patty, I can envisage their real-life counterparts, hear their voices and recall their experiences – the reality of it is, I simply couldn't make the raw bones of some of these stories up. I have used poetic license when creating scenes and plots, which may not be factual. Any mistakes made are my own, but only after hearing first-hand how terrifying it was to live through the Sheffield Blitz could I put pen to paper and serve our real women of steel the justice they rightfully deserve.

I truly hope, as a Sheffielder (well just about – I've been here 27 years) I have served the women of this hard-working industrious city well and you have enjoyed reading this book as much as I have writing it.

Acknowledgements

Firstly, I would like to thank every female steelworker of the First and Second World War and their family members, who over the course of the last six years have so generously given up their time to talk to me, recalled memories and answered my endless questions. Without these women, the Steel Girls series would not be possible. Although the characters are fictional, they are created from the true-life stories which have been shared with me. I am also so grateful to the women and their relatives for their ongoing and tremendous support, which means so much. At every step of the way, they have been my biggest cheerleaders, and for that I will be forever grateful.

I am indebted to every author, historian, journalist and social commentator who enabled me to look at this period of time in extra detail, allowing me to understand the wider issues and feelings of the women who lived and worked through World War Two, creating a new way of life in the most troubled and hardest of times.

I must say a huge thank you to the fabulous Sylvia

Jones, whose own 'little nannan', Ada Clarke, was a Woman of Steel. Sylvia has become my 'go to' expert on anything Attercliffe or Darnall based. Sylvia has taken me on several walking tours of the area, pointing out all the old shops, picture houses and pubs, so I could envisage all these landmarks, which was utterly invaluable. I'd like to add my thanks to the late Dick Starkey, who recorded his wartime RAF memories in his book, *A Lancaster Pilot's Impression on Germany*, which I have read from cover to cover, after another reader, Sandra Kay, pointed me to it. I must also express thanks to Mary Walton and J.P. Lamb for their excellent book, *Raiders Over Sheffield*, which became a constant source of reference while writing my latest novel.

I must also say how grateful I am to every book blogger who has been kind enough to support me, continually shouting about the books and offering immense support.

Enormous thanks must be given to the extremely dedicated Elizabeth Counsell, at Northbank Talent Management, who is always on hand to offer reassurance, encouragement, and invaluable advice.

I must also offer the greatest of thanks to my former editor at HQ Stories, Katie Seaman, without whom the Steel Girls series would never have seen the light of day. I am also hugely indebted to my new, extremely conscientious and talented, editor, Priyal Agrawal, who has shown so much enthusiasm and passion for this book, for which I am eternally grateful.

I must offer my sincere thanks to my magician-like copyeditor Eldes Tran. A huge thanks to Anna Sikorska for designing the most fitting and beautiful of covers. I'd also like to extend my gratitude to Hanako Peace for helping create the marketing for the Steel Girls and to Georgina Green, Fliss Porter, Angela Thomson and Sara Eusebi in sales, for getting this book on actual shelves.

I am so grateful to each and every one of my family members and truly amazing friends, who have offered unfaltering support in writing the book. As always, I can't fail to mention my good friend and long-suffering running mate, Leanne Hawkes, who has very patiently lived every one of my books with me, listening to me three times a week as we pound the hills of Millhouse Green, and kept me sane throughout. I think at least two of my characters are named after members of her family – including Ivy, (Leanne's lovely mum & now Betty's landlady), which we decided on during one very particular rainy and windy run. I must also thank Ann Cusack for offering relentless support and being the greatest friend anyone could ever wish for.

I would also like to say the biggest thank you to the truly amazing and quite frankly fabulous group of people I work with at The University of Sheffield, who have always been my greatest cheerleaders.

I cannot end this passage of gratitude without acknowledging my two amazing children, Archie and Tilly. They are simply the best, even if my now teenager son rolls his eyes when I mention anything that isn't gaming focused. I sincerely hope I have instilled into them that if you work hard enough for something, you can achieve your dreams, no matter how big or insurmountable they might feel.

There is one person who I constantly think about while writing my books and that is my late mother-in-law, Coleen, a hardy Steel Girl in her own right. I would give anything for her to still be here to see this book. I can imagine her shouting from the rooftops about it, telling all her friends they must read it. Coleen was an avid local history fan and I wish she were still here for so many reasons but she would have loved to check the minutiae of this book, the accents, the landmarks, the Yorkshire traditions. I know she would have been there, going through the details with a fine-toothed comb.

But I gain so much happiness and comfort at how proud and excited she would have been to see little old me writing this series, seeped in historical fact about the remarkable women of the city she loved so much. Coleen, like our hard-working and caring Steel Girls, you will never be forgotten.

Make sure you've read all the books in the heartwarming *Steel Girls* series!

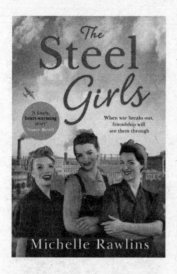

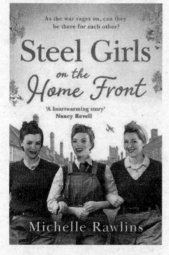
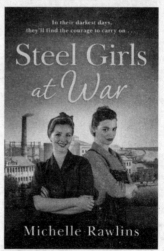

Go back to the beginning of the Steel Girls series

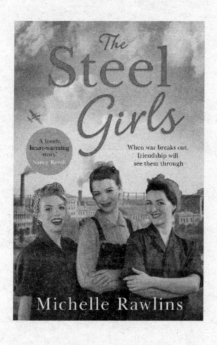

With war declared, these brave women will step up and do their bit for their country . . .

The Steel Girls start off as strangers but quickly forge an unbreakable bond of friendship as these feisty factory sisters vow to keep the foundry fires burning during wartime.

Don't miss this festive tale of courage and friendship on the Home Front

As the Steel Girls face their first Christmas at war, can they come together this winter?

In the harsh winter of 1939, our feisty factory sisters must rally around each other to find hope and comfort this Christmas season.

Catch up with the third heartwarming book in the Steel Girls series

As the war rages on, can they be there for each other?

In spring 1940, the war is raging on but the Steel Girls find themselves fighting battles closer to home . . .

Be swept away by the next gripping tale
of bravery in the Steel Girls series

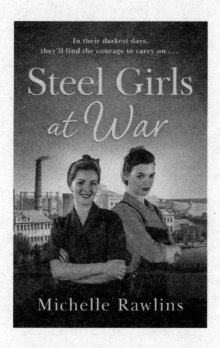

In their darkest days, they'll find the courage to carry on . . .

As the Steel Girls come together to be there in Nancy's hour
of need, will life ever be the same again?

ONE PLACE. MANY STORIES

Bold, innovative and
empowering publishing.

FOLLOW US ON:

@HQStories